The Fifth Key

by

Mirabelle Maslin

Augur Press

THE FIFTH KEY
Copyright © Mirabelle Maslin 2008

The moral right of the author has been asserted

Author of:
Beyond the Veil
Tracy
Carl and other writings
Fay
On a Dog Lead
Emily

British Library Cataloguing in Publication Data.
A catalogue record for this book is available from the British Library.

ISBN 978-0-9558936-0-5

First published 2008 by
Augur Press
Delf House,
52, Penicuik Road,
Roslin,
Midlothian EH25 9LH
United Kingdom

Printed by Lightning Source

The Fifth Key

To all who value my work and my writing

Chapter One

Captain Todd could see the storm clouds gathering on the horizon, and he knew that there was trouble brewing. To navigate his ship so near to the rocky shore in calm waters was challenge enough, but with turbulence it would be a very risky proposition.

He considered the options. Dropping the anchor here would be certain to attract the kind of attention that he wanted to avoid, but going on carried with it the possibility of ending up at the bottom of the sea, cargo and all. How was he to ensure the safety of the ship, the crew and its precious load – the load that would guarantee them all an easy life for the rest of their years?

The journey had been long and arduous. They had set sail many months ago. Each man had known the dangers from the outset, but every one of them had good reason to throw in his lot with the venture. Most were beggars and escaped convicts. Todd had selected only those who could prove that they had lived at sea for at least a year in their miserable lives. He had his ways of telling who was lying and who was not, and no one slipped through his scrutiny. These were men who clung with fierce desperation and tenacity to the fragile hope of a new life, and had enough experience to know that together they had a chance of making the long crossing to fulfil their dreams of life with the riches they carried. Although nearly exhausted, they were survivors and they struggled on. And now, their final goal beckoned.

So near, and yet so far. How were they to work their way along this treacherous stretch of coast, and reach the safe haven where there were those who had been instructed to keep watch for them, and would hide them and their booty?

The dark clouds were racing across the sky, and Todd reckoned that the storm would be on them within the hour. Even waiting here would not ensure safety from it. The rocks were perilous, and if the ship were swept towards them it might not survive. He made the decision to carry on.

Shouting terse orders to steer away from the shore, he instructed his crew to make haste for their destination, which in favourable conditions was less than a few hours away. With luck, they would find a cove or an inlet that might shelter them through the storm.

The crew worked with the precision of one man, but with the strength of many. There was little swearing now, as every one of them was only too aware of their plight, and threw all their energy into the hope of salvation.

Todd made no move to leave the deck. He watched the face of the sea change from hope to menace as the storm approached more rapidly than he had predicted. The only option left now was to bring down the sails and ride the storm. At least they had managed to put more distance between the ship and the worst of the rocks here. He barked the orders. The sails shrunk down the masts, and they waited.

Todd opened his eyes. Everything hurt, and he could not see anything that made any sense. He tried to move, but a scream jumped into his throat, and he gave up quickly, as a long-established sixth sense told him that making a noise might not be in his best interests. His hands and feet were numb, and he knew that he was soaking wet. He closed his eyes again, and drifted into semi-consciousness.

He had no idea what time had elapsed before he opened his eyes again. Still there was nothing that he could recognise, but now he realised that this was because everything was so blurred, and that even if he were surrounded by familiar things, he would not be able to identify them.

He gave a low moan, and once again slipped into a state that allowed no coherent thought.

When he next came round, things were different. He was sure that he could hear voices, and his hands were no longer numb. Although he could not see properly, he was sure that he was in a shelter, or a dwelling of some kind. He felt up and down his body, and found that he was wrapped in a rough blanket. He could find no evidence of his own clothing. Any other movement was impossible, and he realised that although he had no pain, he could not move his legs at all.

What looked like the shape of a person appeared beside him, and very slowly began to trickle some liquid into his mouth. He was able to take a little in, before once again, he lost consciousness.

'What happened next?' asked Nicholas anxiously.

'He was buried in a shallow grave near the cliff top,' his great-uncle John replied. 'A curiously-shaped stone marks the spot.'

'How do you know?' asked Nicholas.

'My grandad took me to see it when I was about your age.'

'That was a long time ago,' Nicholas reflected.

'It was. But I remember it as if it were only yesterday.'

Nicholas fell silent, and then surprised his uncle by demanding, 'Draw it for me.'

'Artistic skills were never my strong point, but I'll do my best.'

John picked up a pencil and began to sketch on the back of an envelope that happened to be on the table.

Nicholas watched quietly. At thirteen he was already beginning to look like a man, and had to shave at least twice a week. He had grown several centimetres in only the last six months, and he felt hungry all the time. Yes, that was no exaggeration. That physical hunger never left him, and if he did not follow its command, he felt so tired that he could hardly stand up.

As the image of the stone took shape, he could see why his uncle had thought it to be unusual. In fact, it reminded him of the shape of a very rough-hewn key, and he said so.

'You're spot on,' said his uncle.

'But you can't have a key made out of stone.'

'Maybe I could tell you the rest of the story.'

'There's more?'

John looked slightly evasive, and Nicholas thought he saw a troubled shadow flit across his face. He wondered if he should not have pressed his uncle. After all, he was now a very old man of nearly ninety. He had been the oldest of three brothers by many years. His youngest brother had been Nicholas' grandad, but he had died long before Nicholas was born, so Nicholas himself had never known him.

John gathered himself, and said with a note of uncertainly in his voice, 'There's quite a bit of the story still to tell.'

Nicholas stared at him. 'Why did you only tell me part of it?' he asked carefully. 'And... why didn't you tell me the story before now?'

Nicholas had known his great-uncle John as far back as he could remember. He lived in a quaint single-storied house, on the edge of the village where Nicholas lived with his parents. The outside of the house was in need of repair, and Nicholas sometimes heard his parents talking about how they might persuade his uncle to let tradesmen do the work, but they never seemed to get any further than that. Nicholas was not bothered. His uncle's house had always looked the same to him, but he did remember his parents saying how, as a younger man, his uncle had always kept the house and garden looking smart. Whenever Nicholas thought about it – which was not often – he realised that he rather liked its dilapidated appearance. The garden was overrun with all kinds of trailing and thorny plants, the brickwork on the chimneys was falling off in places, some of the windowsills had rotted and the front door was jammed shut. The wooden garage had more or less collapsed, and the timber was a mess.

Nicholas had a much older brother, Jake, who was thirty-five, and spent most of his time travelling the world, carrying only bare essentials with him. Nicholas saw him only very rarely. He liked spending time with Uncle John. He liked the idea that Uncle John was himself an older brother, albeit to two generations before, but unlike Jake, he was there all the time, and he could see him nearly every day.

'Go on,' he urged. 'Tell me everything.'

'I couldn't tell you before, because that's a part of the story,' John explained hesitantly.

Nicholas had never seen his uncle behave like this before. He had always seemed so predictable, reliable and calm. And now, he could see all kinds of emotion passing through him, and he looked quite agitated.

Nicholas wanted to know the story. He wanted to know the whole of it. *Now*. But he did not want to stress his uncle, who was obviously struggling with something.

He wanted to be able to reassure him that it was okay, and that he did not really need to know the story. But that would be a lie, because he felt an urgency and a passion for having that knowledge.

At last his uncle looked him straight in the eye, and said, 'If the story is true, we are both Todd's descendents.'

Nicholas felt stunned. How could that be? The man had died almost as soon as he had been rescued. But had he? Maybe he had lived for a while? More questions crowded into his mind, and he stared at his uncle, asking nothing, and waiting for the answers.

'There's a pledge that goes with the story.'

Nicholas noticed that his uncle's voice was now strong and steady. He continued to wait.

'And that's why I told you nothing of it until now.'

Nicholas nodded.

'The story was never to be handed on until the chosen one was thirteen or more. Oh, I know that makes it sound like one of the fantasy books and films your generation is so fond of, but it's what I was told.'

'Did you know anything about it before you were thirteen?' asked Nicholas quickly. He realised that although he was now learning more, he was feeling quite upset that his uncle had not told him before of the existence of this story.

John shook his head. 'No, it was kept from me until I was well past my thirteenth birthday.'

Nicholas relaxed. 'So I'm younger than you were.'

'That's right – by a good few months.'

'How old was my dad when he was told about it?'

'He doesn't know.'

Nicholas was struggling. 'But he has to…'

John continued to look straight at him with a steady gaze. He paced his words slowly and clearly as he said, 'The story is not passed from each generation to the next. It's passed from grandfather to grandson.'

Nicholas tried to absorb this information. 'So my dad knows nothing…'

'Yes, your dad knows nothing,' John repeated, waiting for Nicholas to grasp the significance of this.

'And… must it stay like that?' Nicholas' voice was almost a whisper.

'Yes, it must stay that way,' his uncle confirmed gravely.

'Why?' It was a simple question, and one to which Nicholas required an answer. 'Why?' he repeated.

'It's part of the pledge.'

'But why? Why is it part of the pledge?'

'I don't know the answer to that.'

'But we've got to find out,' said Nicholas urgently. 'Can't you see, Uncle John? It's really important.'

'I know it's important,' his uncle acknowledged gently, 'but let me tell you more of the story.'

Nicholas opened his mouth to ask more of the questions that poured into his mind, but he could see that his uncle could not be swayed, and he shut it again.

'I'll tell you everything I know,' John promised. 'It was difficult for me to make a start, and I held quite a lot back. First, I needed to

5

have your reaction to the part I told you. Until I had that, I didn't know if you were ready to prepare to take the pledge.'

Nicholas struggled hard with himself. He wanted to ask question after question until he was certain that there was nothing else his uncle could tell him. But he managed to stay silent, telling himself to trust this man who had never failed him. He had been stunned by the revelation that there was something huge that his uncle had kept from him, and then by the discovery that his father did not know, and was never to know. Fleetingly he touched his chin, and he realised that he had almost expected to find a full beard there, as he suddenly felt years older.

He heard his uncle say, 'It was complicated in my generation, and only I knew the story.'

'Is it that only one out of each second generation is told?'

'Yes. And as you must have realised, it isn't always the oldest son who is given the knowledge.'

Nicholas had not realised. He had got as far as thinking that his uncle John knew because he was the oldest of three brothers, but he had not worked out why he, Nicholas, rather than his brother Jake, was being told. But then, there were plenty of times when he forgot that he had a brother. Jake was such a shadowy figure to him.

'What about my grandad?'

'That's a very good question,' replied John. 'And the answer's a story in its own right. Are you ready?'

'Of course, I am,' replied Nicholas. Why was his uncle asking him this, when it was so obvious?

'My own grandad was worried that my parents would have no more children after me. My father was his only child. Grandad knew that he would not live much longer, but he told me that he sensed that I was not to be the chosen one. How he knew this we'll never know, but that's what he said. He certainly came to know that I would not always be an only child – that there were to be three of us, and that he wasn't going to survive long enough to know the other two. He was in a quandary, and that's why he left it for several months after I was thirteen before he made a start. After he had told me everything and showed me the grave, I took the pledge. Then his health began to fail quickly. He made me promise never to have children, and to hand on the knowledge to a grandson of my youngest brother. I was completely confused. I had no brother, and there were no signs of any hope for that. I doubted his belief that there would be a brother, let alone two brothers. But about five years after my grandfather died, my first brother was born, and two years after that, my other brother – and that was your grandad, James.'

'Yes, I know that,' said Nicholas. 'Go on, Uncle John. Go on.'

'When James was thirteen, I began to tell him the story, but he refused to listen. He covered his ears, and ran away.'

'How much had you told him?'

'Very little. I had only said that there was something our grandad had said he should be told when he was thirteen, and that he wasn't to tell Dad.'

'That wasn't much,' Nicholas observed.

'Well, it was too much for him, and he was very wary of being alone with me after that. I had been living away from home for a good few years by then, so I was a bit of a stranger to him, and at his age he didn't like the idea of not being able to tell Dad everything. James must have gone and said something to Dad, because one day Dad told me in no uncertain terms that I wasn't to frighten James with my tales.'

Nicholas digested this information, and then said, 'I know what I can feel like when I see Jake. Maybe it was a bit the same for Grandad James about you.'

'Certainly the thing about me being much older and being away from home must have been a part of it, but I wasn't all that far away, and I saw the family much more than you've seen Jake. I've a feeling that your grandad had some instinct about the story, and that was what frightened him, not me.'

'I'm a bit frightened,' Nicholas confided, 'but not much. Most of my feelings are to do with wanting to know everything straight away. I'm even more hungry for that than I am for food.'

'And that's saying something,' said John, smiling. 'We'll have to take it slowly though.'

'Okay,' Nicholas agreed. He felt like a man, and he liked that. It was a good time for him to hear the story. His parents were away for the weekend, and he was staying the night with his uncle. There was plenty of time. He was beginning to accept that there was no way that his uncle could have told him any of this before. He felt trusted – as if he was being welcomed into some kind of special circle. He waited attentively, sitting in the battered old armchair that matched the one his uncle was sitting in – one on each side of the empty fireplace.

Although it was only seven o'clock, it was dark outside. That evening in late November was not particularly cold, and the old Dimplex radiator that stood in the middle of the room gave out enough heat.

'Fancy a fire?' asked John.

Nicholas nodded vigorously. He jumped up and ran out to the woodshed, where he gathered some kindling and logs. John closed the tattered curtains and lit the fire, while Nicholas made a pile of sandwiches. It was not long before a warm glow was spreading out into the room.

'Now,' said John, 'where had I got up to? I was telling you about James. Wasn't I?'

'Uncle John, why is it me and not Jake?' asked Nicolas, feeling secure about his importance.

John explained. 'I could never have a proper conversation with Jake about anything, let alone this. Don't get me wrong. I tried, and I kept on trying, but there was never anything between us that would have given me a chance of telling him, and I had to accept that he wasn't the one.'

Nicholas was sure he could feel himself growing even taller.

John went on. 'It was very hard for me. As I said, my grandad had made me promise never to have children, and that meant no marrying. And as you know, at first I had no brothers at all. Then when I had them, and later told my young brother – your grandad James – I just about lost all contact with him. And when I later tried to prepare Jake, it was much the same.'

'It's all right, Uncle John. You've got me. I know you've had to wait a long time, but we're together now. Really together.'

In the safety of the old armchair, the fire, and his uncle's undivided attention, Nicholas felt at one with himself and the world, and he felt ready for anything.

John gathered himself. His great-nephew had a lot more to take in.

'You've learned about sex at school,' he said. This was more a statement than a question, but he waited to see if Nicholas wanted to say anything.

'Yes... Why?'

'Todd had been taken to the cottage of a shepherd. The shepherd was a widower, but he had an unmarried daughter who kept house for him. She cared for Todd in his last weeks, and eight months after he died, she gave birth to a son.'

'Was that Todd's son?'

'That's what I was told. The shepherd's cottage was quite isolated, and anyone who visited or passed by never saw Todd, but that's not to say that he never had any lucid moments in the weeks he was being cared for there.'

'Wow!' said Nicholas. 'Was he my great, great, great, great...' Here he gave up.

'As I said before, as far as I understand, we're both direct descendents of his.'

'I want to go and see his grave,' stated Nicholas determinedly. 'Can you take me?' he added uncertainly. He knew that his uncle had not travelled far in recent years, and he felt a stab of anxiety. He was not yet old enough to go alone. How could he explain this to his parents when he was not supposed to divulge the story, and even if they asked no questions and helped him to go, how could he find the spot only by following directions given by Uncle John?

'Nicholas,' said John gently, 'when I last went back to see it, the cliff had been eroded by the sea, and the grave had disappeared.'

Nicholas' shoulders sagged. He was intensely disappointed, but equally he was relieved.

His uncle went on. 'Later I can show you some old black and white photographs I took of the surroundings last time I was there. But let me tell you more about the ship.'

'Go on, Uncle John.' Nicholas' voice was full of eagerness.

John smiled, and then continued. 'It was carrying a cargo of treasure. No one knew what, and none was found, but there was a merchant who lived some miles south of where the ship was wrecked. He had a large house that was set above a small harbour that he kept as his own. It's believed that the ship was making for that harbour, and that the merchant and his family and workers knew what was on board. Apparently, preparations had been made as if a large company were to arrive and be integrated into the household. But no one came.'

'Are there any clues?' asked Nicholas breathlessly.

'The fifth key,' his uncle replied.

Nicholas was by now perched on the edge of his chair, leaning forward, trying to ensure that he missed nothing. Startled, he asked, 'What do you mean?' But then he noticed that his uncle was looking grey and drawn, and he added quickly, 'You don't have to tell me any more now, Uncle John.'

John leaned back in his chair and shut his eyes for a moment.

Nicholas searched his mind for something to say that might help him. 'Why don't we have an early night?' he suggested as calmly as he could manage. 'We can talk again tomorrow.'

John smiled inwardly at his great-nephew's attempt to sound mature and in charge of the situation. He was more than happy to go along with it because he felt exhausted. He had been alone with this secret for more than seventy-five years, and his advancing age, and the strain of the responsibility of imparting it to Nicholas was apparent. He had known that he must not wait much longer before raising it with him, but he had been so afraid that Nicholas would have reacted adversely, and then not only would he have lost the nephew he loved so much, but also he would have been left with an insoluble dilemma.

John stood up slowly. 'You're right,' he agreed. 'I'll get off to bed now. You can sit up for a while if you want.' He left in the direction of the cold bathroom, and his bedroom beyond.

Nicholas sat up late, watching the embers of the fire die down. His mind was full of what he had learned. But exactly what had he learned? His uncle had told him a story, but what did it mean? For a second, his confidence wavered. Maybe after all it was just fantasy? But that did not account for the way the story had been handed down, his grandfather's strange reaction, and even Jake's reaction. From what Uncle John had said, his grandfather had showed all the signs of fear, and Jake's detachment from their great-uncle had been even more than Nicholas might have expected. When he compared the reaction of both these relatives to his own reaction, there was no connection at all. He concluded that not only did the story bear more than a grain of truth, but also it had most certainly been for his ears, and his alone.

Not wanting to leave his chair, he fetched a blanket and covered himself. He supposed that part of his reluctance to go to bed was to do with the fact that he would have to leave the room that still felt full of this evening's revelations, and that he wanted to wait here until his uncle returned the next morning, so that they could talk again, and he could learn about the fifth key.

He gazed around the room in the dim light. Occasionally, a larger flame would burst out of one of the remaining pieces of wood, and would push back the shadows, but it would not last long. The room was furnished very simply. In addition to the old armchairs, there was a plain wooden table with three chairs around it that did not match. His uncle had made the table when he was a young man, and there was an interesting story behind each of the three chairs. But Nicholas knew those stories so well that he did not think through them. He wanted only to fill his thoughts with what he was learning now. Old wooden boxes, stacked on their sides along one wall, made perfect bookshelves, but although they were crammed with books, he had never seen his uncle reading any of them. Maybe there were clues amongst them? The only other objects of any note were several large battered metal containers that were stacked in one corner of the room. Although he had never seen inside any of them, he had never wondered about their contents before. Yet now he wished he knew what they held.

He finally fell asleep in the middle of making plans about how to ensure that he never revealed to his parents how his life had changed. Yes, his life had changed completely, and he knew that it could not go back to what it had been.

Chapter Two

Nicholas woke with a start. For a moment he wondered where he was. He could hear the sounds of someone moving about. Then he remembered that he was in his uncle's living room, and he realised that it must be morning.

He wriggled out of the chair and went to the kitchen, where he found his uncle stirring a large pan full of porridge. His stomach rumbled loudly.

'Done plenty,' his uncle announced. 'How did you sleep?'

'Fine, thanks.'

Nicholas was relieved to find that his uncle looked more himself. His face had lost its grey pallor of the night before, and the hand that stirred the porridge was steady and purposeful. He curbed his desire to rush straight into asking more questions, and instead said, 'We've got all day, because Mum and Dad won't be back until quite late.'

'I remembered that,' John replied. He said nothing more as he filled a large bowl with porridge and handed it to his nephew. 'Get that down you first. You need it.'

Nicholas took the bowl, and sat at the table in the living room. His uncle joined him, and they ate in a silence that was only broken by John saying, 'Make sure you empty that pan. I've had all I need.'

Nicholas needed no persuasion. Then, warmed by the food, he waited expectantly.

'There are logs to be chopped,' said his uncle abruptly.

Nicholas could not hide his disappointment.

'Young bodies need to be worked,' John stated matter-of-factly but not unkindly.

Nicholas felt like a boy again, and he did not like it. He heard his uncle say, 'It's no good telling you everything if I don't help you to get ready for whatever you might be facing.'

Then Nicholas surprised himself. He did not want to be a boy any more, especially as he had felt last night what it was like to be a man, and he said, 'Uncle John, I'll do the logs for you, but there are other things we'll have to get down to soon.'

'I know. We'll get on to that later this morning.'

'I'm talking about something else.'

John stared at his nephew. There was something about him that was different. 'What is it?' he asked.

'You're going to have to teach me how to do some of the work around here.'

'But you do the logs just fine.'

Nicholas drew himself up and said firmly 'You know there are things that need doing to the house – outside and in. You can't pretend any more. It's time we worked out how to see to it. There's plenty I could do if you teach me.'

John began to stand up. He was going to take his dish to the kitchen. There was something about the way things were going that was making him feel intensely uncomfortable.

'Sit down, Uncle John,' Nicholas ordered. 'I've a lot to learn from you about the pledge and about the fifth key.'

'I'll just take my dish,' John said, a little evasively.

Nicholas was determined to act like the man he knew he was.

'Look, Uncle John,' he insisted, 'you know you need more help around here, and I'm old enough now to do plenty of it. And while we're doing all that together, I'll learn a lot more about what you want to tell me than I would if I was just sitting in a chair, listening to you telling me the story.'

John viewed his nephew's sturdy body. Although Nicholas had always been a willing helper, John had limited his requests to a minimum, and had only asked him to do things that he knew a boy could accomplish quite easily. For a long time he had been worried about the state of his house, but he had told no one of his concerns, as he feared the intrusion of incompetent workmen. Oh yes, Nicholas' parents had tried to persuade him, but he had fobbed them off, letting them believe that he was not bothered about any of it, when in fact, underneath, it gnawed away at him. Nicholas had grown a lot in the last year, and the way he was going he was likely to end up as he himself had been as a young man – a good six feet tall and plenty of strong muscles.

'All right, Nicholas,' he agreed. 'I see what you're getting at.' He smiled, and reached his hand across the table. 'We'll make a good team, young man.'

Nicholas hesitated only for a fraction of a second, and then grabbed his uncle's hand and held it tight. 'Where shall we start?' he asked breathlessly.

13

'We need to check all the guttering and down-pipes first,' said John briskly. 'There's a good ladder trapped under the wreckage of the garage. Let's work to free it.'

John put on his thick coat, a woolly hat and some old gloves. Nicholas grabbed his anorak, and followed his uncle to the remains of the garage.

'Hm,' observed John ruefully, 'I think we'll convert this into kindling. Go and fetch the saws. We'll start cutting it up, and stack as much as we can in the woodshed.'

They sawed in silence for an hour, and then Nicholas glanced at his uncle's face and said, 'Time for you to get a mug of tea, Uncle John.'

'That's a polite way of telling me that I look awful and need a rest. Isn't it?' John smiled. 'You're right, of course. I'll go and sit down for a while. Come in whenever you've had enough.'

Nicholas worked on. He had no feeling of having had enough. In fact, the more he did the more he wanted to do, and his strength seemed to increase as he worked. He only stopped when his stomach rumbled so loudly that the sound of the saw could not drown it out.

When he went into the house, he found his uncle fast asleep in his armchair, an empty mug on the floor beside him, and the Dimplex heater drawn up to the side of the chair. He made himself a thick sandwich, heated up some of the soup from the large pan that they had filled the previous morning, and took his food to the table. There he sat, quietly eating his way through his lunch. His uncle barely stirred, and the only sound he made was an occasional gentle snore. Nicholas did not feel worried about him, as he was warm and relaxed, and his face was a good colour.

Another hour's work, and Nicholas had cleared much of the mess, and the ladder was long freed. It was an aluminium one – quite similar to his father's – and he wondered if he could lift it and set it up so that he could start looking in the guttering.

Then he heard his uncle's voice. 'That's a grand job. Want a hand with the ladder now?'

'Ye... Yes.' Nicholas' voice adopted a note of confidence. 'I thought I'd start at the back of the house.' Then he faltered. 'Er... Um...'

'Spit it out.'

'I noticed there's some water running down the wall just inside the back door.'

'I saw that too. You're right. We should start there. You'll probably have spotted that the outer wall is stained around there.'

Nicholas had not noticed this before, but he could certainly see it now.

Together they had no difficulty in setting up the ladder, and John stood at the bottom, while Nicholas climbed up to look. He could not hold back a yell when he looked in the guttering, and then noticed that the down-pipe was detached, and that he could swing it back and to with ease.

'It's a total mess up here,' he called.

'No surprise to me. I've known it, but I've done my best to turn a blind eye for a long time. Come down for a minute.'

Nicholas was soon standing in front of his uncle.

'If we get a trowel and a bucket, would you scoop some of that mess out?'

'That would be great!' exclaimed Nicholas excitedly.

John raised an eyebrow quizzically, while Nicholas rushed off to get what he needed. John was cheered by his nephew's enthusiasm, and he began to look forward to their doing some more of this basic work together.

They spent the rest of the daylight hours working their way round the guttering, and checking the down-pipes.

Back in the house, they made an inventory of what they had found. John clipped some paper onto an old piece of board and picked up a pencil.

'Brackets missing on most of the down pipes. That makes them unstable,' said Nicholas. He liked using the word 'unstable'. It made him feel even more like a working man.

'You said you found small holes rusted through some lengths of guttering,' his uncle reminded him. 'Tell me again which sections.'

'And there were some slates too,' Nicholas added. 'I could see where some of them had come from. There weren't any actual holes in the roof, but missing slates aren't a good thing, are they?'

'Certainly not. How many in total, and whereabouts?'

The list completed, Nicholas asked, 'Shall I look in the loft next?'

His uncle was about to brush off the idea, when he realised that such an examination was so long overdue that he could not remember the last time anyone had been up there. If there were any minor leaks in the roof, a search of the loft would soon reveal them.

'There's a step-ladder in my bedroom,' he said. 'But it doesn't reach far enough.'

'Let me try,' Nicholas suggested. He collected the ladder, and was soon putting it up under the hatch that was in the hall.

'Maybe you will manage,' his uncle commented. 'If you lift the hatch up and slide it to the left it will be out of the way.' He steadied the ladder as Nicholas manoeuvred the hatch, swung lithely into the loft, and disappeared from view.

A moment later, his head appeared at the hatch, and he asked, 'What about a light?'

'Sorry, I forgot. Wait there, and I'll get the big torch from under my bed.'

John returned to climb the ladder to hand the torch to Nicholas. But he had only progressed to the first step when the ladder began swaying about in an alarming way.

'Stop!' Nicholas shouted agitatedly. 'It's not safe.'

John retreated back on to the floor. He felt frustrated and upset. 'Can't even go up a few steps of a ladder,' he muttered angrily.

'Hold it steady,' Nicholas directed. He was soon standing beside his uncle.

'I'd better give up,' said John miserably.

'Look,' Nicholas replied, 'I can't do this unless you hold the ladder for me. It was the same outside. There are things you can't do without me, and there are things I can't do without you. Let's just get on with it.'

John nodded, and steadied the ladder. Nicholas disappeared into the loft again, but this time John could see the beam from the torch flashing back and to.

'Seems all right,' Nicholas reported as he returned to the hall, 'but I can have a look again some time if you want. Tell me if there are things you want me to look out for.'

'Holes, wet and any rot. That'll do for now.'

'No holes and no wet,' Nicholas assured his uncle.

'Nicholas, it won't be long before you're off home again, and I haven't answered any of your questions,' said John apologetically.

Nicholas drew himself up, saying 'Remember I'm a man now, Uncle John. We must get our priorities right. We've got to make your house shipshape, so it can survive all the storms!'

John grinned, and winked at his nephew. 'I see what you mean. There's a lot to do, so we'll be spending plenty of time together. There are winter jobs that we can do, and plans to make for the good weather. Plenty to be doing and talking about...'

Nicholas smiled broadly, picked up the step-ladder, and took it back to his uncle's room. Before he left to go home he said, 'I'll be here on Tuesday and Thursday evenings, and most of each weekend.'

John made the thumbs-up sign, and then waved as his nephew disappeared down the road.

As Nicholas neared his home, he had no worries about how to avoid telling his parents about his wonderful secret. He would tell them everything, but tell them nothing.

'Hi, Dad,' he greeted his father, who had just put the car away in the garage.

'Hello, Nick,' his father replied. 'Good to see you. How've you been?'

'Tell you inside,' said Nicholas cryptically.

He liked his father's strong chunky body and greying hair. He thought that was what a proper dad should look like.

His mother, Sarah, was busy preparing the evening meal.

'Hi, Mum,' he said cheerfully.

'Oh, Nicholas. It's you,' she replied, pleasure showing in her voice. 'Had a good weekend?'

'It was great. I can't remember where you went, but I hope you had a nice time,' Nicholas added generously.

Nicholas had never thought of his parents as being old. He had never known Uncle John as being anything but quite old, and his parents were a lot younger than that. Yet certain children at primary school had sometimes teased him about them, saying that they were his grandparents. He knew that they had had their fiftieth birthdays before he went to secondary school, but with Jake being more than thirty, that made sense.

His mother laughed, and the lines round her eyes crinkled. 'We went to a sculpture exhibition in London,' she reminded him. She flicked her hair out of her eyes, and continued preparing the meal with quick, deft movements.

Over the meal, he made his announcement. 'I'll be at Uncle John's on Tuesday and Thursday evenings, and for most of the weekends,' he stated confidently.

'What about homework?' his father enquired.

'Monday, Wednesday and Friday evenings,' he replied.

'What about gym club and football?' asked his mother.

'I've got a job.'

His parents looked at each other, mystified.

'Uncle John and I are working on his house.'

'But...' Prompted by a sharp kick on the shins from his wife, Nicholas' father, Colin, stopped himself just in time. 'That's good news. Where have you started?'

Nicholas went on to tell his parents about the progress they had made so far with the garage and the roof.

His father was clearly impressed. 'I'm proud of you,' he said warmly. 'I'll come...' Again he experienced a painful kick on the shins. 'I mean... Don't hesitate to let me know if you think there's anything I can do to help you both.' He was rewarded by seeing a glowing smile on his wife's face as she looked at him across the table.

'Okay,' replied Nicholas, as he hungrily devoured a second helping of casserole that his mother had heaped onto his plate.

Colin valued Sarah's perceptiveness and her quick action that had guided him. He admired her greatly, and in many ways. Physically, she was easily recognisable as the person he had married before she was twenty. Her slender but strong frame and her thick auburn hair were little changed, and although now fifty-four, she could easily be mistaken for someone much younger.

Later, as he lay in bed, Nicholas thought about how perfectly his plan had worked. He was going to spend all the time with Uncle John that he needed. Uncle John's house would slowly be repaired, and he would learn everything he knew about the fifth key. He wondered when he would be ready to make the pledge. But that did not worry him. He and Uncle John would know when the time was right. Meantime, he would learn a lot about house repair and maintenance. The results of that would keep Uncle John warm and safe for years to come. And all the while, his parents would help, suspecting nothing of his wonderful secret.

He hugged himself tightly in bed, and drifted off to sleep through a night that was full of the sounds of stormy waves crashing onto a rocky shore.

Chapter Three

On Thursday of that week, Nicholas and his uncle were sitting in their usual seats. The fire was blazing, and the room was so warm that Nicholas had taken his jumper off.

'Is any of the garage in the fire?' he asked.

His uncle laughed. 'No, and there won't be for a while. The wood will have to dry out a good bit first.'

Nicholas stared into the flames and fell silent.

At first his uncle thought nothing of this, but as the silence continued, he asked, 'Is something bothering you?'

Nicholas shook his head, but then burst out, 'You said you've found someone to do the roof. That's my job. I wanted to do it.' Tears sprang into his eyes.

'Now then,' said his uncle, 'there's nothing I would have liked better than to teach you myself, but that would take time, and we need to get the place watertight before we can work together on the inside.'

Nicholas looked at him. 'You really mean that?'

His uncle nodded. 'I know that you want to do the outside work, but teaching you would have taken quite a while.' He laughed. 'We would have had to fix something low down for you to practise on first, because we both know that me and climbing up ladders don't mix. So I've done the next best thing. I phoned round a few places, and by luck I came across a firm who can send someone in the middle of January.'

'But that's weeks away!' Nicholas protested.

'I didn't think I could get someone this side of Christmas, and the middle of January is pretty good.' John paused, with an air of suspense.

'What is it?' asked Nicholas. 'There's something you haven't told me yet. Isn't there?'

John could not hide the smile that spread across his face. 'The man who's coming is the son of a very old friend of mine. My friend died more than ten years ago, but his son remembered me, and he's more than willing to do me a favour.'

Nicholas was puzzled. What could the favour be? He could not guess, so he waited for his uncle to continue.

'He said he'd need an extra pair of hands. You know, someone to hold things for him, and hand things to him. I told him about you, and he's agreed to come at weekends so that you can work together.'

'Him and me!' exclaimed Nicholas. 'He'll let me help?' he added incredulously.

'He'll teach you quite a bit about the job along the way.'

Nicholas could hardly speak. 'I can't wait!'

'You won't be doing much waiting, because there's plenty we can get on with before then,' said his uncle. Nicholas looked at him expectantly, and John continued. 'We've got a lot to talk about. Haven't we?'

'Yes...'

'And in amongst all that we'll make our plans for what we'll do to this house once it's watertight. I've been thinking. I've still got all my old tools. Haven't used them for years, and they're pretty out of date by modern standards.'

'Where are they?' asked Nicholas.

John nodded towards the metal chests that stood in the corner of the room. 'In there.'

'Can I look?'

'Good idea. Fetch the top one over here.'

Nicholas lifted the first chest across. It was very heavy. He tried his hardest not to let it show that it was a struggle for him. His uncle seemed not to notice, and he stood up and lifted a wooden box down from the end of the high mantelshelf that was nearest to where he sat. The box was something that Nicholas had always admired, but as he had never seen his uncle use it, he had not asked about it. It was roughly the size of an adult's shoe box, although deeper and not so long, and it was made out of wood that was so dark that it was nearly black.

'Not sure where the key is,' his uncle muttered as he balanced the box on one arm of his chair, and he went off in the direction of his bedroom.

Nicholas could now see that although the lid of the box was covered in dust, there was an inlaid pattern consisting of various shades of lighter-coloured pieces of wood. He stared at it, but did not reach out to touch it.

His uncle returned. In his hand he carried a small ring of simple keys, each of which he tried in the lock. None of the first few fitted.

The fourth went in, but made no useful connection.

'Number five,' said John, almost to himself.

Nicholas held his breath as his uncle inserted the key and turned it. There was a faint sound as the lock clicked open. His uncle lifted the lid.

Nicholas leaned forward in his chair to see what was in the box, and found to his astonishment that it was full of keys of all shapes and sizes.

John explained. 'Don't worry. The keys for the chests are easy to spot. They're the four biggest ones, and there's a small blob of gold paint on each. I fixed that before I put them in here. I'll let you hunt them out.'

He passed the box across to Nicholas, who began to sift through the contents.

'Here's one!' he said triumphantly as he identified it. 'Uncle John, where did this box come from?' he asked as he continued to search.

'I don't rightly know. My grandfather left it to me when he died.'

'You were lucky. I don't have anything that belonged to either of my grandads,' said Nicholas. 'Here's another one...' He passed the key across. Then he stopped his search and looked straight at his uncle. 'Does this box have anything to do with the pledge?' he asked.

'I wish I knew,' John replied. 'I've often wondered.'

'How did you know that it was for you?' asked Nicholas. But before his uncle had time to reply, he found another of the keys. 'Got one!' he said, and handed it across.

'He'd written a letter to my father.'

'What did it say?'

'I never saw it. All I know is that when my father opened it after my grandfather's death, he learned that I was to have the box.'

'Did your dad know where the box came from?'

'Not as far as I know. If he did, he never said anything to me.'

'I've got the other one now,' said Nicholas. He shut the lid of the box and handed it to his uncle, who carefully replaced it on the mantelshelf.

'You can find your way into the chest,' his uncle suggested, handing the keys back to Nicholas so that he had them all.

His uncle watched as Nicholas examined the four. There were only minor differences between them, so there was no clue about which belonged to the chest in front of him. He leaned forward and tried one without success, but the lock yielded to the second, and he lifted the lid.

'These are my planes,' said John quietly.

Nicholas reached forward to pick one of them, but then drew back.

'It's all right,' his uncle reassured him. 'Have a look through them all. They're different sizes. If you look at the blades, you'll see some of them are shaped.'

This conversation then led to the telling of many interesting stories about their past use, while Nicholas carefully arranged them across the floor. Then, just as carefully, he packed them back in the chest.

'What's in the other chests, Uncle John?' he asked.

'There are saws, hand drills, a spokeshave or two...'

'Can I look?'

His uncle nodded, and soon they were exploring the contents of the second and third chests.

'The bottom chest doesn't have tools in it,' John explained. 'It's full of old papers of one sort or another.'

'Can we have a look anyway?' asked Nicholas.

His uncle hesitated. Nicholas was about to say that it did not matter, when he had a strong feeling that it did matter. In fact, it mattered very much.

He looked straight across at his uncle and said, 'Uncle John, I think that we have to look in it.'

'If you're that sure, then we'd better,' his uncle agreed. 'But what time is it?'

Nicholas looked at his watch. 'Oh, no, it's ten o'clock already! I promised Dad I'd be back. I've got to go.' He grabbed his coat and rushed out of the door, calling over his shoulder, 'See you soon.' He did not want to do anything that would risk his parents stopping him from seeing his uncle on weekdays, and he sprinted down the road, arriving home out of breath. He was glad to find that his parents were absorbed in watching a DVD, and he went into the room to join them.

'Hi, Nick,' his dad greeted him warmly. 'How're you doing?' He pressed the switch on the remote control to silence the film.

'Hungry,' replied Nicholas with a broad grin on his face.

'We knew you would be,' said his mother cheerfully. 'I've left you something in the kitchen.'

'Thanks, Mum.' Nicholas went straight to see what there was.

'Why not bring it in here?' his dad called after him. 'You can watch the rest of this with us if you want.'

Nicholas had noticed that the DVD was about sculpture from around the world, so he called back, 'School tomorrow. See you in the morning.'

His parents looked at each other.

'He's behaving really responsibly,' said his mother.

'It's a good sign,' replied his father. 'We've got to keep an eye on things. He's planning to be spending a lot of time at John's, but if he keeps this up, it'll be fine.' He was about to switch the DVD back on, but he became thoughtful, and then said, 'I'll be working from home tomorrow afternoon. I think I'll take a walk up to John's after lunch. I'll get a better idea of what they're up to, and I can find out if there's anything they need.'

'I could make something in the morning for you to take along.'

'That's a good idea. I'd forgotten you were having a day off.'

'Yes, with that long appointment at the dentist in the afternoon, I thought I'd have the whole day off. I won't be able to concentrate on much in the morning.'

'I think I'd be the same,' Colin sympathised. 'Shall we finish watching this DVD now?'

Sarah nodded, but she could not focus on it. Instead, her mind drifted. She worked in the office of a local branch of a large insurance firm. She had applied for the job as manager of the administrative staff when Nicholas started at secondary school. Before that, she had done a variety of jobs – mainly part time, as she and Colin had always planned that one of them should be around for Nicholas. They did not want to repeat the mistakes that they had made with Jake. Oh, they had done their best, but they had been so young when he was born.

However, things had not always gone smoothly. Not long after Nicholas' seventh birthday, Colin's job was moved much further from home, and he had been working away for weeks at a time. He had met a divorcee during a long lonely evening in a pub one night, and it was not long before he was staying with her whenever he was away. Sarah knew nothing of this for a long time. At first, she had put his distant behaviour down to the stresses of being away, but then one day she overheard him speaking on his mobile to someone who clearly was more than just a friend, and she realised that something was very wrong.

Tackling this had not been easy. When she had asked him about it, he had made up a story that sounded barely plausible. But she persisted – gently at first, and then more forcefully. When everything came out, he spoke little of the woman, but ended up showing a lot of distress about the long separations from home, and together they decided that he should look for a different job. That was when Sarah had gone back to work herself. They had looked at their finances, and decided that he should hand in his notice straight away. In a month's time, he was at home with Nicholas, and she was working as a secretary for a consultant at the hospital, to fill in for someone who was on maternity leave. Having done this kind of work before, she found it straightforward, and the consultant was glad to have her, as it was difficult to get a replacement who understood medical terminology. Colin had said that he would let the woman know that he would not be in touch again, and Sarah had trusted him to do that. At first, she had felt very anxious about the existence of this woman, but when she understood that their association had been merely Colin's desperate attempt to cope with being away from home so much, she gave her little further thought. After all, Colin had assured her that nothing physically intimate had taken place between them. When the consultant's secretary had had her baby, she wanted to reduce her hours, and the post was made into a jobshare. By then, Colin had secured work as regional manager for a chain of retail outlets, and although he still had to travel, he was rarely away overnight – a situation that suited them very well.

Yet, this evening, there was something that troubled her. Why on earth should that be? After all, it had happened more than five years ago. She glanced at Colin. He appeared to be engrossed in the film, but although it was about one of their favourite subjects, she could not connect with it.

'Col?' she said quietly.

He did not seem to hear her.

She repeated his name, this time a little louder.

'What is it, love?' he asked, his gaze not moving from the monitor.

'I think I'm too tired. I can't concentrate. Let's go to bed now, and save the rest for another night.'

'Okay,' he replied good-naturedly, and switched it off.

Sarah felt guilty about not being completely direct with him, but she knew that she needed some time to think. Yet when she lay in bed that night, listening to the gentle sound of his snoring, and feeling wide awake, she wished after all that she had said something. But what could she have said? There had been times over the last five years when one or the other of them had referred to that difficult time in their lives, expressing profound relief that they had found a way through it together. What else was there to say?

Each time she thought she might be about to doze off, she returned to full wakefulness with a start. She had certainly been preoccupied with memories of that time. Why? Her thoughts circled and circled, but got nowhere. Then she began to think about Nicholas. Gone thirteen already. It seemed only yesterday that he was a baby in a cot, next to this bed. Thirteen... Maybe this was a clue. What was happening in my life when *I* was thirteen? she wondered.

It was then that she remembered that not long after she was thirteen, she had had to live with her mother's cousin, Joy, during term time. Her father had found a much better job, and the family moved to London, but everyone thought that she should stay on at the same school – at least until she had done her first external exams. So in the end it was nearly two years before she was with them in term time as well as the holidays. She liked living with Joy. Joy had lots of friends, and she included her in just about everything – concerts, theatre, gatherings at her home...

She shuddered involuntarily, and then she remembered something that was not so good. That creepy man who used to come to some of the gatherings... What was his name? Stanley. Yes, Stanley. She had not liked the look of him when she first saw him, and she soon noticed that he put on a bit of an act around the others, while being nasty to her when unobserved. She had tried to speak to Joy about him, but had found that Joy was dismissive of her concerns. This surprised her, because in every other way she had found her to be warm and closely involved with everything she wanted to say. She had felt hurt and isolated. She had not felt that she could phone her mother to talk it over, because Joy would have been bound to overhear. And when the holidays came, the hubbub of family life took up all the time, and in any case, Stanley was not there, so she felt fine. Stanley... He would pinch her arm in the kitchen, or worse still, he would pinch her bottom. And it would always hurt. One day he even purposely tripped her up, so that she smashed some of Joy's best tea set. She had run to her room, sobbing. Joy had followed her, reassuring her over and over again that the loss of the tea set was not a disaster. Colin was so unlike Stanley. In fact, he was not like Stanley in any way at all. Colin was always gentle and kind. She and Colin had always discussed things openly. Colin had never done anything knowingly to hurt her... Here she stopped. He *had* done something that he *must* have known would cause her hurt, and this was something that they had never spoken about. Together they had found a way to correct the situation, but they had never spoken about how hurt she had felt. She realised then that this was at least half her fault, as she had never said anything about it to him, and she supposed that he had been feeling so churned up at the time, that all his energy was being used in keeping himself afloat.

She resolved to talk to him about it the next day, and after that she soon fell asleep.

Sarah was woken the next morning by what sounded like fragmenting crockery coming from the kitchen. She looked across at Colin, but the bed beside her was empty. The clock showed her that it was past eight. She jumped out of bed, put on her housecoat, and hurried downstairs.

'Sorry, Mum,' said Nicholas, 'I knocked these plates off the worktop.'

'Never mind about that,' his mother replied. 'These pieces of crockery are sharp. Have any of them cut you?'

'I'm fine, but I'll be late for school if I don't go now.'

'Don't worry. I'll clear it up. I'm not at work today.'

'Thanks, Mum.' He put on his coat and picked up his bag. 'Dad left a few minutes ago.'

'Have a good day. I'll see you after school... if I survive the dentist,' she joked.

As she cleared up the mess, she promised herself that she would talk to Colin that afternoon, or in the evening at the latest. Then she showered, dressed, and began to mix a fruit cake for him to take to John at lunchtime. She knew it was what John would like best. He could keep it in a tin, and cut a slice whenever he fancied. She stirred in his favourite spices, and then reached for some of her homemade marmalade to give it the orangey tang that he so liked.

She listened to the radio as she baked the cake, and she also prepared a few things to restock her freezer for days when things were rushed. There was a play on the radio that interested her – a story of life in a small rural community several generations ago. She supposed that some of it represented plenty of what had been familiar to John as a child.

She and Colin had been worried about John for quite a while now. His looking older had been accompanied by his looking considerably thinner, but he would never let them be involved in making sure he got enough to eat. An occasional fruit cake was all that was allowed. Beyond that, he would not go. And his house... Over the years, it had changed from being neat and well kept, inside and out, to a place that was suffering from decay. Colin had done his best to interest John in having people round to help him, but he would have none of it. What a relief it had been when Nicholas had announced their plan. Even if some of it went wrong, there was change in the wind, and surely something good would come of that.

Colin had a relatively relaxing morning. He had only to visit three shops, and there were no hitches. Sales were going well, there were no problems with staff, and the range of stock was being increased. He was looking forward to working at home that afternoon. A leisurely lunchtime visit to John's, and then when Sarah was back from the dentist, they could have a chat before Nick came home from school. After that, they would have a quiet evening finishing that DVD.

It had been quite a surprise when Nick had told them of his plans, but it was a huge relief. It seemed that John was able to trust Nick in a way that he just could not face with anyone else. Maybe it was something to do with Nick's age and personality? It hardly mattered. The most important thing was that something was changing – and for the better.

He arrived home just after twelve, and was hit by the aroma of fresh baking as he entered the kitchen. He sniffed the air appreciatively.

'Perfect timing,' said Sarah, smiling.

Colin gave her a kiss on the cheek. 'I hope your trip to the dentist isn't as traumatic as you think it might be.'

'I'll be fine.' Then Sarah added wryly, 'The waiting is usually worse than the event.' She handed him a wickerwork basket. 'This is for John.'

'Thanks. I'm sure he'll let me give it to him if it's one of his favourite cakes.' He kissed her again. 'See you soon.'

He whistled a cheerful tune as he strolled up the road to see his uncle. Life was good.

When he arrived at the house he was surprised to find that the back door was locked. 'Odd,' he muttered. 'John always unlocks it when he gets up.' He walked round the side of the house so that he could knock on the living room window to catch his attention, but although through the grime he could see him sitting in his usual chair, he did not react to the sound of his banging. 'Very odd,' he said aloud. Surely his hearing can't have got that bad.' Then he froze, as he realised that something must be very wrong.

Determinedly, he went round to the bedroom window, collecting a brick on the way. He covered his arm and head with his coat, and smashed the pane by the fastening, opened the window, and climbed in. He was at his uncle's side within minutes.

John was mumbling, but he did not appear to notice him. Colin could not make out anything that he was saying. He reached for the phone and rang the emergency services. Fortunately, the ambulance arrived very quickly, and the paramedics were soon attending to John.

'We're pretty sure he's had a stroke,' said one of the men. 'The quicker we get him to hospital, the better. You said you're his nephew?'

'That's right.'

'Do you want to come in the ambulance?'

'I think I'd better. I'll just have to leave that window I smashed. I can board it up once I know what's happening with John.'

Colin felt quite shaky as he watched the paramedics caring for his uncle. He was impressed by their professionalism, and their real concern. He reflected that although he had heard many bad stories about the Health Service, there was no chance that this was going to be anything other than a good one. Whatever the outcome, these people were doing their best.

Fortunately, the emergency staff at the hospital were not overloaded, and John was assessed immediately, and then taken to a ward. Colin gave the ward staff his phone number, made a note of theirs, and left for home to wait for Sarah's return.

Once home, he sat in a chair feeling very shocked. John was certainly an old man, and anything could happen at that stage in life, but he'd hardly ever had a day's illness. He thought that he ought to go and do something to secure the window, but he did not feel able to do anything other than wait for Sarah. Maybe he should contact a joiner? He reached for the phone and rang Tom Barker's mobile number. Tom was a neighbour who worked as a handyman.

'Tom? Glad I've caught you. Any chance you could do a patch-up at my uncle's house? I had to break in. He's not well, and had to go to hospital... Your mate can go down? That's great. Thanks. Let me know how much.'

He replaced the phone, took out his handkerchief, and mopped his brow. He felt cold, but his forehead was covered in sweat. Not long now before Sarah would be back. Three at the latest, he calculated.

He made himself a mug of tea, and sipped mechanically. He realised that he felt very upset.

Just then, the door opened, and Sarah appeared. One side of her face looked extremely odd, and when she spoke it did not move. Colin dropped his mug and grabbed her arms, saying urgently, 'Sarah, what is it?' He was shaking from head to foot.

'The dentist had to use a lot of anaesthetic,' explained Sarah calmly. 'It'll wear off in a while, and then my face will work again. What on earth is the matter, Col? You look as if you've seen a ghost.'

He took her hand. 'Come and sit down. I've got some bad news.'

Sarah looked alarmed, and followed him obediently into the sitting room.

'John's in hospital,' he stated baldly. 'It looks as if he's had a stroke. When I went up to the house I had to break in. He was semi-conscious, and was mumbling, so I got an ambulance.'

'Oh, no!' exclaimed Sarah. 'Poor John.'

'I went with him to the hospital, and he's in good hands. He's in Ward Three.'

Sarah relaxed a little. 'I know most of the staff on that ward. I'll give them a ring and see how he is.' She reached for the phone, but stopped to say, 'No wonder you got such a shock when you saw my face. You must have thought I was heading for the same thing.'

Colin nodded mutely, and Sarah phoned the ward.

When she had finished the call, she said, 'The news is better than I thought it might be. He's comfortable, but confused. Not surprising, really. He's never been a patient in hospital before, has he? His left side is weak, and that's distressing him. He keeps trying to reach out with his hand, but he can't manage.'

'Being left-handed doesn't help at a time like this,' Colin commented. 'Yes, poor John.'

Sarah began to make plans. 'We'll go up and see him this evening.' She looked at her watch. 'Nicholas will be home soon. We'll tell him what's happened, and we can all be up there for six, when visiting starts.' Suddenly she smiled. 'I'll go and clear up the tea. It's the second mess I've had in the kitchen today.'

'Let me do it,' said Colin quickly.

'We can do it together,' she replied.

'What was the first mess?' asked Colin as they worked side by side.

'Nicholas had an accident with some crockery before he went to school. I told him not to worry, and I sorted it out.' She paused, and then said carefully, 'It's funny. I was awake in the night remembering how I broke some of a prized tea set when I was about his age.'

Despite his worry about John, Colin detected in the subtleties of his wife's tones that there was more to the story than she was saying, and he said firmly, 'You must tell me all about that once we've got time.'

'I will,' she replied.

Again Colin sensed that her words conveyed a deeper meaning, and he resolved that when the time was right, he would do his best to ensure that he understood what it was.

After they had finished cleaning up, Colin walked a little way down the road in the direction of the bus stop so that he could meet Nicholas. He watched from a distance as the bus disgorged its packed contents of young people onto the street, and he waited until Nicholas had nearly reached him before he spoke.

'Hi, Nick,' he said.

Nicholas jumped. He had been deep in thought about the physics lesson at school, because they had been learning about electricity, and he had listened intently to everything.

'What is it, Dad?' he asked. He knew that his father would not have walked down the road like this unless something important had happened.

'I'm afraid I've got some bad news,' Colin began. 'Come to the house, and we'll tell you straight away.'

In the privacy of the kitchen, Colin told Nicholas what had happened. He watched his son's face turn white as he took in the news. He swayed a little, and Sarah and Colin took an arm each, and supported him into the sitting room and into a comfortable chair.

'Take it easy, son,' Colin advised. 'Take your time. It's been a big shock for all of us. Uncle John's an old man, but he's never been really ill. I'll get you a glass of water.'

'No!' choked Nicholas. 'Stay here.' He gathered himself. 'I've got to see him,' he said urgently. 'I must.'

'It's okay, Nick,' his father soothed him. 'We're all going up to the hospital very soon.'

'Yes, visiting time starts at six,' his mother explained. 'Nicholas,' she added gently, 'he's in very good hands. I know most of the staff well, and they do excellent work.'

Nicholas had been thinking that his head was going to explode, but the sound of his mother's words calmed him a little. So Uncle John had a chance of surviving? He tried to form the question into spoken words, but his mouth felt as if it were full of glue, and he made no sound.

'Take your time, son,' said his father again. 'I'll get that glass of water now. You'll be surprised how much it helps.'

Nicholas took the glass from his father, gulped some water, and then spluttered.

'Just sip it,' his mother advised.

As the cool liquid began to dissolve the mess inside his mouth, speaking became possible, and he asked, 'What will happen to him?'

'He's very weak and confused at the moment,' said his mother, 'but there's a good chance that he'll stabilise. I don't know what movement he'll regain on that left side. It's too soon to know. But the main thing is that he was found quickly, and that really helps. With a stroke, the sooner it's treated, the better the outcome.'

Here his father took over. 'When you left him last night he was fine?'

'Yes.'

'What was he wearing?'

'His baggy cord trousers and that big jumper that you knitted for him, Mum.'

'That's excellent,' Colin replied.

'Why?'

'Because that means he definitely wasn't ill until this morning. When I found him, he was wearing his working jumper – the one with lots of knitted patches on it. That means he must have been in bed in the night, and then got up intending to do some work this morning. At some time between then and when I arrived at twelve fifteen, he's had the stroke.'

'We'll know more over the next few days, Nicholas,' said his mother. 'If he stabilises, there's plenty that can be done to help him.'

Nicholas felt some of the stress soak out of his body. Uncle John wasn't out of the woods yet, but he was in with a chance, and he would do everything he could to make sure that that chance was the biggest one possible.

'I've got to see him every day,' he stated emphatically.

'We all will,' his father reassured him.

'Your dad and I can arrange to take some time off work,' said Sarah. 'We'll take it in turns, and that will mean that Uncle John will have one of us with him every afternoon.'

'And I can go every evening, after school. Can't I?'

'Of course, you can,' his father replied. 'There's a good bus service between here and the hospital, so you'll always be able to get there for six, even if we aren't ready.' He looked at his watch. 'Hm... It's five already. Nick, I think you and I should go and get a couple of things from his house – something familiar that he might recognise. After that, we can come back and pick up your mum, and we'll all go to the hospital together.'

Nicholas jumped out of his chair. He felt much better, and he knew exactly what to do.

Colin collected the spare key, and they set off. At the house, he inspected the boarding on the window, and was reassured that it was secure. Nicholas opened the first metal box and selected two of the planes.

'That's it, Dad,' he stated as he locked the box again.

Colin did not question his son's choice. They collected Sarah and drove to the hospital.

Ward Three was full of people who were lying down in bed, with one or two visitors sitting at their side. There was a low hum of conversation between the visitors, but very little that engaged the patients, who were either too ill or too tired to talk. Nicholas saw straight away where his uncle lay, and he hurried to his bedside, while his mother went to speak to a nurse. His father held back to let Nicholas have a few minutes with John on his own.

Nicholas sat on a chair that he had pulled tight up to the head of the bed. His uncle lay motionless with his eyes shut, and his face had a greyish hue. Nicholas leaned forward until his mouth was near his uncle's ear, and then he whispered, 'Uncle John, it's me, Nicholas. You don't have to say anything. I'll do all the talking. If you can hear me, you only have to move a finger of your... right hand. Don't try to move your left hand. It has to be your right.' Nicholas took a breath and said, 'You are the one who knows the secret of the pledge.' He

32

waited. To his utter joy, he saw his uncle's fingers twitch.

'You're there!' he said with suppressed elation.

Again he saw the fingers move a little.

'Mum and Dad are here. They know it'll be a shock for you to be in hospital, and they're fixing to come and see you every afternoon. I'll come every evening. This evening I've brought two of your best planes for you to see. Can you open your eyes?'

He watched his uncle's face intently. He thought he saw the right eyelid move fractionally, but he could not be sure. But when he looked at his hand, he saw the fingers moving a little more.

'I won't leave them in the hospital,' he told him. 'I'll keep them at home so they'll be safe, but I can bring them again.'

Sarah had finished speaking to the nurse, and she and Colin approached the bed. She took hold of John's right arm, leaned towards his head and said, 'Hello, Uncle John. It's me, Sarah. I've come to see you. I know most of the staff here, so I can phone any time to see how you're getting on. We'll visit every day, and I want you to know that you're in the best place for now.'

She fetched a chair, and sat at the foot of the bed.

Then Colin took his uncle's hand and said quietly, 'We're all here, John. Colin, Sarah and Nicholas. We'll come and see you every day. You're in good hands. I know that everything will be feeling strange at the moment, but we'll sort something out. Don't worry.' He felt his uncle squeeze his hand weakly, and tears sprang into his eyes. 'I'll get a chair and I'll sit here for a while.'

'You stay there, Dad,' Nicholas directed quickly, 'and I'll bring you a chair.'

Colin was glad not to have to let go of his uncle's hand. He felt calmed by the brief response that he had felt. He sat down on the chair that Nicholas brought.

The three sat mostly in silence. Sharing only an occasional comment, they were content. When seven o'clock came, a small bell rang, and all the visitors began to collect up their belongings and stack their chairs.

Nicholas whispered in his uncle's ear, 'See you tomorrow.' Then they left. They were on their way home in the car when he asked, 'Mum, can you phone the ward just before I go to bed?'

'Yes, of course. I'd already planned to. I found out from the nurse that they are hoping it was only a minor stroke – a small bleed in his brain.'

'But surely he wouldn't be so unwell if it were only that,' Colin reasoned.

'I'm coming to that,' said Sarah. 'They've found he's got a chest infection. The two together can easily result in someone of his age being as ill as he is. They're giving him a course of an antibiotic, and they're hoping that he'll start feeling a bit better after a couple of days.'

Nicholas did not feel very hungry that evening, but he made himself eat some of the food that his parents prepared, and then he went to try to concentrate on his homework. It was important to him to look at what he had learned about electricity that day. He was sure it was going to be very useful.

Just before ten, his mother came to let him know that his uncle was stable.

Chapter Four

When Nicholas woke the next day, he was very glad that it was the weekend. He and his father soon decided to spend some time at John's house.

'Now we know that he's doing not too badly, I think it would be a good idea to have a look at what needs doing,' Colin announced.

'After Uncle John and I looked at the roof, he fixed for someone to start working on it in January,' said Nicholas. 'I'm going to be helping,' he added importantly.

'Maybe you and I could look round inside,' his father suggested. 'It might be a long time before he'll be able to come home again, and when he does, there'll need to be some improvements.'

'What do you mean?'

'It's really too soon to be able to say. Meantime, you and I can collect any washing, strip his bed, and clean round a bit.'

'Okay, I know where everything is,' said Nicholas confidently.

They worked at John's house until lunchtime, and then gathered up the washing to take back with them.

Sarah was pleased to see them, and willingly loaded up the washing machine. She had made a pile of sandwiches for them to share before they all set off for the extended weekend visiting time at the hospital.

'There are quite a few jobs at the house that Nicholas and I could do together,' Colin began. 'He's kept everything clean, but there are things that need to be replaced, and things that we could improve for him.'

'I think you should go ahead,' Sarah confirmed.

'Are you up for it, Nick?' asked his father.

Nicholas felt a warm glow spread through his body. 'I'm your man,' he said.

Colin continued. 'I know you'd already planned to spend weekends there.' He smiled. 'How about being a working man at weekends and a schoolboy through the week?'

'Definitely!'

'You might get some surprises with your dad,' said Sarah.

'What do you mean?' asked Nicholas.

'Before we were married, we managed to buy a small terraced house, but it needed everything doing to it. Your dad did it all, with me as the apprentice – although that was interrupted when I was pregnant with Jake. We moved here when I was pregnant with you – a few years after Jake left home. Hardly anything needed doing, so you've not seen your dad in action.'

'I have,' Nicholas protested. 'I remember when he built the garage.'

Colin was puzzled. 'But you were only three.'

'I remember the huge lorry with all the bricks. The heaps were massive. And you were this big superman who made a garage sprout up out of the ground. But I haven't seen you doing anything else. What can you do?'

His mother continued. 'He did a kitchen and a bathroom, and we did all the decorating together.'

'Wow! Dad, can we do the whole of Uncle John's house?'

'That would take a long time, but we can certainly revamp some parts of it,' his father agreed.

'And I'm going to be the apprentice,' said Nicholas happily. He felt as if he wanted to run all the way to the hospital to tell his uncle.

When they arrived at the ward, John was propped up in bed, looking a bit better. He was too weary to say much. Nicholas could see that the left side of his mouth still did not look right, but it was not as odd as it had appeared at first. His left arm was curved in front of him, and in his hand was a strange-looking plastic ball that was covered in soft spikes.

'Can I have a look?' asked Nicholas curiously.

His uncle gave a slight nod.

'It's squeezy,' Nicholas commented as he tried it out.

'It'll be for exercising his hand,' Sarah explained. 'They start as soon as they can with this kind of thing. I'll leave you here and have a chat with one of the nurses.'

Nicholas and his dad told Uncle John how they would take care of the house for him meantime. They did not tell him about their plans, as they both knew that this could make him feel agitated, and he did not have the strength to cope with those feelings at the moment.

Sarah joined them, looking cheerful. She looked at John, saying, 'The news is good. They say you're doing very well.'

Again they talked in a way that did not require John to answer, but this time they involved him more, and he would nod, or shake his head slightly. And when they got up to leave after an hour, he tried to cling on to Nicholas' hand.

'Hey! That's good,' said Nicholas, admiring the minimal movement in his uncle's hand, and he noticed that a flicker of a smile lit his face in response.

The following week saw a considerable improvement in John's condition. The physiotherapist was seeing him every day, and the doctors were talking about transferring him to the rehabilitation unit. They wanted him to have more physiotherapy, to gain some weight, and to be assessed to see what kind of support he might need when he finally left hospital.

It was when he was transferred to that unit that Colin made the decision to tell him what he and Nicholas had begun to do in the house. When he raised the subject, John looked distressed, and Colin thought he had done the wrong thing.

He was surprised when John said, 'I'm very grateful to you both. It's been on my mind, and I've been worrying a lot.'

'Why didn't you say?' asked Nicholas.

'I didn't want you to have any bigger burden.'

'But it's great!' Nicholas insisted. 'Dad and I are working together, and he's showing me how to do all kinds of things. We're drawing up the plans for your kitchen and bathroom.' Here he clapped his hand to his mouth. 'Oh no! I wasn't supposed to say anything about that yet.'

John chuckled. 'I know your dad. Whenever he gets his hands on a job, it's got to be done to perfection. That's one of the things that worried me about asking for his help. I thought he'd end up wearing himself out, and you and your mum would see hardly anything of him.'

'Well, it's all working out perfectly,' Sarah assured him. 'Colin and Nicholas are thick as thieves most of the time.'

'I couldn't be happier, John,' said Colin. 'The age Nick is at, it wouldn't be surprising if he wanted to pull away from me a bit, and I was bracing myself for that, but this project has brought us closer together.' He put a hand on Nicholas' shoulder and squeezed it affectionately. Then he added, 'I just wish it hadn't been that you had to get ill first.'

'I knew that things had to change,' John admitted, 'but I couldn't face making a start. Fortunately, Nicholas helped me with that before I fell ill, so the whole thing has been less of a shock. Nicholas, promise me one thing.'

'What?'

'We were in the middle of some interesting chats before all this happened. Can we keep on with those?'

'We *must*,' Nicholas stated emphatically. 'I've been waiting for you to get better so that we can.'

John drew in a deep breath, and relaxed. 'Then everything's fine,' he murmured. He shut his eyes, and soon began to doze.

'I think it's time for us to go,' whispered Sarah. 'The staff say he'll be in for a good few weeks. There will be plenty of time to talk things through.'

'Mum, now that he's a bit better, I think I can come and talk to him on my own sometimes.'

'That's easy to arrange,' said Colin. 'I'll help if you need transport.'

'Yes,' Sarah encouraged. 'I can see that he's looking forward to your chats. It'll do you both the world of good.'

In bed that night, Colin turned to Sarah and said, 'There was something you were going to tell me about broken crockery.'

Sarah took his hand. She smiled in the darkness, and replied, 'I think it can wait.'

Chapter Five

Visiting time at the rehabilitation unit was quite flexible. The treatments and doctors' visits were well past by three o'clock. Then the patients were given some tea, and from four until seven, visitors were welcome to come and go. With Christmas approaching, the staff had put up some decorations.

Nicholas would go there straight from school, his father would come and stay for a while after work, and then they would go home together. Sarah would visit at weekends, when Nicholas and Colin were busy at John's house.

At first, Nicholas and John would talk about everything that had happened since John had fallen ill. But as he gained a little more strength, their conversation went back to their secret – talking over what they had shared so far.

When Colin joined them, they would discuss what he and Nicholas had begun at John's house, and what they could accomplish. With Nicholas' help, Colin's plans for the kitchen had been finished, and he had estimated how much it would cost.

'There are advantages in myself and Nicholas doing the work,' he told John, 'although depending on how well you are when you go home, the social services might fund necessary adaptations to your house, once they've assessed the situation, but they'll probably use their own tradespeople.'

'I don't want that,' said Nicholas hurriedly.

His father turned to him. 'It's up to your uncle to decide.' Then he addressed John. 'Think it over, and remember there's no pressure from us.'

'But I want to work on it over my Christmas holidays,' Nicholas objected.

Again his father turned to him. 'It's a very exciting proposition, but it's your uncle's house, and he has to make the final decision.'

Nicholas hung his head. It felt for a moment as if the bottom had dropped out of his world. He had not thought about social services before, and he could see what his dad was getting at.

'Someone came to see me this morning about my house,' said

John. 'She said she was an occupational something-or-another, and she was talking about grab rails and things like that. I said I was too tired to think about that at the moment, and she said she would come back again next week, and after that she would speak to you.' He suddenly looked very weary.

'I'll let Sarah know, and she can find out who it was, and have a word with her,' replied Colin hastily. 'Nicholas, I think we should go now, so that John can have a rest.'

'No, don't go yet,' said John urgently. 'I've got something to say. It's about money.'

'We don't have to talk about that now.'

John looked straight at Colin. 'Yes, we do,' he insisted. Nicholas noticed that he seemed to gather strength, and for a moment looked almost back to his old self. 'I've got plenty saved up. I knew a day might come when I needed help. If you and Nicholas really want to go ahead with all that work, then I've got all you'll need. Never mind about Mrs Grab Rails – she can do the frilly bits later if she wants.'

Nicholas laughed out loud. His uncle was right. The grab rails were the frilly bits. He and his father would be doing the real work, and they would do it properly.

He heard his father say, 'You might eventually be grateful for the frilly bits, John, but I know what you're getting at.'

'Colin, when you come in again, I need a cheque book from the house. Nicholas will get it.'

'Where is it, Uncle John?' asked Nicholas, puzzled.

'In that other metal box. It's right on top of everything else. You'll see it as soon as you open the lid.'

'Okay.'

'Colin, I don't want you to be out of pocket,' said John decisively. 'You'll be ordering things up soon, and I'm going to make sure you've got enough for everything.'

Colin was about to protest, but he thought better of it, and instead promised to bring the cheque book.

On the way home in the car, he began to explain to Nicholas why he had agreed, but Nicholas interrupted, saying, 'Look, Dad, it's obvious. If you treat Uncle John as if he can't do anything, that will just help him to stay ill.'

Colin was impressed, and said so. They travelled the rest of the way in companionable silence.

Over the evening meal, Colin said, 'Now that John has given us the go-ahead, we need to agree on a plan of action.'

'But I thought we'd worked it all out already,' Nicholas protested.

'We've worked some of it out,' his father agreed, 'but there's more. Sarah, I'd like to use the whole of the Christmas break to work on this with Nick.'

Sarah smiled. 'I had the impression that you'd already made up your mind.'

Colin went on. 'This time of year is one of the busiest for me at work, but I've got someone who could cover for me. It's one of the experienced shop managers I've been training up. He's very ambitious, and he's hoping to get a move to another part of the country as a regional manager. He's unattached, and I'm certain he'd jump at the chance of the experience of acting up. What do you think?'

Sarah looked at him knowingly, and repeated, 'I thought you'd already made up your mind a while ago. But there's one thing you've missed.'

Colin looked perplexed. 'I thought I'd covered everything.'

'What about me? Oh, I'm willing to bring up the rear with provisions for the workforce, but I'm going to do my bit, too. Col, don't forget that there's another pair of experienced hands here.'

A slow smile spread across Colin's face. 'Okay, it's the rewiring first. I'll go down to the merchant's on Saturday and get everything we need.

Chapter Six

'Uncle John, can we have a proper talk about the pledge today?' asked Nicholas as he arrived for one of his evening visits.

He was surprised to see that John looked round nervously.

'Yes, lad, but keep your voice down.'

'But no one will know what we're talking about,' Nicholas protested.

'You can never be too sure,' his uncle replied. 'You don't know all of what you're dealing with yet, and to be honest, neither do I.' He looked intensely at Nicholas, and then observed, 'You've been very patient while I've been ill.'

'I knew it wasn't right to try and talk about it until now,' said Nicholas modestly. 'And in any case, Dad and I have had plenty to do that's helping me to prepare.'

John nodded knowingly. 'That's right. The man in you is definitely coming to the fore with the work we're doing together. But the impatience of the boy will have had a hard time waiting.'

Nicholas hung his head for a moment, and then burst out, 'I was so worried!'

John put his finger to his lips, and Nicholas dropped his voice before continuing. 'I was worried that I was going to lose you, and I was worried that I wouldn't be able to take the pledge, because without you I would never know enough about it. I couldn't talk to Dad about it because I'm not supposed to, and in any case, he doesn't know anything.' Here he paused for breath before saying, 'I even found it hard to tell him how worried I was about you, in case something else slipped out at the same time.' He bent forward and hid face in his hands.

'You've done well, Nicholas. Being a man can sometimes be very hard, and you are already facing things that some men don't have to face until they're a lot older.'

Nicholas looked up. His face was flushed. 'Am I? Am I, really?'

His uncle inclined his head. 'Surely you can see for yourself?'

'No... Well, yes... sometimes.'

'And now let's get down to business. Your physical strength is developing quickly, and your skills will develop working alongside your dad. Our talks must feed your mind, ready for the pledge. I'll tell you the first part of it. It will not surprise you. You have to swear that you will never tell your father or your son anything about it.'

Nicholas broke in. 'I may never have a son anyway.'

'Don't be too sure,' replied his uncle. 'You've a lot of life to live.'

'Tell me, Uncle,' urged Nicholas, desperately.

'Just one more bit, and then we have to let you have time to absorb it,' said his uncle firmly. 'If by the time your grandson is thirteen, you have not understood the full meaning of the fifth key, then you must pass on all your knowledge about it to him, and help him all you can.'

'That's what you're doing now. Isn't it, Uncle John? My own grandad couldn't face it, so it had to be you and me.' Nicholas thought for a moment, before adding slowly, 'Wait a minute. You told me that only one out of each second generation is to know. Your grandad had told you about it, so you shouldn't have tried to tell my grandad. You should have waited for Jake to be born.'

'I follow what you're saying, but I didn't see it like that. I wanted to tell the person that my grandad would have told, had he lived on.'

There was a silence, and then Nicholas asked, 'Do you think that somehow my grandad James might have known that he would die young?'

'I hadn't ever thought about that,' said John. 'I'd always thought it was all to do with him somehow not liking me, but maybe it was deeper than that – a kind of instinct. Maybe that was why he was frightened.'

'It was really hard on you that your grandad told you that you weren't to have children.'

'He was a man I respected greatly, and I wanted to follow his wishes, but it was hard when I was younger.' Here John smiled. 'I had to steer away from the lasses, when I could have done with chasing a few.'

'It wasn't just that,' said Nicholas seriously.

'What do you mean?'

'You weren't the chosen one, so you had to be only the bearer of the pledge.'

His uncle stared at him. 'I never really thought about that.'

'Anyway,' pronounced Nicholas confidently, 'you and I are going to find out everything about the fifth key, and then it won't matter if I have children and grandchildren.'

His uncle smiled again. 'It's wonderful being together now. I've been so alone with this for all these years.'

'Is there anything that's happened to you that might be connected to it all?'

'Not really. Except...'

'Except what?' Nicholas pressed.

'That box on the mantelshelf.'

'Is there something about it that you haven't told me yet?'

His uncle hesitated. 'It's nothing...'

Nicholas waited.

'I just get a feeling about it. It's not anything I can put my finger on.'

'There must have been a reason why your grandad wanted to make sure that you got it when he died.'

'I've often puzzled about that. I can't understand why he didn't say something to me when he was still alive.'

Nicholas noticed that his uncle had begun to look very tired. 'I'd better go now,' he said quietly. He stood up, took his uncle's hands in his, squeezed them tight, and then left, saying, 'See you tomorrow.'

On his way home on the bus, Nicholas made a decision. Next time he saw his uncle, he would ask him if he could take the box home to his bedroom.

The rest of the evening was spent discussing more of the renovation plans with his father, and they planned to spend Saturday morning searching out more of the supplies and equipment that they would need over the Christmas holidays and beyond.

Before Nicholas went to bed, his father said, 'I've made up my mind to get central heating installed. I know John's been managing with his portable heaters, but I think he needs something that will heat the whole house whenever necessary. There's a gas pipe comes in at the kitchen, because there used to be a gas cooker there years ago. You and I can install all the radiators, and I'll arrange for someone to do the boiler.'

Nicholas' face shone. 'That's great, Dad.'

He went to bed and dreamed of Uncle John's house looking good, outside and in, with a welcoming warmth there to greet him when he came back home at last.

Colin and Sarah sat up late, discussing where John might live until his home was ready for him.

'He's coming along well,' Sarah began. 'I think the rehab unit will be ready to discharge him in a few weeks.'

'I've been thinking about that, too,' replied Colin. 'We need somewhere local for him to stay – perhaps even for a few months.'

'I've been doing a bit of research.'

'Already?'

'If I'm going to work, and helping you and Nicholas as well, I can't look after John,' said Sarah, 'so I've got a list of local homes that we can check out. Remember, we might have to book a place in advance.'

'Good thinking,' replied Colin admiringly. 'My head's been full of radiators, wire, brackets and a million other things, while you've been thinking about people.'

'A good division of labour, don't you think?'

'I can tell by the look on your face that you've already got something up your sleeve,' Colin observed. 'Spill the beans.'

Sarah smiled. 'I've been in touch with three places, and looked at two. I fell in love with the second one straight away.'

'Okay, tell me all about it.'

'It's a couple who've got quite a big house. They live upstairs, and the residents live downstairs. They're registered to take people for respite care. The woman – Maggie – used to be a nurse.'

'How many do they take?'

'Usually four. Five at the most. They come for a fortnight at a time, and then the couple have a week off, before taking another group for a fortnight.'

'But that's no good for us. We'd need somewhere for longer than that.'

'I know. That's the only sticking point. But I had a long talk with them, and they're going to think about it. It rather depends on how well John is when he's discharged. They aren't planning to go away again until around Easter. They're going to get back to me before Christmas, and if the answer is yes, they would like to go to the hospital and meet John once we've put the proposition to him.'

'You're a marvel,' said Colin. 'Exactly how far away are they?'

'Ten minutes' walk. And I've told them that if they want to be out for an evening, and John can't be left on his own, I'll go round. I think that should clinch it,' Sarah added confidently. 'I loved the atmosphere. It was so friendly and relaxed, and the residents looked well cared for and content.'

Chapter Seven

It was the end of term at last, and Nicholas was in his art class. He did never particularly looked forward to it, as he preferred to have practical things to do. However, today felt different. He was looking forward to Saturday, when he and his father would set to work in earnest. The materials that they had bought together were stacked in Uncle John's living room, where they had already cleared as much of the floor space as they could. They had been doing further preparation – taking up some floorboards, and making several extra inspection hatches where they needed them. His mind was so full of it that he did not hear what the teacher was saying.

It was only when Laura, the girl who was sitting next to him, nudged him that he remembered where he was.

'What are we supposed to be doing?' he whispered.

She handed him a large sheet of paper. 'We can choose today,' she replied. 'We can paint anything, so long as we're willing to stand up and talk about it afterwards.'

'Thanks,' he said gratefully.

The girl offered to share the tray of paints she had brought, and he went to collect a brush. When he returned, she was already making a simple sketch that he guessed was going to be a large bunch of flowers.

Lost in thought once more, he absentmindedly dipped his brush into the nearest container of paint, and drew it across his sheet of paper as he thought about what his father had said last night about earth wires. No good attaching them to plastic pipes...

Briefly he noted the colour of the stripe of paint, cleaned his brush, and thought about his uncle's special box. Uncle John had promised that he could have it in his bedroom, and he was going to collect it at the weekend.

Half an hour later, the teacher's voice penetrated his inner world.

'Time to start clearing up,' it boomed.

Nicholas reflected that it sounded a bit like the foghorn he had heard when watching an old film recently. He had liked the film because it was all about lifeboats in action in days gone by. With a

46

start, it was then he became aware that he had covered his paper with a painting of a stormy sea, and a ship that was perilously near some rocky cliffs.

'Oh, no!' he said aloud.

'What's that, Nicholas?' asked the teacher.

'Er... um... nothing,' Nicholas stumbled.

The teacher went on. 'Hurry up and tidy away. Then we'll have time to discuss everyone's art work.'

Nicholas felt desperate. There was no way that he wanted to talk about what he had painted. What could he do? Quickly, he grabbed a container of dirty water, and tipped some of its contents over his painting, pretending that it was an accident. Then he snatched a cloth, and in a staged attempt to clean up the mess, swiftly blurred his painting beyond recognition.

He glanced around him. Fortunately it was only Laura who had noticed what he had done. She looked astonished, but mercifully said nothing and busied herself with other things.

He heard the teacher's voice. 'Oh, bad luck, Nicholas. Never mind. You can still describe the painting and tell us about it.'

Nicholas relaxed. He screwed up the soggy sheet, and buried it in the bin.

When it came to his turn to talk to the class, he told them of a lifeboat scene, and most people were quite interested and asked him questions about it, which pleased the teacher.

'Thank you, Nicholas. That was a good contribution,' he commented before turning to ask Laura to talk about her flower painting.

'That was a close one,' Nicholas muttered under his breath. 'I'll have to be more watchful. Mustn't let anything slip.'

'What?' hissed James, the boy to his left.

'Er... You...' He began to whisper back. He stopped himself just in time, realising that he had nearly told James that he had the same name as the grandad he never knew. 'Nothing,' he finished.

Only Friday morning left, and then the holidays. At last he would be able to immerse himself in work with his dad, and in his conversations with Uncle John.

That last morning, Nicholas had a long conversation with his two best friends, Rab and Louis.

'How's your Uncle John getting on?' asked Louis.

'Not too bad,' replied Nicholas. 'It's going to take a while, but I think he's going to be okay.'

'You were really worried,' said Rab. 'I could tell.'

Nicholas nodded, remembering how hard it had been to think about not having Uncle John around any more. Aloud he announced, 'I'm going to be working on Uncle John's house this holiday.'

'What? On your own!' exclaimed Rab incredulously.

'Dad'll be working there... and probably Mum.'

His friends looked impressed.

'I wish I had something like that to do,' Louis grumbled. 'Mum and Dad are working, and I've got to go away and stay at my gran's. She'll make me eat all the time.'

Nicholas tried to cheer him up. 'If you're as hungry as I am, that won't be too bad.'

'It's not just the food. It's having to make polite conversation to her friends, and not having anything else to do. Ugh! They *still* ask me what I'm going to do when I grow up. One day, I'll think of something really way-out,' Louis finished rebelliously.

'Well, think of me on the holiday-of-a-lifetime, stuck with my big sister, and my mum and dad,' said Rab.

Louis stared at him. 'I prefer Gran's. At least I'll get money to go to the swimming pool most days,' he admitted. 'It's a fifty metre one.' Louis was a very good swimmer, and belonged to the local amateur team.

Fleetingly, Nicholas wished he could tell his friends about the fifth key and the pledge, but the moment passed. That secret belonged to him and Uncle John, and no one else.

Friday evening saw Nicholas and his dad hard at work. Sarah had been to visit John, so they had been able to start at six. They packed up at around ten o'clock, and Nicholas collected the box from the mantelshelf, covered it in bubble-wrap, and put it in a stout bag. He carried it very carefully down the road to his house.

'Lovely box,' his father commented. 'You were right to ask John if we could take care of it meantime.'

Nicholas smiled to himself, and said nothing. As soon as he got home, he went straight upstairs, and put the box on a shelf that was near his bed. Then he lay down and reached out to it, to check that he could touch it whenever he wanted.

'We've an early start in the morning,' his dad announced when he appeared downstairs for his supper.

'I'll be ready at seven thirty,' Nicholas promised between mouthfuls of wholemeal fruit bread that his mother had baked.

Soon afterwards he disappeared off upstairs, leaving his parents staring after him. The idea of Nicholas being downstairs before eight in the school holidays had previously been inconceivable.

In bed that night, Nicholas lay awake in the dark, thinking about the next day, and from time to time reaching out and touching the box. He had set his alarm clock for six forty-five, so that he was certain to be ready on time.

The following morning, Sarah was sitting, bleary-eyed, at the breakfast table.

'Are you sure you want to come?' asked Colin. 'You could easily join us later.'

'I've made up my mind,' she replied determinedly, her voice thick with sleep. 'I'm coming, and that's that.'

Nicholas started to giggle, and his mother looked across at him, clearly annoyed.

'What's so funny,' she snapped.

'Your hair, Mum,' he replied. 'It's standing up on end. You look as if you've had a fright.'

Sarah went to the mirror in the hallway. Nicholas was right. He and Colin came into the hall and collected their coats, ready to go. 'I think you two can go on ahead,' she conceded. 'But I won't be long.'

After they had left, she spoke to herself sternly. 'Come on, Sarah. You're just tired from the week's work. You had all those staff appraisals to do on top of everything else, *and* there was the Christmas night out. Go and work at John's this morning, and then leave the boys to get on with it while you go to the hospital.'

Now she felt fully awake. She went upstairs, rummaged in the wardrobe for her ancient overalls, dressed herself, and tied her hair in a scarf. She was about the leave when the phone rang. It was Colin.

'I've forgotten to bring the rawlplugs, love. They're in a bag behind the kitchen door. I had a bit of trouble getting the right size, so it was only yesterday I bought them.'

It was Sarah's turn to chuckle. 'Good job I'm still here,' she said.

She went to get the bag, and was soon walking purposefully down the road.

They worked hard all morning, with only a short break for a hot

49

drink. When lunchtime came, she went back home to eat something and get changed, before taking the bus to see John.

When she arrived, she found him in good spirits.

'I've been doing some walking practice up and down the corridors,' he told her. 'I'm doing well.'

Sarah could see that his face was a healthier colour than it had been for a long time.

He went on talking animatedly. 'And if I don't slip back tomorrow, they're going to wrap me up and walk me around outside for a few minutes. I can't wait.'

Sarah smiled at his boyish excitement. 'That's such good news. I'll tell the others when I see them again this evening. I'm glad to report that they're working hard.'

'Fresh air,' said John as he savoured the concept. 'I've been dreaming about it every night for the last week, and now it's within my grasp!'

'You must promise me that you won't overdo it.' Sarah wagged her finger at John with mock severity.

'There's no chance they'll risk letting me do that,' John assured her.

'Nevertheless, remember, your progress is all to do with building things up in small steps. And now, down to business.'

'What's this about?'

'Now you're doing so well, I think it's time to introduce you to my plan.'

John felt a little apprehensive. He had managed to incorporate Colin and Nicholas' plans for his home, but now Sarah had something else in mind. He tried to look relaxed, but he did not feel it.

Sarah noticed that his face had taken on a tense expression. She touched his hand 'There's nothing to worry about,' she assured him. 'A while ago, I realised that you would be ready to leave this unit long before your house was in order, so I made some enquiries. I've found a very homely place not far from us, and the couple who run it are looking forward to meeting you.'

John felt his eyes fill with tears. 'I'm very grateful,' he said. 'I was so worried about what would happen next, and I had no way of arranging anything myself.'

'The couple are called Ken and Maggie Hogg. They're off for a week over Christmas, and so am I. I could bring them to see you.'

A look of anxiety passed across John's face. 'I'm not at my

best...'

'Look, Maggie used to be a nurse,' Sarah reassured him. 'And they'll explain everything about the setup when they come.'

'Do you think Nicholas will come to see me tomorrow evening?' John asked. 'I've a few things to talk over with him.'

'I'll tell him,' Sarah replied, 'but I won't tell him about your walking. You can give him a surprise.'

Although Nicholas had become accustomed to physical work, by the time he and his father finished that evening, his body was aching in places he had never noticed before.

'Phew!' he exclaimed as they washed their hands and prepared to leave.

'I agree,' Colin responded with considerable feeling. 'Today has shown me that I'm a bit out of shape. Never mind, though, we'll both soon limber up.'

Sarah had kindly made a stew for them all to share, and Nicholas ate two large platefuls without saying a word. When he stood up to get himself some fruit, his muscles objected, but it was a very good feeling. Things were proceeding now in exactly the way he wanted.

Sarah told him that John was looking forward to seeing him the following evening, and Nicholas sighed contentedly. 'I'm looking forward to that too. I think I'll go to bed now, so I'll be ready for another early start.'

His parents glanced at each other knowingly.

'I'll not be long after you,' said Colin.

By the time Nicholas got into bed, he felt as if he were almost asleep on his feet. He managed to reach out to touch the box, and then he remembered nothing else until he woke to the insistent sound of his alarm clock the next morning.

He dressed quickly, and then went downstairs to make some porridge for them all. He did everything he had observed when his uncle had made it. When he had finished, he could hear no movement from upstairs, so he lifted the pan off the cooker, ran upstairs and knocked on his parents' door. He heard a muffled groan, and he knocked a little louder.

'All right,' called his mother. 'I'm awake now. I'll give your dad a poke.'

Nicholas heard a yelp, and soon afterwards, his father appeared on the landing in his pyjamas.

'I've made breakfast,' said Nicholas cheerfully.

'Thanks, I'll be down in a minute.'

They all set off a little later that day. This time, Sarah stayed with them. She and Colin were still working when Nicholas left at five to get ready to visit John.

'Give him our love,' his mother called after him as he left.

When Nicholas arrived at the hospital, he was delighted to find his uncle waiting on a seat inside the entrance doors.

'Surprise!' said John.

'Uncle John!' exclaimed Nicholas. 'How on earth did you get here? It's a good way back to the ward.'

'I've been doing some secret practising,' his uncle confided. 'I'm allowed to come this far on my own now, and I saved it up today until I knew you were about to arrive. Will you take my arm on the way back? I'm feeling pretty tired now, because I was allowed outside for a few minutes under supervision earlier today.'

'That's great news, Uncle,' replied Nicholas as they walked slowly down the corridor together. 'How much longer do you think you'll be here?'

'They're talking about another couple of weeks if I've got somewhere suitable to go afterwards. Your mum's kindly fixed something up for me, so there shouldn't be a problem. I'm to meet the people next week. She's bringing them to see me.'

'Your house looks a bit of a mess now,' Nicholas told him, 'but it's for the right reasons.'

'How are you getting on?'

'Dad's teaching me so much. This holiday's going to be the best I've ever had. Mum's good too. I'd never seen her in baggy overalls before. She looked really funny at first, but I'm getting used to it.'

By this time they had reached the ward, and John was grateful to be sitting down again.

'Perhaps I've done a bit more today than I should,' he admitted. 'But tomorrow will tell. If I'm none the worse, I'll do the same things again.'

'You must be careful,' said Nicholas anxiously. 'We want you to get well so you can enjoy your house when we've finished. And we've got something very important to do together.'

'I haven't forgotten, Nicholas,' his uncle assured him. 'And I wanted to see you today not just because I was missing you, but because I've got things to tell you.'

Nicholas sat right on the edge of his seat, and leaned forward so that they would not be overheard.

John began. 'The metal chest that has the papers in...'

Nicholas nodded. 'The one I got your cheque book from.'

'There are one or two things in there that we should look at together.'

'Okay,' said Nicholas with barely-suppressed excitement. 'But what sort of things?'

'Remember I told you that I had to wait to see how you reacted to everything?'

'Yes.'

'You have done very well. You have worked hard like a man. And you rightly asked to take the box to your room for safe keeping.'

'Do you mean that I've passed a kind of test, and there's more you can tell me now?'

'That's nearly right,' his uncle replied. 'It isn't the sort of test that has specific answers, though.'

'Uncle, are you saying there's more you can tell me now?' Nicholas repeated urgently.

John looked at him straight in the eyes. 'Not quite yet. Nicholas, I promise you that this isn't some kind of game I'm playing with you,' he added. 'I'm following what I was told to do.'

Nicholas' tense body relaxed, and he asked, 'What do you want me to bring from the chest?'

'There's something that looks to me as if it could be a measuring instrument. It's quite crudely made, and I can't be sure what it's for. It's in a small tin case. Bring that. The other thing is a letter. Well, it isn't really a letter. It's a sheet of paper inside an envelope.'

'Is it the only envelope?'

'No, but it's the only one that I've written on. It's blank apart from my name – and I wrote that in the bottom left-hand corner.'

'Can you tell me what's on the paper?'

John paused for a moment before saying, 'It's a list.'

Nicholas could not contain himself. 'What kind of list? You must tell me. I *have* to know,' he pressed.

'Now, now,' his uncle chided. 'Knowing won't solve anything.'

Nicholas hung his head. He knew that he should wait. He was sure that when he brought these things from the chest, his uncle would show him what was inside the envelope, but everything in him was screaming to find out straight away.

'Nicholas,' said his uncle gently, 'it's a list someone drew up when he was trying to work out what the fifth key meant. Whoever it was didn't get very far, though. I'll tell you what I remember of it, and we can look at it together when you bring it.

'The writer was thinking about what kind of key it might be. He had assumed at first that it must be a key that opens a lock, but then had realised that there were several different kinds of key – a key to a code, keys on a musical instrument, a key in music, and even a quay.'

'I hadn't thought about any of that!' exclaimed Nicholas.

'Neither had I until I read the list. Nicholas, that envelope was in the wooden box, together with the measurer.'

'So you've had it for ages. How old were you when your grandad died?'

'I must have been in my twenties.'

'So you've had these things all that time,' mused Nicholas. Then he added decisively, 'I'll ask Dad if he can manage without me again tomorrow evening. If he can, I'll be back then.'

John smiled. 'Remember I'm not going anywhere, so if we have to wait a day or two, it'll be fine. The only appointment I have this week is when your mum brings Ken and Maggie Hogg to see me on Wednesday evening.'

'I'll be back before then,' Nicholas promised determinedly as he stood up to leave.

At home, he found he had no difficulty in persuading his parents to let him go back the following evening.

'I'm off all this week,' said his mother, 'so your dad and I can carry on while you go back to the hospital. You've been working so hard that you haven't seen so much of your uncle, so I'm not surprised you want to spend a bit more time with him.'

Chapter Eight

The following day, Nicholas opened the metal chest just before leaving for the hospital. His parents were working in his uncle's bedroom, so he had no need to explain anything. He soon found a small metal box, and when he opened it he knew that this was the one, because inside was the object to which his uncle had referred. He did not stop to examine it, but shut the lid, and put the box in his pocket.

Now for the letter... He hunted through several bundles of papers and correspondence, and was beginning to feel that he would never find it, when at last he saw it – right at the bottom of the bundle that he was examining. With trembling hands, he slipped it into a plastic cover that he had brought from home to protect it, replaced all the contents of the chest, and locked it. Then he called goodbye to his parents, and left in the direction of the bus stop. A bus came almost straight away, and he arrived at the hospital in good time.

Uncle John was waiting for him at the entrance, and Nicholas could see his face light up as he spotted him coming across the car park. In fact, he looked quite animated. They walked down the corridor together, and were soon deep in conversation.

'I found the things okay,' said Nicholas, as he took the metal box out of his pocket, and the plastic cover from under his jacket. He handed them to his uncle.

'I knew I could count on you,' replied John. 'Let's wait until we're sitting by my bed, and we'll have a look.'

When they were seated, John silently took the paper out of its envelope and handed it across to Nicholas, who unfolded it slowly and carefully. The style of handwriting that he saw was entirely unfamiliar, and it took him a while before he could make anything out. Eventually, he found the word 'key'. Even that was a struggle, despite knowing that it must appear somewhere.

John watched his nephew, but said nothing.

At length, Nicholas sighed. 'This is really difficult, Uncle John. How on earth did you read it?'

'It took me a long time, and I never did manage to read it all,' his uncle confessed. 'Bring your chair beside me, and I'll show you exactly what I'm sure about.'

Nicholas handed the sheet back to his uncle, and eagerly moved his chair.

John began. 'This is a heading at the top.' He pointed to a row of letters that to Nicholas had no meaning at all. 'It says "For him who seeks". The next line says "The Fifth Key", and the writer had drawn a miniature key.'

'So that's what that shape is!' exclaimed Nicholas. 'I thought it had to be a couple of letters joined together, and I could make no sense of it at all.'

John continued. 'I think that the next line includes a number of characters that don't belong to the English language.'

'How on earth did you make that out?' asked Nicholas. 'Nearly all the writing on this paper looks nothing like anything I know.'

'I'm no expert on foreign languages,' said his uncle, 'but in my life I've seen some samples of characters from around the world, and the more I looked at this over the years, the more I thought this was the explanation.'

'So that was why you decided the person was thinking about a code?'

'I could be entirely wrong, but it would make sense. It's certainly a possibility that the fifth key is something about the key to a code.'

'What's the next bit supposed to be?' asked Nicholas. 'It looks blank to me.'

'A couple of lines of music.'

'How on earth can you see that?' Nicholas squinted closely at the paper as his uncle held it in front of him.

'It always was extremely faint,' said John, 'and it might have got more faint as it has aged. My eyes aren't up to it now, so I'm just going from memory.'

'Well, we're both going to have to go from your memory,' Nicholas replied matter-of-factly, 'because I promise you, it's disappeared!'

His uncle looked disappointed. 'I'm very sad about that, because I'd hoped your sharp eyes would have picked it up.'

'Never mind, Uncle John. I'll draw some staves, and if you tell me the notes, I'll put them in.'

John passed him his writing pad, and Nicholas drew lines using the side of the plastic wallet as a ruler. He could now see the value of those recorder lessons he had suffered at primary school. The teacher had been so boring, and it had really put him off, but somehow he had managed to take in enough of the basics.

'Key signature?' he asked briskly.

John shut his eyes and thought for a moment before saying, 'It's an F sharp. And the first note is G.'

Nicholas inserted these on the first stave that he had drawn.

John looked at Nicholas. 'My memory isn't what it was,' he said tiredly. 'Nicholas, I don't like disappointing you, but I'm not sure what comes next.'

Nicholas held his breath and waited.

John shut his eyes again. 'Ah, I can see the second line after all. It's A and then G and then E.' Then he added, 'It's a good job I joined that choir when I was young, otherwise I would hardly have known it was music.'

Nicholas quickly drew the notes, and then said, 'Don't worry, Uncle John, I expect you'll remember any others later.'

'You could be right, Nicholas, but I've had to keep all this to myself for so long, it might take a while.'

'You've remembered a lot already,' Nicholas encouraged. 'And I didn't know you'd sung in a choir. When was that?'

'It must have been soon after my grandad died. The couple I was lodging with invited me along to their church. They were short of people to sing, so I volunteered. I didn't do it for long, though, because I moved away.'

'But will you look at the rest of the writing now, and tell me what it says.'

John peered at it. 'That's easy. It says "maybe the quay".'

'Is that everything?'

'I'm pretty sure that the long squiggle at the bottom must be a signature, but I've never been able to work out what the name is, and I don't suppose I ever will. Let's have a look at the measuring thing now.' John opened the container, took it out, and handed it to Nicholas. 'What do you think?'

'It's weird.'

'It's certainly a bit of a puzzle.'

The device was a flat plate of metal about the length of Nicholas' hand. On each side of it a series of holes had been drilled, through which were attached needle-like additions that could be swung out at any angle. A roughly-etched pattern could be seen on the face of the metal plate.

'My best guess is that this pattern might be something to do with the way the needles are to be arranged.' There was a note of uncertainty in John's voice.

'Uncle John,' said Nicholas suddenly, 'how do you know that these things have something to do with the pledge? You told me that you didn't know you were to have the wooden box until after your grandfather died. Had you seen it before?'

'Not that I can remember.'

'Why on earth didn't he tell you about the box when he told you the story?' Nicholas burst out. 'All this gets more and more complicated.'

'The box might have nothing to do with it,' his uncle pointed out. 'It might merely have been a convenient way of giving me the letter and the measuring device. And maybe I wasn't to know about them until he died.'

'Oh, I hadn't thought about that,' said Nicholas, feeling stupid.

'Look, Nicholas,' his uncle replied, 'I've had a lot longer to think about it than you. And remember, I haven't got all that far with it, and I'm mightily relieved to have you with me now.'

Nicholas cheered up immediately. This was something they were doing together, and who could tell what would come from that?

'Will you take these things home with you and keep them in the box?' his uncle asked.

Nicholas could see that he was tiring now. 'Of course I will,' he replied. 'I promise I'll keep them safe.' Then he picked them up, put on his jacket, and bid his uncle goodbye.

Chapter Nine

The meeting with Ken and Maggie Hogg went well. John liked them straight away, and he was looking forward to living with them for as long as necessary after he left hospital. They agreed to keep a room for him from the end of January, and said that if he left hospital before then, they could make a temporary arrangement by having him upstairs with them, using their spare room. This was something they had done before when caring for a relative, and they were happy to do the same for John.

Nicholas and his parents decided that they would continue to work in John's house on Christmas morning, but take the afternoon off to be with him in the hospital.

'This is the best Christmas I've ever had,' Nicholas told his parents over breakfast. He was feeling so relaxed that he almost told them about his recent conversations with his uncle. He quickly took another spoonful of porridge, and almost choked on it.

'But we haven't had time to buy your present yet,' said his father.

'And we haven't decided what it's to be, so we can't even tell you what you'll be getting,' his mother added.

'I've got all I want,' Nicholas replied. 'You're both teaching me things at Uncle John's house that will help me for the rest of my life, and Uncle John is...' Again he nearly said something. '... Uncle John's getting better,' he finished. He jumped up. 'It's time to get going. If you really want to buy me something, I'd like tools, please.'

He grabbed his jacket, and started to jog down the road. There were things he could safely get on with at his uncle's house before his parents joined him. He knew only too well what he must not attempt to do alone, as his father had taught him about potential dangers.

He moved with ease. He knew that he was getting stronger and fitter by the day, and he revelled in it. Not long ago, if he had jogged down the road like this, he would have arrived panting, but not now. Not long ago his muscles had ached each night, but now he felt only a healthy tiredness. And when he woke each morning, he felt refreshed and eager to start work again.

Colin and Sarah were left staring at each other across the kitchen table.

'I'm so proud of him,' said Sarah, her eyes moistening.

'At this rate, he could end up being a top-quality tradesman with his own business,' said Colin. 'He takes things in so quickly, and he's always hungry to learn more. And on a couple of occasions, he's spotted ways of doing things that are better than mine.' He chuckled. 'It's a good thing I've kept up my trips to the gym. Otherwise, I wouldn't have the energy to keep up with him.'

'It's a pity I've got to be back at work after Boxing Day,' Sarah commented with considerable regret. 'This is so different from working at the office, where even though the staff are good, there can be niggles and back-biting.'

Colin laughed. 'I'm trying not to think of life beyond the holidays. I know I'm putting blinkers on. But why not?'

'At least I get another couple of days at New Year,' Sarah reminded herself.

'And the weekends are ours, too,' Colin pointed out.

'I wonder how Nicholas will react to going back to school?' said Sarah.

'We'll have to cross that bridge when it comes,' Colin replied. He glanced at his watch. 'We'd better get going. He'll be wondering where we are.'

When they arrived, Nicholas was hard at work, stripping the paper off the walls of the living room. They left him working there while they continued with the rewiring, calling him only when they needed his help under the floor. At this time of year, the daylight was at its minimum, and from the beginning, Colin had fixed up a number of battery-powered inspection lamps.

Apart from a short break, they worked all morning, stopping at one o'clock in time to wash and change before Colin drove them to the hospital. Sarah took a large flat parcel, and a basket of some packets of Christmas specialities that she had ordered from the local delicatessen.

'What's in the parcel?' asked Nicholas curiously. He poked it, and it felt squashy.

'It's a dressing gown,' his mother explained. 'John could do with a spare one.'

There were few patients on the ward. Most had been able to go to friends or relatives for the afternoon. The nurses, too, had brought some Christmas fare, and when everyone pooled their contributions, there was quite a spread.

The patients nibbled carefully at the less challenging items, while Nicholas took at face value the invitation to eat as much as he wanted.

One of the nurses watched him with amusement. 'You remind me of my younger brother,' she commented. 'He's always hungry.'

'You should try being him for a day,' Nicholas replied. 'It's hard.'

The nurse, who was small in height and of slight build replied, 'I'm not trying to make fun of you. I like seeing people enjoying their food. It's a fairly rare sight here. I've never needed much myself, even though I'm on my feet most of the day.'

'You have to keep it pretty warm in here,' Sarah remarked. 'That won't do much for your appetite.'

The nurse nodded, and then hurried off to answer a phone.

John was very pleased with his dressing gown. 'You've taken another weight off my mind,' he said gratefully. 'I'll need this when I'm with Ken and Maggie.'

'You must say if there's anything else you need,' Sarah insisted.

'I don't like to bother you,' replied John. 'You're already doing more than I could have dreamed.'

'Now,' said Colin firmly, 'I want to get it into your head that what we're doing with your house is benefiting us all.' John opened his mouth to say something, but Colin would not let him speak. He went on. 'This is a family project, and you're letting us use your house for it.'

'He's right, Uncle John,' Nicholas added.

'One thing's been worrying me about you, Nicholas,' said his uncle.

'What's that?' Nicholas asked.

'What about your friends? A young lad like you needs time with his friends. You don't want to be spending all of your time with an old man like me, and working on my house.'

For a moment, Nicholas wondered why his uncle had not mentioned this before, but then he realised that he had waited until they were all there before saying anything.

'Don't worry about that, Uncle John,' he replied, 'my two best friends, Rab and Louis, have gone away. They won't be back until it's nearly time for school again. Rab and his family have gone on an expensive holiday, and Louis has gone to stay with his gran while his parents are working. Actually, both of them were really envious when

I told them what I'd be doing.' He chuckled. 'Louis was moaning about how he'd be expected to sit at table for hours and make polite conversation.'

John looked relieved. 'It's another thing that had been preying on my mind,' he admitted. 'We might have to talk about it again some time after the holidays.' He drew himself up. 'And now, I've got an announcement to make. It looks as if I'll definitely be able to leave hospital in a couple of week's time.'

'That's great news!' said Colin excitedly.

Sarah got up and hugged him warmly. 'I'm so pleased. I'll give Ken and Maggie a ring in a couple of days.'

'That would be a help,' John concurred. 'I don't find it easy using the phone from here.'

Nicholas could not stop smiling. He was very happy that his uncle was clearly on the mend. The fact that he would soon be living not far away meant that he could easily visit him every day, and keep on with the work in the house.

The afternoon passed very pleasantly, and it was with reluctance that they left for home, having stayed a full hour beyond the usual visiting times.

Nicholas made himself a substantial snack, and then went to his room to look at the box and its precious contents. Colin and Sarah decided to have a quiet evening and an early night.

In bed, Colin turned to Sarah. 'We never got round to talking about that broken crockery,' he reminded her.

'Never mind about that,' Sarah replied quickly. She was feeling so content with the day that she did not want to think of anything else.

But Colin persisted. 'Come on now. This would be a good time. We've had a great day, and things are going in the right direction with John's house and his health. There's something we've got to clear up, and there's no time like the present.'

Sarah sighed. 'You're right, Col, but I don't want to start talking about something that might end up with us not feeling too good.'

'Why on earth do you think that could happen?' asked Colin, mystified. 'I remember when you mentioned it at first, I could tell that there was more to it, but how could it make us feel low?'

'It'll mean that I'll have to talk again about that bad time we went through,' Sarah informed him unwillingly.

Colin took her hand and held it in his. 'In that case, we *must* talk about it,' he insisted. 'Where are you going to start?'

Sarah shut her eyes, and said through gritted teeth, 'Col, I never really talked about how hurt I felt. I was so glad we worked out a way through it that I was happy to get on with our life.'

'Of course you were hurt.' Colin held her hand tightly. 'Anyone in your position would have been. But why didn't you say something?'

'I think I know now, but it's quite a story.'

'And there's something about broken crockery in it?'

'That's right.' Sarah then went on to tell him about how Stanley had tormented her during the time she was living with her mother's cousin, Joy, and she finished with the story of the smashed teaset.

'I certainly remember you telling me about those years,' Colin reflected. 'But you've always made them sound really good. You've never mentioned Stanley before.'

'Joy brought so much into my life, and I'll always be profoundly grateful for that.' Sarah began to talk animatedly about trips to the theatre, but Colin stopped her.

'We can talk about that later,' he said firmly. 'What I want to know is why you didn't tell anyone about what he was doing to you, and why you haven't said anything to me before.'

'But I did!' Sarah burst out. 'I tried to talk to Joy about him, but she kept brushing me off.' She began to cry.

Colin reached for the box of tissues, and waited until Sarah was ready to speak again.

'Col, I could never understand why she wouldn't listen.'

'Didn't you say anything to your family?'

'When I was at home, it all seemed a long way away, and I was involved in other things.'

'Mm...' said Colin. 'I'm beginning to understand now why you didn't talk to me about how hurt you'd been by my behaviour. You didn't have any success about the Stanley episode when all that was happening. And because with us, we fixed something better up for ourselves, that must have seemed to be all that was needed.'

'I just didn't realise at the time.'

'I'm not surprised. Sarah, I've often wondered why I ended up doing what I did.'

'It's obvious. You hated being away from home so much, and you told me so.'

'But why didn't I tell you straight away, instead of getting in a mess?'

'I assumed you thought you had to get on with your job. It wasn't until we discussed alternatives that you could see you didn't have to.'

'That's part of it.'

'Oh!' exclaimed Sarah. 'You mean you think there might be something like Stanley for you?'

'Not exactly like Stanley, but something about being forced to be away from home for some reason when I was small.'

'I hadn't thought about that before,' said Sarah slowly.

'But don't let's concentrate on that at the moment. We've got to talk about how hurt you felt about what I did.'

'We have,' Sarah pointed out. 'And now we're going to think about you being forced to be away from home. Your mum once told me that she was quite ill on and off when you were small, so I wouldn't be surprised if there were times when she was at home but you were being looked after somewhere else. Col, I'm really sleepy. Would you mind if we think about this later?'

Moments afterwards, they were asleep, curled up closely together.

Chapter Ten

On his next visit to the hospital, Nicholas and his uncle decided that they would leave any further conversations about the fifth key for now. Nicholas wanted to concentrate on working alongside his father, and since Uncle John had shown him the letter and the measuring device, he already had a lot to think about.

The rest of the holiday passed all too quickly, and on the last Friday evening, Nicholas and his parents sat round the table at home to plan the next weeks. Sarah had gone back to work straight after New Year, and Colin would be starting again on Monday. The school term began on Wednesday.

Colin began. 'Nick, I'm afraid you won't be able to work at John's house during the day on Monday and Tuesday.'

'I'll be fine, Dad,' Nicholas assured him. 'I'll keep on with the job of cleaning the internal walls.'

'But you'd be on your own for hours,' his father pointed out. 'And I'd never forgive myself if something went wrong.'

'Please, Dad,' Nicholas pleaded. 'You know I'd be very careful.'

Colin looked at Sarah. 'What do you think, love?' he asked.

'I agree with you, Col,' Sarah replied. 'It's better to be safe than sorry.' She turned to Nicholas and said, 'We trust you completely, but it would be wrong for us to take any risks. We can all spend the evenings there on Monday and Tuesday, but you mustn't be there on your own.'

'Not even a couple of hours in the mornings?' he begged. 'Mum, I could phone you at work when I get there and when I finish. Then you'd know I was fine. I could visit Uncle John in the afternoons.'

Sarah looked uncertain. 'Your dad and I will have to think about it. It's a big decision.'

Nicholas was satisfied with that. He thought for a moment, and then commented, 'The roofer will be coming the weekend after next.'

'Let's hope the weather will be right for him,' Colin remarked. 'Any high winds, and there'll be delays. But when it's done, we'll be able to work on the mess inside the back door. And not before time.'

Nicholas was very excited. 'I can't wait,' he said. 'There's always more to learn.'

'I've chosen the gas boiler,' Colin announced. 'I'll have to work out when to get the man to come and install it.'

'How about the end of February?' suggested Sarah. 'We don't want it to be there while we're still making a lot of mess. It would be another thing to keep clean.'

'Good thinking,' Colin replied. 'I'll make the booking on Monday, when I'm on my lunch break.'

Nicholas stood up. 'I'm off to bed. I don't want to waste any time tomorrow.'

'We'll come up soon,' said his mother, yawning.

On Sunday evening Sarah and Colin decided that they would let Nicholas work at John's house between ten and twelve on Monday and Tuesday. Nicholas was ecstatic, and he jumped up as high as he could, trying to touch the ceiling.

'Hey, steady on,' said Colin. 'Don't injure yourself, or you won't be able to go at all.'

'No chance of that.' Nicholas was adamant. 'I'll get up early in the morning and make a start on the bit of homework I should have done this holiday. It's only one subject.'

Colin smiled indulgently. He admired his son's directness. Over the last weeks he had watched him take several competent steps into manhood, and he respected what he had achieved.

'I'll miss you tomorrow, Nick,' he said with considerable feeling.

'I don't think I'll miss you too much, Dad,' Nicholas replied cheerfully. 'I'll be quite busy. Goodnight both of you.' He went upstairs.

Nicholas lay awake for a long time that night, thinking about the days and weeks to come. From time to time, he reached out and touched his uncle's special box, knowing that the letter and the measurer were safe inside it. Tomorrow afternoon, he and his uncle would resume their talks about the fifth key.

When he finally slept, his dreams were full of storms, rocky cliffs, and shipwrecks.

The following morning, he completed some of his homework, and made his way up to his uncle's house, where he phoned his mother to say that he was about to start work. He was satisfied with the progress

66

that he made, and at lunchtime he cleared up, and phoned her again. He did not feel bothered about having to stop. He had done more than he had planned, and he was looking forward to seeing his uncle again. After that there was still the evening for working.

The day was relatively mild, and when he arrived at the hospital, he found his uncle at the door, dressed and ready to go out.

'Where are you going?' he asked worriedly. 'We were going to have a long talk this afternoon.'

His uncle smiled. 'I haven't forgotten. I've got permission to stroll round outside with you for ten minutes first. Come this way, and I'll show you. There's an open area at the back that catches the sun at this time of day.'

John took his great-nephew through the hospital, and they went outside into the open. It was sheltered, and felt surprisingly warm.

'I've got some questions,' said Nicholas.

'Don't forget any of them,' his uncle replied. 'We'll think about them as soon as we're back on the ward.' He sighed contentedly. 'They've been very kind to me here, but I'll be glad to leave. I could do with a bit more freedom. Ken's coming to pick me up in a week's time. I can hardly wait!'

Nicholas looked at his uncle. For a moment, he appeared almost boyish in his excitement.

Later, sitting beside John's bed, Nicholas began. 'When you first told me the story, and drew the gravestone, you said you had some photographs of it you could show me. Where are they? I'd like to see them soon.'

'I certainly meant to show you, but I can't tell you exactly where they are.'

'Haven't you got some idea?'

'I know they're somewhere in my bookshelves, sandwiched between the books.'

'Oh no!' said Nicholas. 'It's not going to be easy to get at them. We've put them face-to-face in the middle of the room, with some heavy canvas over them. It looks as if I'll have to wait.'

'Never mind,' replied his uncle. 'We'll get to them later. They'll give you a general idea of the place. There's nothing very specific. What's your next question?'

'Where was the cliff?'

'Didn't I tell you?' asked his uncle, surprised. 'It's on the east coast of Yorkshire. Curiously, on the news today I saw how one village there is gradually crumbling into the sea. Next question?'

'What do you think the treasure might have been?'

'That's something I've pondered over long and hard. I like to think it's Spanish gold that had been plundered somewhere along the south coast of Spain.'

Nicholas' eyes shone.

'Any more questions?' asked his uncle.

'When do you think the shipwreck happened?'

'It's only a guess, and I could be wildly out, but possibly sometime in the 1600s.'

Nicholas fell silent. His mind was filled with images of sacks of doubloons, and he could not think of anything else to say.

John closed his eyes. There was a lot for the lad to take in. He wished he could tell him things that were more concrete, but in all his years of thinking about what little he knew, he had never really got any further forward. He had felt such relief at being able to talk to Nicholas. Instead of running away, the lad was hungry for more. It had been hard to test him by holding some of it back, but he had to be sure. Trying to tell his young brother, Nicholas' grandfather, had only resulted in a rift between them – one that had never healed. How hard it had been when he had tried to approach Jake. And then Jake had made it very clear that he did not want anything to do with him. He had found this hurtful, but if he were honest with himself, he knew that Jake already had enough problems of his own, and he could understand that he might want to avoid the kind of close contact that would have been involved.

Colin and Sarah were such good people, but they had been so very young when Jake was born, and added to that, much had gone wrong for them. He had been pleased when they managed to get their little terraced house. Colin had made an excellent job of it. But then his mother had fallen ill, and she was never the same again. Her personality seemed to change. She became irritable, and sometimes quite erratic, and she would shout, and hurl things across the room. Colin had been very worried about her, and he and Sarah spent many hours at her home, trying to help her, and often staying overnight. But this had not gone well, and as a small child Jake must have heard and witnessed things that frightened him. At first, he was viewed as a child who was self-contained, but as time went on, it was clear that he was actually quite withdrawn, and if anyone tried to be closely involved with him, he would back away.

How sad it had all been. He remembered being surprised when James had introduced him to his wife Millie. She had seemed such a happy-go-lucky person, and for a while he had hoped that James' marriage to her would mean that he and James could have some regular contact after all those years. But the ill health that Millie suffered when Colin was small wore her down, and she never got back to her former bounciness. Then after James died, she struggled on as best she could to get Colin through school. Maybe she was angry that Colin had married so young. But it must have been more than that, as in the end they had to have her taken into mental hospital. Poor woman. There had been nothing he could do to help.

He wondered where Jake was now. He never liked to ask Colin if he had heard from him. Perhaps he was wrong, but he could not think of the best way of doing it.

The sound of Nicholas' voice startled him from his thoughts.

'Uncle John, I've been thinking about that music. Have you remembered any more of the first line?'

John shook his head.

'Are you sure there were more notes?'

'Not exactly,' replied his uncle. 'There was something, but I suppose that could have been rests.'

'If there weren't any more, then the letters of all the notes spell GAGE, and that would be a funny way of spelling gauge,' Nicholas commented. 'Maybe the metal thing is a gauge.'

John sat bolt upright. Perhaps the lad was onto something. 'Let's think about that,' he said excitedly. 'If you're right...'

'If I'm right, it doesn't exactly get us anywhere. Does it?' Nicholas was puzzled by his uncle's attitude.

'I know. I know. But this is the first time for years and years that I haven't felt completely stuck about it all. Bit by bit, I've told you what I know. I've watched you very carefully along the way, and all I've seen is evidence that you're maturing into a man because of what we're sharing. That's helped me to tell you everything. You've got to remember, Nicholas, that not only have I had to carry the secret alone, but also for a long time I've been afraid that sharing it would mean loss rather than gain.'

'And with me, you're gaining more and more!' said Nicholas triumphantly.

'I can see it with my own eyes, but it's taking a while to sink in,' his uncle admitted.

'Well, it'll sink in more and more, because there's no other way for it to go,' Nicholas stated confidently.

'And now, you've come up with an idea about the music.' John paused, and then asked, 'Have you by any chance had any ideas about the line above it?'

'The bit we think might be a code? Nothing definite, but I've been planning to look in the school library and on the Internet. I should be able to make a start in the lunch break on Wednesday.'

'Good lad!' said John.

'Uncle John, do you think there was a quay in the harbour belonging to the merchant?'

'There could well have been something, but I don't think there would have been anything substantial. After all, as far as we know it was more of an inlet than an actual harbour.'

'I've not been looking forward to going back to school,' Nicholas grumbled, 'but I'll be doing some useful research.'

His uncle winked at him. 'Yes, and you never know what you might dig up.'

Chapter Eleven

Wednesday lunchtime saw Nicholas poring over the large dictionaries in the school library. His parents had a row of reference books on the shelves at home, and there was quite a good dictionary amongst them. He had thought of looking in it, but he wanted his researches to be private.

Quay. He was very interested to find that an earlier spelling of this word was in fact 'key'. Uncle John will be keen to know that, he thought, as he made a note about it in his jotter. Now for 'gage'. He turned the pages and found that there were several entries. There was quite a lot of information in the first entry, so he read the other entries first. That's interesting… it was the name of a quart pot or a quart pot full. He was sure his uncle would want to know that. And it is short for greengage… 'That's pretty obvious when you think about it,' he murmured, as he copied both meanings. Then he turned his attention to the more lengthy entry.

Gage
Something deposited to ensure the performance of some action, and liable to forfeiture in case of non-performance; a pawn, a pledge.
A pledge (usually a glove thrown down) of a person's appearance to do battle in support of his assertions. Hence, a challenge.
To stake, wager; to risk or bet. To pledge. To bind as a formal promise. To assert on one's own responsibility that… To fix. To bind or entangle.

Nicholas' head was swimming. He realised that he had stopped breathing. He pushed the dictionary away, and laid his head on the table. Breathe, breathe, he told himself. He was eternally grateful that there was no one sitting at the same table, as anyone that close at hand would be bound to notice that there was something wrong. He was certain that he had now found something crucial to the understanding of what he and his uncle had to achieve.

The bell went for afternoon lessons. The librarian would surely notice him. Gingerly, Nicholas lifted his head from the table, and was glad to find that he felt able to sit upright. Another minute passed, and then he picked up the dictionary and returned it to its shelf. He felt just about all right now, so he collected his things and made his way to the games corridor. Thank goodness it was swimming this afternoon. He would see Louis and find out how he had got on at his gran's, and the swimming would clear his head. After that, he could come back to the library and copy these entries to show to Uncle John.

In the changing rooms he learned that Louis' holiday had been much better than he had expected. Not only had he been able to go swimming almost every day, but also he had been invited to join a racing team at that pool, and now he was desperate to get back to his gran's whenever he could.

'How did you get on?' asked Louis when he had finished his news.

'It's great working with Mum and Dad,' said Nicholas, his eyes sparkling. 'I'm learning so much. There's the rewiring, and the central heating. I can't do any of that on my own, but I help a lot. There are plenty of jobs I can get on with, though. I'm getting really good at stripping the walls. And the weekend after next will be the first one on the roof.'

Louis was impressed, and said so. 'Do you think there's anything I could do?' he asked rather longingly.

'You haven't got time,' Nicholas pointed out.

'Suppose not,' Louis conceded.

'But I can ask,' Nicholas added generously.

'Thanks.'

Soon the boys were chasing each other up and down the pool.

Nicholas was much refreshed, and was looking forward to returning to the library briefly before going home. As they changed back into their clothes, he asked Louis if he had seen Rab.

'No. Maybe he's been captured,' Louis replied dramatically.

'Hope not,' said Nicholas. He grabbed his things and headed off in the direction of the library calling 'See you!' over his shoulder.

Although that afternoon the bus to the hospital seemed to take forever, it was running to time, and as usual, John was waiting for Nicholas at the door.

'I've got clues,' Nicholas announced breathlessly as he reached him.

'Do you think it's private enough on the ward?' asked John uncertainly.

'It'll be fine,' Nicholas reassured him. 'I don't think anyone will know what we're talking about.'

Minutes later, they were seated.

Nicholas took out his jotter, and handed it to his uncle saying, 'I only had time to look in the dictionary today, but I've found this.'

He watched as his uncle turned the pages.

'Good lad!' John exclaimed in low tones as he studied the notes that Nicholas had made. 'Why didn't I think of doing this myself?'

'It needed two of us, Uncle John,' said Nicholas calmly.

'So quay and key are one and the same thing. I suppose the ship fits there, and that's the gateway to its cargo. But all this other stuff is almost more than I can take in. To have such a strong link between the music and a particular kind of pledge is beyond what I could have dreamed of. And the music itself is a simple code that tells us.'

'That's what I hoped you'd say,' said Nicholas eagerly.

John rushed on. 'Maybe the line above the music will tell us what the pledge is about, if only we can understand it. No wonder my grandad was so insistent about the pledge, and I thought it was only to do with having to promise to hand on the knowledge to the right person if I couldn't understand it myself. But now I know that there is a pledge embedded in the knowledge itself.'

'I was so excited when I found the entries that I stopped breathing, and nearly fainted,' Nicholas confided.

John was wriggling irritably in his chair. 'I hate being here,' he snapped. 'I want some strength back so that I can get on with these important things.'

Nicholas felt upset to see his uncle struggling like this. In fact, he felt tearful. He took a deep breath and said firmly, 'Look, Uncle John, I'd like that for you, too. But for now we'll have to use my strength for both of us, and the best thing you can do is to make sure you're better enough to go to the Hoggs soon.'

'I'm sorry, Nicholas,' his uncle apologised. 'I know that's the next step, but now I know I've got some life ahead of me, it's hard not to have it straight away.'

'I've never been ill like this, but I don't think I'd like it either,' said Nicholas, doing his best to be sympathetic. 'And if you ask me, I think you're doing really well.'

John leaned back in his chair. 'Thanks, Nicholas. That helps. Sometimes I think you must get fed up with me. I'm so slow.'

Nicholas gaped at him. 'But... but I couldn't do any of this without you. Look,' he added urgently, 'you've got to concentrate on getting to the Hoggs. Once you're there, it'll be a lot easier to see you, and for us to have our talks. Have you got a date?'

'It's a week on Friday.'

Nicholas' face broke into a smile. 'That's only a week and a half away,' he said excitedly. 'And on the Saturday, the roofing man starts.'

'Bernie's coming already?'

'Yes, it'll be the middle of January. You arranged it for then. Don't you remember?'

'I remember very well, but when you're in a place like this, most days are the same, and it's all too easy to lose track of time.'

'I'd better go now,' said Nicholas, 'but please keep thinking about that line above the music.'

Chapter Twelve

The post usually arrived before Nicholas left for school, and this Friday was no exception. His dad had already left for work when Nicholas heard the letterbox.

'I'll go and see if there's anything interesting,' he told his mother as he rushed into the hall.

There was hardly ever anything for him, but today, amongst the circulars, he found two postcards, both of which were addressed to him. He stopped to read them.

The first was from Rab. It said:

Hi,
Bomb scare. Flights cancelled. See you Monday with luck.
Rab

It was a relief to know that his friend was okay. Underneath the light-hearted attitude he had shown to Louis, he had been worried.

He turned to the next card. He did not recognise the writing, and it was difficult to make out what it said. He looked at the picture on the front. It was stunning – coral reefs. Then he tried the writing again. Thank goodness it was not as bad as the list in his uncle's box. He screwed up his eyes and concentrated as hard as he could. Eventually, he made out the words:

Hello. Am doing some diving. Thought you might like this. J

Who could this be? Everyone except Rab was back in class. He had not been going to any clubs because of the work he was doing at his uncle's house, and in any case, he could not think of anyone he knew there whose name began with 'J'. Maybe he had misread it. He peered at it again, and tried to see it as another letter, but no, it was definitely a 'J'. And the address section clearly said 'Nicholas' on it, so there could be no confusion there.

Then a thought struck him. Could it be Jake? He dropped the circulars on the mat and ran upstairs to his room, where knew he had a book with Jake's signature inside. He grabbed it from its place on the shelf, and compared the handwriting. It certainly looked the same. How strange. Why had he sent this card now? Mum and Dad heard from him about once a year. They always told him about it – a short phone call, or a letter consisting of a single paragraph. He was always moving around, and he was always fit and well. That was about all they knew. But for Jake to send him a postcard... Nicholas thought he had never done that before, unless it was when he was so small that he would not have realised what it meant.

He ran back downstairs again, took the rest of the post to the kitchen, and put it on the table in front of his mother.

'Thanks, Nicholas,' she said. 'I'll look at it later. I'd better get ready now.'

He nearly told her about the postcard from Jake, but instead he said, 'Bye Mum. See you later.' Then he went off to catch the bus.

All day at school, the postcard was on his mind. He wished he knew why Jake had sent it. He could not wait to show it to Uncle John, and ask him what he thought of it. He tried his best to concentrate on his work, but there was so much on his mind – the weekend's work ahead, the line in the list that he and Uncle John were trying to decode, and now the postcard.

When he saw his uncle at the hospital, he took the postcard out of his bag straight away and handed it to him.

'What do you think of this?' he asked.

'It's a stunning picture,' his uncle commented.

'Yes, I know. But what do you think of the message? It's from Jake.'

'Jake! Are you sure?'

'Of course I'm sure,' said Nicholas irritably. 'I didn't know who it was at first, but I went and compared the writing with something he'd written inside a book.'

'Very resourceful. Now I wonder why he's writing to you after all these years. Have you any ideas?'

'No. That's why I'm asking you.'

'Let's go to the ward and sit down,' John suggested. 'I'm getting a bit cold standing near this door.'

Nicholas immediately became concerned about his uncle, and they walked together to the ward. Once there, he asked, 'Is there something about Jake that you know and I don't?'

'What I had in my mind is that the last time your mum and dad spoke to me about him, they said that if he sent a postcard, they were likely to get a visit from him some time over the next months.'

'The last time he came, I was about nine,' Nicholas reflected. 'He stayed only for an afternoon. He talked to Mum and Dad, but he didn't say much to me.'

'Have you shown this card to them yet?'

'No, it came just before school, and Dad had already left. I didn't want to say anything to Mum. I'll show it to them this evening.'

'I think that's the best thing.'

'Uncle John, I've had an idea about that line of writing on the list,' said Nicholas suddenly.

'Tell me.'

'I think we should make a much bigger version of it.'

'There'd be no harm in doing that. In fact, it's a very good idea. Then I won't have to peer at it.'

'I'll do it soon,' Nicholas promised.

'And once I'm settled in at Ken and Maggie Hogg's, we can put our heads together about it, and about the pledge that's embedded in the mysteries of the fifth key.'

That evening, after supper, Nicholas made his announcement. He had meant to make a casual comment, but it did not work out like that.

'I've got something important to tell you,' he began.

'Fire away,' said his father. 'Your mum and I are all ears.'

'I've had a postcard from Jake.'

Nicholas noticed that for a moment both his parents seemed to turn into statues. Then he saw his mother's eyes mist over, and his father's face lose some of its colour.

'When?' asked his father.

'This morning. Just as I was leaving for school.'

'Are you sure it's from him?' asked his mother.

'I'm certain. Do you want to see?'

'Please,' said his father.

Nicholas went to the hall to get it out of his bag, and he could hear his father saying something to his mother, but could not pick up what it was.

'Here it is,' he said, putting it on the table in front of his father.

He watched as his father picked it up as if it were very fragile.

'It's a lovely picture,' his mother commented in a voice that was not quite steady.

77

'Do you mind if we read it, Nick?' asked his father.

'No. He doesn't say much, though,' Nicholas replied.

His father cleared his throat. 'Nick, when Jake sent a postcard, it always meant that he'd be coming home for a visit quite soon. We haven't seen him for more than four years, so this is a big thing for us.'

'Has he ever sent me a postcard before?' asked Nicholas curiously.

'No,' his mother replied. Her voice sounded a little choked. 'He's never sent anything to you before.'

Nicholas was about to say that none of this particularly bothered him, when he remembered that he was nearly a man, and that he should be involved, whether or not it bothered him.

'How will we know exactly when he's coming?' he asked.

His mother looked surprised, and explained, 'He'll phone the night before.'

'That doesn't give us much warning.'

'He likes it that way,' his father commented quietly.

'But how can we get ready?' asked Nicholas. It seemed obvious to him that if you had not seen a person for years, you would want to get ready to welcome him, and if it was your son, you would want to even more.

'We just make sure there's something in the freezer,' his mother explained.

'But you do that anyway,' Nicholas pointed out.

'I know,' his mother replied. She looked quite tearful.

'Do you think he'll stay the night?' asked Nicholas. 'The spare room's a mess with all Uncle John's clothes piled up in it. He can sleep in my bed if he wants.'

At this, his mother began to cry.

'What is it, Mum?' asked Nicholas.

It was his father who replied. 'I think your mum's affected by the fact that even though Jake's never paid you any attention, you're doing your best to help with his visit.'

'He sent me that postcard. And after all, he *is* my brother. Anyway, I'll make a space in the spare room.'

'He hasn't stayed with us ever since you were born,' his father said gently.

'That doesn't mean he never will,' Nicholas replied firmly, and he went upstairs to his room.

78

He lay on his bed, and reached out to touch the box. There was so much happening that he found it difficult to keep track of it all. School work. Work at Uncle John's house. The roofer due to come soon. The pledge with the hidden pledge. The meaning of the fifth key. The coded line on the list. And now Jake... Why was he coming now? Had he in some way sensed that something was happening? But that was impossible. There was no way that he could possibly know. It must be pure coincidence that he had decided to come. And yet... Nicholas struggled with something that was rumbling around at the back of his mind.

'He must know that I'm thirteen now,' he said aloud.

That night, in bed, Colin and Sarah had a long talk about Jake and Nicholas.

'I so hope that this is the start of a change for the better,' said Sarah, trying to hold back her tears.

She could see that Colin looked tearful, too.

'I never thought he would ever acknowledge Nick,' said Colin. 'I've longed for it ever since he was born, but I've got so used to Jake ignoring him that it comes as a shock to see that card.'

'He doesn't ignore him completely,' Sarah protested.

'Yes, but a word here and there over a number of visits you could count on one hand doesn't add up to much.'

'I wish I knew what to get ready so that he would feel welcomed when he comes,' said Sarah, her voice full of longing.

Colin responded patiently. 'I think he can't experience that kind of thing as being welcoming. In fact, I think he would feel it to be somehow unpleasant, and that's why he makes sure we can't do much.'

'But maybe underneath he wants it really,' Sarah pointed out.

'That might be true, but my instinct tells me it's best not to try to get through to that,' said Colin.

'Why not?' Sarah spoke sharply.

'It might frighten him,' replied Colin quietly.

'I think you're right,' Sarah conceded. 'If this is to change, I can't just go on what I want.'

'Shall I put the light out now?' Colin suggested.

Sarah nodded. She would get the usual few things ready, and then wait for the phone call.

Chapter Thirteen

Nicholas and his parents worked hard all that weekend. Nicholas noticed that his mother looked slightly pale, but apart from that she seemed to be her usual self. They planned that when they moved Uncle John from hospital to the Hogg's, on the way they would bring him to have a look at the house.

On the Sunday afternoon, Nicholas did a lot of clearing up and cleaning. He had finished stripping the wallpaper in all the rooms, and he had washed down the walls, so that they were ready to decorate when all the other work was complete. The rewiring was finished, and they had done some of the pipework for the central heating. They had begun installing units in the kitchen, where they had already replaced the sink. Secretly, he hoped that he and his uncle might have a few moments together in which they could look amongst the books for the photographs, but he knew that he could not bank on that.

During the week, Nicholas found that he could concentrate quite well on his schoolwork. Rab was back safely, and that was a big relief to him. Although Rab made the story of his extended holiday sound very amusing, it had been a potentially very dangerous situation.

Now that the time for Uncle John leaving hospital was very near, Nicholas realised how difficult it had been for them all. Although they had known relatively quickly that Uncle John could be helped, it had been a very worrying time, and they had not known how well he would be. So far, he was doing very well. He was walking a bit further every day, and once he had moved to the Hogg's, visiting him would be quite a different experience.

That week, Nicholas did not have time to do any further research, and although initially he had planned to make an enlarged version of the incomprehensible line in the list, he decided to leave it for now. He had cleared the bed in the spare room, so that whenever Jake arrived, it would be ready. That way it would be much easier to behave as if he were assuming that his brother was staying for at least a night. Then a sudden thought struck him. Jake had travelled the world since he left home. He was bound to have come across all kinds of unusual things. Maybe he could help with that line from the list? But it was secret. Nicholas could not show it to him. But why not? If he copied it, Jake would not know that it was part of a list, and he would not need to know it was anything to do with Uncle John, either. But how could he explain how he had come by it? Here Nicholas felt stuck. He did not want to have to lie to his brother, but he would have to think of something, because he would be very likely to ask. But would he ask? For that matter, would he agree to look at it? And in the unlikely event that Jake would speak to him at all, and would take an interest in it, he could just say it was a secret. Jake's whole life was such a secret that he would have to respect Nicholas'. But Nicholas decided to talk to Uncle John about the whole thing first, and get his reaction. Monday would be a good time for the copying. Uncle John would be settled in his room at the Hogg's, and they could do it together.

Colin took a half day from work on Friday. He wanted to be able to collect John from hospital while it was still daylight. That way he would see more of his house when they called in. The pale sun had taken the chill out of the air, and he set off for the hospital in good time, arriving just before three o'clock.

When he reached the ward, John was sitting ready, with a broad smile on his face.

'I've said my goodbyes to all the staff,' he said. 'Let's go!'

Colin thanked the senior nurse on duty, and took John's bags. Then they walked together to the car.

'Freedom!' said John as he climbed in slowly.

'We're to meet Nicholas at your house,' Colin explained. 'He should be there about four. I thought I'd take you for a bit of a drive first. Where would you like to go?'

'I don't know... Anywhere. Just anywhere,' said John happily.

Colin drove carefully round some local lanes with the heater on.

After a while, John asked, 'Can we turn that down now?' He laughed. 'It's even hotter in here than it was in hospital.'

'I've got to look after you properly,' said Colin jovially, as he turned the dial.

'Colin, could we go to my house a bit early?' asked John.

'Yes, of course. But why?'

'I'd like to give Nicholas a bit of a surprise if I can fix it. And I'll need your help.'

'If you explain, I'll do my best,' Colin replied.

'He told me you've got my bookcases in the middle of the living room, facing each other.'

'That's right. And we've covered them so they don't get splashed.'

'I'm very grateful for that, but I need something from them.'

'I can certainly give you a hand with that,' said Colin.

'The trouble is that I don't know exactly where to look, and the other thing is that it's a bit of a secret,' John added lightly.

'That's okay,' Colin reassured him. 'I'll take the cover off, prise them apart, and then leave you for ten minutes or so. I've got some measuring up that I can get on with. You can whistle when you're ready. Shall we head for the house now?'

John nodded, and they were soon drawing up outside it.

As Colin helped John slowly down the uneven path, he said, 'We'll have to do something with this eventually, but we'll leave it to the last.'

John nearly protested, and he almost said that he would see to it, but instead he said, 'Thanks.' Inside his house he was greatly impressed by what he saw. 'You haven't had all that long, but you've done so much.'

'We're a good team,' Colin conceded modestly. 'Take your time looking round. I'll go and move the bookcases.'

John moved around his home, touching things as he went. His mind filled with images of what it would be like being back again – images that he had determinedly blocked all the time he had been in hospital.

In the living room, Colin said, 'I'll leave you to it then,' and disappeared in the direction of the kitchen.

John ran his hands along his books. 'Now, I wonder where they are,' he muttered to himself. He chose a book at random, and flicked through its pages. But he rapidly realised that he had no time for this now, and replaced it quickly. He focussed his attention, and worked his way along the spines to see if they would prompt a memory of where he had stored the photographs. Ah! Now he remembered. They were in that old cardboard writing case. Where was it? He peered along the rows of books until he could see it, and he lifted it out.

Just then he heard a door bang shut, and he heard Nicholas' voice asking where he was.

'I'm in the living room,' he called.

Nicholas burst in. 'What do you think of it?' he asked proudly.

'It's incredible,' said his uncle warmly. 'You must show me round.'

Colin appeared in the doorway, and winked across at John. 'Let Nick give you a grand tour, while I finish off what I was doing.'

'I've got the photographs,' John told Nicholas, handing the writing case to him.

'Great! I'll put this in my bag,' said Nicholas excitedly. 'I promise I'll keep them safe.'

Nicholas hardly stopped talking as he showed his uncle everything he had been doing. Eventually, John had to admit that he was tired, and they locked up the house and set off for the Hoggs'.

Maggie Hogg was waiting for them to arrive, and when she saw the car draw up, she opened the front door and came to help with John's possessions.

'Welcome!' she said expansively, as she led them through the porch and into the large hallway. 'John, one of our booked residents cancelled last week, so you can have a ground-floor room straight away. His niece and her family are giving him a surprise holiday in the sun for his ninetieth birthday.'

She opened a door into a spacious room that had a window on the side of the building looking out onto a shrubbery.

'I'm nearly ninety myself,' John commented.

'And you don't look a day over eighty!' Maggie exclaimed.

John enjoyed her cheerful approach. However, by now he felt exhausted, and all he wanted to do was lie down.

As if sensing his thoughts, she said brightly, 'You're probably needing a rest. I'll go and bring you a pot of tea.'

'I'll put your things away for you,' Nicholas offered.

'Thanks, lad,' replied his uncle wearily, as he sat down in a comfortable reclining chair beside the window and leaned back gratefully.

He shut his eyes, and Colin saw that he fell asleep within seconds. He touched Nicholas' arm and whispered, 'He's nodded off. I think we should slip out now. One of us can easily come back later.'

As they went into the hall, Maggie appeared with the pot of tea. 'Asleep?' she commented. 'Don't worry about a thing. I'll keep an eye on him, and when he wakes up, I'll show him where everything is.'

Nicholas was in bed early that night. His mother had been to see John, and had come back with a glowing report. He would go tomorrow evening, with news of what he and Bernie were doing with the roof, and he would take with him the photographs so that they could study them together. He reached out and touched the special box with its precious contents, glanced across at his bag where the photographs were safely stored, switched off the light, and was soon asleep.

Chapter Fourteen

'Working with Bernie's great!' said Nicholas as soon as he saw his uncle. 'I can't wait until tomorrow. We've got to get as much done as we can before dark.'

'I thought you'd get on well together,' his uncle replied.

Nicholas took the writing case out from under his jacket, and handed it to his uncle.

'Have you looked through them?' asked John.

'Of course not!' replied Nicholas, offended. 'They're yours.'

'They belong to both of us now,' his uncle pointed out quietly. 'They're a part of what we're doing together.'

He opened the case, and laid out the photographs on the rectangular coffee table that was beside his chair.

He pointed to three, and explained, 'I took these from the beach when the tide was out. It gives some idea of the cliffs.'

Nicholas stared at them. He imagined that when the tide was in, the whole scene would look pretty scary.

His uncle pointed to another. 'This is a heap of stones that looked as if it must have been a dwelling at one time.'

'The shepherd's cottage?'

'There's no way of telling. The original one could have slid over the cliffs long before I got there, but I thought I would take this to set the scene.'

Nicholas had wanted to see the cottage where his ancestor had died. He felt disappointed, but did not say anything.

His uncle continued. 'Here's a view out to sea. It was pretty stormy on the day I took that one.'

Nicholas could see that huge waves had been whipped up near the shore.

John went on. 'I didn't go down to the beach that day.' He paused to give Nicholas time to look at it. Then he said, 'And here's one looking inland. It's mainly moorland.'

Nicholas could see only flattish land, covered in low vegetation, with no building in sight. It looked pretty bleak.

He heard his uncle say, 'And here's the one of the stone.'

Nicholas reached out and picked it up. He recognised the shape of the stone straight away, as it was as his uncle had sketched for him. His hand trembled a little. If the story were true, this man had lived just long enough to father a child, and if he had not, then he, Nicholas, would not be here now.

'How can we find out for certain?' he said almost to himself.

Then he realised that he must have spoken aloud because his uncle, sensing what he meant, replied, 'I don't think we can. That far back, the only records of commoners were kept in the churches, and I think it's very unlikely that anyone would have wanted to record Todd's death. And that's borne out by the stone. If you think about it, that stone was something that most wouldn't give a second glance to.'

Nicholas could follow the logic of what his uncle was saying. 'But what about his son?' he asked urgently. 'Won't his birth be recorded?'

'We can't be sure it was his son,' his uncle reminded him gently. Then he surprised Nicholas by saying, 'I tried to follow it up, though. I looked in a lot of old registers, but I didn't see anything that looked promising. It was like looking for a needle in a haystack. All I had was the location. I didn't have a date, and I didn't have a name.'

'But we *do* have a name,' Nicholas objected.

'There's no way the birth of any such child would have been recorded under Todd's name,' his uncle explained patiently. 'Remember that in those days it was considered unacceptable to have a child outside marriage. The shepherd and his daughter might well have tried to pass the child off as belonging to a relative to conceal the truth.'

'Oh... I see,' said Nicholas slowly. But he was not sure that he really did see. He found the whole concept very odd, and could not understand why on earth people used to behave like that. Many people at his school had parents who lived separately, and it was not uncommon for parents not to be married. He normally would not give this a second thought, but as he struggled to understand the situation of people living in Todd's time, he realised that life then had been very different indeed.

His uncle continued. 'Even when I was a boy, it was either marriage or risk your children being social outcasts.'

'I hadn't thought about all of that,' said Nicholas, feeling somewhat bemused. 'But I'm really glad you did your best to see if you could find anything out about the baby.'

'For obvious reasons, it mattered a lot to me. And it still does.' John fell silent for a minute, and his face became set. 'I want to know,' he finished emphatically.

Nicholas could see that although his uncle had stopped searching for information long ago, inwardly he had never given up the wish to find out, and he felt reassured.

'There's something else I want to talk to you about,' he said.

'Go ahead.'

'I was thinking I might show Jake that strange line from the list.'

His uncle suddenly looked very worried. 'You mustn't,' he said flatly.

'I don't mean to show him the list,' Nicholas explained. 'Remember how I'm going to copy that line, and make it bigger? I could show him that. He's been all over the world. There might be something in it that he recognises.'

'I see what you're getting at,' his uncle acknowledged. 'But I still think it's risky.'

'He wouldn't know where it came from, and if he asked, I'd say it's a secret. He couldn't say anything against that.'

'I still don't feel happy about it.'

'Anyway, he might not come,' said Nicholas.

'He'll be coming for sure,' his uncle insisted. 'There's no doubt about that.'

'I'll do the copying here on Monday,' said Nicholas.

'And we'll talk about it again then,' finished his uncle.

From then on, the weeks seemed to fly past. Every weekend, in most of the daylight hours, Nicholas worked with Bernie on the roof, and then would join his father doing inside work. His mother continued to put a lot of hours in. He and Bernie replaced all the guttering and many of the downpipes. That work was complete by mid-February, and then the rush was on to advance the central heating system in time for the boiler installation.

John settled in so well at Ken and Maggie's that it was almost as if it were a second home to him. Little by little his health was improving, and he began to find that he could walk to the local shop to collect a newspaper each day. This greatly improved his confidence, and most days he had a twinkle in his eye that Nicholas had not seen for a long time.

Nicholas and he had done their best to make an accurate, enlarged copy of the mystery line, and John kept this in his room, taking it out from time to time and studying it. He valued having a version that he could see properly, and he and Nicholas often looked at it together. They had not yet made a final decision about showing it to Jake.

With only a few weeks left until Easter, Sarah and Colin had a discussion about John.

'There's no way the house will be ready for him before Ken and Maggie go away,' said Colin. 'A younger person could camp in the house, but after what John's been through, that's completely out of the question.'

'He's improved so much that I've been wondering about having him at our house while they're away,' Sarah replied. 'You and I get a few days off around Easter, and Nicholas gets more than two weeks.'

'I haven't had time to tell you yet, but I've just fixed to have the second week of Nicholas' holiday off work. I want to push ahead with the work on the house, and that's the time to do it.'

'I feel quite envious,' Sarah admitted. 'I can't get any time off that week. With others away, it's not possible.'

'If it weren't for the man who covered for me at Christmas, I'd be in the same position. It suits me very well that he's so ambitious.'

'What do you think about having John here?' asked Sarah.

'I think he's ready. Are Ken and Maggie going to be away for the full two weeks?'

'I'm pretty sure they are.'

'Well, out of that time, there are only three days when I'm not going to be around. The rest of the time, I'll be just up the road, and only a quick phone call away.'

'I'm pretty sure that Nicholas will sit with him on those days,' said Sarah. 'Those two... they're as thick as thieves! They never seem to run out of things to say to each other.'

'Do you think there'll be a problem with our stairs, though?' asked Colin.

'I've thought of that,' Sarah replied. 'Apparently, Maggie's had him practising on theirs. It's a thing she does with all her residents, as it's all too easy to lose confidence with that kind of thing.'

'Good for her,' said Colin. 'All we've got to work out now is whether he goes in the spare room or uses Nicholas'.'

Sarah smiled. 'I think I know what the answer to that will be.'

It was nearly the Easter holidays, and Nicholas was feeling very excited. Uncle John's house was beginning to look good in places, and he was sure that they could do a lot more over the next two weeks. He whistled as he walked home briskly from the bus stop that day. He was looking forward to his uncle staying with them. He had insisted that he should use his room – with the special box still on the shelf near the bed.

He had learned that Louis was being despatched to his gran's again, but Nicholas could tell that this time he did not mind at all, now that there was plenty for him to do with the swimming club there. Rab was not going to be too badly off, either. A cousin of about his age was coming to stay, and plenty of activities had been arranged.

Despite this, Louis and Rab continued to feel envious of Nicholas' position, and the three boys had been discussing how they might get together in the summer to do some work for John. The plan so far was to suggest that they worked in the garden, and Rab had ideas of asking if they could grow potatoes there. Nicholas had promised to talk to Uncle John about it.

The house was empty when Nicholas arrived home. His parents would not be in until after six. He hung up his bag and coat, and sat with a long drink. The heating was still on at school, and with the milder weather it could be far too hot.

Having finished his drink, he ran upstairs to get changed – spending extra time in his room as he opened the special box and examined its contents again. He did not know how long he was there, but when he began to feel hungry, he closed the box and returned to the kitchen.

He was cutting a slice of walnut loaf, when the phone rang. He ignored it. It was bound to be for his mum or dad, and whoever was ringing could try again later. In any case, they should be home quite soon.

He took a bite, and the phone started ringing again. He would have to answer it now. He gulped down what he had in his mouth and reached for it.

'Hello,' he said, in a neutral kind of voice.

'Is Colin there?' It was a man's voice.

'He'll be back soon.'

'I'll phone again.'

'Do you want to leave a message?'

'No.'

Nicholas heard a click as the caller put down the phone, and he was left staring into the handset. There was something odd about this call. He suddenly wished his dad had been at home. Fleetingly he considered calling his mobile, but dismissed the idea because he did not want to worry him. After all, there really was nothing to worry about.

He looked at his watch. Five thirty. Half an hour to go. He switched on the television, but somehow it irritated him.

Then he heard a sound at the front door, and moments later his mother appeared in the living room.

'Hi,' she said. 'How're you doing? How was school?'

'Okay.'

Sarah looked at him intently. 'Is something the matter?' she asked.

'Not really... There was a phone call for Dad.'

'Oh... Who was it?'

'That's just it. Whoever it was didn't want to leave a message.'

'Never mind. I expect they'll phone again,' said his mother, returning to the hall to take off her coat. 'I'll be back in a minute. I'm going to get changed,' she called. But the phone rang again almost immediately, and she added, 'I'll get it.'

Nicholas relaxed. He picked up the newspaper and flicked through its pages. There were parts of it that he found interesting, and he often talked through some of these things with his dad.

His mother came into the room.

'It's Jake,' she announced. 'He'll be here soon.'

Nicholas could see that she looked flushed.

'I hope he talks to me this time,' Nicholas stated. 'He's bound to notice that I'm not a child any more.'

'I don't know if that will make a difference,' his mother warned him. 'We'll have to wait and see.'

'Well, there won't be any early bedtime for me,' said Nicholas with a smile. 'So he'll have to put up with me being around. And at least I can thank him for the postcard.'

That seemed to calm his mother's agitation. 'Yes... yes... of course,' she agreed. 'He'll have to let you say something about that.'

Colin put his head round the door. 'Hello, you two.'

'Col... I didn't hear you come in,' said Sarah.

'You were too busy nattering,' he said playfully. But then he saw the expression on Sarah's face, and asked, 'What is it, love?'

'Jake phoned. He'll be here soon.'

Nicholas noticed that his father looked pleased. In fact, he looked very pleased.

'Excellent!' Colin exclaimed. 'I've been looking forward to this. Do you want a hand with the cooking?'

Sarah dropped the chopping board that she had just grabbed from its hanger on the wall, and it landed with a loud clatter on the floor.

'I think I do.'

'I'll go and move my pyjamas,' said Nicholas. He ran upstairs and transferred the special box, a clean shirt and his nightclothes into the spare room, before returning to join his parents.

It was not long before the doorbell rang.

Sarah gave a stifled yell. 'I've nicked my finger,' she said desperately. 'There's blood going everywhere.'

Nicholas took charge. 'I'll get the door.'

'Good lad,' said his father, searching for a dressing for Sarah's finger.

Nicholas opened the door confidently, and there was Jake standing on the path outside. Although he was tall, he definitely seemed smaller than Nicholas remembered. And he had far less hair. Last time he came, he was covered in long black hair – all over his face and head – and now there was very little of it. He was clean-shaven, and his hair was cropped quite short. Last time he had looked quite thin, but this time he was more substantial. And his clothes looked okay. He was wearing dark grey trousers instead of jeans, and had a shirt that was covered by a navy jumper that seemed in good shape. On his feet he was wearing a pair of dark-coloured trainers that could be new, and he was carrying a small backpack.

'Hi!' said Nicholas casually. He stood to one side so that Jake could pass him in the hall. Then he followed him into the kitchen, where his mother was wiping traces of blood off the worktop.

Her face lit up. 'Jake!' she exclaimed happily, and she moved forward as if to hug him.

Nicholas watched as Jake rapidly stepped backwards and turned to his father saying, 'I've got a couple of hours.'

'It's great to see you, Jake,' said Colin. 'Will you have something to eat?'

Jake hesitated.

'It's nearly ready, anyway,' Sarah stated.

Jake was by now staring intently at Nicholas.

'Got your postcard,' said Nicholas. 'Thanks.'

Jake nodded, and turned as if to go to the living room.

'You can have my room tonight,' Nicholas offered.

Jake froze.

Colin began to speak, 'Nick…' But he stopped as Sarah stuck a spoon into his ribs.

'I've … got … two … hours,' said Jake, emphasising each word.

'The room's ready for you to use,' said Nicholas calmly. Then he went straight to the cutlery drawer, and made a noise by selecting the knives and forks.

For a moment, Jake looked as if Nicholas had hit him.

'Come and sit down, Jake,' his father invited, 'and you can tell me what you've been up to.'

When they left the kitchen, Sarah whispered to Nicholas, 'Would you mind staying here with me for a little while?'

'Okay,' Nicholas agreed. 'I'll help carry the food when it's ready.'

He toyed with the newspaper, but he was not reading it. He was thinking. His mother stood at the cooker, stirring something in a pan.

So far, so good, thought Nicholas. Jake's got to see that I'm a man – like him.

About ten minutes later, Nicholas and his mother took the food to the living room, and put it on the table. Without saying anything, Jake took a seat.

'Uncle John's been very ill,' Nicholas began.

Jake flinched.

Nicholas continued. 'He's a lot better now. We've been doing up his house for him.'

Jake started to tremble.

His father put down his knife and fork, looked him straight in the eye, and said, 'Your mother and I have often talked about how we spent more time looking after our house and other people than you when you were small. Will you please stay here tonight, and let us start to try to find a way to make amends?'

Jake said nothing, but stood up and went straight into the hall. Nicholas heard the door bang behind him as he left.

'Nick, I am so grateful to you,' said his father.

'But I was just talking to my brother,' Nicholas pointed out.

'In a very mature way,' said his mother. 'I'm proud of you.'

'You don't need to be,' Nicholas insisted. 'I'm hungry. Do you two mind if I get on with my food?'

After he had finished his meal, he announced, 'I'm off up the road to see Uncle John. You can phone Maggie if you want me to come back.'

But as he went into the hall, he saw that Jake's bag was still there, and he went back into the living room.

'I don't think I'm going yet. Jake's bag's in the hall,' he explained. 'He can't be far away.'

'I think I'll have a stroll round outside,' said his father.

'Good idea,' Sarah agreed. 'I'll stay here.'

'You coming Nick?' asked his father.

Nicholas shook his head, but then immediately changed his mind, and joined him.

'I haven't a clue which way to try,' said Colin as they walked down the path together.

'I don't think it matters all that much,' Nicholas replied.

His father looked at his watch. 'I'm going to give it about twenty minutes, and then go back to the house. We're unlikely to see him.'

'Let's go up to Uncle John's house,' suggested Nicholas suddenly.

'Any particular reason?'

'We could check round it, and then go home. If Jake's back by then, it would give a reason for us being out.'

'I like that idea. Come on.'

When they reached the house, they checked round the outside and found nothing that was of any concern.

On the way back home, Nicholas asked, 'Where he might have gone?'

'I don't know. He's never done this before.'

Back home, they found Sarah sitting staring blankly at the television screen, with Jake's bag on the seat beside her.

It was late evening before Jake reappeared. Colin had left the front door unlocked, and he just walked in. Nicholas noticed straight away that he no longer looked agitated.

'I've come to pick up my bag,' Jake announced, as if nothing had happened.

Not able to think of anything to say, Sarah handed it to him, and he turned to leave.

'I'll show you where my room is,' said Nicholas. 'Come on.' He quickly stepped into the hall in front of his brother.

93

Jake began to push past him.

'Or… you could stay in Uncle John's house,' Nicholas suggested, thinking fast. 'He's not living there while we're doing it up.'

Jake stopped in his tracks.

'You'd have to take a sleeping bag,' Nicholas advised. 'There's plenty of cold water, but no food.'

'Fine,' said Jake. 'You coming?'

Nicholas reckoned that Jake must know where Uncle John's house was, and that his question indicated a softening of his attitude.

'You set off. I'll catch you up,' he said over his shoulder as he ran upstairs to collect his sleeping bag.

Although Jake walked quickly, Nicholas had no difficulty in catching him up.

'You're fit,' Jake commented, looking straight ahead.

Nicholas said nothing, but stayed alongside his brother.

When they reached the house, Nicholas used his key to let them in through the now fully-functional front door.

He switched on the hall light, and said, 'You'll find your way around.' Then gave his sleeping bag and the key to Jake, and left.

Back at home, his parents were waiting to speak to him.

'We didn't say much,' he reported. 'I'd better get to bed. Let's hope he comes again tomorrow evening.'

'John will be here then,' said Colin. 'I'm to collect him from Ken and Maggie's around six o'clock.' He thought for a moment and added, 'I think it's going to be a good thing in more ways than one.'

Chapter Fifteen

At school the next day, Nicholas felt strange, but more real, both at the same time.

Lunchtime came, and he looked for Rab and Louis.

'What's up?' asked Rab, when he found him.

'My brother's come,' said Nicholas.

Rab stared at him incredulously. 'I didn't know you had a brother.'

'I didn't...' said Nicholas, 'but I do really.'

Rab was clearly perplexed.

Then Louis joined them. 'Exciting news?' he asked cheerfully.

'Nick hadn't got a brother, but he has,' said Rab, bemused.

'What?' Louis turned to Nicholas. 'What's going on?'

Nicholas explained. 'My brother is twenty-two years older than I am. I've hardly ever seen him, and I don't really think about him. He came yesterday, and he might be here today.'

Rab had sometimes thought that Nicholas' parents must be a bit older than his, but you could never be sure of these things. And anyway, what did it matter? But now it mattered, because otherwise Nicholas could not have this brother.

'Twenty-two years!' exclaimed Louis. 'That's ages. Nick, are you sure?'

Nicholas nodded, and then said, 'I'm starting to look a bit like him.' There was a note of pride in his voice.

'Can we see him?' asked Rab curiously.

'Probably not this time,' said Nicholas. He was surprised to discover he had a gut feeling that it even if Jake went away today, it would not be all that long before he was back again.

'I've got to leave for Gran's straight after school,' Louis announced regretfully.

'My cousin's not coming until Sunday,' said Rab, 'so text me if there's any chance.'

'Okay.'

The bell went for afternoon lessons, and the three friends parted.

After school, Nicholas wondered whether to go straight home, or detour by John's house. He deliberated about this on the bus, but came to no conclusion. Then he decided that the best thing was to go to the Hoggs' to see Uncle John.

His uncle was packing the rest of his things, and was very surprised to see him.

'What you are doing here?' he asked. 'I'll be at your house very soon.'

'I know,' said Nicholas, 'but I thought you should know what's been happening.'

His uncle sat down and waited.

'Jake phoned yesterday and came round. We were eating together and Dad said something to him about the past, and he just took off. But he left his bag behind. When he came back much later on, I took him up to your house with my sleeping bag, and left him there.'

'Oh, good lad!' his uncle exclaimed. 'That was perfect.'

Nicholas looked surprised. 'It seemed obvious.'

'If you hadn't thought of that, he would have left,' his uncle insisted.

'How do you know?' asked Nicholas.

'Just believe me,' his uncle replied. Then he fell silent, and when he spoke again, he said, 'So we're all waiting now to see if he reappears this evening.' It was more a statement than a question. 'It's not a bad thing that I'm going to be at your house, Nicholas. I think that now I might be able to help. I hope your dad comes soon. We need to do some preparation.'

John continued with his packing.

Nicholas looked at his watch. It was more than an hour before his father was due to come. He could not sit still, and instead paced around the room.

His packing finished, John said, 'Can't you sit down? You're making me dizzy.'

'It's really hard,' Nicholas replied. 'I want Dad to come now, so that we can take you home and start talking about Jake.' Then a thought struck him, and he began to feel very agitated. 'What if Jake's gone to our house? There'll be no one there, and he'll go away.'

His uncle attempted to reassure him. 'Try not to worry. When you left him at my house, did you give him the key?'

'Yes.' Nicholas could feel his agitation reduce a little.

'That means he's got somewhere as a base. If he's left, he'll be far away by now. If he hasn't, I've a hunch he's unlikely to go to your house until later this evening.'

Nicholas took a deep breath, and tried to relax. He realised now just how important it was to him to make further contact with his brother. He felt that he had made a small start, and this had opened up a longing that he had never consciously known before. He swallowed hard to choke back his feelings.

'You did very well yesterday,' said his uncle. 'You couldn't have done better. We'll have to wait to see what he does next.'

Nicholas opened his mouth to speak, but nothing came out.

'Would you like a game of dominoes?'

Nicholas nodded mutely, and his uncle produced the battered pack from his bag.

'You must have been no more than five years old when I first taught you how to play,' John commented.

This broke the tension in Nicholas. He smiled, and engaged in the game.

It was only half an hour later when Colin appeared in the doorway.

'Surprise!' he said. 'I managed to finish a bit early.'

Nicholas jumped up. 'Come on, Uncle John,' he urged, taking both his bags.

John quickly gathered up the dominoes, and followed Nicholas into the hall, where they found Ken and Maggie waiting to see him off.

'Thanks for everything,' he said sincerely, as each of them hugged him.

'Be sure and come back to see us,' Ken invited, his eyes clearly showing his affection for John. 'I'll miss our conversations.'

'Yes,' Maggie agreed, 'you must come and have tea with us one Sunday. We'll look forward to that.'

Nicholas and his uncle said nothing during the short drive, but when they were seated in the living room with mugs of tea, John turned to Colin saying, 'Nicholas has been telling me about Jake's visit.'

'I thought he would,' replied Colin. 'I couldn't wait to finish work today. I didn't want to miss any chance of seeing him again.'

Nicholas was very pleased to hear his father say this. He found it comforting that he had not been alone in his concern about missing

Jake.

Sarah's head appeared round the door.

'I thought you wouldn't be back for a while yet, love,' said Colin, surprised.

'I couldn't concentrate,' she replied. 'I just had to be here, so I left at the same time as the others. I'll go in early on Monday instead. Let me get my coat off. I'll be with you in a minute.'

She disappeared, and Colin went into the kitchen to get her a mug of tea.

When they came back, the four were soon deep in conversation.

'I still haven't worked out why he sent the postcard to you, Nick,' said Colin. 'It's always been addressed to me and your mother before.'

'And he's letting you make contact with him,' Sarah added.

'It's not much,' Nicholas pointed out.

'But it's a huge change,' said his father.

'When did you last hear from him?' asked John.

Sarah looked at Colin. 'It was around this time last year. Wasn't it, Col?'

'Yes, he phoned late one evening – around eleven o'clock. He didn't speak for long, but he sounded quite warm.'

'That's right,' Sarah remembered, looking tearful. 'It raised my hopes. He usually sounds so matter-of-fact. It made me think that things were changing.'

'Maybe they were,' said John wisely.

'What shall we do?' asked Sarah in agonised tones. 'I don't want to lose him again. He's just up the road, and he may be about to leave any minute for another unknown destination.' She began to sob. The stress of seeing him so little over the past fifteen years rushed to the surface, and she could not contain it.

Although Nicholas was sad to see his mother so upset, he was profoundly grateful that she was able to show at last how she really felt about his brother's absence from their lives.

'If he's in the middle of leaving, there's nothing we can do right now to deter him,' said John calmly. 'In fact, trying would just make things more difficult.'

Colin looked at him. 'That's my feeling too. We're going to have to be patient.'

'I've got a plan,' said Nicholas suddenly. 'If he hasn't come by nine o'clock, I'll go up to the house and see if he's still there.'

'That sounds sensible,' Colin agreed. 'What do you think, Sarah?'

Sarah's sobs had reduced a little, and she managed to reply. 'Yes, I think that's the best plan.'

'Why don't you sit here with Nick and John?' Colin suggested. 'I can make something for us all to eat. Anyone for beans on toast?'

'Not much for me, Col,' said Sarah. 'I don't feel hungry.'

It did not take Colin long to produce the food, and when they had finished eating, John announced, 'Sarah and Colin, I've got something I'd like to say to you both. For what it's worth, I think you did the best you could when Jake was small. Millie was struggling, and it was understandable that you tried your hardest to help her. I'm only sorry I couldn't help, but James had left her with the feeling that I wasn't to be trusted, and she couldn't accept anything from me.'

'Who is Millie?' asked Nicholas, puzzled.

'She was your gran on my side,' his father explained. 'After my dad died, she didn't manage very well, and as time went on she became pretty unstable mentally.'

'I was so sad about it,' said Sarah, tears again welling up in her eyes. 'We did all we could to prevent her from having to be taken into a home, but in the end we had to give up. The whole thing was too much for us.'

His father continued the story. 'We used to take Jake with us when we went to see her. Sometimes we stayed there for a few days, to see if that would help to stabilise her. But nothing worked. In fact, I sometimes thought that our being there made her worse.'

'But she couldn't have been left alone,' Sarah explained. 'Neighbours were concerned about her behaviour, and one day she had even attacked the postman.'

'We didn't want to leave Jake with anyone else,' said Colin. 'He was very young at the time. But it was wrong that we exposed him to witnessing her odd behaviour, which could be quite aggressive.'

'Sometimes even we were frightened,' Sarah added.

'Jake would have been bound to pick that up,' Colin observed. 'He became very quiet, and we noticed that he began to try to do everything perfectly all the time. We found somewhere where my mother could be looked after, but by then the damage had been done.'

Sarah continued. 'After a while, we thought it might help Jake if we took him to nursery to be with children his own age. We found somewhere small and homely. At first he seemed to settle in all right, and I found myself a small local job with flexible hours. I needed something like that because by then I was feeling pretty low. But this arrangement turned out to be a terrible mistake, because Jake suddenly became even more withdrawn.'

'How did he manage at school?' asked Nicholas. He wondered why on earth his parents had not told him all this before, and he was hungry for every detail.

'The structure there seemed to suit him,' his father replied. 'He did all his work with great precision, and this calmed him. He didn't make friends, but the other children liked him.'

Then John spoke. 'As you know, I tried to speak to him when he was about your age, but got nowhere.'

Colin went on. 'He did well in his exams at secondary school, and I wanted him to apply for university, but he was adamant that he wanted to travel round the world, and he's been doing that ever since. Nick, I expect there's a lot more you'd like to ask, but do you mind if we leave it for now? I feel shattered.'

'That's all right, Dad,' Nicholas replied. 'I don't want to wait, but I will.'

'That's very generous of you,' said his father. 'You've had to wait a long time already, and I'm very sorry about that.'

'I'm going out for a bit,' Nicholas announced. 'I'll take my mobile, so phone me if he comes.'

No one tried to dissuade him, and he set off in the direction of the local shops. He thought that he would buy an evening paper for something to do. He knew that his father did this when he wanted time to think things over, and he could see it was not a bad idea.

But he had not gone far before he changed his mind, and instead began walking in the direction of his uncle's house. Then he began to run.

'Please be there, please be there, please be there,' said his feet as he sped up the road.

He ran so fast that he arrived panting. But now what? He took a moment to take stock of the situation. The house looked deserted, but from where he was standing there was no way he could be sure. Jake had his key, so if the doors were locked, he would not be able to get in.

He moved silently up the path to the front door. It was locked. Then he went round to the back door. It was ajar. He froze in his tracks, and held his breath. He assumed that Jake would not be so careless as to leave the door like this, so he could not be far away. He slipped round the side of the house to his uncle's bedroom window, and as he neared it, he could see a glow of light. Flattening himself on the wall, he edged his way towards the part of the window that was covered by a curtain, and peered round it. There he saw Jake sitting motionless on the floor, in a strange posture. He drew away from the window, and stood with his back leaning up against the wall to think.

Should he go in, and risk making him angry by disturbing his ritual?

'No,' he murmured.

He waited only another few seconds before creeping back down the path and running home as fast as he could. He arrived covered in sweat.

'What on earth...' exclaimed his mother, as he appeared in the living room.

'He's still there,' Nicholas announced. 'I saw him in Uncle John's bedroom. He's sitting on the floor – really still.'

Colin glanced at Sarah, and then turned to Nicholas. 'He used to do that kind of thing when he lived with us.'

'I think he'll come, and he won't be long,' said John quietly.

Colin felt instinctively that John was right, and he was content to sit, thinking about the enormous step that he and Sarah had taken in explaining so much to Nick. And Nick had seemed to take it all in. Again he was deeply impressed by his son's mature response to what must have been to him a disturbing revelation.

John leaned back in his chair and shut his eyes. He suddenly felt very tired. The upheaval of the move was a quite a big thing, but the change in the situation about Jake was enormous. Nicholas was involved at last, and he was responding to the challenge in exactly the same way as he had done in relation to the knowledge of the pledge and the fifth key.

Sarah felt quite calm, but she could not rest. She went to the kitchen and tidied it, feeling supported by accomplishing familiar tasks.

Nicholas went into the hall, opened the front door, and sat on the step. He wanted to be in a position to see Jake as soon as he came into view.

It was not long before he spotted him, walking down the road at a leisurely pace. He jumped up and rushed into the living room to let the others know, before returning to his position on the doorstep. He sensed the moment when Jake caught sight of him, and he was pleased to see that he did not falter.

Nicholas stood up when Jake reached the gate. 'Come in,' he said.

He let Jake go into the house ahead of him. It was then he noticed that Jake carried nothing with him – no bag, and no sleeping bag. This had to be a good sign, he thought.

He heard his father's voice as Jake went into the living room. 'Hello, son.'

He followed Jake into the room, and saw him wince slightly as he saw Uncle John sitting there.

'John's staying with us for a couple of weeks,' Colin explained.

'The place I was in is closed for a holiday,' said John quietly. 'But in any case, I'm just about better now.'

Colin went on. 'Nick and I are planning to push on at John's house over the next two weeks. We're hoping to get it ready enough for John to go there after that.'

'Gran...' Jake began.

'It's not like it was with Gran,' said Colin.

Jake was quiet, as if he was taking time to let this sink in.

'Would you like some beans on toast?' asked Sarah.

Jake looked uncertain for a moment, and then nodded.

Nicholas felt worried. If Jake wanted to stay on, where would he sleep? If they were working at Uncle John's, surely Jake would not want to be there. He wanted to speak to his father, but was unable to think of any way of attracting his attention without Jake being involved. His thoughts whirling, he bit on his lip, and he tasted the saltiness as it started to bleed.

His mother appeared with the food, and Jake ate it silently.

When he had finished, he asked, 'What time are you starting in the morning?'

'Eight o'clock,' said Nicholas before anyone else had time to answer. He quickly added, 'I can come early and wake you if you want.'

Jake flashed a look at Nicholas that seemed to carry with it a hint of gratefulness.

'Okay,' he said abruptly. Then he stood up, turned, and was gone.

Nicholas went to the front door and watched him disappear into the distance before rejoining the others.

'So far, so good.' The relief in Colin's voice was almost palpable.

'I was really worried,' Nicholas admitted.

'So was I,' his father confided. 'I couldn't think how to make him feel welcome to stay on. You hit on exactly the right thing.'

'I'll stay here in the morning,' said Sarah. 'I don't suppose he'll come down, though.'

When they all went to bed, Colin and Sarah talked late into the night, but eventually they had to accept that they could not plan a way forward. Instead they would have to wait to see how things evolved.

Chapter Sixteen

Nicholas slept well, but when he woke at the sound of his alarm clock, he found that his bedding was in a tangle on the floor beside him, and for a minute or two he was unable to remember anything about the previous evening.

When it all came flooding back to him, he leapt out of bed, and was soon ready to leave, having first made himself a sandwich to eat on his way up the road. When he arrived at the house, he decided that the best thing was to ring the doorbell. Thank goodness they had connected it up.

Jake appeared at the door, and opened it wide to let him in. 'I want to do some work here too,' he stated bluntly. 'But not today.'

'Okay,' replied Nicholas. 'We'll be working from eight o'clock every day until around nine in the evenings.' He paused. 'You can keep my sleeping bag here,' he added casually. His heart was thumping, but he showed nothing of his feelings. He looked at his watch. 'It's seven forty-five.'

Jake grabbed his bag and went down the path.

Colin arrived at the house not long afterwards, and Nicholas told him what had taken place.

His father was astounded by the news that Jake was planning to work on the house. 'But I don't know what to suggest,' he said worriedly. 'I know he's experienced in all kinds of things, but I don't know what he'll want to do.'

'He'll probably tell us,' Nicholas replied, filling a bucket with water.

His father went on talking as if Nicholas had not spoken. 'He won't want to work with us.'

'He'll just tell us,' Nicholas repeated, raising his voice.

His father looked at him as if he were speaking a foreign language, but then he seemed to understand. 'Thanks, Nick. Let's get on now.'

Nicholas and his father packed up at eight o'clock that evening to make sure the house was free long before Jake returned. At home, they told the others about the progress that had been made – with Jake, and with the house.

Sarah was very tearful when she had the news of Jake. 'If he's really going to be working there, I think it's best I don't come up at all, unless something else changes.'

'We didn't get as much done today as we could if you'd been there,' Colin told her, 'but I think you're right.'

'John and I did some talking today,' Sarah informed them. 'It's been very helpful, and I expect we'll do some more tomorrow.'

When Nicholas arrived at his uncle's house the following morning, he could hear noises suggesting that Jake was already hard at work. He went round to the back door, and let himself in. He found Jake in the living room, mending a piece of skirting board to the right of the fireplace. Jake turned, looked at him, and went on working. Nicholas said nothing, and began his own tasks.

From that day on, Jake worked alongside them. He always chose things that he could do alone, and was invariably working in another room. But he was there. He said very little, and only spoke when he needed something for what he was doing. His work was flawless.

Colin and Sarah spoke to each other a lot about what was happening. Sarah continued to spend her free time at home with John. This arrangement worked well. She found that spending relaxed time with him allowed her to air much of the private sadness she had carried for most of Jake's life. Although she and Colin had shared their worries about Jake, and had discussed their feeling of inadequacy, she realised now that she had bottled up much of her misery in order to keep going. When he had left home and was rarely in contact, she had felt devastated. It had been one night when she had allowed those feelings to spill out that Nicholas had been conceived. Once they were certain about the pregnancy, they had decided they did not want to live in a house that seemed to them to be full of their failure as parents, and so they moved. Sarah had been on edge, fearing that Jake would not make contact again until after they moved, and she was terrified about the risk of losing touch completely. She and Colin had made a specific arrangement with the buyers of their house so that they would ensure he was told their new contact details. However, he had phoned not long before they left, and had come to see them. Sarah had been worried about how he would react to her pregnancy, and she and Colin had made preparations. When Jake had arrived, Colin opened the door, and gave him a letter they had written together, stressing that it was important and that he should keep it safe. It included their date of removal, new address and phone number. He had put it in his bag without opening it. As Sarah had feared, as soon as he saw her, he turned and ran out of the house. It had been well over two years before they heard from him again, and he had not come to see them until Nicholas was nearly five.

Towards the end of the first week, Jake approached his father and said abruptly, 'I'll do the tiling in the bathroom and kitchen.'

Colin nodded, but said nothing. He was pretty sure that Jake knew where the boxes of tiles were stacked, and in any case, Jake would ask if he were short of anything.

'I'll get Nick,' Jake added, and went off to find him.

Colin stared after him. He felt completely stunned. It had been a miracle that Jake had stayed. It had been a miracle that he had been working here at all. And now... Now, he was going to work with Nick – the brother that he had never been able to accept. He shut himself in the spare bedroom, and began to paint the frame of the window.

Nicholas was securing one of the inspection hatches when Jake appeared.

'Tiling,' said Jake.

'Okay,' Nicholas replied. 'I'll finish this later.' He jumped up and followed his brother to the kitchen, where he began to discover what it was like working with him.

Jake demonstrated everything carefully, while saying very little. It was clear that he was determined to teach Nicholas how to do it himself, rather than using him as a spare pair of hands.

Colin continued to keep well out of the way, as he wanted to avoid doing anything that might disturb what was taking place.

At six o'clock, he decided to try leaving them together. He cleaned his hands, packed up his things, and put his head round the kitchen door.

'I'm just off to see Sarah and John,' he said casually.

'Okay, Dad,' Nicholas replied without looking round.

Jake grunted, and continued with his silent encouragement of Nicholas' efforts.

Not long after Colin left, Jake astonished Nicholas by saying,

'You can stay all evening.'

Nicholas continued to concentrate on what he was doing, but nodded.

They worked together until after ten o'clock, when Jake said, 'You've done fine. See you tomorrow.'

At home, Colin asked Nicholas if he would prefer to be on his own with Jake the next day.

'No, that wouldn't be right,' Nicholas replied. 'We're trying to get the place finished, and we don't want to lose any time.' He turned to his mother and added, 'But I think you shouldn't come.'

'Your dad and I had more or less decided that,' answered Sarah.

The following day, Jake continued to teach Nicholas how to do the tiling, and Colin made sure that he was working elsewhere. Again he left early, leaving his sons together.

Not long after he had gone, Jake stated, 'We'll stop at eight.'

Nicholas was so surprised that before he had time to think, he asked, 'Why? We could get more done.'

'We'll talk,' said Jake cryptically.

At eight o'clock precisely, Jake put away the tools, and took his brother into the living room, where they sat in the battered armchairs – one on each side of the empty fireplace. The chairs were covered with thick dustsheets.

'This is how Uncle John and I used to sit before he got ill,' Nicholas commented.

Jake further surprised Nicholas by saying, 'He had these chairs when I was young.'

They fell silent for a few minutes, and then Jake said, 'You're doing okay, Nick.'

Nicholas felt very pleased to hear this. From Jake, it was praise indeed. Until now, he had said nothing except give directions. These had always been precise and accurate, but he had never given any encouragement, and certainly no praise.

'Thanks,' said Nicholas.

'I'll stay until you go back to school. We'll get plenty done.'

Nicholas could not conceal his delight. 'That's great!'

Jake winced, got up from his chair, and went to the kitchen.

Nicholas froze. He wished fervently that he had not said anything.

Jake was away for a full ten minutes, during which Nicholas tried his best to think of something that would bring back the connection with his brother. But he could not come up with anything, and he sat motionless, waiting.

Then Jake was back in the room again, and he had something in his hand.

'Here,' he said, holding a piece of cake out to Nicholas.

Nicholas took it carefully. 'Thanks.' He took a bite, and found that it tasted very good.

'Walnuts,' Jake commented.

Nicholas wondered if Jake had made it, but decided not to ask. Instead, he quietly ate his way through it.

When he had finished, he stood up, saying, 'I'd better get off. See you tomorrow.'

Again Jake surprised him – this time by going with him to the door.

Nicholas was about to walk down the path, when he turned and said, 'I've got something I want to ask you about. I'll bring it with me one day soon.' He did not wait to see Jake's reaction.

As he walked back down the road, he realised that he did not want to tell the others about what had taken place. Not yet.

From then on, the brothers worked together until eight o'clock each evening, and then they would sit and talk a little. Their father had continued to leave around six, and Nicholas had more than once encouraged him to stick to that.

After a few days, Nicholas took with him the copy he had made of the line of strange writing from the list, and when the time came for him and Jake to have their talk, he produced it.

'This is what I wanted to ask you about,' he began. 'Mum and Dad always said that you travel a lot. I don't know where you've been, but I thought you might be able to help with this. I think it's in foreign writing.'

He handed it to Jake, and waited while he unrolled the strip of paper.

Jake studied the characters intently for a while, before allowing the paper to roll itself up again.

He handed it back to Nicholas. 'It's not a language I know.'

Nicholas felt disappointed, but he was very glad that Jake had been willing to look at it.

'Where's it from?' asked Jake.

'I copied it from something else,' Nicholas explained.
Jake looked at him, clearly waiting for more information.
'I can't tell you any more because it's a secret,' said Nicholas carefully.
'Hide it well, then,' Jake replied, smiling.
Nicholas relaxed, and smiled back.

But as they sat together the following evening, Jake picked up on the subject again.
'I've been thinking about your secret,' he began.
Nicholas felt very alert. He wondered what Jake might come up with, when last night there had been nothing more to say.
'I think it's a private code that someone's devised. I've sometimes done that myself.'
Nicholas digested this information. Then he burst out agitatedly, 'But how will I ever understand it?'
Jake watched him with a look of amusement on his face. 'You'll never understand it if you get in a frenzy about it.'
Nicholas was crestfallen, and hung his head.
'Patience, Nick. Patience,' said Jake.
'Can you give me any clues?' Nicholas pressed desperately.
'I've just given you the most important one,' Jake pointed out. 'You'll get there in the end.'
Nicholas had an urge to get out of his chair and shake his brother, but he knew it would do no good. Jake's arms were strong and of considerable length, so it would be physically impossible. Added to that, he knew that his brother was likely to turn away from him if he behaved in a way that was anything other than mature. Very slowly, he had been gaining Jake's respect, and it was vital to him that he did not lose this. He realised that Jake had trusted him immeasurably by confiding that he himself used personally-devised codes. Despite his frustration, somewhere inside him he knew that at least for now, this information was more important than worrying about that line on the list.

The end of Nicholas' holiday was looming fast. There was only the weekend left. His Friday evening chat with Jake had been brief and stilted. This was not because Jake was particularly reticent. In fact, he was telling Nicholas a little about the various options of where he might go next. Although Nicholas knew that this was another huge step forward in his relationship with his brother, he did not feel warmed by it. Instead, he felt withdrawn, and for once, Jake spoke more than he did.

With the addition of Jake's considerable input, John's house was nearing completion, and John would certainly be able to move there very soon. There was not much left to do apart from finishing touches, and Nicholas and his father would be able to see to them with John in residence.

Nicholas parted from Jake earlier that evening, and Jake made no move to encourage him to stay. He walked down the road very slowly, feeling miserable. When he reached home, he hesitated outside the front door, unwilling to go in, and he knew that he was about to cry. He took out his grimy handkerchief and wiped his face, but this did nothing to stem the tears. He stood on the doorstep, uncertain about what to do. He could not go back to John's house, and he could not face explaining anything to his parents and Uncle John. He was in a quandary.

Then another option occurred to him. He had left his uncle's house early, so no one here would be expecting him yet. He could spend a while wandering round the streets, trying to clear his head.

The air was clear and spring-like. He headed for the track that had been made from the route of an old railway. As he walked along, he met several people, but they were deep in their own thoughts, and did not give him a second glance. He was glad not to feel drawn into having to exchange a greeting.

His time with Jake had been amazing, and he did not want it ever to end. Jake had taught him so much, they had worked together, and then they had begun to talk together. If anyone had asked him two weeks ago if he thought any of this to be likely, he would have been completely bemused. Yet it had all happened, and it reached the ache that had been deeply buried inside him. He had not known how much he had longed to be in contact with Jake, and to know him as his brother. And now that this contact was a real part of his life, he could not bear to let it go. The thought of it ripped him apart.

He had learned much from his parents about what had gone wrong when Jake was young, and it had helped him to understand why Jake had avoided them all, and himself in particular. His acceptance of that had enabled him to reach out to Jake, and he had got something back that was bigger than anything he could have imagined.

But now he was about to lose it all. He could not face this, and he wanted to run away. He stopped suddenly as this thought came into his mind. It was exactly what Jake had done, and look what had happened... Jake had run away from something he found unbearable, and this had resulted in a separation from their parents that ate away at them inside, and an unknown emptiness in Nicholas himself that no one had recognised, or understood.

He stopped. 'I can't run away,' he said aloud. 'So what am I to do?'

It was then he realised that somehow his relationship with Jake had become tangled up in his mind with his promise to Uncle John never to let his parents know anything about the pledge. Of course he could talk to the others about how he felt about Jake. And it was not just that he could – he *must*.

Now, life began to feel possible again. Although it had been a great disappointment that Jake had not been able to read the code line, in a way it had been a very good thing. If he had, that would have linked him inextricably with the secret he shared with Uncle John, and then his relationship with Jake would have run the risk of remaining largely a secret, too.

At this, he turned and walked purposefully back home.

As soon as he entered the hall, he heard his father call, 'Hi, Nick! We've been looking forward to seeing you.'

Nicholas put his head round the living room door and grinned.

'We've been having a long talk since your dad came home,' said his mother, 'but there's been a missing element – you.'

'I'm hungry,' Nicholas stated emphatically.

'If you look in the oven, you'll find something that'll fix that,' his mother replied.

'I'll get it,' said his father. 'You sit down, Nick.'

His father brought a plate with three large baked potatoes and various fillings.

'You get stuck into that,' Colin encouraged, 'and we'll tell you where we've got up to.'

Sarah began. 'It's been hard for me to stay away. I've wanted to come.'

Nicholas swallowed a mouthful of hot potato, and said, 'Mum, if you'd come we couldn't have done everything we did. Jake's brilliant.'

'He's made me redundant,' Sarah observed with a smile. 'But the time John and I have had together has been good for me.'

'For us both,' said John firmly.

Sarah looked sad. 'I wish I could have seen more of Jake.'

Colin touched her arm. 'Of course. I've had something quite different with Jake this time, but you haven't.'

'Mum,' said Nicholas, 'I think that if you'd tried to keep coming round, even if Jake had stayed on, he wouldn't have talked to me.' At this, he felt upset, and nearly choked on a piece of potato.

His mother thought about this. 'I think I've been selfish,' she admitted at last.

Nicholas was about to say something else, but she stopped him.

'No.' She struggled for a moment, and then went on. 'I've been wrong... very wrong. I thought that because you weren't born until after Jake left home, he was nothing to do with you.'

Colin groaned. 'And I thought the same.'

Sarah continued. 'And the fact that he ignored you just confirmed it for me.' She looked at Colin. 'We should never have let that happen.'

'You're absolutely right, love,' Colin agreed. 'Even if Jake couldn't accept Nick, that shouldn't have meant that we behaved to Nick as if Jake was nothing to him.'

Nicholas relaxed. The hot potatoes had certainly helped, but this conversation was exactly what he had needed. His parents seemed to understand now what had been dragging at him, and it was no longer something that he had to manage on his own.

'I don't want him to go away,' he said, but he no longer felt the misery about it that had been dogging him.

'None of us want him to go,' his uncle stated quietly. 'I'm an old man, and when he goes, I might never see him again.'

'Don't say that!' said Nicholas sharply. The thought of losing both Jake and his uncle was too much for him. And what about the pledge and the fifth key? He could say nothing about that at the moment. He glared angrily at his uncle.

'Nicholas,' said John, 'I'm a lot better than I was, and I'm looking forward to spending time with you at the house that you have all rescued for me. But realistically, if Jake disappears for another few years, I may not be around when he comes back.'

Nicholas had to accept this. Uncle John was right. But he did not want it to be like this. He did not want Jake to disappear for another few years. He could not bear the thought at all. And it was clear that

Uncle John and his parents could not, either.

It was this last consideration that helped him, and any child-like thoughts of insisting that his parents sort all this out receded. Instead, he said, 'We'll have to work out what to do.'

His parents stared at him, and then stared at each other.

It was his father who spoke first. 'We've been stuck behaving in one way for years and years.'

'You've started to change, though,' Sarah observed. 'When I saw you with Jake, you were a bit different.'

'I felt it,' Colin agreed. 'And it carried on at John's, although you haven't been there to see it.'

'That's probably why Jake's been able to talk to Nicholas,' commented John wisely.

'So what's the next stage?' asked Sarah, with a note of desperation in her voice. 'It's Friday evening now. By Monday morning he'll be gone, and we won't have a clue where he is.' Her voice had risen as she tried to suppress a feeling of panic.

'I've been doing a lot of thinking,' said Colin. 'I don't think it's going to help to suggest that we all meet here or at John's for an hour or so. In fact, I think being in any kind of building isn't the right thing.'

'I think I follow what you mean,' Sarah agreed. She was still feeling very agitated, but was concentrating hard on everything that Colin was saying. 'We could do something together outside. But...' Here she stopped, feeling disappointed. 'But it would mean that John couldn't be with us.'

'Don't worry about me,' said John. 'The most important thing is to get your family together.'

'But you're our family, too,' Colin pointed out.

'What if we did something outside for a bit, and then Jake could show Uncle John round his house?' Nicholas suggested.

'That's perfect!' exclaimed his mother. 'And I could make something to eat that we could leave in the house for them.'

'I don't think that's a good idea, Sarah,' said Colin gently. 'I don't think it would help.'

'You're right, Col,' she acknowledged. 'I'm just trying to race ahead again.'

Colin was sympathetic. 'I know, love. We all know where we'd like to be, but we've got to work out the right steps to get there.'

'I can tell Jake,' Nicholas offered.

'Thanks, Nick,' replied his father, 'but it's my job. In fact, since time's short, I'll phone him now to let him know what we're thinking.'

'He might not answer,' said Sarah worriedly.

'I know,' Colin agreed, 'but that doesn't mean I shouldn't try that first.'

As Sarah had guessed, there was no reply, so Colin got a notepad and envelope, and wrote a note to Jake.

'I'll take this up the road with me,' he said. 'I'll ring the bell, and if there's no reply, I'll post it through the door.'

'I can run up with it,' Nicholas offered eagerly. Colin was about to reply when Nicholas added, 'But I mustn't, because it's your job.'

'Correct,' said Colin. 'I won't be long.'

He was soon back. 'Mission accomplished. I posted it through the door. And now I'm going to think about what I'm going to say to Jake before he leaves.'

When Nicholas arrived to start work the following morning, Jake said nothing to him about the letter. When his father arrived, Nicholas heard them exchange a few words, but he was in the bathroom at the time, and could not make out what was said.

However, when he and Jake sat down for their evening chat, Jake referred to it straight away.

'Was it your idea?' he asked, with a penetrating stare.

'No it wasn't!' Nicholas exclaimed indignantly.

'Okay.'

There was an awkward silence between them, and then Nicholas made himself ask, 'Are you coming?'

'Think so,' Jake replied. He was clearly struggling with something.

Nicholas again contained a strong urge to shake his brother. Instinctively, he knew that Jake was doing his best, but waiting for the promise of any reliable contact with him was very hard. He reminded himself firmly that once Jake had started to spend time with him, he had been consistent in what he had given out. To have had a time like that was amazing, and he must wait now to see what might unfold.

Then to his astonishment, Jake said through clenched teeth, 'I'll miss you.'

'I'll miss you too,' replied Nicholas, trying to keep his face from showing emotion, but not quite succeeding.

'I've got something for you,' Jake told him.

Nicholas watched as Jake felt inside his pocket, and brought out a small object that was wrapped in a coloured handkerchief. He handed it to Nicholas.

Nicholas slowly opened the handkerchief and instantly recognised a piece of coral.

'It's coral,' said Jake unnecessarily. 'Like on the card.'

'I'll keep it safe.' Nicholas knew that what he really meant to say was that he would keep the memory of this moment with Jake safe until he saw him again. Suddenly, he found that he no longer needed to know when that would be.

'So you're coming to work in the morning, and then we're all going out in the afternoon,' Jake stated.

Nicholas stood up. 'That's right,' he replied happily.

Soon he was running down the road, desperate to tell the others the news. But although he told them that the plans for tomorrow were on track, he said nothing about the coral, and he put it in Uncle John's box, to join the list and the measuring device.

Chapter Seventeen

As Nicholas strode up the road to his uncle's house the following morning, he felt on top of the world. He was confident that whatever happened today would be good, and he gave it little thought. He and Jake would spend the morning together, and then they would set off for the path he had walked along the other night. His mum and dad would deliver Uncle John to his house and leave the car there, and then join them at the railway walk. After that, Jake would show the work to Uncle John, and Dad would take John home again afterwards.

The morning passed pleasantly. The brothers said very little to each other as they made the place tidy for their great-uncle's visit.

Then it was time to set off for the walk. There was warmth in the sun as they strolled along together to the agreed spot.

Once there, they stood watching the passers-by – people on bikes, young parents with smallish children and people walking dogs. Nicholas wondered how Jake felt when he saw the children with their parents, but he did not ask. It was not the right thing to be talking about at the moment. Although he had felt confident about this meeting, he found himself holding his breath when his parents came into view.

He said nothing as Jake greeted their father, and then made an effort to speak to their mother. 'You came,' he said to her, and then quickly moved so that he could walk abreast of his father, leaving Nicholas with Sarah.

Nicholas surprised himself by making casual conversation about birdsong and dog breeds, and in this formation, they made their way along the pleasant walkway.

After about half an hour, Colin looked at his watch, and said, 'Time to get back, folks.'

For a moment, Nicholas thought he saw Jake falter, as if he wanted to continue walking. But then he dismissed the idea when Jake began to stride ahead, as if the only thing he wanted to do now was to get back to the house.

When they arrived, Sarah patted Jake's arm briefly, saying 'Bye, Jake.'

Nicholas was pleased to note that although Jake looked a bit stiff, he did not flinch, or turn away.

Colin took Jake's hand and shook it warmly. 'It's been a real pleasure to work with you,' he said. 'Keep in touch. I hope we'll see you again soon.'

Nicholas remained quiet. He knew that he would have his precious time with his brother in the evening. He was deeply impressed by the way that his father was behaving.

Then he heard him say, 'Jake, we could come and see you sometime, if you let us have an address.'

Colin did not wait for a reply, and instead turned to Sarah. 'Come on, love. We'll let Jake and John get on.'

Nicholas and his parents walked back home, leaving the car at John's ready for Colin to collect him later.

'Mug of tea, anyone?' asked Colin as soon as they were through the door.

'Watching you is all I needed,' Sarah replied.

'I'm only sorry I haven't been able to do it before, love.' Colin gave her a hug. He looked at Nicholas. 'And if it weren't for you, I doubt we'd have got as far forward as we did.'

'We're a family,' said Nicholas. 'Everyone does their bit.'

About an hour later, the phone rang, and Colin picked it up. It was John, ready to return.

'I'll be up in a few minutes,' Colin told him.

He walked briskly up the road to find John standing beside the car, and Jake nowhere in sight.

'Leave him,' John advised. 'He's exhausted.'

Colin nodded, and helped John into the car. 'Nick'll be seeing him later. That's enough.'

As soon as John saw Nicholas, he said admiringly, 'You've all done a grand job on my house.'

'When would you like to move in?' asked Colin. 'We can do the rest around you.'

'Give Jake all the time he needs, and I'll move in as soon as he's gone,' replied John.

'I can get shopping in for you,' Nicholas offered immediately. 'You can make a list of things...' He stopped and looked at his uncle meaningfully.

'Ah... yes... Lists can be very useful,' John replied. 'I'll certainly follow your advice.'

117

Nicholas had no agenda for his time with Jake that evening, and their hour was spent browsing quietly through their great-uncle's bookshelves.

'There are some very interesting things here,' Jake commented. 'I wish I had more time to study them.'

Nicholas knew that he was referring to something much greater than the books themselves, and he made no comment.

'The school library's not too bad,' he said. 'I sometimes go there.'

'Study all you can, while you can,' Jake advised, picking out another book and skimming its pages. 'And I'll send you a card or two.'

Nicholas' heart leaped. Jake was going to keep in touch with him. But he would like to send things to him as well.

As if reading his thoughts, Jake said, 'I don't stay in one place for long.'

Nicholas was sure that he was thinking about giving him some way of contacting him, so he did not press him. He was surprised that he was feeling quite calm, as if when he left Jake this evening, it would not be long before he saw him again.

He stayed a little longer, and then announced, 'I'd better go now. School tomorrow.'

'Let John know I'll be gone by tomorrow evening,' Jake told him.

On the doorstep Nicholas said, 'See you.'

Jake touched his shoulder lightly. 'See you.' Then he turned and disappeared back into the house.

The warmth of Jake's touch stayed with Nicholas.

Chapter Eighteen

As soon as he saw his friends, Rab and Louis, in the corridor at school, Nicholas burst out excitedly, 'My brother stayed for the whole two weeks, and we've nearly finished the house. Jake's brilliant!'

Rab and Louis looked at each other. Nicholas rarely showed such excitement. At times, he would say that he was excited about something, but this exuberance was new.

'By the way you look, it must have been good,' Rab commented. 'And I don't think Louis and I are going to get a word in about our holidays.'

'Probably not,' replied Nicholas grinning at them. 'No, that's not true. I want to know, but give me time to say a bit more, and then I'll be able to listen.'

'Okay then.' Rab and Louis spoke together.

Rab looked at his watch. 'The bell will go in a minute. You'll have to be quick.'

'He taught me how to do loads of things,' said Nicholas.

'Like what?' asked Louis.

'Tiling,' Nicholas replied proudly. 'And we talked.'

Rab and Louis looked at each other. 'What do you mean?' asked Rab.

'Yes, what do you mean?' Louis echoed. 'What's so amazing about talking?'

'Because Jake's travelled since before I was born, it's as if I never existed,' Nicholas explained. 'But it's not like that now.'

'Okay,' said Louis, as he began to understand the impact on Nicholas of being around his brother. 'You can tell us more about it later, if you want.'

'I will,' Nicholas answered. 'And because having Jake meant we did much more of the work, Uncle John's back in his house now. It's not exactly finished, but we've done enough. Dad and I can do the rest at weekends. And I'll ask soon about us doing the garden in the summer.'

'Great!' said Rab enthusiastically. 'Having my cousin staying was all right for a couple of weeks, but I want something real to do in

119

the summer.'

'Me too,' Louis agreed.

'But what about your swimming?' asked Nicholas.

'I'll do that as well.'

The bell above their heads rang loudly, and Nicholas put his fingers in his ears. 'I hate that,' he muttered.

'I suppose without it we'd just stay here chatting all day,' Rab joked. 'See you later. I'm off to German.'

It was later that week before Nicholas and John sat down together for a serious talk about the fifth key. All the time John had been at Nicholas' house, there had been no privacy for such a conversation, but neither had missed this. Jake's presence in their lives had rightly taken precedence over everything else. It had been crucial to everyone, and would continue to be so. An unbelievable amount of progress had been made, and now Jake's absence no longer meant an inexplicable disappearance that was punctured only rarely and temporarily. And while all this change had been taking place, John's house had undergone rapid transformation.

'I showed Jake the copy I'd done of that line in the list,' Nicholas began.

His uncle looked worried. 'Did he come up with anything?'

'I got the impression he knew quite a bit about languages. He couldn't recognise any of it, though. But later, he said he thought it might be a code the writer had invented.'

John relaxed. 'It's the only other thing I can think of, but how on earth we work out what it means is a real puzzle. I've racked my brains, and I don't know where to start. By the way, did he ask where it came from?'

Nicholas nodded. 'But he accepted that I couldn't tell him.'

'Have you got the copy with you? I'd like us to study it.'

Nicholas produced it from the pocket of his jacket.

John took it to the table, unrolled it, and put a book at each end to secure it.

'Let's do the simple things first,' he suggested. 'How many characters are there?'

'Seventeen,' Nicholas replied instantly. He did not have to count them. He had already done so, many times.

'And do any of them repeat?'

'Only one.' Again Nicholas had no need to look.

'Let's see,' John mused. 'That's the fifth and the eighth.'

It was then that Nicholas joined him at the table. He stared at the line. His uncle was right.

'What would you say the shape is of those two?' asked John.

'Like a capital E that has fallen on its back and has thick legs sticking up,' Nicholas replied. What could his uncle be getting at?

'That shape reminds me of a simple key, but without a handle,' said John.

Nicholas wondered why he had not thought of this himself, but until he had spoken to Jake, he had been sure that the line was written in some mysterious foreign language, and he suspected that his uncle had thought the same.

Suddenly something occurred to him. 'Uncle John, if you add together the two character numbers – five and eight – it comes to thirteen. That's how old I am.'

'Yes, the age you had to be before I told you the story and about the pledge. And you never know, but maybe it's significant that the first "key" character is the fifth along the line.'

Nicholas felt excited. 'Maybe the rest of the characters in the line are clues to the embedded pledge,' he suggested.

'Could you bring the list with you next time you come?' asked John. 'In fact, could you bring the box back? It would be handy to have it and its contents here for whenever we talk.'

'I copied the line very carefully,' said Nicholas. He sounded a little offended.

'I've no doubt about that,' his uncle replied. 'That's not what I'm getting at. We need all the information whenever we're concentrating on this.'

Nicholas could see the sense of what his uncle was saying, but he still felt resistant. The box had been in his room for many weeks, and it would feel very strange without it. And there was the coral that Jake had given him. Where would he keep that, if the box were here?

John was aware of Nicholas' hesitation. 'What is it?' he asked. 'You can come and see the things here whenever you want.'

'I know that,' Nicholas replied. 'I... I'll bring it up when I come tomorrow.'

John became thoughtful. 'I'd like to let you have something to keep in its place.' He went to the bookshelves, and selected what looked like an old book. It had quite an ornate cover, and a substantial spine. He handed it to Nicholas. 'Have a look inside,' he directed.

Curious, Nicholas opened the book, intending to skim its pages. But he found that the cover concealed a wooden compartment.

'Oh, wow!' he exclaimed. 'I haven't seen this before.'

'You'll have seen it all right,' said his uncle, 'but you won't have looked inside it before.'

'It would be great if I could borrow it for a while.'

'You can have it for as long as you want. I know you'll take good care of it.'

Now that there was somewhere special to keep his precious coral, Nicholas was content. 'Shall I go and get the box now?' he asked.

'No, tomorrow will do fine. Let's spend the rest of our time this evening thinking about the possibility of their being an embedded pledge. Since you brought the information about the meaning of 'gage' to me when I was still in hospital, I've put a lot of thought into it.'

'Have you still got the notes I made?'

'Yes, I kept them very carefully.' John searched through a small heap of papers at one end of the table, and found a manilla envelope. 'They're in here.' He took out the sheet of paper and said, 'I very much like the idea that GAGE could be a sign someone is about to do battle in support of his assertions. That sounds noble and correct. But if it's being used as another way of saying "pledge", it doesn't have to mean more than we already know. Certainly the pledge I had to take was binding me in a formal promise – just as this definition says.'

'Uncle John, maybe the code line isn't to do with an embedded pledge at all. Maybe it's a clue to where the treasure ended up!'

'It's all questions and no answers,' his uncle replied. 'But asking the questions is a start.'

'I'd better go now,' said Nicholas suddenly. 'I've got some homework to do before I go to bed.'

'Take the book box with you,' his uncle reminded him, 'and I'll see you again tomorrow…'

'With your grandad's box,' Nicholas finished. 'And I'll bring the photographs back here too.'

Nicholas whistled happily as he walked down the road with the box-book under his arm. Although he was going to miss Jake and all the hard work they had been doing over the holidays, Uncle John was back in his house, and they were going to concentrate on the mysteries. He thought back to the evening before Uncle John had fallen ill. That had been several months ago. So much had happened since then, and it had delayed their focussing on the puzzles that they were to address. But in a way, everything that had happened had helped to prepare him for now. He remembered how his uncle had told him a little at a time, so that he could observe his reaction. He felt he had understood why he had had to do that, but that kind of testing out was negligible compared with the challenges he had had to face since then. At first, he had been so worried that his uncle would die, and that not only would he have lost someone very special, but also he would be alone with the pledge and the mystery of the fifth key. That danger passed, and he had grappled with all the new skills that he was being given a chance to learn. And Jake...

Nicholas felt that he had been filled up with life – the kind of life that did not depend on having large quantities of money. He had his uncle, and he had acquired skills that he could use to support himself in his life. And he had his brother.

What was ahead, Nicholas could not predict. But one thing was certain. He and his uncle were now going to put a lot of their time into trying to move forward with the puzzles they had been bequeathed from generations before. Nicholas liked the idea that these had been handed down for a very long time, and the thought that he and his uncle might be the last ones to study the puzzles was breathtaking. He could hardly wait for tomorrow evening.

Chapter Nineteen

Nicholas arrived at his uncle's soon after four thirty the next day. He had first gone home to collect the box and the photographs. He carried the box carefully in his emptied school bag, with the photographs in the side pocket. As soon as he went into his uncle's house, he unpacked his bag.

He placed the box on the mantelshelf. It looked right there. His uncle was back home, and so was the box.

'I went for a walk up to the newsagent's today,' John told him. 'I was pretty tired afterwards, but it's given me a bit more confidence.'

'I can get you anything you want,' Nicholas reminded him. 'Please be very careful,' he added anxiously.

'I would have turned back if I needed to,' his uncle assured him. 'I had to go slowly, but I was fine. And I had a plan.'

'What was that?'

'Your dad bought me a mobile phone when I came home,' John explained. 'At first I didn't want to have to think about using it, but he insisted on giving me instructions. And now I'm glad, because it means I can go out, and if I need help to get back, I can phone a taxi.'

Nicholas stared at his uncle, wide-eyed. He had always refused to have anything to do with taxis before, so this was a big change.

John continued. 'Anyway, enough of that. I've got something to show you.' He picked up his newspaper from beside his chair, and passed it across to Nicholas. 'Page thirty.'

Nicholas turned the pages. 'What's it about?' he asked.

'It's an interesting article about ships that were carrying treasure that's ended up on the sea bed.'

'You mean shipwrecks?'

His uncle nodded. 'Some of them foundered in bad weather, and some were sunk deliberately by rivals. According to the reporter, there are fortunes to be made by anyone who can salvage the treasure.'

By this time, Nicholas had found the page. There was a map of Spain, pinpointing a number of known shipwrecks – mainly in the sixteenth and seventeenth centuries. 'Wow!' he exclaimed. 'It lists gold, silver and jewellery set with precious stones.' He laughed. 'Jake could be rich. He can dive, so he could get some and sell it.' Then he became serious. 'I wouldn't want him to even try. Jake's too precious. I don't want to risk losing him in the sea.'

'If you read through the article, it says there was a ship that sank off the Scilly Isles in the seventeenth century. That's a bit closer to home.'

'Yes, I've got it,' Nicholas replied. 'It was in 1641.' He sat quietly and read through the article. Then he asked, 'Uncle John, where you do think Todd's ship had come from?'

'Good question,' his uncle replied. 'I imagine it could have come all the way from somewhere like the New World. But who can tell? It could have set off from somewhere nearer home – the Spanish coast for instance – and then made its way through the English Channel, and up the east coast from there.'

'Do you think it was carrying gold?'

'Almost certainly, but it might have been carrying things like spices too.'

'What for?'

'In those days, spices were very valuable, and only the rich could afford them.'

'Just about everybody uses them now,' Nicholas reflected. Then he added, 'But people don't use gold and silver coins any more.'

'When I was a child, I remember seeing some gold sovereigns that my father had saved,' his uncle mused. 'And I remember thrup'ny pieces made out of silver. Even the shillings had silver in them.'

Nicholas was impressed. 'I wish I could see some sovereigns,' he said wistfully.

'Maybe when I'm a bit better, we could get on the bus and go to see what there is in the museum,' his uncle suggested. 'We...'

'I could go by myself,' Nicholas interrupted hurriedly. He did not like the idea of Uncle John going on a journey, even if it was only into town. The reality of how ill he had been was still clear in his memory. He decided to change the subject. 'Can we look at the measurer now?'

'Good plan,' his uncle agreed. He took it out of the box, and Nicholas sat on the arm of his uncle's chair so that they could look at it together.

Although Nicholas had looked at it many times when the box was in his bedroom, its impact on him had always been the same. It was rough and simple, yet at the same time it had a potentially complex meaning.

'We don't know when it was made, who made it, and what it was for,' said John. He chuckled. 'That's a very good starting point. Isn't it?'

Nicholas smiled. 'You missed something out.'

'What was that?'

'We don't know why your grandad left it for you.'

'Thanks for reminding me of that one.'

Nicholas groaned. 'How are we going to get anywhere with it?'

'We could make up a story about it,' his uncle suggested suddenly. 'It'll help us to relax, and then who knows what we might begin to see.'

'Okay,' said Nicholas enthusiastically. 'Who's going to start?'

John began. 'My grandad came across the measuring device not long before he died, and he thought I might be interested to have it.'

'Mm...' Nicholas hesitated. 'But why did he put it in the box with the list about the fifth key? Putting it there made it special.'

John continued. 'My grandad didn't want me to have the device until after he'd died.'

'I'm sure that's right,' Nicholas agreed.

'And it's definitely something to do with the fifth key.'

'I'm sure that's right, too,' said Nicholas. 'Maybe you had to know about Todd and take the pledge when you were thirteen, but you weren't supposed to know much about the fifth key until after your grandad died.'

'There's no doubt that I had to be told about Todd and the pledge when I was thirteen,' his uncle replied. 'And... maybe because I was only a carrier of the knowledge, I wasn't allowed to have the rest of it until my grandad died.'

'That fits!' Nicholas exclaimed excitedly. 'Your grandad had to keep it to himself, just in case he lived long enough for my grandad James to be born, and reach the age of thirteen. He was pretty sure that he was going to die before then, but he could never be absolutely certain.'

'Who can be sure when their time has come?' asked John, almost to himself. 'I might have died when I was ill. Todd could have drowned, but if the story is right, he lived long enough to father a child. Neither Todd nor I could have predicted what actually happened to either of us.'

'You might live for years and years now that you're better,' said Nicholas happily. 'No one knows.'

'I think we've worked that one out,' John affirmed. 'My grandad thought he would never live to see the chosen one, so when I was thirteen, he told me enough to prepare me to be the carrier. He told me no more than was necessary, and this was in case he was wrong in his belief about his death. Then he made sure that the box and its contents would be given to me when he died – so that I would have as much information as possible to hand on.'

'But my grandad James wouldn't have anything to do with it,' said Nicholas, 'so you had to wait. You tried Jake, but that was no good either, and so you had to wait for me.'

'Right,' John agreed. 'Back to the device. It's central to the fifth key.' He fell silent for a minute or two, and then added, 'Maybe it's something that will give us directions.'

'Directions...' Nicholas repeated. He fingered the needles. 'They just flop about,' he said, sounding frustrated.

'Will you go and get some greaseproof paper from the kitchen?' asked John.

'Okay,' Nicholas replied cheerfully. He jumped to his feet.

'There's a pack hanging behind the door,' his uncle called after him.

Nicholas soon returned, and handed the sheet to him. John picked up a pencil, placed the sheet over the metal plate, and began to scribble lightly on the paper.

'You're doing a bark rubbing,' Nicholas observed, 'but it's our directions instead.'

John continued, very carefully working to produce a copy of the rough design that was etched on the plate.

'Do you think it could be like a sun dial?' Nicholas asked suddenly.

His uncle immediately stopped what he was doing. 'Why did you think of that?' he asked, trying not to sound elated.

'I don't know,' Nicholas replied. 'It just came into my head. I was thinking about how the plate could lie flat, and needles could be arranged pointing almost vertically, and how shadows could be cast if the sun was shining.'

'Let's go down that route for a while,' said his uncle carefully. As he had been working on copying the design, he had become almost certain that some of the marks were intended to convey the sun or the moon. 'Will you go and get the torch from my room?'

Nicholas was back with it in a few seconds. 'But if we stick the needles up, they'll only flop down again. And how would we know which way the plate would have to be placed, or where to put it?'

'One step at a time,' advised his uncle kindly.

Nicholas wanted to be sensible, but he felt restless and paced around the room, while his uncle put the device flat on the table, and put the torch next to it.

'Seven needle extensions,' said John, 'and three are slightly shorter than the others. Perhaps the long ones go horizontally.'

'And maybe it has to be put on the key-shaped gravestone,' Nicholas moaned dolefully. 'In which case, we're wasting our time.'

'None of this is wasted,' said his uncle firmly. 'Come over here. I've got something to show you. I'm pretty sure there's enough on the design that suggests directions for four horizontal needles.'

To his surprise, Nicholas found that he became absorbed in what his uncle was showing him. 'Uncle John, I could try holding the points of the three short ones together in a sort of wigwam.'

'You do that, and I'll position the torch by this sun or moon shape,' said his uncle.

Together, they produced the full effect of what they had planned.

'Todd's gravestone, the two symbols in the third line of the list...' John murmured quietly to himself.

'Uncle John,' said Nicholas suddenly, 'what if the other writing on that line is just there to distract anyone who reads the list?'

John stared at his great-nephew with a dawning realisation. 'We've been so hooked up on the idea that we had to understand what the whole line said, when in fact it may mean nothing. The other writing might be there only to disguise the fundamental significance of the two "key" characters.'

Nicholas was now certain that they were getting much closer to solving the many puzzles that surrounded the whole subject of the fifth key. 'We've *got* to work out what this metal thing is trying to tell us,' he said urgently.

'We can't go to the gravestone,' John stated, 'but it can come to us. Nicholas, get the photographs. I put them in that metal chest where my papers are.'

Nicholas laid the three needles down, and fetched the photographs.

128

John spread them out on the table, carefully placing them to give the best idea of the stone and its surroundings.

'I think we should make a reproduction of the stone,' said Nicholas suddenly. 'We could make it out of papier maché. How big was it?'

John took a piece of paper, and once again drew a rough sketch of the stone. Then he marked it with measurements. 'It's only guesswork, but at least it's informed guesswork.'

Nicholas' mind was racing. 'We've got to have it so that we can experiment with the measuring device and the stone together.'

John gazed at him with admiration.

It was then that Nicholas saw the time on his watch. 'Oh, no!' he exclaimed. 'I've got piles of homework to do, and it's after seven already. But I don't want to go.'

John was as reluctant as Nicholas to stop what they were doing, but he knew that he had to help Nicholas to behave in a responsible way.

'Tell you what,' he said. 'You phone your parents and say you're eating with me.'

'But that won't get my homework done.' Nicholas' voice was almost a wail.

'Have you got any of your books with you?'

'No, I left them all at home when I collected the box.'

'Then there's nothing else to do but stop for this evening.'

Nicholas felt very dejected. He knew well enough the sense of what his uncle was saying, but everything in him wrestled with it.

'I could work on the reproduction tomorrow,' John offered. 'I'll do my best to have it finished for when you come after school. What do you think?'

Nicholas hesitated before replying. He would have liked to work with his uncle on that part of their project, but it would probably take up the whole of the following evening, and would delay things. Then he realised how important it was that he was fully involved in each step of what they were trying to achieve, and that trying to push forward in this way was likely to be counterproductive.

'Please will you have everything ready for when I come?' he asked. 'And we can make it together.'

'It's a deal.'

Chapter Twenty

Rab and Louis were concerned about Nicholas. He had been so desperate to tell them about his Easter holiday, but now he was quite withdrawn. They had both wanted to tell him their news, but when they tried to speak to him, he did not seem to take in anything they said.

'Maybe he's going to be ill,' Louis remarked dolefully.

Rab was unconvinced. 'He doesn't look ill.'

Louis went on. 'I'm worried, though. He's been quiet before, but I don't ever remember him not taking things in. And he can look completely glazed over.'

'It's not as bad as that.'

'I've definitely seen him like that today,' Louis insisted.

'Well, there's nothing we can do at the moment. Let's hope it's just a passing phase.' Rab had often heard his parents refer to his own behaviour in that way. It had always irritated him intensely, but now he could see some value in such an interpretation.

Rab and Louis made sure in the lessons they shared with Nicholas that they would sit beside him whenever possible, and give him a nudge from time to time. That way, with luck, the teachers would not notice his lack of concentration.

At the end of the day, Nicholas began to rush out of the building, but Rab stopped him.

'What's up?' he asked.

'Got to go to Uncle John's,' said Nicholas, trying to push past.

At this point, Louis caught up with them. 'Is he ill again?' he asked, concerned.

'No, he's fine... but I've got to go,' Nicholas repeated. Then he seemed to connect with what was happening, and added, 'Look, I'm really sorry. It's just that there's something we're doing together. Promise I'll catch up with you properly next week.'

He tugged his sleeve away from Rab's grasp, and ran off towards the line of buses.

'See,' said Rab. 'He's okay really.'

'I hope he remembers to ask about the summer,' Louis remarked.

'I want to be in on what's going on.'

Nicholas jumped on the first bus in the queue as it was setting off. This time he went straight to his uncle's, and he arrived not long after four o'clock.

He rushed through the door to find a large heap of shredded newspaper and a bucket of paste. Beside them stood a makeshift wooden structure.

His uncle welcomed him warmly. 'I was busy with this all morning. Then I rested after lunch, and since then I've been waiting for you to arrive. I made this wooden thing as the core for the stone. We can construct the papier maché around it.'

Nicholas dropped his bag, and gave his uncle a hug.

John handed him an old shirt. 'You'd better put that on over your uniform,' he advised.

'Oh, I forgot about that,' Nicholas replied. 'I'm so used to being here in my overalls.'

Over an hour later, they stood back and admired their work.

'It's pretty good,' said John. 'In fact, it takes me right back all those years to when I saw the real thing.'

'Thank goodness you had the photograph,' Nicholas pointed out. 'Your drawing was okay, but it didn't give quite the right impression.'

'Let's get something to eat, and leave it to dry out a bit,' John suggested.

Nicholas' stomach rumbled loudly. 'I've been hungry for ages,' he said, smiling, 'but the stone was far more important.'

Over their meal of scrambled eggs on toast, John enjoyed watching Nicholas as he worked his way through several pieces of toast and most of the egg. It was a long time since he himself had felt much enthusiasm about food. He always liked the feeling of companionship when Nicholas was eating with him. Observing the ease with which he demolished quite considerable quantities of food meant it was easier for him to eat a little more than usual.

When Nicholas had cleared his plate, John said, 'I've got some of last year's marmalade, if you'd like some more toast.'

This was a tempting offer. John's home-made marmalade was something special. But Nicholas was keen to carry on what they had begun.

'I can stay on longer this evening,' he said. 'I was in the library at lunchtime and did some of my homework. Can we get back to the stone?'

'And you can have marmalade later,' added his uncle knowingly.

They made large mugs of weak tea, and continued to sit at the table.

'The stone will have dried out quite a bit by tomorrow evening,' John remarked, 'so we'll be able to make more use of it then.'

'If the measurer is to sit on the stone, we've got to work out how,' said Nicholas.

'The real stone was positioned so that the back of it was facing out to sea – almost due east. I would guess that the measurer should have been placed either along the back, or at right-angles to it. And for what it's worth, I think the ship went down in late September, or some time in October.'

'Why?' asked Nicholas.

'That's one of the times when there are very high and very low tides, and storms are more likely, too. It would make sense that wherever they'd come from, they would have tried to make their crossing over the summer months.' John stood up, looked along one of his bookshelves, pulled out a battered map and opened part of it on the table. He poked his finger at Spain. 'Let's assume they'd picked up a cargo from somewhere along the coast. They were pretty daring to have then sailed right round past France and into the Channel. Once there, all eyes from England could have been on them. And then they made their way right up the east coast. They must have had very strong reasons to head for that particular spot. They must have been absolutely certain of a safe haven there, or they would never have attempted it. I wonder what the connection was between Todd and the merchant. Some deal must have been struck long before Todd set off on his mission.'

Nicholas' mind was struggling with the enormity of what his uncle was laying out.

'Would there definitely be gold?' he asked.

'Almost certainly. That alone would make the journey worthwhile. You see, in those days people could buy things with gold.'

'You couldn't do that now,' said Nicholas seriously.

'And if you tried, the police would be at your door,' his uncle added. 'But in those days, there was little or no way of tracing the origin of much of the gold, so you were free to spend it.'

'I wonder if the merchant tried to salvage any of it,' said Nicholas.

'We don't know how far he would have had to travel to get to the spot. And there might well have been strong reasons why he did not want to risk being conspicuous.'

'But if there weren't many people living around there, there wouldn't be anyone to notice.'

'Even if only one or two people saw something, the word would get round,' John observed. 'They would have had to be ready to move a heavy load, and that would have meant transport that would surely attract attention. It would be one thing having an intact ship calling in at your own personal harbour, and the number of servants in your house increased, but it would be quite another going to the site of a shipwreck with a squad of men and large horse-drawn carts, and making a slow journey back home.'

'I see what you mean,' Nicholas agreed. His uncle had described a picture for him that was very clear. The mission had not succeeded, and the only safe thing that the merchant and his household could do was to go on as if nothing had ever been expected.

John continued. 'What the relationship was between Todd and the merchant is another puzzle.'

'Cousins,' Nicholas pronounced, with a note of such certainty that his uncle was rendered speechless.

Nicholas looked over his shoulder, but there was nothing to see. He had suddenly felt a bit cold, and he now had a feeling that his uncle had said something that he had missed.

'What did you say?' he asked.

'Nothing.' John began to doubt that he had heard Nicholas speak. 'I was just wondering where Todd and the merchant had first met.'

'Maybe they were related,' Nicholas suggested.

'Todd couldn't have been very old,' said his uncle. 'You'd be mad to be on the high seas on a mission like that once you were past forty. The merchant could have been older – quite a bit older.'

'If they were cousins, they would have had the same grandfather,' Nicholas commented.

'Nicholas,' said his uncle carefully, 'a little while ago, I thought you said the word "cousins". Do you remember anything?'

Nicholas felt cold again, and once more looked over his shoulder. 'Uncle John, I've got a weird feeling that someone's standing behind me. I had it a few minutes ago, too.'

'That's odd.' John folded up the map and put it away. Then he collected up the photographs. 'I think it's probably time to wind up

133

for the evening. I'm pretty tired after the day's events. We can talk about this again soon. Are you coming tomorrow evening?'

'I wish I could, but I've got to stay on late at school. They need people to shift the scenery in the school play, and I promised ages ago that I would do it. I've only got to do it for one night, though. They've got people for the other nights.'

'What are they putting on?'

'Romeo and Juliet. I wish they'd chosen something a bit more exciting. The only worrying thing is the balcony.' Nicholas laughed and said, 'It fell off in one of the rehearsals. I don't think it was meant to!'

'I hope no one was on it at the time,' his uncle replied. 'Juliet could have had a nasty accident.'

'No, it was only a rehearsal for the sets.'

'Nicholas,' said John, 'I think it won't be a bad thing for us to have a break from what we're doing. There's so much to think about.'

'But we've had a long wait already,' Nicholas objected, 'and more happens when we're together.'

'I know, but without time in between, it might not be like that.'

Nicholas could accept what his uncle was saying, and was content to leave for home, knowing that they could resume their investigations very soon.

John sat up late that evening. He had been disturbed by what he had experienced, and was in doubt as to whether he had really heard Nicholas say 'cousins' or not. John knew that he had been pushing himself a bit too much recently. Maybe he had merely been overtired, and had imagined it. He knew that older people, like himself, could fall asleep for a few seconds at a time. Perhaps that was what had happened, and what he heard had been a fragment of a dream. But in his heart of hearts, he knew that this interpretation did not really fit.

The new Head of English at Nicholas' school had been keen to reintroduce the influence of traditional literature and plays into the department. This was the first play that had been planned. Mr Forster had recruited promising actors, mainly from sixth year, but help was needed from younger pupils as well.

Nicholas had been interested from the outset, and had been keen to become involved. But he had signed up before he knew which play was to be put on, and when he had heard that it was to be Romeo and Juliet, he was disappointed.

The Tempest would have been much better, he thought, as he joined the others who were helping behind scenes. 'Full fathom five thy father lies...' he repeated several times under his breath. But he realised that a satisfying replica of a shipwreck on stage would be a pretty tricky thing to achieve, and he could see why Mr Forster had settled for Romeo and Juliet. He thought of Todd, who was several 'greats' back from his father, and how his bones must have landed in the sea when the cliff eroded. But the rest of the crew had disappeared with the ship. The words ran on. 'Of his bones are coral made...' He did not suppose that the coral Jake had given him was made from Todd's bones, though. Although the school hall was warm, he shivered a little.

'Come on, Nick. Give us a hand with this,' said a voice from behind him.

He turned to see two boys trying to move a huge section of painted blockboard. He quickly pushed his deliberations aside and took a corner of it, while a girl helped at the other end.

Nicholas was very preoccupied at school the following day, so much so that this provoked a number of pointed comments from his teachers. He was greatly relieved when the day was finished, and he could set off once again for his uncle's house. He was glad it was the end of the week.

When he arrived, his uncle was at the front door, looking out for him.

'Come in. Come in,' he said as Nicholas reached the path up to the house. 'And how did the play go?'

'It was quite good.' Nicholas surprised himself by admitting this.

'It's a good tale,' his uncle commented, 'and its dilemmas reappear time and time again through history.'

'Todd's story stayed almost completely hidden,' Nicholas reflected.

'Yes, his situation has been quite different. And there are many things about it that I'd like to know. For instance, I wonder what the shepherd's daughter was called. I realise that all these years, I've thought of her merely as the bearer of Todd's child, and not a person her in own right.'

'Abigail,' said Nicholas, glancing over his shoulder. He shivered. 'Uncle John, I feel really cold.'

'Go and put the kettle on,' his uncle directed. 'We could both do with something hot.'

Soon Nicholas was warming his hands on a steaming mug. 'That's better,' he said.

John waited as Nicholas relaxed. Then he asked, 'Nicholas, do you remember saying something just before you felt cold?'

'No. Why?'

'I'm certain I heard someone say "Abigail". And I was convinced it was you.'

'I don't remember saying anything, but you were talking about the mother of Todd's child.'

'That's right. And then it was as if someone told me her name.'

'Uncle John, that's really strange,' said Nicholas in a low voice. 'What do you think is happening?'

'I can't explain it. There's a lot in all of this that we don't understand.'

Nicholas said nothing. He sat sipping his drink and thinking about what his uncle had just told him.

At length, he asked, 'Uncle John, can we do some more with the stone and the measurer this evening?'

'That's what I'd intended,' John replied. 'We could try different positions for the measurer and its needles, and then shine the torch from different angles.'

The rest of the evening passed quickly as they tried a number of different arrangements. But they did not come to any conclusion.

'Can I take it home with me?' Nicholas asked suddenly.

'You mean the measurer?'

'Yes. I'll look after it. I can put it with my... I mean, I can put it in the book box you lent me.'

John felt curious to know why Nicholas had had this sudden urge, but he decided that he would simply go along with it for now, leaving any questions for later.

'I'll see you tomorrow morning,' Nicholas reminded him. 'Dad and I are coming up to work.'

'I'll look forward to that.'

Nicholas went to bed early that night. He felt more tired than he had felt for months. And it was a completely different kind of feeling from the one he had after doing a good day's work. Instead of a satisfying tiredness, he felt drained – as if something had been sucked out of him.

He woke with a start. It was pitch dark, and he could hear a rattling sound – near his bed. Where on earth was it coming from? By the sound of it, it was certainly inside his room – not under the floorboards, or in the loft.

He switched on his bedside light. There was nothing unusual in the room. Everything looked as normal. But the rattling sound continued, and if anything it was louder, and more insistent. It was then that he realised it was coming from the box book on the shelf beside his bed. He had placed it more or less where the other box used to stand, so he was able to reach it without getting out of bed.

He stretched out his arm, and touched the box. He had been right. There was certainly something rattling about inside it. But how could that be? It contained only his precious piece of coral... and the measurer. The measurer! How could he have forgotten even for a minute that it was there?

He leaped out of bed, and picked up the box. The noise stopped immediately. He stared at it, puzzled, and then opened the lid. The two objects lay side by side, where he had placed them before going to bed.

Nicholas did not know what to make of what had happened. Eventually, he shrugged his shoulders, put the box back on the shelf, got back into bed, and switched off the light.

He was dozing off when the noise started up again. This time it was even louder and more insistent. What on earth was going on? He sat up, switched the light on again, and picked up the box. The sound stopped instantly.

What should he do? He did not want to disturb his parents. In any case, he could not tell them anything, because he could not reveal the existence of the measurer. And he knew that he was not ready to talk about the coral, either. He decided that the best thing was to try to ignore the whole thing, and he could talk to his uncle about it the next day.

He settled himself once more, but this time hardly any time passed before the rattling began again. It rapidly became more and more intense. Then suddenly there was a crash, and silence.

Nicholas sat bolt upright, switched on the light and stared at the shelf where the box had been. Then he looked on the floor. The box was lying there – open. The coral was still inside, but the measurer was nowhere to be seen.

Quickly he jumped out of bed and searched underneath it, and then around the floor. He could not find it anywhere. Although he was certain that it was not there, he repeated his search several times before getting back into bed. By this time he felt chilled, and he lay awake shivering for several minutes before he began to warm up again. But he found it difficult to settle, and he spent the rest of the night turning from one side to the other, in an unsuccessful attempt to sleep.

He must have slept eventually, because the next thing he knew was that his father was in the room.

'Time to get up now, Nick.' He spoke as if he had already said it several times before.

Nicholas slowly opened his eyes. He felt strangely battered, as if he had been on a cross-country run and had fallen into several ditches.

'When you didn't appear, your mum and I decided to let you sleep in for a bit,' his father explained.

'What time is it?' asked Nicholas.

'Nine thirty.'

'Nine thirty!' Nicholas echoed. 'I can't believe it.'

'Why don't you lie in a bit longer,' his father suggested. 'Your mum and I can go up to John's and start work, and you can come when you're ready.'

'Don't leave me!' The words were out of Nicholas' mouth before he had time to think.

His father looked startled. 'But we'll only be up the road...' he began. Then he realised that there was more to this, and asked, 'Would you rather we waited for you?'

'Yes.' Nicholas jumped out of bed. 'I'll only be a minute.'

'Don't worry,' said his father. 'And just take your time.'

When he arrived downstairs five minutes later, his mother handed him a plastic box. 'Breakfast,' she explained. 'You can have it when we get there.'

'Thanks, Mum.' Nicholas was grateful that his parents were not asking any questions.

They walked up the road together, discussing what they hoped to achieve that day.

When they arrived, Colin and Sarah set to work with the decorating in the spare room, and Nicholas sat at the table in the living room.

As soon as he was sure that his parents were out of earshot, he said, 'Uncle John, look in the box.'

John was about to ask the reason for this request, but thought better of it. He stood up, and opened the lid of the box.

'That's odd,' he muttered. 'I'm sure Nicholas took that home with him.' Then he turned and said, 'I thought you took the measurer away with you.'

'I did,' Nicholas replied.

John frowned. 'Then how did it get back in here?' Then his face cleared. 'You're quite a magician.'

'No, I'm not. It must have come back by itself.'

'I think that's taking things a bit too far,' said his uncle with a reproving note in his voice. But seeing the look that came on Nicholas' face was enough to make him apologise. 'I'm sorry. It's just that I can't see how that could have happened.'

'Neither can I,' Nicholas replied. 'But I'd better tell you now what went on last night.'

John sat down in his armchair and listened, while Nicholas told him everything he could remember.

When he had finished, his uncle said, 'Poltergeist activity. That's all I can think of. You're the right age for it. But I haven't heard of anything transporting itself like this before.'

'Please will you explain?'

'Sometimes people of your age find that objects around them might move, or a radio might somehow seem to turn itself on. Some put that kind of thing down to the fact that when youngsters are changing fast, they're vulnerable to certain spirit entities attaching themselves to the rapidly-evolving environment. Such entities are called poltergeists. That's all I know.'

Nicholas looked impressed. 'I'd heard the word, but I hadn't bothered to find out what it meant. He thought for a few minutes, and then asked, 'If that's what it is, when will I grow out of it?'

'That I don't know. Maybe sixteen or seventeen... but I'd be guessing.'

'But that's years,' Nicholas objected. 'I don't want to go on being surrounded by things that bang about and disappear.'

'I'm not saying that this is poltergeist activity,' his uncle pointed out. 'Maybe it's some specific reaction to what we're doing at the moment, and when we're further on, it'll stop.'

'That sounds more hopeful,' said Nicholas, relieved. He stood up. 'I'm off to help Mum and Dad. This evening you and I will push ahead with everything else. I want to cut short this haunting,' he finished determinedly.

'Haunting,' John repeated quietly to himself as Nicholas went into the hall. 'He's put his finger on it. There was the voice that said "cousins" and the one that said "Abigail", and now we've got a presence that brought the measurer back here. It's pretty unnerving, but whatever the haunting is, I think it's trying to help us.'

Colin and Sarah left that evening not long after six o'clock, and after Nicholas and John had made themselves something to eat, they settled down to consider their situation. John took the measurer out of the box again, and laid it on the arm of his chair.

'We'd better keep it here,' he stated decisively.

'It's obviously supposed to be in the box, with the list,' said Nicholas.

'At least for now,' added his uncle. 'I've been thinking about what happened to you. It wasn't pleasant, but I'm pretty sure that whatever force was involved means no harm, and might even be trying to help us.'

Nicholas considered this. 'I hope so. We could do with some help. But if it's trying to help, I wish it was easier for me to accept.'

'A lot of help in life isn't all that easy to recognise, let alone accept,' said his uncle wisely.

'If this is anything to go by, I agree,' replied Nicholas wryly.

'First, "cousin", and then "Abigail",' mused John. 'Todd and the merchant having the same grandfather... And... the secrets of the pledge and the fifth key are passed from grandfather to grandson.'

'Do you think there was a secret before the shipwreck?' asked Nicholas suddenly.

'It's not inconceivable.'

'But why would two grandsons know about it? It's only supposed to be one,' Nicholas observed.

'It could have been that only one knew. Obviously, they would both know about the treasure, because a lot of preparations had been made, but there might have been something else that only one of them knew.'

'Wow!' said Nicholas. 'And it would have to be the merchant.'

'I think that's the most likely.'

Nicholas began to feel very uncomfortable, and although the day was warm, there suddenly seemed to be a chill in the air. 'Uncle

John,' he said, 'I've just had a horrible thought.'

'What's that?'

'If the merchant knew something that Todd didn't, maybe he was planning for something to happen to him, and when something did, that saved him the bother.'

His uncle was startled. 'That had never occurred to me. I'd always seen the two as being accomplices.'

Nicholas' thoughts ran on. 'There would be even more reason for the shepherdess not to let anyone know who her son's father was.'

'You're a bright lad,' said his uncle admiringly. 'Yes, there would be more than fear of social exclusion at stake – his life would have been in danger.'

After this, both fell silent for a while.

Then John said decisively, 'I want to go along this track for a while. And first, I think it's time we had another look at that list.' He stood up, and took it out of the box. 'To him who seeks,' he read. 'The fifth key...' He looked at Nicholas. 'There's definitely a lot more to all of this than I ever imagined.' He turned to the list again. 'Then there's the line that we think masks the fifth and eighth characters. After that we've got GAGE, and then "maybe the quay". What was in the writer's mind about the quay? If the quay belonged to the merchant...' Here he stopped.

'Perhaps the quay was nothing to do with the fifth key itself,' Nicholas suggested.

'It could have had something to do with what was going on underneath the surface relationship between the cousins. But I still think there's a particular connection between it and the fifth key.'

'Let's set up our stone again,' said Nicholas. 'I want to have another go with the measurer.'

He lifted their model of the stone into the space between the chairs.

'You're the sea, and I'll be the land,' he began, turning the stone with its flat side towards his uncle. 'Oh, no! Here comes that cold feeling again. Can I borrow one of your coats?'

John was feeling comfortably warm, but he could see quite clearly that Nicholas' fingers were blue with cold, and he was shivering again.

'Of course you can,' he replied.

Nicholas hurried to the row of pegs in the hall, and came back wearing his uncle's overcoat.

'That's much better. Look, Uncle John, I'm now convinced those characters in that line we used to think was code are two references to this stone, and they can't have been written in the fifth and eighth places by accident.'

'And I'm pretty convinced now that I know the meaning of GAGE,' said John. 'It's got to be the first on your list from the dictionary – "something deposited to ensure the performance of some action, and liable to forfeiture in case of non-performance". That's the key... The fifth key! The gage that had been deposited was the fifth key, and the action had been that Todd was to deliver the treasure. Because he failed in his mission, he and his descendants forfeited the fifth key. Despite the fact that the merchant was family – his cousin – he held Todd to the pledge, and kept the gage – the key.'

Nicholas clutched his uncle's coat tightly around himself, and looked over his shoulder. 'The key must have had huge value,' he whispered.

'It's anybody's guess as to where it is, and whether it still has such value,' his uncle replied in a low voice.

'Uncle John,' said Nicholas, 'I'm a bit scared.'

'I'm not surprised. There have been some dark forces at work, and we're somehow required to make sense of it all, and do something about it. Having a ghostly aide is a bit of a mixed blessing, in that neither of us is used to that kind of thing.'

'The whole thing happened such a long time ago,' Nicholas said with desperation in his voice.

'And we're caught up in it because our ancestors failed to do whatever was necessary – apart from handing the story down so that it was never lost.'

'I wish that we could have a conversation with whatever it is that's hovering around,' said Nicholas passionately.

Then John surprised him by saying, 'Maybe we can. The words "cousin" and "Abigail" that seemed to come from you were replies to questions – although I'd never thought we would be given any.'

Nicholas began to shiver, and kept on shivering.

'I've got to stay here tonight,' he managed to force out between his chattering teeth.

'You won't be very comfortable,' his uncle began.

'This chair will be fine,' said Nicholas firmly. 'I can't possibly go home while all this is going on.'

'We'll phone your mum and dad in a while to let them know.

With it being the weekend, it should be fine.'

'Please do it now,' Nicholas begged through clenched teeth.

John needed no persuasion, and he was soon speaking to Colin. 'Is it okay if Nicholas stays up here tonight?' he asked. 'Yes ... we've got things we'd like to get on with. See you tomorrow.'

He replaced the phone, and addressed Nicholas. 'That's it fixed.' He looked at Nicholas' shaking body and white face, and said, 'I'll put the heating on for a while. I can always open a window if it gets too hot for me.'

Knowing that he did not have to leave his uncle that night helped Nicholas greatly, and although he still felt cold, he began to relax. As the heat from the radiators permeated the room, he gradually warmed up, and instead of having the coat wrapped round him, he merely hung it on his shoulders.

'That's better,' he commented. 'Now let's get on with the stone and the measurer.'

They decided to set the measurer in the same way as they had done previously, and they put it in different positions on their stone, shining the torch from different directions and different angles. Although they found it an interesting exercise, nothing remarkable came to their notice.

'Never mind,' said John as they put the measurer away and moved the stone to a corner of the room. 'That was something we had to try out.'

'But the measurer is definitely important,' insisted Nicholas doggedly. 'Why else would it have been returned to the box to be with the list?'

'It's important, all right,' his uncle agreed. 'It's just that we don't yet know why or how.' He looked at his watch. 'Let's sleep on it, and try something else in the morning.'

When Nicholas woke the next morning, he felt warm and relaxed, and he knew that he had slept surprisingly well.

He stood up and stretched. There was no sound from his uncle's room, so he went to the kitchen to start making porridge.

Time passed, and he was finishing a large bowlful when his uncle appeared, looking perplexed.

'Have you seen my torch?' he asked. 'I was sure I'd put it back under my bed, but I can't find it anywhere.'

'But I remember you taking it when you went to bed,' replied

Nicholas, surprised. 'Why not have some porridge, and then we'll have a look round together.'

John thought that was a good idea, and soon he was enjoying his breakfast.

Colin and Sarah arrived just as he was finishing.

'Hi, you two!' Sarah greeted them cheerfully. 'Here come the painters and decorators. Had a good night?'

'Yes, thanks,' John replied. 'But I can't find my torch. It's not in the usual place under my bed.'

'Don't worry,' said Sarah. 'I'm sure we'll come across it soon. I expect you got distracted when you were meaning to put it away.'

Although John went along with what Sarah was saying, he was certain that he had put the torch away the night before. When she and Colin and Nicholas started work, he wandered round the house, looking everywhere for it. But he finally gave up and went to his armchair, intending to sit and read through yesterday's paper.

It was then that he saw the torch. It was on the mantelshelf, next to his grandfather's box. He blinked, as if trying to clear away an illusion. But the torch was still there.

'I most certainly did not put it there,' he stated emphatically.

He was about to sit down, when something told him to look at the stone he and Nicholas had made. He went to the corner where Nicholas had left it, and found it was not there. Instead, he found it in the corner behind the chair where Nicholas had slept that night.

'Flying torches and walking stones,' he muttered. 'Maybe Nicholas moved them in his sleep. After all, he was pretty disturbed in the evening.'

He settled down to read his newspaper, but he could not concentrate. He turned the pages, but they had no meaning for him. In the end, he gave up, refolded it, and put it on the floor beside his chair. Nicholas could have moved the stone in his sleep, but he could not have come into his bedroom in the night, taken the torch, and put it on the mantelshelf. Of that, he was certain.

He decided to look at the stone again, and he moved it out of the corner so that he could see it better. It was then that he noticed a series of cuts on it. He wanted to call Nicholas to come and look, but as he did not want the others to be involved, he knew he would have to wait. Instead, he examined the cuts. They seemed to form a rough pattern, and as he studied them, he realised that the pattern was one that he recognised.

He collected the measurer, and carefully compared the marks on its plate to the ones on their stone. Yes, part of the pattern had been replicated in an enlarged form.

His longing to show Nicholas became so intense that he called out to him.

'Nicholas, can you come here for a minute, please.'

'I'm coming,' Nicholas replied.

Sarah popped her head round the door. 'Anything I can do?'

John hated feeling that he was dissembling. He wished that he could be open with Sarah and Colin with what was happening, but he had taken a solemn pledge more than seventy-five years ago, and he must not break it.

Fortunately, Nicholas appeared, saying, 'Do you want a hand with something?'

He had a blob of cream paint on the bridge of his nose, and John could not help but laugh when he saw it.

This broke the tension, and Sarah said, 'I'll leave you to it, then.' And she went off to rejoin Colin.

As soon as she had gone, John said in a low voice. 'Look what I've found.' He pointed to their stone.

Nicholas saw straight away what John was pointing out, and he crouched down to examine the cuts.

'I've compared them with the pattern on the measurer,' said John, 'and they correspond to the part in the middle.'

Nicholas ran his finger along the cuts, but could think of nothing useful to say.

His uncle went on. 'And the other thing is that I found the torch on the mantelshelf next to the box. Nicholas, I definitely took it to bed with me last night.'

'I know,' replied Nicholas. 'I do remember.'

'The only thing I can think is that our friend was with us again last night,' said John. 'And he's trying to tell us something else.'

Nicholas was excited. 'One thing is that we now know which way to put the measurer on the stone. Pass it to me.'

Silently, John handed the device to his great-nephew, and watched as he matched the centre of the pattern on it to the pattern of cuts on the stone. The measurer was at right angles to the back of their stone, and the top of it was pointing outwards, along the middle one of its side-pieces.

'The torch appearing by the box suggests only one thing to me,' said John. 'It has to be that we're on the right track when we're using it.'

Just then, Colin's voice came from the doorway. 'Are you busy, Nick? I could do with a lift for a minute.'

Nicholas was startled out of his concentration. He jumped to his feet and swiftly moved across the room and into the hall.

John could hear Colin and Nicholas banging about in the hallway for a while, so he moved the stone back into a corner of the room, and replaced the measurer in the box. It was best to have these things out of the way now. He did not want to have to explain anything to Colin or Sarah. He and Nicholas could resume their conversation that evening.

But when six o'clock came, and Colin and Sarah were about to leave, Nicholas knew that he would have to go back with them. Despite his desperation to continue what he and his uncle had started, he had to face the fact that he had homework to attend to, as it had to be handed in the following day. Reluctantly, he said goodbye to his uncle, promising that he would come round again after school.

Chapter Twenty-one

Nicholas had sat up late to finish his homework, and when his alarm woke him the next morning he felt unusually tired. Determined not to be late, he washed and dressed quickly, and hurried downstairs for breakfast.

'That's early,' he commented, when he saw the post on the table.

'Yes, I just brought it through,' his mother replied. 'But I haven't had time to look at it yet.'

Nicholas sat down to eat his toast, and pulled off the rubber band that held the items together. It all looked like the usual sort of stuff that was nothing to do with him.

'Hang on a minute,' he mumbled through a mouthful of food. 'There's a letter here for me.'

It was then that he realised the address was written in Jake's handwriting. He was glad that his mother had gone into the kitchen. It seemed terribly important to be alone when he opened this. He quickly folded it in half and thrust it into the pocket of his shirt, underneath his school top.

He stuffed the rest of the toast into his mouth, grabbed his bag, and shouted a cheerful goodbye to his mother. Then he ran down the road in the direction of the bus stop.

The bus was not a place that was private enough for him to open his precious letter, and he began to doubt the sense of having brought it with him. There would be no opportunity to read it at school, and he did not want to risk losing it while he was there. It was fortunate that the timetable for today included nothing that would mean he had to change his clothes.

When he arrived at school, he saw one of the girls from his year, and he approached her. 'Kerry,' he said politely, 'do you know who might have a safety pin? Er... I think the hem of my trouser leg is a bit loose.'

'I always keep a small pack of pins in my bag,' she replied efficiently. She opened the front pocket of her schoolbag and produced a small selection of safety pins.

Nicholas was impressed. 'Can I borrow one?'

'You can have one to keep, if you want,' Kerry replied. 'Choose.'

The bell went, and she held them out. 'Hurry up.'

Nicholas took a small gold one, thanked her, and rushed to the toilets. Inside a cubicle, he pinned the letter firmly to the material of his shirt, and then went to the first lesson, arriving just in time.

The day passed uneventfully, and with the warm feeling generated by the knowledge of the letter on his chest, Nicholas found he could concentrate very well on everything.

Rab and Louis searched him out at the end of the day.

Louis grinned at him. 'Have you been avoiding us?' he asked.

''Course not,' said Nicholas. He was pleased to be with his friends for a few minutes before he left. 'I looked for you at lunchtime, but couldn't find either of you. Where were you?'

'We went to the new music club,' Rab explained.

'Any good?' asked Nicholas.

'Most of it was taking names down, and deciding what to do,' said Rab.

Louis continued. 'There were ten of us. We might split into two groups, because some of us want to do band practice, and the others want to try writing a song.'

'We'll might all go to a concert together at the end of term,' Rab added.

'Sounds okay, if you like that sort of thing,' said Nicholas. The only music he was interested in at the moment was in the list, and even that was not uppermost in his mind since his discovery of the meaning of 'gage'.

'Have you fixed with your uncle yet about the summer?' asked Louis.

'Summer...?' Nicholas looked vague.

'Clearing the garden,' Rab reminded him.

'Oh, no!' exclaimed Nicholas. 'I'm really sorry. We've still got some finishing touches to do inside the house. I haven't said anything yet. Look, I'm going to Uncle John's now. I'll ask him as soon as I get there, and let you know tomorrow. Okay?'

Rab and Louis looked at each other and nodded. 'Fine,' said Rab.

'See you tomorrow, Nick,' said Louis, and he set off to walk home.

By now, the buses were about to leave, and Nicholas had to run to catch one.

When Nicholas arrived at the house, John was sitting at the front door on one of the chairs from the table in the living room.

'Thought I'd get some fresh air while I was waiting for you,' he said. 'I was too tired to go for a paper today.'

'I could go and get one,' Nicholas offered. 'It won't take me long.'

'We've got more important things to do.' His uncle looked at him meaningfully.

Nicholas dropped his bag on the ground and sat on the doorstep. 'I've got a letter from Jake,' he announced proudly.

'That's good,' his uncle replied. 'What's he saying?'

'I haven't opened it yet. I wanted it to be private,' Nicholas explained.

'Oh, sorry. I didn't mean to pry.'

'I don't mean that,' said Nicholas quickly. 'Dad had gone to work when it came, and I wasn't ready to tell Mum. After that, I had to rush to get to school.' It was then that Nicholas remembered about Rab and Louis. 'And there's something else,' he added.

'What's that?'

'I've kept forgetting to say to you that my friends, Rab and Louis, want to come in the summer and help me to clear your garden.'

'That's a surprise! It's kind of them, but I don't want them to use up their holiday for me.'

'They've been really envious about me working in your house, and they're wanting to be in on it,' Nicholas explained. 'They want some real work to do.'

'Well, if it's like that,' said his uncle, 'then of course they can come.'

Now that was settled, Nicholas reached inside his top, unpinned the letter, and took it out of his pocket.

'Here it is,' he said. He studied the postmark. 'It's from Carlisle.'

His uncle handed his penknife across to him, and Nicholas slit open the envelope. Inside was a single sheet of paper. The address was simply 'England', and there was no date. Nicholas read the letter aloud.

Hi Nick,
Will stay in UK for a while.
Jake

'That's good news,' said John.

'It doesn't say much.' Nicholas was not disappointed, but the letter said very little.

'I would have expected him to have left for some far-flung destination as soon as he was finished here,' his uncle explained.

'Oh...' said Nicholas. His mind whirred. Maybe this meant that Jake might come back to see him again soon. But that was more than he dared hope for, and he said nothing.

He heard his uncle say 'We'll just have to wait and see what happens next.'

Nicholas nodded.

'Why not go and get yourself a sandwich?' John suggested. 'Then we can get on with our talking.'

Nicholas went into the house, and soon returned with a large sandwich.

'Did anything happen last night?' he asked.

His uncle smiled. 'Everything was quiet and stayed in its place.'

Although this was a relief to Nicholas, he realised that he also felt a little disappointed.

'I wish I knew whose ghost it is,' he said impulsively.

'I'd been thinking the same myself,' his uncle replied. 'If you ask me to guess, though, I'd put my money on it being Todd.'

Nicholas stopped chewing, and stared at his uncle. He had never expected this response from him. 'Have you ever seen a ghost?' he asked.

'No, and I hope I don't,' said his uncle emphatically. 'But I've heard some stories... from people who don't make things up.'

'Tell me.'

John shook his head.

'Please...' Nicholas pressed.

However, his uncle would not be persuaded, and Nicholas had to accept his silence. But he was puzzled, and a little hurt, although he did not want to admit it.

'Let's do some more with the stone when you've finished that,' John suggested. 'I haven't touched it myself. I wanted to wait until you were here again.'

Nicholas was immediately cheered by this, and very soon they were together in the living room, with the stone, the measurer and the torch. But although they now knew that the measurer was to be placed on the stone, and how to locate it there, they got no further

150

forward.

'I'm beaten,' said John with a sigh.

'Don't give up yet,' Nicholas urged.

'One last try, and then we must call it a day,' said his uncle. 'I feel terribly tired. I'm going to have to go to bed as soon as you leave for home.'

Nicholas looked at him worriedly. 'But you've got to eat something, Uncle John.'

His uncle looked at him, surprised. 'I suppose you're right. I'd completely forgotten,' he admitted. 'I'll have a bowl of my chicken soup, and perhaps that'll perk me up a bit.'

'You stay there, and I'll get it for you,' said Nicholas, and he dashed off to the kitchen.

It was while John was sitting waiting that something occurred to him. Maybe they had been wrong about the positioning of the measurer. Maybe it was not meant to sit on the stone at all. Maybe it was supposed to be placed somewhere in front of it.

Nicholas soon appeared with a bowl filled to the brim. He was moving very carefully so as not to spill it. He put it on the table, and produced a spoon out of his pocket.

'There you are,' he said. He wagged his finger at his uncle playfully, and put on a parental voice. 'Now make sure you eat it all up.'

They both laughed heartily. Then while John was waiting for the soup to be cool enough to eat, he told Nicholas what had occurred to him.

Nicholas nodded. 'So we must put it on the floor, but make sure it's turned the right way.'

'We'll give it a try.'

Nicholas sat on the floor and started to play about with this new idea, while his uncle sipped at the soup.

Suddenly John put down his spoon, and said, 'Nicholas, I wonder if we've been thinking this is more complicated than it really is.'

Nicholas looked at his uncle attentively.

'The cuts might just have been to confirm that the measurer is related to the meaning of the stone ...' his uncle began.

'And the meaning of the stone is Todd,' Nicholas finished for him.

'What if the measurer is to help us with the fifth key?' said John.

'Then it can only help us when we've found out what the fifth key is.' Nicholas lay down on the floor as if exhausted, and groaned. 'It's like hunting for a needle in a haystack – only worse. Uncle John, we need more help with this.'

To Nicholas' surprise, his uncle replied, 'I agree.'

'But we can't get any, because we're not supposed to say anything,' moaned Nicholas. He felt completely stuck.

'We're not beaten yet,' said John. 'We'll think of something. You go home soon, and I'll have an early night. We'll sleep on it. Will you be able to come tomorrow?'

Nicholas looked at his watch. 'If I go now, I'll have a couple of hours to get on with homework. Yes, I'd be able to come tomorrow if I do that.'

'Good lad,' said John. 'And remember to tell your friends that they'll be welcome any time in the summer.'

Back at home, Colin and Sarah were sitting down to their evening meal.

His father greeted him. 'Good to see you, Nick. How's John today?'

'He's fine. He's having an early night, and I've got homework to do,' Nicholas replied.

'Have something to eat with us first,' his mother suggested. 'There's plenty.'

Nicholas was about to say that he would leave it until later, when he remembered Jake's letter.

'Thanks,' he said. 'I had something at Uncle John's, but I'm still hungry.'

Once he was settled, he announced his news. 'I got a letter from Jake today.'

His parents stopped eating.

'It didn't say much – just that he's staying in the UK for now.'

'That's very good news, Nick,' said his father.

'Yes, very,' his mother agreed. 'Did he give an address?' she asked carefully.

'No...' Nicholas hesitated before adding 'Well, it says "England", and the postmark is "Carlisle".'

Sarah and Colin looked at each other.

'I want it to mean that we'll see him again soon,' stated Nicholas.

Sarah took Colin's hand across the table, and she touched Nicholas' arm with her other hand. 'So do we,' she said.

Chapter Twenty-two

Although Nicholas called round to see his uncle the next day, he did not stay long. He was reassured to find that nothing untoward had happened in his absence. He had been given a lot more homework that day. It did not have to be handed in until the following week, but they agreed that it would be best if he worked on it straight away. It would be finished well in advance of the weekend, when they could spend more time concentrating on the mysteries that occupied their thoughts.

Nicholas had made sure that he had spoken to Rab and Louis, who had been ecstatic about the news that they would be welcome at John's house that summer.

It was Friday before Nicholas and his uncle concentrated once more on the fifth key.

'I've been doing a lot of thinking,' John began. 'And the more I consider the whole picture, the more I feel we need to go to where the gravestone used to be.'

'We can go in the summer holidays,' said Nicholas excitedly.

'That's exactly what I'd like to do, but I'm not fit.'

Nicholas' shoulders sagged. He knew his uncle was right. Now that he was so much better, it was all too easy to forget how limited he was in what he could do. He was well able to look after himself in his house, and quite often he would walk to the local shops, but he could not go further than that.

'You might be able to by the summer,' suggested Nicholas cautiously.

'I can't see it,' his uncle replied. 'I might have a bit more strength by then, but I wouldn't be fit for a journey like that, or for walking across a distance on rough ground. I'd stopped travelling about before I fell ill, and I'm not as well as I was then.'

Nicholas fell silent. He knew that he could not go alone. His parents would never agree to it, and he could see why.

'I can't ask Dad to come with me,' he said. 'He would be bound to want to know what it was all about, and he would want to come

153

everywhere with me. Even if I managed to persuade him to take me there on a long weekend holiday, we'd have to be together all the time.'

'I've thought all that, too,' said his uncle. 'But I've been toying with another possible solution.'

Nicholas brightened up. 'What is it?' he asked eagerly.

'Maybe we could get Jake to help.'

'But he's not here.'

'Not at the moment,' John agreed, 'but I've a gut feeling it won't be long before he pays us another visit.'

Nicholas said nothing as he considered this.

John continued. 'Mind you, I can't vouch for how he'll react when we ask him.'

'If he comes, and if he will talk to us about it, there isn't much we can say because of the pledge,' said Nicholas worriedly.

'My view is that if Jake comes and stays for long enough for us to raise anything with him, he won't ask questions. What will be in his mind is whether or not he's willing to help by taking you somewhere you want to go.'

'You mean, we'd just ask him if he'd take me to East Yorkshire?'

'That's more or less it. And if he agrees to it, he wouldn't think it strange if you wanted a bit of time on your own.'

'So we wouldn't have to break the pledge,' said Nicholas, relieved.

'No, not at all. But there's another consideration.'

Nicholas waited to see what his uncle would say.

'The situation is changing, and the pledge may become redundant.'

'It can't be redundant,' Nicholas burst out. 'The story's been handed down for ages and ages.'

'But why was it handed down, and in the form that needs the pledge?'

'Because... because...' Nicholas' voice trailed off.

His uncle continued. 'It's because the mystery of the fifth key has never been solved. Once that has happened, then the story, and the way it is handed on, changes.'

Nicholas began to see what his uncle was getting at. 'I always wanted it to be that *we* solve this,' he said.

'Yes, I remember when I was talking about you having a grandson to hand the story on to, you were quite indignant, because you wanted to believe that it would end with us.'

Nicholas sighed. 'There's so much to remember and so much to think about. I can't hold it all in my head at once.'

'Neither can I,' his uncle pointed out. 'And never forget that in my view you're doing very well.'

'Thanks.' Nicholas felt much reassured by his uncle's attitude, and he turned his mind back to the possibility of including Jake. 'So we could end up telling Jake about it.'

'We'd have to be certain of being quite a bit further on with it. But, yes.'

'I hope he comes soon,' said Nicholas, his voice full of longing.

'So do I, but there's nothing we can do about it at the moment, whereas there's plenty we can do in preparation. Let's work out how you'd go about the trip.'

Nicholas was immediately enthusiastic. 'How many days do you think I'd need?' he asked.

'It'll depend a bit on train times. But you'll have plenty of daylight, and that will help. Let me see... If you got a train around eight or nine in the morning, you'd be there before lunchtime. Then a bus...'

'I can get times on the Internet,' Nicholas interrupted eagerly.

His uncle continued. 'When I was there it was quite a walk from where the bus stopped. But that was years and years ago, so it's no use going by that. Things will have changed. Nicholas, we're going to need a good map. Can you go and get one? I'll write down the names of the places that must be on it.'

'I can go into town tomorrow,' said Nicholas. 'I remember the place where Dad bought one when we went on holiday to Wales the year before last.'

'Good lad!' replied John. 'I think there's a chance with modern transport that the trip could be done over a weekend. You might be able to get there after school on a Friday, have all day Saturday to look around, and then come back some time on the Sunday. What do you think?'

Nicholas' face was flushed with excitement. 'I wish I was old enough to go on my own,' he said. Then he added quickly, 'No, I don't. I wish Jake was here now, and that we were planning it together.'

Nicholas had no trouble persuading his parents that he needed to go into town for something for his uncle. They only asked if he had enough money, and he assured them that John had given him plenty. He set off early, soon after they had left to finish the paintwork at the house.

His memory of where the bookshop was that stocked a range of maps was accurate, and he had no difficulty in finding it. He was soon scanning the shelves, with his uncle's prompt in his hand. But to his great disappointment, he could find only the maps to the north, south and west of the one he needed. He felt so upset that a lump formed in his throat.

Just then, an assistant wearing a short-sleeved top bearing the shop logo approached him. 'Can I help?' he asked.

Nicholas was about to say that he was fine, and that he was just looking, when he changed his mind. He pointed to the row of maps, and said, 'The one I'm looking for isn't here.'

'I'll check through in the back,' the assistant offered, and he disappeared out of sight.

While he was waiting, Nicholas checked and rechecked the maps on the shelf, but to no avail.

When the assistant returned, he was carrying a map, and Nicholas' heart banged in his chest.

'I only have this one,' he told Nicholas. 'I'm afraid it's damaged. But you can have a reduction on it.'

'I'll definitely take it,' said Nicholas firmly.

The assistant led the way to the till. 'It's half price,' he informed him.

Nicholas handed over the money, and took the bag with the precious map in it. Fleetingly, he clutched it to his chest. Then realising that this might look odd, he carried the bag by his side, although from time to time he had to check its contents.

On the bus to his uncle's, he took out his prize and examined it. The cover was quite badly damaged. It was slightly ripped in places, and there were score marks across the picture on the front. However, when he opened it a little, he was sure that the map itself was intact. He could hardly wait to give it to his uncle, and for them to study it together.

When he arrived at the house, he ran into the living room, and handed the bag to John.

'It was the only one,' he explained breathlessly as his uncle took the map out of the bag. 'But I got it cheap.'

John stroked the cover of the map. 'You did well, Nicholas,' he said. 'I'll put it away for now, and we can look at it together this evening.'

Nicholas was surprised how quickly the time passed. He worked with his parents for several hours, and felt quite content, knowing that in the evening he could continue devising his plans with his uncle.

Six o'clock came, and as his parents left, his father called, 'We'll leave you two to plot whatever you're up to.'

Nicholas stared at him for a moment, startled. Then he realised that his father was joking, and he smiled.

Close study of the map helped Nicholas to get a clear picture in his mind of the latter part of the journey. He knew now what place names to type in for his Internet search.

'It would be a good idea to carry copies of my photographs with you,' said his uncle. 'But I've only got these prints, no negatives.'

Nicholas thought for a moment. 'Do you think it's something we could ask Dad for help with? You see, he's got a scanner at home, and I could copy the photographs onto his computer.'

'I don't see why not,' his uncle replied. 'No one would know what they mean. They just look like holiday snaps from years ago. Shall I ask him, or will you?'

'I will,' said Nicholas. 'There's a good chance he'll let me do them myself. He's shown me how to do it before.' Then he turned his attention back to the map. 'And you think one whole day there will be long enough?'

'I can't promise anything,' his uncle replied. 'But one thing's certain, you'll come back a lot wiser than when you set off. We'll have to see where that takes us next.'

'But what will we do if Jake doesn't come soon, or if he doesn't want to go with me?' asked Nicholas worriedly. 'What on earth will we do then?'

'We'll have to wait until you're old enough to go alone,' replied his uncle.

Nicholas was aghast. He could not possibly wait that long. He was sure that it would be years before he could travel alone to an unfamiliar place, and there was no one else they could ask to go with him.

'Remember, Nicholas,' said John gravely, 'there's a lot more to this than either of us can guess. If you have to wait a long time to go and see these places, so be it. Don't forget that we've made a lot of headway in this very room, and although we can't yet see them, there must be other ways to advance things. I don't want to rely on our helper, but whoever it is, or was, has been very close at hand.'

'And we don't know what else will come from that,' Nicholas finished for him.

'I think it's time for a few games of dominoes now,' said John, smiling.

Chapter Twenty-three

The next two weeks passed uneventfully. Nicholas and his parents worked less intensively at John's house now that it was more or less finished. There were a few things to be improved, but there was no urgency to see to them. The weather was warm and pleasant, and John often had his windows open. He greatly enjoyed the simple act of opening and shutting them, since many of them had been completely jammed for a long time. He liked to sit outside when the sun was shining on the front of the house, and would sometimes take a book to read.

To his surprise, Nicholas found that he was content to let things drift. He was kept busy at school, and after the months of focussing energetically on the work at his uncle's house, it felt quite good not to be bound by a very rigid timetable for a while. His urge to solve the mystery of the fifth key as quickly as possible had quietened, as he had realised that at this stage, there was little to be gained by constantly trying to delve into it.

Then, one evening, just before ten o'clock, the phone rang.

Sarah picked it up. 'Hello,' she said. 'Oh! Jake, it's you!'

Nicholas had been sitting reading a book. As soon as he heard his mother say Jake's name, he looked up, and he could see that her face was a study of delight mixed with a flustered state. He was not surprised, because underneath he felt much the same.

He heard his mother say, 'Jake, it's so good to hear you. You want to speak to Colin? I'll hand you over.' She passed the phone across.

Nicholas waited. He hoped fervently that this call meant Jake might be coming again soon.

'You're passing through at the weekend?' said Colin. 'Of course we'd like to see you ... Jake, the more we see you, the better ... Yes, I can assure you that's how we all feel ... You don't need to worry about the timing. We'll make sure there's someone here on Saturday ... Oh, okay ... Do you want a word with Nick?'

Nicholas' heart missed a beat. His father handed him the phone.

'Hi Jake. Yes, on Saturday ... Jake, there's something I want to

159

ask you … Okay … Bye.'

'He said not to worry about being in on Saturday, because he'll go up to John's if we're not here,' Colin told them.

'Col, I've got to be here,' Sarah declared emphatically.

'I know, love. I feel the same,' Colin replied.

'I'll probably be at Uncle John's,' said Nicholas, 'but you must phone when Jake gets here.'

'Of course,' promised his mother.

'I've got to tell Uncle John.' Nicholas spoke almost desperately.

'You can tell him tomorrow,' said his father. 'That'll be soon enough.'

'No… now,' Nicholas insisted.

'Why not phone him?' suggested his mother.

Nicholas hesitated for only for a second before saying. 'I've just got to see him.'

'Off you go then,' said his father. 'I'll give him a ring to say you're on your way. It's a bit late, and he might wonder who's at his door.'

'Thanks, Dad.'

Nicholas ran as fast as he could up the road, and when he arrived at his uncle's house, he was gasping for breath.

John was standing at the door in his pyjamas, ready to let him in. 'Hey, steady on,' he said.

Nicholas rushed past him, collapsed in the familiar armchair, and managed to gasp out, 'He's coming on Saturday.'

'Your dad told me when he phoned,' explained John gently. 'Do you know how long we'll have with him?'

Nicholas was still trying to catch his breath, and he shook his head mutely.

'Did you speak to him yourself?'

'Yes, but I didn't have long. I told him there was something I wanted to ask.'

'That's good. He'll be thinking.'

'I suppose I'd better go back now,' said Nicholas reluctantly.

'I've got to go to bed myself,' John agreed. 'Will you be coming in after school tomorrow?'

Nicholas brightened immediately. 'We can talk about Jake, and after that there'll only be Friday left before he comes.'

Jake arrived not long after noon on that Saturday. Colin and Sarah had decided to leave the door ajar, and he strolled into the house as if he had never left it. Sarah was in the kitchen making some sandwiches and a salad, and Colin was out at the back of the house, clearing weeds.

Sarah jumped as Jake entered the kitchen. 'Oh!' she exclaimed. 'Jake, it's so good to see you.' Impulsively, she reached out to hug him, but when she saw the startled look on his face, she touched his hand instead. 'I'll call your dad.'

She went to the back door. 'Col, Jake's here,' she said quietly.

'Excellent,' he replied in a low voice. 'I'll come in straight away.'

He put down his spade, slipped off his gardening shoes, and went into the house. He took Jake's hand and shook it warmly. 'It's great you could come,' he said.

'Where's Nick?' asked Jake.

'He's at John's,' his father explained. 'I'll give him a ring to let him know you're here.'

Jake shook his head. 'Not yet,' he said emphatically.

Sarah put the food on the table. 'Have something with us,' she invited.

Jake sat down and allowed her to fill a plate for him. He ate slowly, saying nothing.

Sarah sat next to him, and Colin sat opposite.

What was so striking, Colin thought, was that the atmosphere between them was one of ease. This was exactly how they should have been together, years ago.

When Jake had finished, he stated, 'I'd rather phone Nick myself.'

'That's fine,' replied Colin. 'We'll be around the house here all day. Come and go as you want.'

Jake picked up the phone. Then he hesitated.

Sarah quickly scribbled the number on a slip of paper, and handed it to him. He keyed it in.

'Hi, John,' he said. 'I'll be up in a minute. Tell Nick.' He put down the phone. 'See you later,' he called as he left the house and strode off up the road.

Sarah watched through the window as he receded into the distance.

Colin joined her and took her hand. 'Things are still changing, love.'

161

'Col, this is one of the happiest days I've had since Jake was small.'

As Jake neared John's house, he saw Nicholas sitting on the front doorstep, waiting for him. As soon as Nicholas spotted him, he jumped up and rushed towards him. He could not contain his obvious delight, and he was very pleased to see that Jake did not back away from it. Instead, he pushed Nicholas playfully, as if he were a rather exuberant overgrown puppy.

'Where's John?' asked Jake.

'Inside,' Nicholas replied. 'You go first.'

John's face gave a very clear picture of how he was feeling about seeing Jake again. 'Welcome home,' he said.

'It's yours,' Jake corrected him.

'You've put a great deal into it,' his uncle insisted, 'and the spare room is yours to use whenever you want.'

'And the same with my bedroom,' Nicholas added.

Jake looked overwhelmed.

Quickly, Nicholas changed the subject. 'My friends, Rab and Louis, are going to help me with the garden in the summer.'

This tack seemed to help Jake, and he looked more relaxed again. 'Now tell me what you wanted to ask.'

Nicholas glanced at his uncle. John nodded. 'Go ahead,' he encouraged. 'Tell him what we talked about.'

'I want to go to the Yorkshire coast,' Nicholas began. 'I don't want to go with Dad, and I'm not old enough to go by myself.'

'And I'm too old to go with him,' John added. 'It's something I'd like to do, but it's not feasible.'

'What about your friends?' asked Jake.

'I need someone older,' said Nicholas, trying to contain the desperation that threatened to creep into his voice.

'Me?' asked Jake.

Nicholas looked straight at him. All his intentions of raising the subject in a matter-of-fact way had disappeared, and his eyes were full of pleading.

'What exactly have you got in mind, Nick?' asked Jake bluntly.

'A weekend…' Nicholas' voice trailed off.

'And?'

Jake's voice had continued to sound friendly, and this gave Nicholas what he needed. He continued, hardly pausing for breath.

'Set off by train on Friday after school, catch a bus, have all day

162

there on Saturday, and come back on Sunday. I've got travel times from the Internet.'

'So far, so good,' said Jake. 'Where are you planning to stay?'

'Er... I haven't done that bit yet,' Nicholas admitted, suddenly feeling inadequate.

There was an awkward silence, which John broke by saying calmly, 'I'll pay.'

'I've got a tent,' Jake stated without emotion. 'It sleeps two.'

'Where?' asked Nicholas, surprised.

'In a garage.'

Nicholas was puzzled. In a garage? And where was it? He said nothing, and waited to see if Jake would say more.

'A lockup,' said Jake. This statement carried with it a note of finality, and Nicholas knew not to expect any further information.

There was another silence, and then John reminded them, 'If you two decide to go away together, I want to pay for the travel and the sleeping arrangements.'

He stood up and went off in the direction of the kitchen. Then Nicholas heard the tap running briefly, followed by the sound of the door being shut.

'He's left us to get on and decide,' said Jake, smiling.

'Can we go?' asked Nicholas.

'Think so. I'll let you know for sure tomorrow.'

'Okay.'

'I'm off now,' Jake finished.

Nicholas felt disappointed that he did not stay longer, but he noticed that as Jake left, he did not seem in such a rush, and he was sure he was going back down the road to see their parents again.

'I'll stay here with you for a bit longer,' he told John.

'I'd like that,' John replied. 'And there's another thing. I think you're wise. Jake could do with some time with Colin and Sarah.'

They smiled at each other conspiratorially.

'By the way, Uncle John, I talked to Dad a while ago about using his scanner. He said I could, but I didn't want to do anything straight away in case it seemed important.'

'Good lad!' John put a hand on Nicholas' shoulder. 'I'll give the photos to you before you leave.'

'Uncle John, do you think Jake will go with me?'

'I think there's a very good chance.'

They then took out their map again, and had another close look at the areas that John had marked earlier. And when Nicolas left, he was carrying not only the photos, but the map as well.

At home, he found that there was no sign of Jake, but his parents were looking very happy and relaxed.

'Jake's coming again tomorrow,' his mother announced contentedly.

'And I get the impression he's intending to stay around for a while,' his father added.

'Dad, can I use your scanner this evening?' asked Nicholas.

'For John's photos? Yes, of course. Come and get me if you need anything.'

'Thanks, Dad.'

Nicholas had no problems with the scanner, and he made two copies of each photograph, carefully storing them in the cardboard envelope his uncle had found for the purpose.

'Did it go okay?' asked his father when Nicholas joined his parents again.

Nicholas nodded. 'Uncle John will be pleased,' he said. 'Er... do you know what time Jake's coming?'

'He said after lunch,' his mother replied. 'And he wants to go for another walk with us.'

'Same place?' asked Nicholas.

'Yes, that's right,' his father confirmed. 'He thought we might go a bit further this time.'

'Even without walks, we're already a lot further on,' said his mother proudly.

It was good to see her so happy. Although Nicholas had always known his mother as someone who was cheerful and positive most of the time, she must always have been doing her best to hide the unhappiness that she felt about Jake's absence. And she had done it very effectively. Now that he saw his parents in a properly relaxed state, he could see the difference.

When Jake arrived the following day, he spoke to Nicholas straight away.

'You're on,' he said. 'Weekend after next.'

'What's this?' asked Colin. 'Secret plans?'

'We're having a weekend away,' Jake told him.

Colin could not hide his surprise. 'Where are you off to?'

'Not all that far,' Jake replied. 'Don't worry. We'll look after

164

each other.'

Colin persisted. 'Can Sarah and I help?'

'We've got everything we need,' Jake assured him.

Nicholas noted that Jake had told his father everything he needed to know, but had given away nothing.

Colin was bowled over by the news, and went to find Sarah, leaving Jake and Nicholas together.

'I've got all the kit,' said Jake. 'There are quite a few campsites along that stretch of coast.'

Nicholas' eyes shone. 'That's great! I've got a map. I'll show you where.'

'Okay,' replied Jake. 'Shouldn't be too busy at this time of year.'

Nicholas dashed upstairs for the map.

Jake studied it for a while. 'Ah, yes. Should be easy enough. All you'll need to bring is walking boots, waterproofs, a change of clothes, and your sleeping bag. I'll get the train tickets and book the campsite. I'll meet you here after school, a week on Friday.'

'I'll let Dad help me check my clothes,' said Nicholas with a mischievous grin. 'He'll feel better if he's got something to do.'

Just then, Colin and Sarah appeared at the door.

'I hear you're planning an expedition,' Sarah began. 'Let me know what food you want to take, and I'll make sure I've got it ready.'

'That's kind of you, Mum,' Nicholas replied, 'but Jake and I are going to fix all that.'

Jake nodded. 'It's an essential part of the deal,' he said, winking at his mother. 'Walk now. Then I must go.'

Later, Sarah wondered if she had imagined the wink, but when she checked with Colin that night, she found that he too had seen it.

In bed, Sarah and Colin had a long conversation about what they had learned that day.

'If someone had asked me what I wanted most in the world,' said Sarah, 'I wouldn't have dared think that we could have Jake and Nicholas planning a trip together.'

'To be honest, I don't think I've taken it in properly yet,' Colin replied.

'I wonder if John knows anything about it,' said Sarah suddenly.

'I'd be surprised if he didn't,' Colin replied. 'And actually, if I look back, I'd say there's been something brewing for a long time.'

Sarah was puzzled. 'But it can't have been the trip with Jake, because Jake being around is so new.'

'I know. That is the puzzling thing. If you ask me, it's as if Jake was drawn back because something was going on.'

'What on earth do you mean!' Sarah exclaimed.

'I don't know. There is something, but I can't put my finger on it.'

'Try,' Sarah insisted.

'The last thing that happened before Jake said he and Nick were going away together was that Nick scanned those old photos of John's. Oh, I know he asked weeks ago if he could do it sometime, but there was something about how he went about doing it that was almost too ordinary.'

'How can something be too ordinary?' asked Sarah.

'I just get the feeling that there's something behind it,' said Colin irritably. 'That's all.'

'Col, I'm sorry. You've been around Nicholas at John's more than I have over the last months. You'll have seen things that I haven't. But why didn't you say something to me before?'

'That's just it,' Colin replied. 'There wasn't anything I could put my finger on, so there wasn't anything to tell you. But now we've got Nick and Jake about to go off together, I can look back and see there's been something gradually building up that's made this possible. If you want a particular example, there was that time recently when I needed Nick to help me. I went to the living room, and he and John were deeply engrossed in something. As soon as I spoke to Nick, he rushed to help me.'

'He's usually like that,' Sarah pointed out.

'Yes, but not quite at that speed. As I said, there have been a number of signs so small that each of them has been unremarkable, but when I started to put them all together after hearing Jake and Nick's news, I could see something significant had been afoot for some time.'

'I wonder what it is,' mused Sarah. 'We can't ask. Col, I've never wanted to interfere between Nicholas and John, and I don't want to now.'

'I agree. It's important to let them have their own relationship. And the same is true with Nick and Jake. If they want to tell us more, they can, but we mustn't pry.'

Sarah was horrified at the thought. 'Nothing was further from my mind.'

'Maybe the photographs have something to do with the trip,' Colin suggested.

'And maybe not,' said Sarah firmly. 'Col, it's been a wonderful day, and I'm not going to do anything that risks spoiling it.'

Colin gave her a peck on the cheek. 'One thing's for certain,' he said, 'I'm going to take Nick shopping next weekend. His boots will be on the small side by now, and his waterproofs need replacing. A decent backpack wouldn't go amiss, either.'

'I couldn't agree more.'

'Right,' Colin finished, 'now that's settled, I'm going to put the light out.'

At school, Nicholas was tempted to tell Rab and Louis about his impending trip with Jake, but he knew that they would ask a lot of questions he was not prepared to answer, so he said nothing.

The shopping trip with his father went well. They enjoyed looking round together, and ended up buying some good-quality items. In addition to what was on their list, they bought two pairs of thick socks and a camping mat. Nicholas was both pleased and relieved that his father made no attempt to question him about the purpose and location of the planned weekend. In fact, he was very impressed. He was sure that if their positions were reversed, he would have been trying his best to elicit information. How his father managed to maintain the conversation without straying into details of the trip itself, he did not know.

When they arrived home, Sarah insisted on examining everything they had bought, and giving it her approval. Nicholas was desperate to show his kit to his uncle, and as soon as she had finished, he loaded everything into his backpack, and set off up the road to see him.

'This looks like a good pair of boots,' said John remarked. 'Your dad's done the right thing here. You've got everything you need if it pours with rain or you have to walk through a bog.'

'Uncle John, we've got to talk about the things I must do while I'm there.' Nicholas spoke urgently.

His uncle surprised him by saying, 'The main thing is to follow your intuition.'

'But there are things I've got to see,' Nicholas protested.

'We can certainly go through the places I know about,' said John.

167

'We can pencil them onto the map. But we can't predict what will happen once you're there, and you've got to feel free to go where you must.'

'It's sounding more and more difficult.'

'Come on, let's get the map out,' John directed.

Soon they were poring over it together, and with John's guidance Nicholas made some identifying marks on it.

'And you'll be taking a set of the prints,' John reminded him. 'There's likely to be a lot of change, but that doesn't mean they won't be of any use.'

'Is there anything else I should take with me?' asked Nicholas. 'Jake said he'd bring everything we need, but he doesn't know what I'm going to do.'

'The measurer!' said John suddenly. 'It's a good thing you asked. You must take it with you.'

Nicholas felt full of panic. 'I can't.'

'Why not?' asked his uncle reasonably.

'What if I lose it?'

'That's a risk we'll have to take.' His uncle was adamant. 'It's no good going without it. You might need it. Now listen, I've had an idea.'

Nicholas listened attentively.

'What we need to do is think of a way you can keep it strapped onto your body the whole time.'

'How can we do that? Even if we find a way, it'll probably dig in and make me bleed, and that's bound to show.'

'Just a minute,' said John. He went to his bedroom, and Nicholas could hear him rummaging through the chest of drawers.

He returned with a triumphant expression on his face. He handed a pouch to Nicholas that was made out of material, with a long cord attached to it. 'See if it will fit in there,' he instructed.

Nicholas collected the device from the box, and began to fit it into the pouch.

'It's perfect!' he said, as it slipped in with ease. He hung the cord round his neck, and pushed the pouch underneath his shirt.

John was pleased. 'It'll be safe in there. The only other thing now is the money.'

'Jake said he would get the train tickets.'

'I'll give you enough for those, and for everything else.' John turned to the table, and Nicholas could see that there was a bulging envelope waiting there. 'There's a cheque, and a pile of cash. You can hand it over to Jake when he comes to meet you.'

Nicholas did not know what to say.

'Don't say anything,' said John. 'This is the only way I can come along with you. We're in this together, remember.'

Nicholas took the envelope and zipped it into the pocket in the lid of his backpack.

'You can put the prints there too,' his uncle advised. He sorted out one of each, and put them in a plastic cover before handing them to Nicholas. 'Now be sure and come and see me during the week.'

'Of course, I will,' Nicholas assured him. 'I always do. And we need to keep talking. Uncle John, just because I'm going away with Jake, it doesn't mean that you don't matter any more. You're even more important now.'

Nicholas saw his uncle's eyes become watery.

'Uncle John, I don't know if I'll be able to phone, but I'll take some change with me in case I can get to a phone box. There's not much point in taking my mobile, because I won't be able to recharge it.'

Chapter Twenty-four

True to his word, Nicholas called in to see his uncle after school every day that week. When Thursday came, their parting was quite emotional.

'Good luck, Nicholas. Good luck,' his uncle called after him as he left.

That evening, his parents were almost as emotional as John had been, although they were trying hard to cover it up. His mother fussed about food for a while, and his father tried to give him extra money, but Nicholas was firm with them, and would take nothing else. His parents both knew that when they arrived home on Friday, the house would be empty, and their sons would be on their way to an unknown destination. This was a big moment.

By comparison, Friday morning's parting was almost casual.

'Bye Nick,' said Colin, as he was about to leave for work. 'Hope it all goes well.'

'Thanks, Dad. I'll see you on Sunday.'

Sarah squeezed his arm, and then saw him out of the door. 'Have a good trip,' she called after him.

At school, Rab and Louis could tell that something was up. They put increasing pressure on Nicholas to tell them, but he refused to say anything other than he was seeing Jake again, and they eventually gave up.

The last bell of the day rang, and Nicholas was free to race to catch the first bus in the line. He made it ahead of everyone else, and took the seat nearest to the door.

When he arrived home, he was delighted to find that Jake was waiting for him.

'You should have said you'd be here early,' he told him. 'We could have let you have a key.'

'I'm not ready for that yet,' said Jake bluntly, but he smiled at his brother with a warmth that was unmistakeable.

Nicholas ran upstairs, changed quickly, and grabbed his backpack. He could not wait to show it to Jake.

'That looks very fine,' Jake remarked as soon as he saw Nicholas

170

descending the stairs. 'It'll come in extremely useful. The train leaves at five thirty, so we've plenty of time, but we should get going.'

The bus arrived at the station soon after five, and they decided to sit on the platform to wait. It was relatively quiet at first, but became packed by the time the train was due.

'People going home from work, and people going away for the weekend,' Jake commented.

Nicholas discovered that Jake had booked seats, and that they were near the luggage shelves.

'Got to keep our things safe,' said Jake with a grin. 'You never know who's going to be around these days. And I've booked a place on a small campsite. It's on a farm, not far from the beach.'

Nicholas was glad to hear that Jake had been so thorough. Although he trusted him completely, he had wondered if they would have had to spend the first night in the middle of a deserted moor.

The brothers sat in relative silence for most of the journey. Occasionally, they would exchange a few words about things that they could see through the windows. For Nicholas, this was as much as he wanted. To be with Jake in any situation was wonderful, and to be with him on this trip felt like paradise.

Although the train had been completely full, at each station more and more people left. There had been one quite long delay, and it was nearly nine o'clock by the time they arrived. Jake hurried Nicholas off the platform in search of the bus, as it was due to leave at nine.

'The next one's at ten,' he said tersely as he strode along, elbowing his way through some groups of people, with Nicholas jogging behind him.

They managed to jump on the bus just as the doors were closing.

At first, the driver was annoyed. 'Hey! What are you two up to?' he said. But when Jake explained that they were on the last leg of a long journey, he realised that they were not out to cause trouble, and he asked where they were heading for.

'Brackhall Farm,' Jake replied.

'I'll drop you off at the end of their track,' the driver offered. 'It'll save you a bit of walking.'

'Thanks.' Jake swung his pack onto a spare seat behind the driver's cab, and sat on the other side of the aisle with Nicholas next to him.

The bus was empty apart from a woman with a small child who had fallen asleep on her lap.

'You staying long?' asked the driver.

'Couple of nights,' Jake replied.

'Hope the wind doesn't get up,' said the driver. 'It's pretty breezy at that site.'

'Got a storm tent.'

The driver fell silent until they were within a few hundred yards of the track.

'Here you are,' he told them, drawing the bus up. 'Good luck.'

'Thanks, said Nicholas and Jake together, as they stepped off.

It was still light, so there was no difficulty in seeing which way to go. The track to the farm was well under a mile long, and the brothers enjoyed stretching their legs after the many hours of travelling.

When they reached the house, they saw a sign directing campers to the rear door, where they knocked a couple of times, and waited.

The door opened to reveal a well-padded woman with grey hair, who Nicholas guessed was probably around the same age as his parents. She looked them up and down.

'You made it,' she observed. 'You're the only tent tonight, so you can choose your spot in the paddock.' She pointed to a fenced area not far from the house. Then she indicated the single-storied extension next to the door at which they were standing. 'Shower and toilets are in this bit here. It's a separate door. You'll see when you go round the back.'

'Thanks,' said Jake, turning towards the paddock.

Nicholas was very surprised when the woman added, 'You can have breakfast with us if you want. Two pounds fifty a head.'

Nicholas looked at Jake, and was further surprised when Jake said, 'Fine. What time?'

'Eight on the dot.' Then the woman closed the door, and left them to organise themselves.

'Have you pitched a tent before?' asked Jake.

Nicholas shook his head.

'Now's the time to learn then.'

Jake went to the far corner of the paddock, next to a flattish rock, pulled a cylindrical bag out of his pack, and put it on the ground.

'I'll sit here,' he said. 'You work out what to do.'

Nicholas put down his backpack, and opened the end of the tent bag.

Jake watched quietly, while Nicholas tried his best. Jake only gave directions when absolutely necessary.

When Nicholas had finished, it was nearly dark.

'Just in time,' Jake commented. Then he added, 'You must be hungry.' He dived into his pack, and produced enough food to more than fill them both up.

They ate in companionable silence, and when they had finished, Jake said cheerfully, 'Sleeping bags and camping mats. Then we'll turn in. There's nothing better than a night under the stars.'

It only took a few minutes to lay them out in the small tent.

Although he was very tired, Nicholas did not fall asleep straight away. It felt good to be lying beside Jake. Jake had slept almost immediately, and Nicholas welcomed the sound of his regular breathing. He was content to lie there, thinking about the events of the day, and considering what might be ahead of him. He tried to concentrate on how his uncle had told him to follow his intuition, but at the moment, this concept was so nebulous that it had no meaning.

The next thing he knew was that Jake was digging him in the ribs.

'Come on, if you want any breakfast.'

Nicholas came to with a jerk. For a second he could not think where he was, but then he knew that he had slept the night with Jake in the tent, and that it was now morning.

'What time is it?' he asked.

'Quarter to eight.'

'Oh no!' Nicholas scrambled out of the tent, grabbed his things, and made for the shower block.

He was back promptly, and he and Jake went to the rear door of the farmhouse, which the owner had left ajar.

Jake knocked and called out, 'Hello!'

'Come on in,' a voice replied.

Jake and Nicholas made their way down a short passage and into a room that had a large table, round which three people were already seated.

'Morning,' said a jovial man with a weatherbeaten face, swinging round in his seat to look at them. Nicholas wondered if it was the husband of the woman that they had seen the night before.

The man held his hand out to Jake. 'I'm Thomas. Glad to meet you.'

'I'm Jake, and this is my brother, Nick.'

The other two men at the table nodded. 'We're passing through,' said one with an obvious lack of interest.

'We do bookings when the local transport café is full,' Thomas

173

explained.

Just then, the woman they had seen the night before came into the room. She was carrying a large tray.

'Can I help?' Nicholas asked politely.

She looked surprised, and then pleased. 'I could do with a hand this morning,' she said.

She put the tray on the table, and beckoned to Nicholas to follow her into the kitchen, where he helped her to gather together what was needed, and carry it to the others.

There was no real conversation over breakfast. At eight thirty precisely, Thomas stood up and announced, 'Taxi service.'

The two men stood up and prepared to leave.

'See you later,' said Thomas. 'Got to take them back to their lorries.'

When Jake and Nicholas were left with the woman, she became quite animated.

'I don't think I introduced myself last night,' she began. 'My name's Fran. Did you have a good night?'

'It was fine, thanks,' replied Nicholas. He wished that Jake was saying something, but he seemed to be concentrating on a piece of toast and marmalade. He searched his mind for something to continue the conversation. 'Um... How long have you lived here?'

'Thirty years or more,' Fran told him. 'And Tom was born here.'

Nicholas was impressed. This meant that Thomas had been there for a very long time. Suddenly he realised that he was likely to be an excellent source of information.

'We were thinking of going down to the beach this morning,' Nicholas began. 'Can you tell us where the path is?'

Fran laughed. 'You're right to be sure. We don't want anyone risking dropping off the cliffs. Follow the fence from the far corner of the paddock, and that'll take you to some rough steps down. And remember, the tide'll be in this afternoon, so you'd best get going soon.'

'Can I help with the washing up?' Nicholas offered.

'No, you've already earned your breakfast. Off you go.' Fran stood up and bustled into the kitchen, where Nicholas could hear her moving crockery.

'Come on,' said Jake, suddenly coming out of his reverie. 'I don't want to have to fish you out of the water.'

They left most of their things in the tent, and tied it shut. Then they took their packs and set off along the fence.

Soon they were on the steep descent to the beach.

'How far along do you want to go?' asked Jake casually.

Nicholas realised that he had no idea about his answer to that question. He just knew that it was important to be on the beach, looking out to sea, and gazing up to the cliffs.

'Let me check your map,' said Jake.

Nicholas took off his pack, and passed the map to his brother, who opened it to show where the farm was. He pointed to the route they had taken, and Nicholas could see that they would reach the beach a little way north of where Uncle John had indicated.

'Can we turn to the right at the bottom?' he asked. 'I'd like to have a look along the cliffs.'

'Fine by me,' replied Jake amiably.

The sun was warm, and there was a light breeze. The sea was fairly calm, with the only waves appearing right at its edge. There was no one about, and in that moment Nicholas felt as if the whole world belonged to him and Jake.

As they made their way along the beach, an occasional seagull dived low, as if to inspect them. Nicholas saw some pieces of driftwood, and wondered if they were remnants of Todd's ship, but he knew that any wood from that source would have decayed long ago.

The sound of Jake's voice penetrated his thoughts. 'I checked the tides when I booked the site. Fran's right. We'll have to watch the time.'

'How long have we got?' asked Nicholas.

'Can you give me the map again? There are a couple of options. I'll show you.'

Nicholas extracted the map from his pack once more and handed it to Jake, who studied it for a few minutes and then pointed. 'We're here, and we're heading south. Less than three miles further on, there's an inlet with a marked track leading back up. We've got another couple of hours of safe time, so we could easily carry on and follow that. Otherwise, we must turn back in another forty minutes or so.'

Nicholas had no difficulty in seeing the sense in what Jake had said. He did not hesitate, saying, 'I want to carry on.'

Jake refolded the map, and handed it back to him. They continued along the beach in silence.

Reaching a corner of the cliffs that had obscured the view ahead,

Nicholas could suddenly see a large area that was covered in rocks, and out into the water he could see more protruding above the sea level.

'This is the kind of thing you have to factor in, when you're working out how long a walk will take,' Jake explained. 'It'll take us a lot longer to work our way round these than if it was open beach.'

Nicholas moved ahead, and at first found ways through the litter of slabs and broken rocks, but soon he found himself struggling in a mass of them. Many of their surfaces were slippery with seaweeds.

'Take your time,' Jake advised. 'No broken limbs.'

Nicholas had already slowed his pace, and was happy to reduce it further. He was wondering if this was the place where Todd's ship had foundered. It would not be surprising, he thought. The only way round it would have been to keep well away from the shore, and if the wind were driving the ship towards the rocks, it would not have stood a chance. Jake had been right to do his calculations including plenty of extra time to reach the other track. Strolling along on a featureless sandy beach was completely different from what they were facing now.

At last they reached a shingle beach, and the going was much easier. By now, Nicholas could see that the tide was coming in quite fast. Another look at the map showed that they were about half a mile from the track, and watching the water moving up the beach was an excitement, not a threat.

Nicholas was glad to be leaving the beach soon. He was only too aware of what had taken place either here, or quite nearby, many years ago, and he had no wish for him and Jake to suffer the same nasty end as Todd's crew had done.

Although they reached the place where they guessed the bottom of the track must be at hand, there was no sign of it.

'It's probably quite easy to see from the top,' Jake commented. 'We'll just have to search this area in sections until we find it.'

Jake appeared to be perfectly relaxed about their situation, so Nicholas did not feel worried, and he began to investigate an area where the cliff had broken away and littered the beach with broken rocks. Having agreed that they would whistle to each other every few minutes, Jake went further along the beach, and then cut up behind another area of recent disturbance.

Water was lapping up near Nicholas' ankles when Jake returned.

'I think I've found the place,' he said. 'The problem is that the

176

lower end of it has been swept away. That's why we couldn't see it at first. I reckon if you stand on my shoulders, you'll be able to climb onto the lowest ledge that's survived the fall. After that, it'll be a bit of a scramble at first, but then you'll be on the path that joins the track.'

'How will you get up?' asked Nicholas. He was feeling very anxious, but trying hard not to show it.

'Come on,' said Jake. 'Let's get you up there.'

He took Nicholas' arm and hurried him to the spot. 'Climb on my hands,' he instructed.

Nicholas flattened himself against the rock face, and stepped into the foothold that Jake created with his clasped hands.

'Now on my shoulders.'

Nicholas did not hesitate. He knew that if he wasted any of their precious time, it would make Jake's task all the more difficult. He clambered onto his shoulders and up onto the rocky ledge. Then he marvelled as he watched Jake using his long arms and legs and strong fingertips to lever himself up onto the ledge to join him.

'Off you go,' said Jake. 'There's not much room here.'

Nicholas scrambled up the next ten feet or so until he reached the bottom of the path, with Jake close behind him. Then the brothers turned and watched the sea covering the sand where they had stood only a few minutes earlier.

'Well done,' said Jake, putting his hand on Nicholas' back. 'We'll have some lunch at the top, and then you can tell me what you want to do next.'

Nicholas was impressed by Jake's confident attitude. He was aware that his own heart was beating rather rapidly, and he could not help thinking about what might have happened if his brother had not been with him.

At the top of the path, they sat on their waterproofs, looking out to sea, and eating some of the food that Jake had brought.

'I'll get the map out,' said Nicholas. 'I want us to look at the other places Uncle John and I marked, and then choose which to go for.'

'I'm not bothered,' Jake replied, 'so long as we stick together.'

Nicholas liked this, but he made no comment. Instead, he pointed to the map. 'Inland, there's a village with a church we could look at, and...' He was about to list more, when he had a strong feeling that the only thing he really wanted to do was to walk southwards, along the top of the cliffs. 'Can we just keep going along here?' he asked, pointing.

'Fine by me.' Jake finished his apple and tossed the core to one side. 'Water?' he asked. He handed the bottle to Nicholas, who drank thirstily from it.

A few minutes later, they were once again strolling alongside each other. Nicholas was looking out to sea and thinking about Todd, his men and his ship.

As time passed, the brothers said very little to one another. Neither felt the urge to speak. It was sufficient for them to be together, sharing this experience.

It was only later that Nicholas turned to his brother and said, 'I'd like to go to that village after all. Can we see the best way to get there?'

'Sure,' replied Jake.

Once more they studied the map together, and they devised a route that led through several fields, and then joined a marked path that led to a road into the village.

'It'll take us a while.' Jake looked at his watch. 'Any shops'll be shut by the time we get there.'

'I wasn't thinking of shops,' said Nicholas, 'but I'd like to look inside the church.'

Nicholas had no illusions about the likelihood of discovering any information that was relevant to Todd, or his son. He wanted to go to a place where, if everything had been right, Todd might have been buried, and his son's birth recorded. An unpleasant thought went through his mind, and he shuddered.

'You cold?' asked Jake.

Nicholas shook his head.

Jake did not press him for any further response, and he was left with his thoughts. What if the baby's birth *had* been registered, but the merchant had subsequently destroyed the record? Nicholas felt shivers going up and down his spine. He wished he could talk to his uncle. He even considered talking to Jake about it. But not only would that be wrong, it would not be fair. Jake had come to enable him to have his time here, and for no other reason. If Nicholas began to tell him details of what he and Uncle John shared, it would force him into that arena. He would have no choice.

Perhaps there would be a phone box in the village? He hoped so. Uncle John would be bound to be in, and he would be able to speak to him for a few minutes in private. He quickened his pace.

'You're speeding along,' Jake commented.

Nicholas decided to be honest with his brother. 'I want to speak to Uncle John,' he explained, 'and I'm hoping we can find a phone box.'

'If there isn't one in the village, there's probably one at that transport café,' said Jake. 'We passed it on the bus yesterday evening. If we have no luck there, Fran's bound to let you phone from the house.'

Nicholas hoped that they would find a phone long before they got back to the house. He could not possibly call from there, and would have to make some kind of excuse.

After another hour of walking, they had left the fields behind, and were near the end of the path, where it was about to join the road. Nicholas could see the spire of the church, and once round a bend in the road, he could see the cluster of houses that formed most of the village itself.

They headed for the church, and as they approached it, to Nicholas' great relief he came upon a phone box.

'You're in luck,' Jake remarked. He pointed ahead. 'I'll wait for you on that seat up there.'

Nicholas took change out of his pack, and keyed in the number. He soon heard his uncle's voice.

'Hello, Uncle John,' said Nicholas. 'It's me.'

The pleasure in his uncle's voice was very apparent. 'How are you doing?'

'Fine,' Nicholas replied. 'It's great being with Jake. I'll tell you everything when I get back, but I had to hear your voice.'

'What is it?' asked his uncle. 'Tell me what's on your mind.'

'What if the shepherd and his daughter registered the birth of the baby, but the merchant destroyed the record soon afterwards?'

'I hadn't thought about that,' said John. 'It's possible.'

'I felt really horrible when it came into my mind,' Nicholas confided. 'We'd walked along the cliffs for quite a while, and I'd been thinking about everything.'

'I'm very glad you rang, and I'll look forward to hearing everything soon. Say hello to Jake for me.'

Nicholas wanted to tell his uncle that he had felt scared and did not like the shivery feeling, but he knew this was a conversation that had to wait.

'I'd better go now,' said Nicholas. 'Jake's waiting for me.'

He put the phone down. He suddenly felt quite a bit better. That had been enough for now. He ran down the road, and sat on the seat with Jake.

'Any news?' asked Jake.

'Uncle John told me to say hello.'

Jake acknowledged this information with a nod. 'Do you want to see inside the church?' he asked casually.

'Could do.' Nicholas was non-committal.

To his surprise, his brother said, 'I wouldn't mind a look myself. You coming?'

Nicholas jumped to his feet. 'Let's go.'

Although the church was dark and rather cold inside, Nicholas felt none of the shiveriness that he had experienced earlier. The interior of the church was quite plain, although a few of the windows were made of stained glass. Jake was impressed by the quality of it.

'The colours and forms are very good,' he said.

'I didn't know you were interested in that sort of thing,' Nicholas commented.

'Oh, I've been around,' was Jake's only reply.

When they left the church, they both blinked as the sunlight outside hit them.

'How long do you think it's going to take to get back?' asked Nicholas.

'You tired?'

'Not really. I only wanted to know how much longer we've got.' Nicholas reached into his sack and pulled the map out.

'See if you can work it out,' Jake suggested.

Nicholas studied the map. He could see clearly where they were now, and where the farm was. He looked at the scale at the side, and then made a rough calculation of
the distance.

'Another couple of hours?' he guessed.

'That's what I thought,' agreed Jake, 'but we could see if there's a bus due once we're on the main road.'

'I don't want to get a bus,' said Nicholas immediately. 'I like walking with you.'

Jake smiled. 'Okay, pal.'

The rest of the walk was uneventful, and they finally reached the tent a little over two hours later. Another tent had appeared in their absence, but it had been pitched on the opposite side of the paddock, and the owner was nowhere to be seen.

'I'm hungry,' Jake pronounced. He dived into the tent and reappeared with a camping stove and a small pan with a folding handle. He handed the water bottle to Nicholas, who quickly filled it at the tap outside the shower block.

Not long afterwards the water was boiling, and Jake tipped a generous quantity of rice into it. Then he picked up a small book he had taken from the tent, and began to read.

The sun still provided some warmth, and Nicholas went and lay on the flat rock for a little while, thinking. He patted his chest, checking yet again that the measuring device was still safely contained inside its pouch. Then he sat up, took it out, placed it on the stone, and began to toy with it.

He was so immersed in what he was doing that he did not notice Jake coming up behind him, and he jumped when Jake said, 'Not long now.' He caught sight of the device and asked, 'What have you got there?'

Nicholas was flustered, and he did not know quite what to say. 'It's... it's something Uncle John lent to me.'

'Can I have a look?' asked Jake curiously.

Nicholas handed it to him hesitantly.

'I won't damage it,' Jake assured him. He stared at it intently, and seemed to recognise something. 'Now this is very interesting indeed. Do you know where it came from?'

Nicholas shook his head, but then added, 'Er... well... Uncle John's grandad left it to him.' This time he was not wishing that he could speak to his uncle. He was wishing that his uncle was there in person. Why on earth had he taken the measurer out of its pouch? It had seemed such a natural thing to do at the time, yet now it felt as if he had done something wrong, and he did not know how to correct it.

Jake studied the measurer again. 'Fascinating.'

'What is?' asked Nicholas, feeling very subdued.

'The pattern in the middle of this has some similarity to something I've seen before. It's only rough, but I recognise it.'

Immediately, Nicholas was alert. He waited to see if Jake would say more.

'It was on a gravestone.'

Nicholas held his breath.

'In a churchyard.'

Nicholas was stunned. He wanted to shout 'where' as loudly as he could, but he remained completely silent. He so much wanted to know the answer to that question, and yet he was afraid to ask.

Jake went on. 'I remember being puzzled by it. I'd never seen anything quite like it before. Actually, it's not all that far from here.'

Questions crowded into Nicholas' mind. Not only did he want to know where that gravestone was, when Jake had seen it, and if they could go there tomorrow, but also he wanted to know exactly what was written on it. And if they could go, he needed a camera. Why had he not brought one with him? It would have been easy to bring a simple single-use type.

Then he heard Jake say, 'Food's ready,' and he followed him to the tent, where the pan was sitting on the grass, covered with an enamel dish. Jake shared out the steaming rice, and opened a can of baked beans to go with it.

'You want to see it?' he asked abruptly.

Nicholas nodded vigorously.

'We'll talk about it before we turn in.'

After this, they sat in silence, working their way through their food.

Nicholas was in a state of intense alertness. Although he was hungry, and he was eating, his whole being was so focussed on Jake's revelation that digesting food seemed a tricky proposition. He ate slowly and carefully.

It was dusk by the time they cleaned their plates and tidied up their things.

The two brothers lay side by side in the tent, with the map lying folded up between them. It was nearly dark, but Nicholas could just make out the shape of Jake's head when he turned towards him.

'When did you see it?' asked Nicholas.

'About seven years ago,' Jake replied. 'I was travelling around the north of England, picking up casual jobs to keep myself going.'

'Can we get there tomorrow, before we go back home?'

'I don't know. We'd need a bus, and Sunday services are usually very limited.'

'Show me where it is on the map.'

Jake switched on his head torch and unfolded the map. He jabbed his finger at it, and Nicholas could see that the place was at least five miles further away than the railway station.

'Do you think we'd have to go to the station, and then get another bus from there?'

'Probably.'

'Jake?'

'Yes?'

'What else was on the stone?'

'Nothing.'

'No writing?'

'No. Just the pattern.'

'Can you remember the time of our train?'

'Seats are booked on the two thirty. There's one train after that.'

'What time?'

'Not sure. Maybe four thirty. I'll check in the morning. Timetable's in my bag. Sleep now.'

'Can we catch the later train?' asked Nicholas sleepily.

There was no reply.

When Nicholas woke, the sleeping bag next to him was empty. He crawled out of the tent to find Jake sitting consulting the train timetable.

'It's at five,' he said. 'You'd be back home after nine. Is that going to work?'

'I've only got one piece of homework. I can look at it in bed.'

'Not ideal.'

'Please.' The note of pleading in Nicholas' voice was unmistakeable.

'Okay. Breakfast now.'

Nicholas obediently followed Jake into the shower block, and then into the house.

As before, Thomas was sitting at the table, but the two men who were with him were different.

'Morning,' Thomas greeted them.

'Hello,' said Nicholas. 'Is Fran in the kitchen?'

Thomas nodded. He pulled out the chair beside him and beckoned to Jake to join him, while Nicholas went to find her.

'Are you on the transport café run again?' Jake asked Thomas.

'I'm leaving at nine. Do you want a lift?'

'Would you go as far as the train station?' asked Jake. 'We'll pay.'

Thomas wrinkled his forehead as he considered this.

At length he said, 'I'll need to check with Fran.'

183

Nicholas appeared with steaming bowls of porridge, and put them on the table before returning to the kitchen.

Fran appeared with a teapot, and Thomas told her about Jake's request.

'You're in a rush,' she observed.

'We're hoping to fit something else in before our train leaves,' Jake explained.

'You can suit yourselves,' she said kindly. 'I'll be busy here all morning.'

When Nicholas came to sit at the table, Jake told him, 'Thomas will take us to the station, but we've got to be ready by nine.'

Nicholas glanced at his watch, and started to eat his porridge quickly. But he burnt his mouth, and Jake had to make him slow down.

Despite his fears about missing the lift, Nicholas was ready with time to spare. He and Jake sat on their packs at the side of the drive until Thomas was ready. Fran had refused to take payment for Nicholas' breakfasts, and had given them a large sandwich each to take away with them.

They squeezed into Thomas' battered old car together with the lorry drivers, and Thomas navigated down the drive to join the road. There was no conversation until they left the transport café.

'Where are you off to?' asked Thomas.

Nicholas did not want to tell him, but Jake explained that they intended to visit a church in the village south of the station.

'Interesting place that,' Thomas remarked. 'Has got some right rum gravestones. But there's been vandalism. Can't understand people any more. There wasn't anything like that when I was a lad.'

Nicholas broke out in a cold sweat. What if the stone had been damaged? Or worse still, wrecked? He could not think of anything to say, so he kept quiet.

When they reached the station, Jake put his hand in his pocket, pulled out a twenty-pound note, and gave it to Thomas.

'Too much,' said Thomas.

Jake raised his hand as if to stop him from saying more, but Thomas took out his wallet and insisted that he took ten pounds in change.

'Come again soon,' he called as he waved through the window of his car. 'Fran and I'll be glad to see you any time.' Then he muttered something that to Nicholas sounded like, 'Should see some fools that come.'

'Better look for a bus straight away, Nick,' Jake directed.

They scrutinised the stands that were near the station entrance until they found a likely route.

'Hm... Sunday service doesn't go that far,' said Jake.

'We could walk,' suggested Nicholas eagerly.

'Good man. Looks as if there's a bus in about fifteen minutes. Get your map out, and we'll see how far we'll have to cover ourselves.'

The bus drew up just after they had ascertained that if they were to see the church, it would involve a walk of three miles each way from where the bus stopped.

Nicholas had a tight feeling in the pit of his stomach as the bus left the town and progressed slowly along a number of country lanes. It was a relief when it reached the end of its journey, and he and Jake got off and began their walk. There was a light drizzle, although it was not wet enough for them to put on their waterproofs. The way was easy enough to find with the aid of the map, and they arrived at their destination not long after eleven o'clock.

At last, Nicholas was standing outside the churchyard. He turned to Jake and asked, 'Can you remember exactly where it was?'

'More or less. Go through the gate and round the right-hand side of the church. It's somewhere beyond that.'

Jake gestured to Nicholas to lead the way. He wanted Nicholas to have the best chance of experiencing a feeling of discovery.

When he rounded the side of the church, Nicholas could see straight away that part of a ruin was standing in the graveyard, about thirty feet from the church itself. Methodically, he worked his way through the stones that were between the side of the church and the ruin. Some were standing, some were flat, and some were tilted rather precariously.

Jake leaned on the stonework at the corner of the church, and watched him. He had come across some strange things in his life, but when he had first seen that stone in this churchyard, it had made a deep impression on him. And now, here he was with his brother, who was carrying with him something that belonged to their great-uncle. And by the design on its metal plate, that object was linked directly to the stone. How long it had been in the family was anybody's guess. All they knew was that it had belonged to Uncle John's grandfather, and there was no information about how he had come by it. Of course, he could have made it himself, but surely that would mean that he had visited this very graveyard at some time. Or... maybe the stone was not the only place where the pattern could be seen. He was certain that the object post-dated the stone, as the stone showed clear signs of age and wear.

Silently, Nicholas continued to make his way slowly between the stones, checking each one as he went. He had almost reached the ruin when he saw it at last – leaning up against the side of the remnants of the wall that faced him. He knelt down on the damp grass in front of it, and touched its surface lightly. To Jake, who was still standing at a distance, it appeared that Nicholas was almost caressing the stone.

Although Nicholas had no doubt that the pattern on the stone was the same style as the centre of the one on the measurer, he wanted to see them together. He felt under his clothing, took the device out of its pouch, and placed it on the grass between him and the stone.

At this point, Jake strolled across to him.

'Look,' said Nicholas, his voice full of awe.

'Unmistakeable,' Jake replied.

'Was the stone like this when you came before?' asked Nicholas.

'No, it was standing next to some of the others, not propped up here.'

'Show me where.'

'I'll try.'

Jake went to the far end of the ruin, and then called for Nicholas.

He pointed. 'I'm fairly sure it was between these two.'

Nicholas looked at the two stones in turn. There was writing on each of them, but it was very difficult to read because both the stones were quite weathered, and moss and lichen adorned their rough surfaces.

At length he said, 'It looks as if there's 16 on this stone.' He showed Jake.

'You're probably right,' replied Jake. He took a penknife out of his pocket, and very carefully scraped the next part of the stone. 'It's an eight or a nine,' he said at last.

Nicholas was excited. 'That means the 16 isn't the date of a month. What comes next?'

Jake continued his work, but neither of them could identify anything further.

'Try the other one,' Nicholas urged.

Jake shook his head, perplexed. 'I don't know what to make of

186

this. I'll give the other one a try, but it looks even more eroded than this one.' He scraped at it a little, but then he stood up. 'I don't want to work on this one. The surface of the stone is too vulnerable.'

Nicholas respected his decision, and did not press him to continue.

'Jake,' he said. 'How can we get a picture of the pattern stone so we can show it to Uncle John?'

'Simple,' Jake replied, smiling. He opened his pack, and lifted out a plastic container, from which he took a small camera.

'Wow!' exclaimed Nicholas, admiring it. 'Why didn't you say you had it?'

'Don't like to rely on it,' replied Jake cryptically.

He took two shots of the stones next to which the pattern one had stood, and then he turned his attention to the stone itself.

'Put Uncle John's thing in front of it again,' he directed.

Nicholas did this, and then stood back out of the way while Jake took a photograph.

'Now put it on top of the stone,' Jake instructed, preparing to take a further shot.

It was then that Nicholas started to feel cold again... very cold. He began to shiver.

'Jake, I don't feel too good.'

Jake looked at him, concerned. 'You're probably hungry. I'll take this last one, and we'll have something to eat.'

Nicholas bent to pick up the device, but it fell out of his hand.

He tried again. Again, the device fell. Nicholas shook his hand vigorously. Maybe if he got his circulation moving he would manage. Yet there had been something strange about the way it had slipped out of his hand that second time. It was almost as if it had jumped. He tried again, and this time it moved away from him before he touched it.

'Jake,' he said in a low voice, 'there's something odd going on.'

'I can see that,' Jake replied. 'I'll try.'

He put his camera in his pocket and walked towards the device. It did not move. Then he bent down, as if to pick it up. Again it did not move.

'Nick, try picking it up now.'

Nicholas picked it up. 'I'm going to put it away,' he said firmly. He fitted it back into its pouch. He was relieved to find that he was not feeling so cold now.

Then Jake searched around in his pack. 'I've got some bits and pieces left,' he announced. 'Nuts, dried fruit, bread, apples...' He handed several plastic bags to Nicholas. 'Take what you want, and I'll have the rest.'

They munched in silence for a while, after which Nicholas felt much better.

'I wonder what would Uncle John make of that when we tell him,' Nicholas pondered. 'Jake, I'm really glad you were there.'

'It was obvious I wasn't going to get that last frame,' Jake remarked lightly. 'But we can come back some time,' he added casually, as he emptied the remains from a bag of peanuts, and tossed the broken pieces into his mouth. He checked his watch. 'We'd better get going.'

They collected their things, and walked briskly back to where they had left the bus earlier that day. They found that unfortunately they had missed a bus, and the wait for the next one would be nearly an hour.

'Better keep walking,' Jake decided. 'You can put your sleeping bag in my pack if you want.'

'No thanks,' Nicholas replied. Although by now he felt very weary, he was determined to be responsible for his own things.

Arriving at the station some time before the later train, they waited in a café, and Jake ordered bowls of soup and some rolls.

Nicholas suddenly realised that in only a few hours' time, he would be back home, and Jake would disappear again.

In his depleted state this prospect seemed gloomy, and without his usual caution, he asked, 'Where are you sleeping tonight?'

'I'll go up to John's.'

'After that?'

Jake said nothing, and Nicholas felt his eyes fill with tears. He put his head down, and wiped them on his sleeve. He became aware that he could no longer hear Jake's spoon in his bowl of soup, and he cautiously looked across at him. To his surprise, he saw that Jake had put his spoon down, and was staring fixedly at his soup.

'After that?' Nicholas repeated, this time more loudly.

'I heard you the first time,' Jake replied. 'The answer is I don't know.'

He picked up his spoon again, and began to consume his soup in an untidy fashion. Then he almost threw his spoon into the bowl and said, 'I missed you.'

Nicholas was lost for words.   He wanted to go round the table to his brother, give him a hug, and tell him that he missed him too. If it had been his dad, he would not have hesitated, but because it was Jake, he was very uncertain about what to do.

'Come again... soon,' he managed to say.

Jake opened his mouth, but did not speak.

Nicholas continued. 'We all want to see you – Mum, Dad, and Uncle John.'

'I'll remember,' said Jake slowly. 'But first there are things I've got to see to.'

'Okay.' Nicholas felt lighter as a result of this exchange, and he enjoyed eating the rest of his food.

Jake, too, seemed brighter, and he told a couple of jokes which Nicholas found extremely funny.

The journey back was very quiet. There were few people on the train, and they were largely scattered along its length, sitting alone. As Nicholas relaxed back into his seat, he suddenly felt overwhelmed with tiredness, and soon his head began to nod.

When he woke with a start, he found that he had been sleeping across Jake's chest, and that nearly two hours had passed.

'Sorry,' he said, quickly sitting upright.

Jake smiled. 'Be my guest. I was asleep for a while too. By the way, a trolley loaded with sandwiches came by. I got some tuna ones. Do you want to share them?'

'Thanks,' Nicholas replied gratefully. Food and sleep were all he wanted at the moment. So much had happened that weekend, and he longed to spend time with his uncle, sifting through it all. But he would have to be at school in the morning, and he doubted his capacity to concentrate on any of the lessons.

His thoughts were interrupted when the train slowed suddenly, and then jerked to a halt.

'I wonder what's up,' said Jake. 'There wasn't any notice of work being done on the line.'

The train did not move for a full fifteen minutes, and then it jerked once more, and started to move backwards.

'Someone will probably let us know,' Jake commented. 'We've more than half an hour of the journey left, so something will have to be done.'

At length, a man in uniform made his way down the aisle,

stopping to speak to every passenger.

When he reached Jake and Nicholas, he explained. 'Intercom's broken. There's a problem on the line. Not sure yet what it is.' He looked evasive, and hurried along to speak to the man a few seats down on the other side of the coach.

'He does know what it is, but he's not going to say,' Jake observed perceptively.

'What will we have to do?' asked Nicholas.

'Just wait,' replied Jake. 'If the train can't go on, they'll have to get a bus for us.'

There was no further news for quite a while, and Jake and Nicholas spent their time trying to devise a simple crossword on a piece of paper that Jake produced from his pocket. Nicholas was so engrossed that he did not see the uniformed man approaching again.

'A coach will be here in about ten minutes,' the man announced as he quickly passed by.

'No use asking him what's happened,' Jake muttered.

'Do you think it's something bad?' Nicholas whispered.

'Can't tell. Don't let's worry about it.'

It was more than half an hour before the coach arrived, and Nicholas could see by the number plate that it was many years old. All the passengers were loaded in, and the driver set off.

By the time they arrived at the station, they were more than an hour overdue.

Their father was waiting for them. As they approached, they could both see him, pacing up and down in an agitated way.

'Thank goodness you're both all right,' he said, hugging Nicholas, and then holding Jake's hand for far longer than a handshake. 'I thought I'd come and meet you, and a message came from the loudspeakers that there had been an accident. I tried to get more information, but no one knew anything. I've been very worried.'

'We've been fine,' Nicholas assured him.

'We weren't given any information either,' said Jake. 'I'd guess it was something that involved the police.'

Nicholas had not thought of this. He hoped that no one had been hurt.

'The car's this way.' Colin pointed in the direction of the station approach.

At Jake's request, Colin phoned John and said that Jake would be along soon.

'Wish I could come too,' said Nicholas. He felt quite dejected. Not only was he losing the constant contact he had had with Jake over the weekend, but also he was desperate to talk to his uncle about everything that had happened. However, that conversation would have to wait until tomorrow, and by then Jake would be gone.

Colin dropped Jake off at John's, and Jake lingered at the gate and waved to Nicholas as Colin drove away. He would have liked to spend more time with his brother, but accepted it was important that Nicholas' schoolwork was not disrupted.

Jake was not surprised to find John's door locked. He banged on it loudly, and John soon appeared.

John greeted him warmly. 'Come in, come in. It was a nice surprise for me when Colin phoned.'

'Nick's got more news for you,' Jake told him. 'I expect he'll be round to see you tomorrow.'

'I was about to get ready for bed,' said John, 'but I'd rather sit up for a while with you.'

Jake was about to brush this approach on one side by telling his uncle not to bother, but he changed his mind, and instead asked, 'Can I talk something over with you?'

John was astonished, but managed to conceal his reaction, and replied calmly, 'Let's sit down. Help yourself if you want anything from the kitchen.'

He went and sat in his armchair, while Jake filled a glass of water for himself and took a banana from the worktop before joining his uncle.

When Jake was settled, John asked, 'What's it about, Jake?' He had wondered if he should merely wait quietly, but had decided against it.

'I want to spend more time around here,' said Jake bluntly.

'You mean, living here, with me?'

'Not exactly.'

John could see that he was struggling with something, and he decided to give him time.

'I want to see more of you and the others.'

This had clearly been very difficult for him to say, and his uncle could see beads of sweat had formed on his forehead.

'But I don't know how to do it.' Here Jake collapsed back into his chair. He inhaled slowly, and then continued. 'I'm away nearly all the time.'

'Yes, that's the way it's been.' John spoke in level tones. He did not want to let his voice show any inflection that Jake might perceive as a direction or a criticism. 'I'm sure we can work out how to change it,' he added carefully.

'I know I can stay here with you,' said Jake, but he sounded distracted.

John was sympathetic. 'It's a big change you're planning.'

Jake looked at him gratefully.

John went on. 'The main thing to bear in mind is that we can work out any changes quite slowly. I can speak for the others as well as myself when I say that we would all like to see more of you if you feel it's feasible.'

'It's hard having more visits,' Jake said in strangled tones.

John thought very carefully, before saying, 'Do you mean that when you see more of us you don't want to go away again?'

Jake opened his mouth, but no sound came out. He cleared his throat. Then he said simply, 'Yes.' He felt deeply grateful that his uncle had grasped this central part of his difficulty.

'So you would like to see everyone more often, but have less coming and going?'

'That's right.'

'But you might not want to see everyone too often yet?'

'That's it.' Again Jake struggled visibly.

John waited patiently.

'I've got my lockup,' Jake burst out.

John could see that he looked exhausted, but he seemed determined to carry on with the discussion.

'I've got money,' Jake stated. 'And I can easily get work.'

His uncle now began to understand what Jake was getting at. He wanted to come home, but could not yet face everything that it would entail. He wanted to be there, but he needed time. He needed time to grow into a situation that was entirely new to him.

'I'll help in any way I can,' John offered.

'Tell them,' said Jake.

This request put John in a quandary. He was more than willing to do anything he could to help Jake, but he was not sure that talking to the rest of the family on his behalf was the best way forward.

'We've had a good talk tonight, Jake. Why don't we sleep on it, and see what tomorrow brings?' he suggested.   'We can talk again in the morning.'

Although he said nothing, Jake was obviously satisfied with this plan, and he began to get his things ready for the night.

Chapter Twenty-five

The day at school seemed to drag interminably. Nicholas looked at the clock at least five times in every lesson. He tried hard to appear as if he were engaging in the course work, but it was a struggle. All the time, in the forefront of his mind, he was longing to be with his uncle, and Jake.

At the lunch break, Rab and Louis searched him out to ask him how his weekend had gone.

'It was great,' Nicholas managed to say.

'Why are you looking so miserable then?' asked Louis.

Nicholas wanted to tell his friends at least something about his time away with Jake, but it just didn't seem possible.

'What's the matter?' asked Rab.

'Got a lot on my mind,' said Nicholas evasively.

'You can tell us,' Louis encouraged.

'Tomorrow,' Nicholas replied firmly. He needed time to sift through everything. So much of it was private, but there must be things he could confide.

'Okay,' said Rab cheerfully. 'Same time, same place?'

'It's a deal,' Nicholas replied, smiling.

When at last the school day was finished, and Nicholas arrived at his uncle's gate, he dashed up the drive and burst into the house shouting, 'Is he still here?'

His uncle met him in the hallway. 'No,' he said.

Nicholas felt a sinking sensation in the pit of his stomach. He had feared that Jake would have left, but all day he had told himself that there was a chance he might still be here. Then Nicholas could see that his uncle was smiling, and he felt confused.

'Why are you smiling, when Jake's gone,' he snapped angrily.

'Something's changing,' John explained. 'Come and sit down. There's not much to tell yet, but I promise that things are on the move.'

Something inside Nicholas told him that his uncle knew more than he was prepared to say at the moment, but as his angry feelings began to subside, he felt he could go along with this. Sitting in the spare armchair that he always considered to be his, he felt more confident.

'I'm sorry I was rude,' he apologised.

'Don't worry,' his uncle reassured him. 'And you've had an important time this weekend. We've got a lot to cover.'

'Tell me about Jake first,' Nicholas urged. 'What did he say? Where is he?'

'Let me get a word in,' his uncle chided. 'There's something I can tell you, but I'd rather you didn't tell your mum and dad, because it'll be better if Jake tells them himself.'

'Okay.' Nicholas could see that he was being given a proper place in whatever was happening, and he felt calmer.

'He wants to spend more time with us all,' John explained, 'but he needs to work out what to do.'

'It's obvious. All he has to do is come home,' stated Nicholas flatly. All his calm had evaporated, and he felt only a surge of impatience. He wanted his brother, and he wanted him now.

'Nicholas, you have been very mature throughout all of this,' said his uncle, 'and I can perfectly understand why you want everything to be sorted out quickly. I'm only sorry that you're going to have to wait longer.'

'I don't want to have to wait any more,' said Nicholas miserably.

'After being with Jake for a whole weekend, I'm not at all surprised,' John sympathised.

'Uncle John, when will I see him again?' asked Nicholas bleakly.

'I don't know.'

'You do!' said Nicholas accusingly.

'I promise I'd tell you if I did.'

Nicholas scrutinised his uncle's face. In his heart, he knew what he had said was true, but he wanted to find a clue that proved his uncle was not being honest. Then he would be able to get the information out of him somehow.

John hated seeing Nicholas in such distress, and he wished he had something to say that would cut it short. Yet at the same time he knew that what was happening was crucially important. Nicholas needed to show these feelings. They were a normal reaction to what he had been through ever since he and Jake started to get to know each other, and even before then. After all, he had seen Jake on a number of occasions through his young life, and he had always known that he was his brother. He must have known people at school who had brothers, and who saw them every day. He must have had to pretend to himself, and to his parents, that it did not matter to him whether Jake was there or not, when underneath, it mattered terribly.

'Didn't he say *anything* about what he was going to do?'

'No, but it was obvious that he was thinking about it a lot.'

'I'm thinking about it *all the time*,' said Nicholas emphatically. 'It all hurts, and I can't concentrate at school.'

'That's to be expected,' replied his uncle gently. 'Look, Nicholas. Jake was quite changed when he and I spoke yesterday evening, but he has to make decisions about many things before he can make any permanent changes to how he lives his life.'

'Permanent changes?' asked Nicholas. 'Why didn't you say that before? I thought you were telling me that Jake was going to visit us more often, so I wanted to know when the next visit was going to be. I *had* to know. But now, you're talking about something different.'

'I'm sorry I wasn't clear enough,' said his uncle. 'It's so important that Jake moves into this himself, without my doing things behind the scenes. But I wanted to say something to you today because I had some idea about how you must be feeling.'

'I want to force you to tell me every word he said,' Nicholas admitted, 'but at the same time I want to be grown up, and trust that everything will be okay in the end.'

'Nicholas, I have no doubt that this will end up okay, but I don't know how long it's going to take. It won't be days, and it won't be weeks. But if you look back in six months' time, you'll be able to see how far you've all progressed.'

Nicholas let out a moan. 'I need to know that it won't be long before I see him again.'

'What you really need is to feel that he's properly in your family, and I don't think that'll be long in coming,' said his uncle wisely. 'Once you're sure of that, his being away for a week or so won't affect you as much. You'd miss him, but it wouldn't hurt any more.'

Although he did not want to admit it, Nicholas was taking in everything his uncle was saying, and he knew that most of it made sense.

'When will Mum and Dad know?' he asked.

'Very soon, I should think.'

'I *hate* having any secrets about Jake. It's okay about the pledge, but it's not okay about Jake.'

'I know. I wondered if it would be best not to tell you about Jake.'

'You had to. And if you hadn't, I would have known there was something you weren't telling me, and I might have guessed wrong.'

Here, Nicholas fell silent for a while. His uncle did not disturb him. He knew that Nicholas needed time to absorb what they had discussed, and become used to his feelings about it.

Suddenly, Nicholas asked, 'Did he tell you anything about what happened in the churchyard?'

'Nothing.'

'Good!'

Nicholas was very glad that his uncle knew nothing of this yet, and he started to feel a bit better, but then he realised that what he really wanted was that Jake was there with them, and that they talked about it together. He leaned forward in his chair, and put his head in his hands.

'What is it, Nicholas?' asked his uncle. 'Would you prefer not to tell me until Jake's with us?'

Nicholas nodded miserably. Then he said, 'But I want you to know now.'

'Why don't you tell me some of it, but save some up until Jake's here again,' John suggested.

Nicholas cheered up at this idea. 'He took some photographs. We'll see those when he comes again. But I can explain what happened.' He went on to tell John how they had found the churchyard, and exactly what had happened there when he had tried to put the measurer on top of the stone for Jake to take another photograph.

'That's astounding!' exclaimed his uncle. 'What on earth can be going on?'

'Don't you remember, Uncle John, that we worked out in this room that the measurer probably wasn't supposed to be on top of our model of the key gravestone?'

'Yes, I remember, but how could the measurer have moved away from you like it did?'

'I was very cold,' said Nicholas, 'so at first I thought it had slipped out of my hand because I couldn't move my fingers properly.'

'But you soon worked out that that wasn't the cause.'

'Do you think our friend might have been there?' asked Nicholas uncertainly.

'It's the only explanation I can think of.'

'Uncle John, I wish you'd been there.'

'I wanted to be with you, Nicholas. Now I'm old, I can't travel, but I'm still with you – in a special kind of way.'

At this, all the misery seemed to drain out of Nicholas' body, and he knew that when he had been away, he had missed his uncle almost as much as he was missing Jake now.

John's voice broke into his thoughts. 'Nicholas, it's sometimes difficult for us both when we have to wait.'

'Especially when it's something to do with the pledge and the fifth key,' said Nicholas, looking across at his uncle meaningfully. And now he felt that he was a man again.

'You achieved a lot in a short time,' John observed.

This made Nicholas feel good, but then he said, 'I don't have any more clues about the fifth key, though.'

'No need to worry about that.' John became thoughtful, and then added, 'But in any case, I'm not sure I agree.'

Nicholas was puzzled. He had found no reference to the fifth key while he was away. He supposed it would have been surprising if he had. Yet finding some small thing that could have been a possible clue would have left him with a feeling of accomplishment. He waited to see if his uncle would say anything else.

John leaned forward in his chair, as if to avoid being overheard, and instinctively, Nicholas looked behind himself to check if anyone were there. Silly, he thought. We're the only ones in this house.

His uncle began. 'I think there's something in the relationship between you and Jake that has to do with the fifth key.'

'How can that be?'

'I'm not sure, but there are two things I've been thinking about.'

Nicholas leaned forward in his chair until their faces were only about a foot apart.

'What?' he asked.

'Something drew Jake back into our lives.'

'But when he came at first this time...' Here Nicholas' voice trailed off. 'Of course, he sent *me* a card.'

'So it was different from the beginning,' John stated. 'I've wondered if the whole thing's gone differently because you aren't a boy any more, but I don't feel convinced.'

'It might have helped,' said Nicholas eagerly. He realised he wanted that his being more like a man had made the difference, but at the same time, he could not help feeling drawn to what his uncle was suggesting. 'And maybe once I was thirteen it was different for him.'

'That's quite a possibility,' John acknowledged. 'But how would he know the significance of that when he never let me close enough to tell him about the pledge?'

'If something drew him back, it doesn't mean that the way we all related to him wasn't important,' Nicholas said very firmly.

'It was crucial,' his uncle agreed. 'Otherwise, even if he'd felt guided back to us, he wouldn't have stayed around. And, Nicholas, the maturity in the way you've behaved towards him has been central.'

Tears sprang into Nicholas' eyes. He had tried so hard... so very hard. And there had been times when he had felt alone with it all. He had known that his parents had been struggling with their own feelings about Jake, and he only knew a little of what that was about. He had felt that he had to act from his own resources, and could not share his uncertainties with them. Before today, he had not even been able to share with his uncle enough of how he had really felt about Jake. It was a profound relief to him that all his efforts had been recognised. His dad had witnessed some of it, and had made positive comments, but Nicholas had needed someone to understand it all.

'I've got to tell you something else,' he choked out.

'What is it?' asked John, with compassion in his voice.

'It isn't about Jake,' said Nicholas. 'It's... about you.'

'Go on.'

'Mum and Dad used to talk worriedly about the state of your house, but I always had to pretend it didn't matter. I pretended so hard, that I believed it didn't matter. But underneath, I was worried about you and your house, and I worried that something might fall down on you, or something horrible like that.' Tears poured down his cheeks.

'Nicholas, I'm terribly sorry,' said his uncle. 'I was being an old ostrich.'

At this description, Nicholas giggled, although this did little to stem the flow of his tears.

John went on. 'I had the stupid idea in my mind that I was managing. I even thought that because I'd learned to ignore the problems, no one else would notice. On the occasions when your dad tried to speak to me, I would find a way of changing the subject, or fobbing him off. Nicholas, you've every right to be angry with me about it. My being an ostrich has been a stress on you, and that has been very wrong.'

Nicholas took out his handkerchief, wiped his face, and blew his nose loudly. Then he said, 'Don't worry, I'll forgive you.' He started to laugh.

'Thanks for being like this, Nicholas, but why are you laughing?' asked John, bemused.

'Why did we all go on pretending for years? You were pretending about your house, and I was pretending with you. Mum and Dad pretended about Jake, and I copied them.'

'But that's what children do,' his uncle explained. 'At first, it's the only way you can learn about life – by copying the people who are looking after you.'

'Well, from now on, I'll work out what's worth copying and what isn't,' Nicholas declared.

'You've already made a very good start,' his uncle pointed out. 'You were pretty determined about me and my house. Without that, I probably would have resisted for so long that I would have ended up in a far worse position than I am now. And your way of relating to Jake gave him something that he could see was different. Before that, he was stuck in all the feelings and memories he had as a child. There's no doubt that while he was living away he was developing his life in all kinds of adult ways, but at home, he became like a young child again.'

Nicholas broke in. 'Uncle John, the camping trip was great! And Jake said we could go again some time.'

'That's excellent news. That will go a long way to changing the fifth key.'

Nicholas was startled. 'How?'

'Supposing we're right about Todd and the merchant being cousins who were as close as brothers... And supposing we're right about something going badly wrong between them...'

Nicholas took up his uncle's train of thought. 'Jake and I are brothers. It all started off wrong, but now we're together, and we're going to be closer than a lot of brothers are.'

John noticed that Nicholas had said he and Jake were together. He was glad that Nicholas believed this now, because whether Jake was here or not, it was true. Judiciously, he made no comment. Instead, he said, 'So it's the right context. And I'm sure things happened on your trip that will help us with the fifth key.'

Nicholas listed them. 'Jake and I getting closer... What happened in the churchyard... What else?'

'I'm pretty sure that you were on to something when you phoned me. And if the merchant was capable of removing an entry from a register, he was capable of doing much worse things.'

Nicholas realised that he was holding his breath. He took a gulp of air, and said, 'Go on.'

'The merchant must have lived on that coast for a long time, and he must have known it like the back of his hand. He knew about the treacherous rocks, and he must have known of ships that had foundered there. In fact, he might have benefited from previous wrecks, and was looking forward to more. Todd was a seafaring man, but maybe he hadn't sailed along that coast before, and had taken it on trust from his cousin that it would be okay. His cousin could have lured him by letting him know about the safe harbour, and the welcome that would await him.'

'This sounds really horrible,' said Nicholas.

'Maybe he even told Todd to approach from the wrong direction. You've been there now, and you've seen the kind of rocks that must have been there at the time. It wouldn't take much bad weather for such a ship to have no chance at all. And the merchant would have known this.'

'But what do you think happened to the treasure?' asked Nicholas.

'As you know, I had worked out a long time ago that it couldn't be moved over land. Maybe the merchant had a number of small boats, manned by people who knew how to navigate along that section of coast, and how to pick the right weather and tides.'

'And half the treasure really belonged to Todd,' said Nicholas. 'So it should have been handed down to us.'

'I think it has been,' his uncle replied quietly.

Nicholas was perplexed. He knew that they had no gold, silver and jewels. He knew that his uncle would not have kept such things hidden from him, pretending that they did not exist.

'The story was handed down to us,' said John.

'But that's not treasure,' Nicholas protested, puzzled.

'The treasure lies within it.'

Nicholas could not understand what his uncle was getting at. He seemed to be talking in riddles.

John went on. 'Think about it. Todd thought that he and his men would be welcomed into his cousin's home and would live a secure life there. It wasn't so much the treasure itself that they had wanted. It was what it would obtain for them. Those men had probably never had anything good in their lives before, and now there was the promise of being a part of a stable community. Such an offer was beyond price. Oh yes, there would be those among them who would plan to steal a cut of the booty. But where would it take them? It wouldn't be much when compared with a life of safety, where everything was provided in return for some relatively light labour? Their mates would already have an eye on such rogues, and wouldn't stand for any nonsense. Todd himself probably had a bit of a history – black sheep of the family kind of thing.'

'Do you really think the men could have believed things could be different?'

'Todd himself knew what life could be. Although at first he would probably get his crew by promises of riches, he had plenty of time to work on them during the passage. The men would have loaded the treasure on board, so they would have seen it.'

'What if the ship had made it to the merchant's harbour?'

'Then more direct murder would have taken place,' said John bluntly. 'Nicholas, I think Todd knows we're able to understand what really happened, and he's giving us nudges of help along the way. And once he's satisfied that we know, we're unlikely to feel him around again.'

'Having my brother is more important to me than anything in the world,' said Nicholas emphatically.

'And that's how it should be,' his uncle replied. 'You're both honest men, who can do a hard day's work.'

'Jake can teach me lots more,' said Nicholas happily.

'And you're teaching him things too,' John pointed out. 'You're teaching him things that he's never been able to manage on his own. And when you're feeling impatient, just remember how patient he was with you when you were learning how to fix tiles.'

Nicholas felt embarrassed, and his face reddened. 'Oh, Uncle John, I hadn't thought about it like that. I'll try to remember, I promise.'

'I know it's hard when it's someone you've waited for all your life, but more waiting isn't wasted time. It will bring you something very special.'

'I want to help Jake, and I want to help Todd,' said Nicholas emphatically.

'You and Jake are helping each other,' his uncle reminded him.

'And we're trying to help Todd,' Nicholas added.

'Nicholas, we've come a long way,' said John. 'When I first told you the story of Todd, what was uppermost in my mind was the fear that you would back away from me. After that, I wasn't sure whether or not you'd be mature enough for the pledge.'

'All that seems ages ago now,' Nicholas reflected.

'And it was only a beginning. Once you began to show your competence as a young man, we began to grapple with question after question that faced us in our quest to make sense of the list, the measurer and the fifth key. Our understanding of the list is far ahead of where I had been with it, we have some ideas about the measurer that we know are right, and we now have clues about the fifth key.'

'And Todd is around,' said Nicholas. 'If he isn't, there's something else. I feel so cold when one of those times comes.'

'And twice, it's seemed that you've answered questions.'

'But we both think it was Todd. Uncle John, we've got to help him.'

'If we're going to be able to help Todd, we've got to be able to work out enough of what happened to him. I'm sure we've pieced together quite a bit of it, but there's more.'

'I think we've got to make more sense of the measurer.'

'I agree with you there. And while doing that I think we'll discover how it's related to the fifth key – whatever that is. I would settle for it being the final clue in the resolution of something that's beyond price, but I can't discount the possibility that there is an actual key, that leads to treasure of financial value.'

'It might be both,' Nicholas suggested suddenly.

John stared across at Nicholas. 'It's obvious when you say it,' he acknowledged, 'but until you did, I'd assumed it had to be one or the other. Let's think again about Todd's share of the treasure. It's either still at the bottom of the sea, or the merchant salvaged it. If the merchant got it, he had no intention of giving Todd's share to any of his descendants. The destruction of the birth record of Todd's son would be an obvious safeguard. When he grew up, even if he knew his ancestry, how could he prove it? Born out of wedlock was bad enough, but his status would be even worse than that. He would have no rights at all.'

'Uncle John, I wonder what his name was,' said Nicholas.

'I'd like to know that too,' John replied.

Nicholas shut his eyes, and screwed up his face in intense concentration. 'I can't think how we're going to work it out,' he said sadly. 'Oh, I know! Why don't we choose a name for him?'

'That's a very good idea. You can choose.'

'But I might choose a name that didn't exist,' said Nicholas worriedly. 'Can you give me some ideas?'

'There's William, John, Robert, Henry...'

'No, none of those. Tell me some more.'

'Let me see. Peter, Arthur...'

'Arthur! Let's have that one,' said Nicholas excitedly. 'That would be great!' He shivered. 'Oh no, here it comes again.'

'Go and get one of my jumpers,' John instructed. 'Then get my coat.'

Nicholas' teeth were already chattering. He rushed to his uncle's room. When he returned, he was wearing a thick winter sweater, and was carrying the coat.

'Put it on straight away,' his uncle encouraged.

Nicholas followed John's advice, and although he was not particularly warmer, he felt a little better.

'I want to try again with the measurer,' he announced.

'Don't you want to wait until you've recovered a bit?' asked his uncle uncertainly.

'I'll manage okay. I'm really glad I had it with me when I was away with Jake.'

'I think that what happened at the patterned stone is very significant.'

'It's a pity we don't have the photographs of it yet,' said Nicholas slowly.

John nodded. 'I'll look forward to seeing them. I'm very interested in that pattern.'

'You won't have to wait long,' Nicholas assured him confidently.

John noticed that Nicholas' agitation about Jake's absence had gone completely.

'Bring our key stone round,' John directed as he stood up to get the measurer out of the box. 'And the torch is in its usual place under my bed.'

They were soon experimenting once more.

'I'm going to place the measurer as an extension to the middle leg of the stone,' said John, 'and this time, I want you to point the four

204

horizontal pins to make extensions to the four most prominent radiating lines on the pattern.'

Nicholas did this. Then he asked, 'What shall we do with the three short pins?'

'I'm thinking,' John replied.

Nicholas waited quietly. He wondered again about the sun and moon signs on the metal plate, wishing that he could work out exactly what they meant. There was no doubt that a beam of light was part of the puzzle, but beyond that they had not determined how to proceed.

'I'm going to shine the torch from the back – like the rising sun,' he said.

'I think we need a bigger space,' his uncle observed. 'Give me a hand to move the table.'

Nicholas willingly took most of the weight of the table. Then he moved the dining chairs, and hung his uncle's coat on the back of one of them.

'I don't think I need this now,' he stated. 'But I'll keep your jumper on.'

He repositioned the key stone and the measurer in the middle of the room.

'Uncle John,' he said suddenly, 'I'm pretty sure the pattern on the stone that Jake and I saw had three grooves in it.'

'You mean there were three deeper cuts in the pattern?'

Nicholas nodded. 'Yes, they were much deeper than the other carving.' He found a notebook and a pencil, and tried to make a sketch to indicate where they were.

'Fascinating,' said John as he studied what Nicholas had drawn. 'This is most unusual. I have never seen such deep grooves on any decorative stone carving. I'm very tempted to think that there's a connection between the short pins and these grooves. You've always been doubtful about holding these pins upwards, and I think that you were right.'

Nicholas stood up, saying, 'I'm going to shine the torch.' He moved behind their stone, and positioned the torch about a metre behind it. Then he stood back to look at the effect. To his astonishment, on the blank wall beyond was the faint silhouette of a figure.

'Uncle John! Look!' he exclaimed, pointing.

But his uncle needed no directions. He was already staring at it. And for that moment in time, the three were as a tableau.

205

Then the spectre faded, and Nicholas and his uncle were left staring at the blank wall in front of them.

'Do you think that was Todd?' whispered Nicholas.

John sat down heavily in his armchair. 'I just don't know what to say,' he replied.

Nicholas looked at him uncertainly, hoping for some kind of guidance, but his uncle seemed unable to offer any direction at all.

'It's really warm in here now,' said Nicholas, taking the jumper off.

At length, his uncle spoke. 'Nicholas, I feel terribly tired. Would you mind if we leave all this for today?'

Nicholas looked at him worriedly. 'Do you feel ill, Uncle John?'

'No, just extremely tired.'

'Shall I get you something to eat?'

'I don't think I could swallow anything at the moment. Will you stay and give me a hand to get into bed?'

Nicholas was now feeling extremely worried, and he said, 'I'm going to phone Mum and Dad.'

'What for?'

'You might need extra help.'

Without waiting for his uncle to agree, he picked up the phone and was soon speaking to his father.

'Could you come up?' he asked urgently.

Colin agreed immediately, asking no questions.

'He's coming,' Nicholas told his uncle.

John was about to protest, but he thought better of it, and waited for Colin to appear.

Minutes later, Colin was in the room with them.

'Want a hand with something?' he asked lightly.

'Not especially,' replied John calmly, 'but it's good to see you. Would you like to get us all a hot drink?'

'I'll get it,' said Nicholas quickly, and he darted towards the kitchen. He wanted his father and Uncle John to have some time alone.

When he came back into the room, carrying a tray with three steaming mugs on it, his father said, 'I'm going to stay here tonight, Nick.'

'I'll be fine, Colin,' John protested. 'I've just done a bit too much today. That's all.'

'Well, *I* won't be fine if I'm lying in bed at home worrying about you,' Colin insisted. He turned to Nicholas. 'Your mum already knows I might stay overnight, so she won't be surprised when you arrive home without me.'

The next fifteen minutes were spent finishing their drinks, and talking about their plans to replace the path leading up to John's front door.

'I'll see you after school,' Nicholas promised his uncle as he left.

Although he felt that his uncle's exhaustion was solely a consequence of Todd's appearance, he felt uneasy, and he was very glad that his father was in charge for the night.

Chapter Twenty-six

'But, Nick, you promised you would talk to us today,' said Rab. He sounded annoyed.

'I'm sorry,' replied Nicholas. 'There's a lot going on.'

'Look,' said Louis reasonably, 'we want to know how you got on at the weekend.' He took a deep breath and added, 'And we're worried about you.'

At this, Nicholas began to think about his friends' concern for him.

Louis continued. 'There have been times when you've seemed completely not there.'

'Glazed over,' said Rab .

'I didn't realise,' Nicholas replied. 'I know I've had a lot on my mind, but I didn't know I was coming across as being odd.'

Now that Nicholas was beginning to see why they were concerned, Rab and Louis relaxed a little.

'You don't *have* to tell us anything,' said Louis.

'But we're interested,' Rab added.

'Of course you are,' Nicholas acknowledged. 'I'm interested in what you're both doing too.'

'You haven't been asking anything recently,' Rab pointed out.

'Yes, that's another thing,' said Louis. 'You always used to be the first one to keep in touch with what was going on for us, but now it's as if you've nearly forgotten that we exist.'

'We're not saying that you've got to take a huge interest in what we're doing,' Rab explained. 'We're just trying to let you see how you've changed.'

'I can see it now you're pointing it out,' agreed Nicholas.

'I don't know how I'd be if I had a brother who suddenly became a brother after never being one before,' Louis reflected.

'I'd be pretty freaked out,' Rab admitted.

'I'm not freaked out,' said Nicholas. 'Not at all. Sometimes I feel as if I've always been close to him, even though it's only happened in the last few months. We had an amazing weekend. He let me put the tent up, and we went for some good walks. The people who own the campsite said we could go back any time.'

Rab looked at Louis and smiled. 'Nick's not gone mad after all, so we can stop stressing about him.'

Nicholas pushed Rab playfully, and then dashed off to get changed for games, with Rab and Louis in hot pursuit. He was grateful to his friends for persisting. He was sorry that they had been worried. He remembered how he had felt when Rab could not get back from his holiday. He had felt very worried then, and it had only been for a few days. He made a mental note to try to remember to talk to them again about their plan for working in Uncle John's garden.

After school, Nicholas found his uncle sitting on a chair outside in the afternoon sun. He was wearing a large straw hat that was positioned at a jaunty angle, and he had a newspaper spread across his lap.

'I keep dozing off,' he said as Nicholas came up the path. 'What time is it?'

'Coming-home-from-school time,' Nicholas replied, laughing. 'How are you?'

'When we ate porridge together this morning, your dad declared me fit and well. I'm fine – just tired. But he said he'd call in this evening.'

'I don't think we should do anything else about the fifth key for a while,' Nicholas began.

John sat bolt upright, and his hat fell to the ground. 'Nonsense!' he exclaimed. 'We can't possibly let that subject drift. It's far too important.'

Nicholas smiled, and picked up the hat. He put it back on his uncle's head, and tried to mimic a parental voice, saying, 'Maybe you'll agree that we'll have to be careful, and take it slowly.'

'Point taken.' John became serious. 'Nicholas, I want to talk to you about what happened. Let's go inside.'

In the cool of the living room, they settled themselves in the armchairs.

'That was a big thing,' John began.

'Very big,' Nicholas agreed.

'I've heard some stories about ghostly presences that I wouldn't like to repeat,' said John cautiously.

'But ours is a helper,' Nicholas pointed out.

'He might be, but I don't feel competent enough to take charge.'

Nicholas was surprised. 'You don't have to. The three of us

seem to be doing it together.'

'Millie used to say she saw things,' John informed him.

Nicholas was stunned by this piece of information. So his grandmother, his dad's mother, used to see... But what did she see?

'What did she see?' he asked, staring at his uncle accusingly.

'We don't really know, because no one else saw them,' John blundered. He hated this situation. Here he was, yet again having to tell Nicholas something new, and entirely out of the ordinary, about one of his direct relatives.

'I can't believe that you didn't tell me before,' said Nicholas.

'All we knew was that she said she saw things,' John repeated. 'No one really knew if she did or not. I didn't want to say anything about it before, because it doesn't help us. But I've been thinking about it since yesterday evening, and I'm sure it's why I felt so worn out. As you know, I wished I could have helped Millie. It was all very sad.'

'At least I know now why you wouldn't talk about ghosts before,' said Nicholas perceptively. 'Do Mum and Dad know?'

'They know what she said, but they never believed her. They assumed it was part of her illness.'

'Well, Todd isn't a ghost, he's a helper,' Nicholas insisted. 'And I think he came last night to let us know we're getting closer.'

'That's what I think too,' said John.

'I wish we knew more about Arthur,' Nicholas reflected.

'If I'd been in his shoes, I wouldn't have wanted to live anywhere near the merchant,' said John emphatically. He shuddered. 'Nasty piece of work.'

'What about the others?'

'You mean the shepherd and his daughter? Mm... Once she realised there was danger from the merchant, Abigail would have had to go away with Arthur. I'd like to think she had relatives who were willing to give her shelter until Arthur was old enough to support himself. In those days, that could have been when he was younger than you are now.'

Nicholas said nothing as he digested this information.

His uncle continued. 'For Arthur to have survived, he would have had to be very resourceful.'

'Like Jake.'

'Even more so.'

'He was younger than I am, but he had to be more resourceful than Jake...' Nicholas murmured. The impact of this realisation upon him was huge. It was one thing learning about past times in history lessons, but it was quite another thinking about Arthur's struggles.

'They were harsh times,' said John solemnly.

'I think we'll stick with Todd's story for now,' Nicholas decided.

'That would be wise,' his uncle replied. 'We're to work out what the fifth key is about, and Arthur wouldn't have been around to see.'

'But someone had to hand the story on,' Nicholas pointed out. 'Todd couldn't, because he was dead.'

'That's right. It needed someone who'd witnessed everything.'

'It must have been the shepherd,' said Nicholas. 'It had to be.'

'He'd have had to stay alive long enough to look for his grandson.'

'Arthur could have made a secret visit to see him.'

'That's a possibility.' John thought quietly about this, and then said suddenly, 'Nicholas, I want us to talk about that line of writing we used to think was a code.'

Nicholas laughed. 'Whoever wrote it was very clever.'

'Yes, it fooled me for a very long time. I'm glad you spoke to Jake about it, because without that, we would have been unlikely to see what it was.'

'We still don't know exactly.'

'That's why I want to talk about it again now,' John replied. 'Can you get the copy out of the chest?'

Soon they had unrolled it on the table, and were examining it once more.

'As we worked out before, the only significant things here – the key-stone shaped symbols – are at the fifth and eighth positions,' John began.

'Out of a total of seventeen,' Nicholas added.

'Surely that means two deaths,' said John. Then he continued with sudden conviction, 'But it could be much more complicated than that.'

Nicholas looked at his uncle, and waited.

'The position of the first one is obviously to do with Todd's death and the fifth key. We thought that five and eight adding up to thirteen was enough explanation for the second one, but now I'm not so sure.'

Nicholas' head began to swim, and he felt unsteady. Something was coming into his mind, but it seemed to be only a jumbled chain of unrelated words. 'Paces...' he mumbled.

His uncle looked at him sharply. He realised straight away that something was amiss, and he said as calmly as he could, 'Yes, I suppose it could be eight paces.'

'Measurer and Todd's stone go together… with other stone.'

By this time, Nicholas was shivering yet again, and John could see that his lips were blue with cold. Although the room was comfortably warm for him, he could see that this did nothing to help Nicholas. He went as quickly as he could to the hall, and returned carrying his coat, which he hung round Nicholas' shoulders, and made him sit down in the armchair that was familiar to him.

'I'm going to put that code away now, Nicholas,' he said firmly. 'We've done enough for today.' Then, instead of rolling it up and putting it back in the chest, he screwed it up, flung it into the empty grate, and reached for the matches, saying, 'In fact, I don't think we need this any more.'

Nicholas watched the flames licking round the edges of the roll, and he started to feel warm again.

John studied his face, and could see that his lips were no longer blue, and his eyes looked clear again.

'Nicholas, I think it could be time to get rid of the list as well,' John said determinedly.

Nicholas did not deter him. 'Can I do it?' he asked.

Silently, his uncle took it out of the box, and handed it to him.

Nicholas tore it into strips and threw it into the fire. Then he took off his uncle's coat.

'That's better,' he announced. 'Uncle John, I felt even worse that time. It was terrible.'

'I could see that,' his uncle replied with considerable feeling. Even though Nicholas now appeared to be all right, he was still all too aware of how worried he had been about him only minutes earlier.

'I'm hungry!' Nicholas announced suddenly. 'Really, really hungry. What have you got to eat, Uncle John?'

His uncle smiled at him. 'Why not go and explore the kitchen?'

Nicholas disappeared, but was soon back, carrying a plate covered in sandwiches.

'You can have some,' he said expansively.

John shook his head. 'Not at the moment, thanks.' He watched as Nicholas worked his way with gusto through his food.

'That's better,' Nicholas said after he had finished the last crumbs. 'I felt as if I hadn't had anything to eat for about a week.'

John smiled. 'I like to watch you enjoying your food. Why not get some more?'

Nicholas patted his stomach. 'No, thanks. I'm full up. Uncle John, I've got something I want to ask you.'

'Go ahead,' John encouraged.

'Do you think we've done enough for Todd? All I really want to do now is get on with my life with Jake.'

John was not surprised to hear this. He had certainly expected that after the recent events, his nephew might have wanted to take a break from their researches.

'What do you think, Uncle John?' Nicholas repeated.

'For most of my life, I've carried Todd's secret alone. You've let me share it with you, and since we've been working on it together, it's felt as if a huge burden has shifted for me. I'd believed that it was up to me to do whatever had to be done.'

'And since you told me about it, I've thought it was up to us together,' Nicholas added.

His uncle nodded, and then continued. 'I realise now that I'd assumed that finding some kind of key that would lead us to hidden treasure was a big part of what we had to do. But now, I'm not so sure.'

'Do you think we might have done enough?' Nicholas needed an answer to his question.

'The truth is that I don't know, and I want time to put some thought into it.'

At first Nicholas felt satisfied with this response. Yet only a moment later, he felt an urgency to say more. 'Can we talk about it now?'

'I'd be happy to do that.'

'I used to think that I had to find hidden treasure, too, but I don't think I want to,' said Nicholas. 'If we found some, it would go to a museum. People who didn't know the story would be looking at it.' He wriggled uncomfortably in his seat. 'That doesn't feel right.'

John considered what Nicholas was saying. 'I see exactly what you mean,' he replied. 'We aren't meant to tell the story, and I think that even if we could, I wouldn't want to.'

Nicholas fell silent for a few minutes, and then said, 'If Todd needs us to find a special key and some treasure, that would be different. I'd probably keep on trying to do it.'

'I think you've put your finger on it,' his uncle affirmed. 'We've got to work out whether or not it's really necessary.'

'I just want to think about what I can have with Jake,' said Nicholas. 'If I have to think about keys and treasure, it gets in the way, because I won't be able to talk to Jake about it. When we went away together, it was all right because he was happy to go wherever I wanted, but I don't want it always to be like that.'

'That trip was crucial,' John asserted. 'So much came from it that helped what we've been doing, and at the same time it cemented the relationship between you and Jake. What you want with Jake from now on will be different.'

'And that's why the fifth key might get in the way. But I don't want to abandon Todd. He's waited a long time for help.'

'A very long time.'

'But I've waited a long time, too,' said Nicholas. 'I've waited all my life for Jake.' Here he stopped. 'Oh, I'm sorry, Uncle John. You've had lots more waiting that I have.'

'Don't worry about that,' his uncle reassured him. 'There was nothing that could be done about much of my waiting, but there's plenty that can be done about yours.'

'We've all done quite a lot about it already,' Nicholas observed.

'Something's just occurred to me,' said John suddenly.

'What?'

'Perhaps Todd will let us know.'

Nicholas liked this idea. 'He might,' he agreed.

'Why don't we leave everything about the fifth key for a while, and see what happens?' John suggested.

'Yes. We can plan your garden instead,' said Nicholas enthusiastically. 'I could bring Rab and Louis round to see you.'

'That's a very good idea,' John replied. 'I'd like to meet them.'

'That's great!' said Nicholas happily. 'I'll tell them tomorrow. Uncle John, we've got plenty to get on with while we're waiting to see who gets in touch first – Todd or Jake.'

Chapter Twenty-seven

At lunch break the following day, Nicholas told Rab and Louis the news.

'Can we come tomorrow?' asked Rab eagerly.

'Good idea,' Louis added.

Nicholas looked uncertain. 'I'll have to ask Uncle John. Friday would probably be best.'

'You're right,' Rab agreed. 'I've got a pile of homework to do.' He looked uncomfortable, and then admitted, 'I've been avoiding it.'

'I'm a bit behind too,' said Louis cheerfully. 'I should be okay for Friday though.'

'Has your uncle got spades and things?' asked Rab.

'I think so,' Nicholas replied. 'But in any case, he'll give us money to buy things we need.'

'I want to start the work as soon as term finishes,' Rab stated decisively. 'I don't have to go away until August. Thank goodness.'

'That suits me,' said Louis. 'I'll soon be fourteen. After that I won't have to stay with Gran again. I'll still visit her though,' he added hurriedly.

When Nicholas called round to see his uncle on the way home, he told him the news.

'Friday will be fine,' said John. 'Tell them I'm looking forward to that. We'll show them round.' He smiled. 'And I'll be able to negotiate terms.'

'What do you mean?' asked Nicholas.

'I'll work out how much an hour to pay them, and what clothing they might need.'

Nicholas looked surprised. 'But we're going to do it for fun.'

'It's real work, Nicholas. If you and your friends weren't willing to do it, I'd have to pay someone to come. Because everything's in such a mess, it's mainly clearing that needs to be done. It will be hard labour from the beginning. If they work well, I'll be able to give them a reference later for any job they apply for.'

Nicholas was impressed. 'I hadn't thought of all that. I'll tell them.'

'That's that fixed then,' said John.

'Uncle John, I'm afraid I can't stay long today, because I've got heaps of homework to do.'

'I'll be fine. It's important that you keep up with your studies.'

'I know,' Nicholas replied. 'Jake said so too.'

He was just walking down the front path, when he turned and ran back into the house.

'Has anything happened today?' he asked meaningfully.

John knew exactly what he was getting at. 'No,' he replied. 'Everything's been quiet. There's nothing to worry about. You concentrate on your homework. I promise I'll let you know if anything comes up.'

On the bus to John's after school on Friday, Rab and Louis found it hard to sit still.

'Stop wriggling about, Rab,' Nicholas said exasperatedly. Rab was sitting on the seat next to him, and his elbow kept digging into him.

'Sorry,' Rab replied. 'I can't wait to see your uncle and his garden.

'I can't wait to get there too,' said Nicholas. He poked Rab playfully. 'Then you won't be doing this to me any more.'

A couple of stops later, the boys left the bus, and Nicholas led the way to his uncle's house. As it came into sight, Nicholas could see John waiting outside on a chair. He pointed him out to the others, and they increased their pace.

'Hello, boys,' John greeted them as they came up the path. 'It's good to meet you. Thanks for coming.'

'Can we look round the garden?' asked Louis eagerly.

'Yes, of course,' John replied.

'I'd like to plant potatoes,' Rab announced confidently.

'That's interesting,' said John. 'Years ago, I used to grow all my own potatoes. I had different varieties – King Edward, Desiree… We can certainly think about putting some in again, if you manage to clear the space. It'll be too late for this year though.'

Nicholas led his friends to the back of the house, and John followed.

'Wow!' exclaimed Rab. 'It's like a jungle.'

'No it's not,' said Louis. 'It's like Sherwood Forest when Robin

Hood was alive.'

'How do you know?' asked Rab loftily.

'I've seen pictures,' replied Louis defensively. 'Anyway, it's thick enough to hide in.'

He proceeded to push his way through some bushes and trailing plants, and soon there was very little of him to be seen.

'Where did you grow the potatoes?' asked Rab.

John pointed. 'There was a large vegetable patch in that area. It's mostly brambles now.'

By now, Louis had disappeared completely.

'Okay, Louis,' called Rab. 'You've made your point. Come on out.'

There was a sound of cracking twigs, and Louis emerged. His arms were scratched, and he had bits of vegetation stuck in his hair. When he saw him, Nicholas could not stop laughing.

John chuckled. 'You're going to need overalls and Wellington boots if you want to go ahead.'

After they had spent more time examining the garden, John invited them in for a drink. They took their mugs, and sat at the front door to talk.

'What do you think now you've seen the place?' asked John.

'I definitely want to come,' Rab pronounced. 'How about you, Louis?'

Louis nodded vigorously. 'Count me in.'

'I'll give you my phone number so your parents can get in touch with me,' said John.

'What for?' asked Rab.

'If I were your parents, I'd want to know where you were,' John replied. 'And I've got to arrange the money for your clothes.'

Louis looked at Rab uncertainly, and Rab returned his gaze. He was not sure what to say.

'Uncle John wants to pay for everything, because if we weren't doing the work, he'd have to pay someone else,' explained Nicholas confidently.

'Oh... yes...' said Rab. Until now, all he had thought about was the challenge of hard work. He had not thought about money at all.

'My idea was to offer a daily rate, with sandwiches thrown in,' John suggested.

'My dad'll phone you,' said Louis hurriedly. He, too, had not thought of this angle on things, and he felt embarrassed.

'You don't have to come if you don't want to,' John reminded him.

'I really, really want to come,' Louis assured him. 'Er... it's just that I don't know about the money.'

'Neither do I,' Rab admitted. 'I haven't worked for money before, and I'm not sure what to do.'

'Don't worry,' replied John. 'I can sort it out when your parents get in touch. And by the way, let them know they're welcome to come and see what the job involves.'

Rab and Louis were comfortable with this arrangement, and they went to have another look at the garden.

'Bows and arrows,' said Louis.

'Rope ladders and hammocks,' said Rab.

Nicholas had followed them. 'Saws and spades,' he said firmly.

'Not many weeks to go,' Louis added contentedly.

Working on the house with his parents, and later on with Jake, had been an amazing experience, Nicholas reflected. He had learned more than he could have dreamed of. Soon he would be working with his friends in the garden. And his uncle was willing to let them grow things there next year. He did not know where Jake would be, except that it would be close to home. Life felt very good.

Chapter Twenty-eight

Another three weeks passed before Jake made any contact, and when he did, it was in quite a different way.

John was sitting at his front door, relaxing in the sun after lunch, when Jake came up the path.

'Hi, John!' he said. 'Mind if I join you for a while?'

John's smile radiated pleasure at the sight of him. 'I can't think of anything better. Bring a chair out for yourself.'

'The step's fine,' Jake replied as he settled himself next to John. 'How've you been?'

'Not bad at all. Nicholas and his friends are coming to do the garden after the school term ends, so I've been poking around a bit.'

'I can do any preparation for you,' said Jake quickly. 'Don't overstretch yourself.'

'Actually, I'm enjoying it. I've found a couple of plants I thought had died long ago, and I've put them in pots for now.'

Jake looked at John and winked. 'I can keep an eye on the work squad. It's not many weeks away, and I should be around by then.'

'I think I'd rather leave them to their own devices. It'll be good experience for them. Whatever they do will be a bonus.'

Jake did not argue. He could see the point of what his uncle had decided. 'Okay,' he said, and then he fell silent.

At first, John was worried that he had offended Jake, but he was soon reassured that this was not the case when Jake began to speak again.

'I've been doing a lot of thinking,' he said slowly. 'Can I run it past you?'

'Two heads can be better than one – if they're the right heads,' John replied. 'Is this to do with what we spoke about before?'

Jake nodded.

'Then fire away.'

'I've got work on a building site near here. Should last at least six months. Could live in my lockup, or...'

John interrupted him. 'I'd prefer you to use your room here,' he stated determinedly.

'It's not my room,' Jake corrected him sharply.

For a moment, John wished he had not spoken, but then he felt glad that he had. Whatever Jake's reaction, the truth was that of late he had thought of that room as being there solely for when Jake came back again, and he wanted to say so. He looked straight at Jake and said firmly, 'As far as I'm concerned, it's yours. And I'd like you to get the use of it.' He stood up stiffly and went into the house, leaving Jake on the step.

Jake made no move to follow him. He was wrestling with his feelings. Only a small part of him wanted to leave. Most of him wanted to talk to his uncle about the room and the rest of his plans, but finding the words was proving very difficult. His brittle reaction to John's invitation had been an example of this.

Eventually, he went into the house in search of his uncle. He found him sitting in his armchair, beside the empty grate.

Jake cleared his throat. 'Sorry,' he said. 'Can we start again?'

John motioned for Jake to sit in the other chair. 'I'm sorry too, Jake. I'm sorry for all the mess that should never have happened. I'm sorry for my part in it.'

'But you didn't do anything,' Jake broke in, puzzled.

'Precisely. I didn't do anything. That's just the point. I should have done something.' He put his head in his hands.

Jake felt glued to his chair, but at the same time there was a force that was compelling him to reach out. With great difficulty, he leaned forward and patted his uncle's head clumsily.

Then John looked up, and took Jake's hand.

Instinctively, Jake tried to tug it away, but John held on with such force that it almost hurt. This gave Jake just enough time to realise what he was doing, and gradually he was able to allow his hand to stay where it was.

'I'll stay,' he said. 'It won't be easy, but I'll stay.'

'I know it might not be easy,' John replied. 'But we'll work on it.' He smiled. 'We'll have plenty of time.'

He changed his clasp on Jake's hand to a handshake.

'It's a deal,' said Jake warmly. This was entirely new territory to him. He felt very uncertain of everything it might involve, but he knew that he and his uncle were together in it, and he knew he was ready now to take this step. 'I'll tell the others this evening, and I'll bring my stuff round after that,' he added decisively.

'Would you like something to drink?' asked John.

Jake stood up. 'No, thanks. I'd better get on. See you later.' He left the room, and John could hear the sound of his footsteps receding down the path.

John leaned back in his chair, and shut his eyes. He had been right. Action was what had been needed. Now that Jake was coming towards the family, a firm nudge in the right direction had been the right thing. And once he was living here, a lot of ground could be covered.

Nicholas had been intending to go straight home that day. He and his uncle had agreed that he should spend as much time as possible advancing a history project that was due to be handed in the following week, and this meant cutting down on visits for a while. Yet something drew him to get off the bus at his uncle's stop, and he went along with this impulse. He need not stay long, he reasoned, and would soon be back home, ready to work on his project.

As he entered the cool shadiness of the living room, he could see his uncle, apparently asleep in his armchair. He turned, and was quietly making his way out again, when John saw him.

'Hello, Nicholas,' he said, 'I wasn't expecting you.'

'I know,' Nicholas agreed, 'but I just wanted to say hello on my way home.'

'Why not sit down for a minute?' John invited. 'I've got something I want to tell you.'

'What is it?' Nicholas perched attentively on the edge of the other armchair.

'Jake's got a job near by.'

Nicholas' eyes shone. 'That's great! How long for?'

'At least six months.'

'Wow!' Nicholas felt that he would almost burst with happiness. 'Where is he now?'

'He called round earlier today, and he's going to your house this evening to break the news.'

Nicholas hugged himself. 'I won't say anything. Mum and Dad will get a huge surprise when he turns up.'

'They will indeed. Especially when he tells them he'll be living here, with me.'

'That means everything's fixed,' said Nicholas. He was so delighted that he could no longer sit still. He jumped up from his chair and leapt in the air, trying to reach the ceiling with his fingertips.

'It's perfect!' he shouted.

'I couldn't have hoped for anything better,' John agreed.

Nicholas became business-like. 'Right, I'd better get back home and do my work. I'll do it in my room, and then when Mum and Dad come home, they won't see the huge smile on my face.'

'Sounds a good plan.'

Nicholas rushed off calling 'see you tomorrow' over his shoulder. He ran home as fast as he could, arriving at the door panting, trying to find his key. He took his work and a drink to his room, and did his best to concentrate. At first, the words swam in front of his eyes, and all he could think about was Jake, but gradually he managed to focus on his project, and became immersed in it.

When Sarah arrived home, she called up the stairs. 'Are you there, Nicholas?'

'I'm doing my history project,' he called back.

'Then I won't disturb you. I'll give you a shout when we're ready to eat.'

Good. His plan had worked. Nicholas continued to concentrate on his project, confident that Jake would soon be with them. And somewhere at the back of his mind, he knew that he had not forgotten about Todd and the fifth key.

Later, he heard his father's car draw up in the drive. Then he could hear the sound of his parents' voices. He worked on.

Then he heard his father's voice. 'Food's ready!'

'Okay!' he called back. 'I'll be down in a minute.' He checked his face in the bathroom mirror to see if he appeared normal enough. Satisfied that he looked cheerful rather than ecstatic, he ran lightly down the stairs and into the living room.

'Working hard?' asked his father.

Nicholas nodded. 'It's a history project I want to get on with. Don't want to be rushing at the last minute.'

'Quite right,' said Colin, handing him a dish of baked potatoes. 'Take plenty,' he encouraged.

Nicholas' stomach rumbled loudly, and he realised that he had forgotten to have anything when he came in from school. 'I'm starving,' he pronounced as he took three of the potatoes.

Throughout the meal, Nicholas said very little. He was listening out for the sound of Jake's arrival. Colin and Sarah exchanged pieces of news from the day, and did not comment upon Nicholas' silence.

They had almost finished when someone knocked on the front

door.

'I wonder who that can be,' said Colin.

Nicholas made no move to get up. Instead, he reached for another piece of fruit, and his father went to the door.

Nicholas heard him say, 'Jake! It's so good to see you again. Come on in.'

On hearing this, Sarah jumped to her feet, a flush spreading across her face, and when Jake came into the room, she said excitedly, 'You should have told us you were coming. I could have had something ready for you.'

'I'm not staying long,' Jake began.

Nicholas saw his mother's face fall.

'Well, I'm not staying long this evening.'

Sarah held her breath, and waited. Colin was looking at her from behind Jake, and she could see that he too was visibly affected.

'I've got work locally, and I'll be staying at Uncle John's for about six months,' Jake announced.

Sarah took out her handkerchief and blew her nose. Nicholas could see that she was trying to conceal the fact that her eyes were filling with tears.

Colin put his hand on Jake's shoulder. 'That's great news, Jake,' he said warmly.

'I'm moving in tonight,' Jake finished.

'There's a potato left,' said Nicholas. 'I've eaten the rest,' he added with a grin.

He handed the dish to Jake, who took the remaining potato, and having ascertained that it was now cold, devoured it in two mouthfuls.

Colin took charge of the situation. 'Sit down, son,' he said. 'I'll get you something else.'

Sarah sprang to her feet, but Colin took hold of her shoulders, and gently forced her to sit down again.

'Where are you working?' asked Nicholas.

'Building site. Not far away.'

'Do you think they'd have me when I've finished Uncle John's garden with Rab and Louis?'

Jake smiled. 'Probably not.'

Nicholas could not hide his disappointment.

'But they'd be missing a stunning opportunity,' Jake added.

Nicholas cheered up immediately. His brother's affirmation was all he needed at the moment.

'We can look round and see what else we can do together,' Jake promised. 'I'm on Monday to Friday, eight o'clock until four. That gives us some leeway.' He winked at Nicholas and added, 'John's warned me off his garden. He says it's your domain.'

'I'll have to see what the others say,' Nicholas replied. 'It's a joint venture.' In his heart, he knew that Rab and Louis would be more than delighted at the thought of Jake's involvement, and he could not wait to tell them.

Colin reappeared with a plate of food which he put in front of Jake.

'Thanks, Dad,' said Jake.

Nicholas noticed the ease with which Jake accepted the food from their father. He knew that the life they would all be sharing from now on would be very different from what they had had while Jake was not with them.

Sarah had said almost nothing. It was sufficient for her to see their sons sitting side by side, relating with ease, knowing that Jake had come home at last.

When Jake had finished eating, he said, 'Must get off now. Got to get my stuff down to John's.'

'Do you want a hand?' Colin asked with a deliberately casual tone.

Jake hesitated for a minute. Then he said, 'Thanks, Dad, but I'd rather do it on my own.'

Colin sensed that Jake had been within a hairsbreadth of allowing the companionship between them, but instead had decided that the more important thing for now was to maintain a clear boundary, and he respected that. He knew that it might not be long before Jake invited him to be involved with something, and he was content to wait.

When Jake had left, Sarah stood up and threw herself into Colin's arms, and they stood together, as one. Nicholas left the room quietly, and went upstairs to continue his project, secure in the knowledge that he would see his brother at Uncle John's the following evening.

Chapter Twenty-nine

Nicholas could not wait to see his friends at school the next day. He searched them out at break time.

'Here comes smiler!' said Rab when he saw Nicholas coming.

'What's the news, Nick?' asked Louis.

'Jake's back. He's got a job on a building site for at least six months, and he's going to be living at Uncle John's.'

'Hey, that means we'll see him,' said Rab.

'Will he be working with us?' asked Louis. He did not know whether to be excited or disappointed at the prospect. He certainly wanted to meet Nick's brother, but he did not want anyone else to be in charge of their project.

'Don't worry,' Nicholas reassured him. 'Uncle John's told him we're in charge of the garden.'

Louis' face fell. 'But does that mean we won't see him after all?' he asked anxiously.

'No, silly,' said Nicholas. 'It means that in the garden he'll only do what we say.'

'Will he mind?' asked Rab curiously.

'Of course not. Any friends of mine are friends of his,' Nicholas assured them. 'He wants to meet you both.'

'That's all right then,' said Louis. 'It's all settled.'

'By the way,' said Rab, 'our parents have been talking to each other about your uncle.'

'Yes, they're really impressed,' added Louis.

Rab giggled. 'I heard my dad talking to my mum about offering to pay your uncle for allowing us to spend two weeks here.'

'What did your mum say?' asked Nicholas.

'She told Dad he mustn't, because she thought your uncle would be offended. Thank goodness I've got one sensible parent.'

Nicholas had met Rab's dad a few times, and he had liked him. 'Your dad's not bad,' he objected.

'He's okay, but he does have some silly ideas sometimes,' Rab replied. He thought for a moment, and then added, 'I suppose we all do.'

Louis laughed. "'Course we do.' The bell went. 'Come on you two. Race you to the science labs.'

'That's a silly idea,' said Rab loftily. 'We'll get into trouble for running in the corridors.

'Power walking,' said Louis cryptically. He set off as quickly as he could, but because of his short legs, Rab overtook him easily.

Nicholas purposely lagged behind. He knew that Louis felt sensitive about his height, and it did not seem kind to rub in the fact that his walking speed was easy to beat.

Four o'clock saw Nicholas arriving at his uncle's gate, hoping to see Jake very soon.

His uncle greeted him. 'Hello, Nicholas. You want something to eat?'

'No, thanks. I'll wait for Jake.'

'He won't be in until around eight this evening. He's been asked to do emergency overtime.'

'Why's that?' Nicholas felt momentary panic when he heard that his brother would be so late home, but now he wanted to know more about the reason.

'He phoned to say one of the men had a bit of an accident. Nothing serious, but he'll be off for a few days, and there's a push on to complete some joinery. Jake volunteered, because all the other men were committed elsewhere.'

Fleetingly, a spiky thought went through Nicholas' mind. 'Jake's committed to me,' he muttered crossly.

'What was that you said?'

'Oh, I was just disappointed that I wasn't going to see him straight away.'

'I'd like you to stay on if you can,' said his uncle.

'I did a lot to my project last night,' Nicholas replied, 'but if I'm going to see Jake later, I suppose I should go home and do some more now.' He felt reluctant to leave, but knew it would be best to advance his project.

'That's fine,' said John. 'I just want to say that I'd like to talk to you about Todd again sometime soon.'

Nicholas immediately changed his mind about going home. 'I want to talk about him now.'

'Are you sure?'

'I won't stay long when Jake comes home. He'll be tired,'

Nicholas observed thoughtfully. 'I can do a bit more to my project before I go to bed.'

'You can have something to eat with me before Jake gets back. I can't eat late in the evenings.'

'Now we've decided what to do, tell me what you've been thinking about Todd.'

John took a deep breath, and began. 'For a very long time, I had no contact with Todd.'

'Yes, it's only since we've been trying to work out what happened to him that we've felt him around.'

'And we thought he'd come to help us,' John added.

Nicholas nodded.

'I think he couldn't come before, because he needed a lot of help first. Then, when he saw we were on the right track, it somehow gave him the energy to join in.'

Nicholas nodded again. What his uncle was saying sounded right to him.

'Twice he joined in our conversation, and on other occasions he moved things that we were working with in relation to the fifth key.'

'Go on,' Nicholas urged.

'The last time was different, and we decided we'd wait for Todd to show us whether or not he needed any more help.'

'We haven't had anything since then. Have we?'

'Nothing. But I've been thinking any sign he gives us might be in the form of helping *us*.'

'But he has been helping us!' Nicholas burst out spontaneously. 'He's brought Jake back.' He clapped his hand to his mouth, looked over his shoulder, and began to shiver uncontrollably. 'Oh, no,' he said. 'I'm freezing again.'

'Don't worry. I'll get something.' John pushed himself up out of his chair, and made his way out of the room. He soon returned carrying the large quilt from his bed, and he placed it round Nicholas' shaking shoulders.

'Thanks, Uncle John.'

'I'm going to get you a hot drink as well.'

'No, don't go away,' gasped Nicholas urgently. 'Something's going to happen. I know it is.' His shivering became more intense.

John sat down, and looked at Nicholas worriedly.

'Don't worry,' said Nicholas through his chattering teeth. 'This is good shivering. I can tell.'

It was then that John became aware of a shadow forming on the far wall, where they had previously seen Todd.

'Look,' he whispered quietly, pointing to it.

Nicholas turned, and as he looked he saw the rough outline of a key silhouetted on the wall. He looked round the room, but could see nothing that could have cast such a shadow.

Then as they watched, the key faded, and it was replaced by what looked like a line of words.

Nicholas leaned forward in his chair, desperately trying to make out what it said.

'What is it, Nicholas?' his uncle asked. 'I can't see.'

'I'm trying,' Nicholas whispered. 'It's really difficult because it's in weird handwriting.' He struggled hard to make sense of it. ' "Beware ... of ..." Yes, that's the first bit.' He screwed up his face in concentration. 'Then it says "losing ..." Uncle John, what on earth can it mean? "Beware of losing ..." '

'Nicholas, is there any more?' John asked urgently.

'Yes. I'm trying to work it out. "Beware of losing ... what ... you ..." That's as far as I can get with it. The rest's a blur.'

'Keep trying, Nicholas. Keep trying.'

Nicholas stared intently at the remaining script. Suddenly, it seemed to clear for a fraction of a second. ' "really ... treasure." That's it, Uncle John! "Beware of losing what you really treasure." That's what it said.'

As soon as he had finished working it out, it faded, and it was replaced by the merest trace of the same shadow of a person that they had seen before.

Then everything was gone, and the wall returned to its usual state.

Nicholas began to feel less cold. He stared at his uncle, and John stared back. It was very clear to them both what had just happened.

'Todd came to say goodbye,' said Nicholas.

'And he told us what the key really meant,' added his uncle. 'There may be a key that opens a secret store of gold, silver and jewels, but that's not for us. What we've got is far more precious that any such things.'

'Yes, Jake's more precious than anything. Uncle John, I hope no one ever finds that secret store,' stated Nicholas emphatically. 'It isn't for anyone really. It has caused a lot of trouble, and I don't want it to cause any more.'

'Todd knew what it was like to lose something that was precious to him,' said John. 'He found that a relationship he had trusted completely turned out to be something quite different. That was a terrible loss.'

'He never knew his son,' Nicholas added sadly. 'He didn't even know he had one.'

'That's an interesting point,' his uncle replied. 'He probably died before anyone knew Abigail was going to have a child, but he's somehow known from beyond the grave.'

'I wish we knew more about Todd and his son,' Nicholas burst out passionately.

'I don't think any more of that knowledge is for us,' his uncle replied.

They both fell silent for a while, each lost in his own thoughts.

Eventually, John said, 'Sometime we'll have to decide what to do with the measurer, but I'll keep it safe in the box here for now.'

'Let's have another look at it,' Nicholas suggested.

John stood up and opened the box, but there was no sign of the measurer.

'It's gone,' he said.

'Todd must have taken it.' Nicholas realised that he felt profoundly grateful it had disappeared. The responsibility of deciding how to dispose of it had felt huge, and he was glad to think that Todd had taken this burden from them.

'I'll have a bit of a look around tomorrow,' said his uncle, 'just in case it's somewhere in the house. But I don't think I'll find any trace of it. Nicholas, it's getting late. We should think about having something to eat.'

'I don't feel hungry,' Nicholas stated flatly. 'I don't think I could swallow a thing.'

'I've got some of my soup left,' said John. 'We could share that.'

Nicholas considered this proposition, and then decided to accept. 'Okay, let's do it together.'

They stood in the kitchen while they boiled and then simmered the contents of John's soup pan. But before they had time to serve it out, Jake came in.

'Hello, you two,' he said cheerily. 'Is there enough for me?'

Nicholas turned round quickly at the sound of Jake's voice, but what he saw was hardly recognisable as his brother. He was wearing a boiler suit, and was covered from head to toe in what looked like a fine white powder. Nicholas could not conceal his astonishment.

'I expect I look like a ghost,' Jake joked.

'Er... Not exactly,' Nicholas hurried to reassure him.

'I'll keep some soup for you,' said John calmly.

'Thanks. I'd better get cleaned up first.' Jake took a black dustbin liner, and disappeared in the direction of his room. Soon afterwards, Nicholas could hear the sound of the shower running in the bathroom.

Nicholas and John had finished their soup by the time Jake reappeared. He looked transformed.

'So it definitely was you under all that mess,' John commented with amusement.

'I must get some masks tomorrow if they want me to keep plastering,' said Jake wryly. 'I had to use an old rag round my face today.'

'I thought it was joinery work they wanted,' John remarked, surprised.

'That's how it started, but it soon turned into other things.' Jake grinned. 'That's how it can be when you're a Jack-of-all-trades.'

'I'm not sure about the "Jack",' said John. 'You've certainly been master of some that I've seen.'

Jake changed the subject. 'How's school, Nick?'

'I told Rab and Louis you're here, and they're really pleased you'll be around when they're working in the garden.'

Jake winked at John. 'Will I be allowed to watch?' he teased.

'You can probably join in a bit,' said Nicholas seriously, 'and there might be one or two things we'll need some help with.'

'I can help you to set up some composting areas,' Jake suggested, 'but only if you all decide you want me to.'

Nicholas glanced at his watch. 'I mustn't stay much longer this evening. I've got a history project to finish. I don't want to get behind.'

'I won't be up much longer myself,' Jake replied. 'I'll get something else to eat, and then I'll be off to bed.'

More than satisfied with how things had gone with Jake, Nicholas said goodnight, and walked slowly home. His mind was full of what Todd had revealed to him and to his uncle.

Chapter Thirty

The rest of the term passed quite quickly. The pressure of schoolwork eased off over the final two weeks, and Nicholas and his friends spent much time planning and re-planning their project. John gave them money to go to the local garden centre to buy spades, forks, secateurs and bush saws, and Colin went with them to help.

Although Jake spent much of his time at work or at John's, he was also a regular visitor to his parents' house – where he would share a meal with them, and then stay on to talk for a while. The conversation mainly consisted of exchanging stories about work, but sometimes Jake would talk about how he remembered watching Colin as he upgraded the little terraced house that they had all once shared. Nicholas never tired of hearing these stories, and would have liked more of them, but he sensed that it was not sensible to press Jake.

One weekend, Jake and John invited the others round for a meal. Nicholas was very impressed at the range of food that they had prepared.

'Some recipes from around the world,' said Jake modestly, when he was asked about where he had learned such culinary arts.

John had bought two extra dining chairs for the occasion, and Colin teased him about the fact that they were a matching pair.

'I did wonder about buying six, and getting rid of my old trio,' said John.

'You must *never* get rid of them!' Nicholas exclaimed. 'They're part of your house.'

'Don't you worry,' his uncle replied. 'That's the conclusion I came to. They've been my companions for so long, it would feel like getting rid of old friends.'

Nicholas relaxed. Uncle John's house would never seem right with new furniture in it. It was okay adding a couple of chairs so that they could all sit round the table together, but replacing anything was unthinkable.

The summer holidays came, and Nicholas, Rab and Louis met in John's garden early on the first Monday morning.

'Where are we going to start?' asked Rab, surveying the jungle that confronted them.

It was then they realised that although they had often discussed the layout of the finished job, they had not made any particular plan for how they were going to go about clearing the ground. The concept had seemed so straightforward that none of them had paid any attention to detail. And it was this they now had to address.

'Anywhere,' said Louis energetically, and he began to slash at the undergrowth with a spade.

'I don't think that'll get us very far,' Nicholas commented, as he observed that Louis' spade made no impression at all. 'Jake said he'd be willing to help us to make some compost areas. We should ask him about that when he comes home today.'

'What are we going to do before then?' asked Louis. He felt deflated.

'I think we've got to stop thinking of this as a jungle,' said Nicholas sensibly. 'It isn't helping.'

'You're right,' Rab agreed. 'It makes me think of films where the hero is slashing his way through the undergrowth.'

'Yes,' said Louis. 'And when I tried that, the spade bounced off and just about hit my nose.'

'It's those brambles. They're everywhere,' observed Nicholas. 'We'll have to get the secateurs and cut them into small lengths.' He took hold of one of the stems. 'Ow!' he yelped. He studied his hand ruefully. It was bleeding, and there were several prickles embedded in it.

Louis helped him to pull them out. 'I don't fancy that,' he remarked.

'Let's go and ask Uncle John for advice,' said Nicholas decisively. He walked briskly into the house, with the others not far behind.

'How do we do the brambles, Uncle John?' he asked.

'You could do with some thick gauntlets,' his uncle replied. 'Now, let me see...' He pulled a box out of the cupboard in the hall, and searched through its contents. 'Ah! Here's a pair.' He handed them to Nicholas. 'Try these.'

Nicholas put them on. He laughed. 'They're a bit big for me,' he said as one fell off and dropped to the floor.

'Have you got any more?' asked Louis. He could see that wearing this kind of protection would make the job possible.

232

'I'm afraid not,' John replied, 'but I'm sure Colin will bring some if we ask him.'

'It's all right, Louis,' said Nicholas. 'I only need one glove. You're left-handed, so I'll give you the right one.'

Louis cheered up immediately. He turned to Rab. 'Nick and I will do the sharp stuff, and you can saw branches and dig up roots.'

They returned to the garden, and decided where to pile the cut brambles. Then they set to work.

By lunchtime, they had cleared a small area completely.

Louis groaned. 'This is going to take ages.'

'Good job we've got two weeks,' said Rab.

Just then, John joined them, and admired their work. 'That's very good. You've been hard at it, and already it's made quite an impression.'

Louis felt a warm glow spread through him.

'This is definitely a good morning's work,' John repeated. 'It's time for some food now. Come in, and wash your hands.'

The boys arranged their tools at the back door, and went inside, where they found that John had everything ready for them on the table.

'I saw at least ten worms,' said Rab.

'That's good news,' John replied. 'We need plenty of them to have healthy soil.'

'I hardly used my spade this morning,' said Nicholas, 'but a robin sat on it instead.'

John nodded. 'Yes, they like to do that. They watch for things they can pick from the soil to eat.'

'I picked up a soggy leaf, but actually it was a slug,' said Louis. He shuddered.

John laughed. 'You'll find plenty more of them. When you're growing vegetables, we'll have to set up ways of protecting the ones that slugs like to eat.'

'Will you show us what to do?' asked Louis.

'Yes. I'm no expert, but I've got a few tricks up my sleeve.'

That afternoon, they cleared nearly as much again of the garden before Jake came home.

'Hard at work? I knocked off at four,' he called across.

At the sound of his voice, Nicholas turned and beamed at him. Then he grabbed at his friends. 'Come on, you two. Here's Jake.'

233

Jake strode over, holding out his hand. 'Pleased to meet you both.' He shook first Louis' hand, and then Rab's.

'Will you help us with the compost bits?' asked Nicholas.

'I'll get a drink of water, and then I'll be right with you,' Jake replied. 'Best to do it before I get changed.'

The rest of the afternoon was spent constructing a row of four three-sided wooden enclosures along the side of the back garden. After that, they piled the cut brambles into the first one, and then put everything away for the day.

Rab and Louis were reluctant to go home. Instead, they and Nicholas lolled around on the slabs near the front door, talking. Jake joined them once he had changed.

'Where did you work before?' Rab asked him casually.

Nicholas was astonished when Jake began to tell them of a number of things he had done over the last years, and stories of some of the different countries he had visited.

It was almost an hour later when Rab looked at his watch. 'Oh no!' he said. 'I've got to go. You coming, Louis?'

Louis jumped up, and they set off jogging down the road together to the bus stop.

The following days were spent in much the same way, and slowly but surely the garden was retrieved. Every part of each day was good – the meeting up in the morning, work, lunch, more work, and then getting together with Jake.

Nicholas noticed how relaxed his brother had been from the outset, and it was not long before he introduced stories he had picked up from fellow travellers. Nicholas found these fascinating, as did Rab and Louis, and they would all do their best to keep Jake talking for as long as possible. Wise to their ploys, he would not be persuaded beyond whatever he had decided, but was always willing to promise more for the following day.

Sunday was their day off. Rab had to go with his parents to visit relatives, and Louis was committed to a local swimming event in aid of charity.

But when they gathered again on Monday morning, the sky was dark and threatening, and they had barely begun their tasks before the rain came pouring down.

'Quick!' Nicholas directed. 'Grab your things and go inside.'

Rab and Louis needed no encouragement, and they headed

quickly for the shelter of John's house.

'Looks as if it's likely to last all day,' John commented. 'And even if it stops, the garden will be too soggy.'

'Can we stay here?' asked Rab politely.

'You're welcome to,' replied John, 'but there's not much to do.'

'Can I show them your tools?' asked Nicholas.

'Help yourselves.'

Nicholas opened the chests, and carefully laid the tools out on the table.

'They're brilliant!' said Louis, touching them one by one.

The morning passed quickly, and after lunch the rain reduced to light drizzle. As John had predicted, the ground was far too wet for them to continue in the garden.

'Looks as if we'll have to give up for today,' said Rab. 'I hope it's not like this tomorrow, or we're not going to finish in time.'

'I listened to the forecast on the radio,' John told them. 'Tomorrow's supposed to be brighter.'

Rab and Louis were clearly reluctant to leave.

'You could get out the cards,' John suggested. 'There are a couple of packs in the bookshelves.'

The boys did not hesitate, and when Jake arrived home, they were still engrossed in their games.

Jake grinned when he saw them. 'Slacking?' he said.

'It was too wet...' Nicholas began. But then he saw Jake wink at him, and he asked, 'Do you want to play?'

'Give me a minute to get changed, and I'll be with you.'

When Jake joined them, they spent another hour learning some games he had picked up on his travels.

'These are all new to me,' said John, bewildered. Patience was the game he knew best, and he felt out of his depth.

'Wet days with workmates,' Jake explained as he shuffled a pack. 'One more game, lads, and then I'll need to get something to eat.'

By the end of the second week, the main part of the garden had been cleared, and John was standing with Nicholas, Rab and Louis, admiring the transformation.

'I can hardly recognise it,' said John. 'It's years since it's looked this tidy.'

Rab looked mournful. 'I wish we could come again next week.'

'Your dad told me you wouldn't be available after today,' said

John. 'He's booked a place for you on an adventure course.'

Rab groaned. 'It won't be as good as this. I bet I'll have to swing from ropes and jump over hedges, or something.'

'It'll be okay,' John encouraged. 'You're bound to find a bit of it that you like.'

Rab hung his head, and kicked a pebble on the path.

'I can't come either, Rab,' Louis pointed out. 'I've got to get in training for the swimming gala at the pool near Gran's.'

'Come in and see me any time you're passing,' John invited.

Rab cheered up. 'Can I come and tell you about the course when I get back?'

John nodded. 'Of course you can. I'd like to hear about it. And, Louis, you must let me know how the swimming goes.'

'I'll do a bit more tidying,' said Nicholas, 'but we can all do the planting next year.'

Jake appeared at the gate, and came to join them. 'Impressive,' he remarked. He turned to Rab and Louis. 'You'll be coming back to see us?'

By now, Rab had recovered. 'We've got to.'

'Yes,' said Louis. 'We'll have to keep the garden looking good. Jake, how long will you be living here?'

'For a good while yet. My contract was for six months, but even then I was told there'd be work beyond that. There's always a shortage of skilled labour, and I've been filling in for every trade since I started. The boss has already said that he wants to keep me on. But I'll see how things are at the end of the year.'

This seemed to more than satisfy Louis, and he and Rab said goodbye to John and Jake quite cheerfully.

When they had gone, Nicholas knew that he would have to ask his brother what he had in mind for the future. He waited until they were sitting round the table, sharing some food that John had prepared.

Then he asked carefully, 'Um… Jake… Do you want to keep on doing that job?'

'I'm not sure, Nick,' Jake replied. 'But it's fine for now.'

Nicholas tried again. 'Do you fancy something else?'

'Haven't been thinking.'

Nicholas fell silent. He did not know what else to say. He certainly wanted to know more. He looked at his uncle, hoping for clues, but John was concentrating on chasing peas round his plate.

In the end, Nicholas went home without having elicited any

further information. But when he arrived, he sought his father out straight away.

'Dad,' he began, 'Jake was telling us his boss wants him to stay in his job.'

Colin looked up from his book. 'That doesn't surprise me, Nick. He won't get anyone better than Jake. He can turn his hand to most things, and he does a good job.' He waited to see if Nicholas would say anything else. 'Is something bothering you?' he asked.

'Er... no... Not exactly. Well... yes.'

'Why not sit down, and we'll talk it over.'

Nicholas was glad that his father had suggested this, and he sat next to him on the sofa.

'What's going to happen to Jake?' he burst out.

'I'm not sure,' said Colin. 'We'll have to wait and see how things develop.'

'I don't think we should,' replied Nicholas emphatically. 'We've got to do something.'

Colin looked surprised. 'What's in your mind?'

'It's great that he's living at Uncle John's, and it's great that he's got good work and we're seeing him a lot.'

'Yes, it is,' Colin agreed quietly. 'It's more than I'd ever dared hope for.' He paused, and then added, 'Nick, I don't want to push things.'

Nicholas thought about this, and then said, 'Couldn't we just talk about ideas?'

'I'd rather leave it for now. I don't want Jake to feel I'm putting pressure on him.'

Nicholas could understand that his father might feel like this, but he was not convinced.

'Well, I'm going to talk to him,' he announced determinedly. Then he stood up, and left Colin staring after him.

As he lay in bed that night, he began to make his plans. Tomorrow was Saturday, so everyone would be around.

Downstairs, Colin told Sarah about the conversation that he had just had with Nicholas.

'I'm not surprised,' she said when he had finished. 'I'm like you. Even though things have changed a lot, I'm worried about frightening Jake off. But it's different for Nicholas, and I think we should follow his instinct and try to be a bit more proactive. Maybe we should have John and Jake down for an evening meal today or tomorrow.'

'I'll certainly go along with that,' Colin replied, giving her a hug.

Having ascertained the following day that John and Jake would join them in the evening, Colin and Sarah set about preparing something a little out of the ordinary.

'We can't have anything too spicy,' said Sarah.

'Why not?' asked Colin. 'I thought a bit of gastro-excitement would be a good idea.'

'I don't think John's stomach would be up to it,' Sarah pointed out.

Colin clapped his hand to his forehead. 'Why didn't I think of that?'

'Never mind. There's plenty we can do that will suit his digestion.'

Having seen his parents deep in conversation about the evening, Nicholas decided to go to his uncle's. There he found Jake in the back garden, tidying up some of the remaining corners.

'Hey!' he protested. 'That's my job.'

Jake smiled. 'There's room for two.'

'Okay,' Nicholas agreed. 'I'll get my things.'

As they worked side by side, Jake surprised Nicholas by saying, 'I think Mum and Dad are up to something.'

'It might be my fault,' Nicholas admitted reluctantly.

'Spill the beans.'

Nicholas stopped what he was doing, and stared directly at his brother. 'I was talking to Dad about what you might be doing later on. He didn't want to ask you.'

'He's worried I'll go away again,' said Jake calmly.

Nicholas gaped at him. He did not think that Jake would ever have said anything like that.

'You'd better shut your mouth before a fly gets in,' said Jake, laughing.

Nicholas pushed him playfully, and Jake quickly grabbed him round the middle and lifted him off his feet.

'Let me down!' Nicholas commanded, wriggling violently and pushing as hard as he could. But Jake was very strong, and had him completely in his power.

'Maybe we should play pistols at dawn,' Jake joked.

'No!' Nicholas shouted. 'That would make us like...' Here he stopped.

'Like what?' asked Jake.

Nicholas said nothing.

'Secret?

Nicholas nodded mutely.

Jake let him down onto the ground. 'Sorry, pal.'

The evening meal was a work of art. Colin and Sarah had been shopping at the excellent local Chinese supermarket, and had extemporised with what they had bought. John found the food not only easy to cope with, but very enjoyable, and he ate more than usual. Nicholas took several helpings of the delicately-flavoured rice noodles, insisting that more should be bought very soon.

After the meal was finished, Colin turned to Sarah and said, 'Well, love, let this be the first of very many. We've got a lot to celebrate, and this is an ideal way to do it.'

'It's been just right for me,' said John appreciatively. 'But I think Jake and I could do one next, though.'

Colin turned to Jake. 'Nick's been telling me about your job. It sounds as if you can be there as long as you want.'

Jake nodded. 'I'll see how I feel at the end of the year.'

'Any other plans?' asked his father, with a studiedly casual tone.

Jake looked at him with amusement. He admired the polished way that his father had put this question, but he knew that underneath he was anxious.

'Look, Dad,' said Jake firmly. 'I'm sticking around. That's enough for now.'

Colin nearly backed off, but he gathered himself and asked, 'Ever thought of going into business on your own?'

'Maybe,' Jake replied cautiously.

Colin glanced across at Sarah, and then said, 'Sarah and I have been talking... We've got a bit of spare capital to invest.' He did not give Jake time to say anything, and finished by adding, 'Think about it.'

Jake nodded, but said nothing.

It was John who spoke next. 'The tools in my chests are pretty out of date, but you and Nicholas can have whatever you want.'

'That's very generous of you,' said Jake.

John tried to brush his response on one side by saying, 'I don't think I'll be using them again.'

'But they mean a lot to you,' stated Jake.

'So do you and Nicholas,' said John, looking straight at him.

Jake turned to his father. 'Leave it with me for a while, Dad. I'll get back to you.'

Throughout this exchange, Nicholas had remained silent. He could see that his parents had taken his views seriously, and what was happening was perfect. Any remaining tension he might have carried had evaporated, and he basked in a feeling of contentment.

Jake nudged him. 'You dozing off there, Nick?'

'No, I just feel full up,' Nicholas replied. He was talking about something far greater than food, but he knew that he did not need to say more.

'You fancy another weekend away?' asked Jake.

Nicholas nodded vigorously.

'Then we've plans to make. Same place?'

'No, I'd like somewhere different. You choose.'

'Okay, leave it with me,' Jake replied. He winked. 'And be ready for a surprise.'

Chapter Thirty-one

It was nearly the middle of September, and Nicholas was once again hard at work with his studies. The summer holiday had passed all too quickly, but the memory of it impacted strongly on him every day. The final week of it had been incredible. Jake had taken him away for a long weekend, and had begun to teach him rock-climbing. Nicholas was desperate to carry this on, and although Jake had not promised anything, it was clear that he was as keen as Nicholas for them to pursue it together.

The next event was to be John's 90th birthday. He had insisted that he did not want any fuss, but he had agreed to the idea of a quiet evening at Colin and Sarah's, with more Chinese food on offer.

It was during that evening that Jake made his announcement.

'I've decided to start my own business,' he said. 'Can we sit down together soon, and talk about finances?'

John's face glowed. 'Hearing that is the best birthday present I could have wished for. You can count me in where money's concerned.'

'You've given me a lot of support already,' Jake reminded him.

'It's been a two-way process,' John replied, 'and I'm still indebted to you. You'll be a great investment.'

'Can I still live with you while I'm getting it all off the ground?' asked Jake.

'I've already told you that the room's yours,' John replied.

The others had so far listened quietly to this exchange, but now Sarah took over. She went across to where Jake was sitting, and put her arm round his shoulders for a moment. 'This is just what Colin and I hoped for,' she said.

Nicholas was overjoyed to see that his brother seemed to be able to accept her approach.

'Sarah and I have worked out what we'll be able to put in,' said Colin. 'Have you thought about where you'll operate from?'

'There's an industrial estate not far out of town where I can lease a small unit,' Jake replied. 'I'll tell you more when we get together to talk it through.'

'Is that at Millbank?' asked Colin.

'That's right.'

'Let's make a start now,' said John firmly. 'I've had enough birthday celebrations. I want to get on with the real things.'

'Are you sure?' asked Jake.

Here Nicholas could not contain himself any longer.

'Come on, Jake. You've got to tell us now.' But without giving Jake time to reply, he said earnestly, 'Take me on as an apprentice.'

'That's an offer I've no wish to refuse,' Jake replied, 'but there'll have to be conditions.' He glanced at their parents, and then turned back to his brother. 'You've got to stay on at school,' he said emphatically. 'We can work together in holidays and at weekends.'

Nicholas could not stop smiling. The only thing he wanted to do was to work with Jake, and if going along with his advice about school meant that he could, it would be fine. 'When do I start?' he asked.

'I've told my boss I'll be finishing up after Christmas,' said Jake. 'He asked me where I was going, and when he heard my plans, he said he'd want me to work as a subcontractor for most of next year. I'll probably take him up on it because it'll give me a steady income while I'm building things up.'

'Jake, when can we have a look at Millbank together?' asked Colin. 'The sooner the better as I see it.'

'I've got to come too,' Nicholas stated firmly.

Colin exchanged a meaningful glance with Jake. 'I'll take an afternoon off work, and we'll go along after four. How about the end of next week, Jake?'

'Suits me,' Jake replied. 'I'll have seen the council's business advisor by then.'

'Jake,' said Sarah, 'bear in mind that I can help with the setting up of the admin system. You've only to ask.'

'Thanks, Mum,' Jake replied.

Nicholas glowed inside. He had felt for a long time now that he had all of his real family, and each step that Jake made to include them more and more in his life was a bonus. His own birthday – his fourteenth – was not far away, and he knew exactly what he wanted – his place in Jake's business, and some of his own tools.

It was the following Easter when Jake first raised the subject of employing regular help in the small office of his business unit. Sarah had worked hard in her spare time to set up the basic systems, but now he needed someone who would spend a few hours there every weekday morning.

He put a small advertisement on the board in the local supermarket, and soon received a number of enquiries. A plump, cheerful, middle-aged woman agreed to work for him until the start of the summer holidays, when she had to go to her daughter's to look after grandchildren. Her involvement was a great success, and they were all sorry to see her go.

After that, Sarah took three weeks of her holiday to cover the work. Nicholas thought it was very funny to have his mother sitting at the desk, talking in a 'business voice' to potential customers on the phone. But they were all wondering what would happen when Sarah had to return to her normal job.

'We could route the phone calls to one of those specialist answering firms,' Colin suggested one evening.

'I'd thought about that,' Jake replied. 'It would keep things going meanwhile.'

'I could carry a special mobile,' Nicholas offered.

'Thanks, Nick,' said Jake, 'but answering that kind of call would get in the way of our work too much. I'd better try putting an ad in the local paper. I didn't want to do that before, because we might have ended up with too many replies.'

However, while at Millbank the next day, Sarah received a phone call from a young woman who had seen the advertisement in the supermarket, and who was willing to come to see Jake and herself at five o'clock that afternoon.

The applicant arrived at ten to five. She was dressed in a simple black suit, and wore black shoes with low heels. Sarah let her in. The woman was of medium build, and was a little taller than Sarah. Sarah guessed that she was in her late twenties, and fleetingly she wondered why someone who was still relatively young would dress in a way that did not enhance her appearance. She showed her round, and soon discovered that although she was a quiet person, she was also businesslike and clearly competent.

Jake was a little late, and burst through the door in his dirty overalls.

'Sorry about the delay,' he said.

'I've been showing Mrs Waters round,' Sarah explained. She gave him a particular kind of look in order to convey her approval.

Jake wiped his hand on his overalls, but it was still filthy, and he said, 'I'd better not shake hands. What do you think of the place so far?'

'This kind of work is familiar to me,' she replied politely. She opened her handbag and took out an envelope, which she handed to Sarah, saying, 'These are references. I trust you will find them helpful.'

Sarah opened the envelope and began to read the references.

'We're looking for someone who'll do eight o'clock until twelve, five days a week,' said Jake. 'You'll be on your own,' he added bluntly.

The woman then surprised Jake and Sarah by asking, 'Will you give me a trial for a month?' This question was delivered with a voice that conveyed little sense of feeling.

'The references are more than satisfactory,' said Sarah.

'Would you mind if we phone you later this evening?' asked Jake. 'I got held up on a job, and I'd like time to catch my breath.'

'Naturally,' the woman replied in the same precise, emotionless voice. She took a pen from the desk, and printed her number on a piece of scrap paper, together with her full name – Mrs Abigail Waters.

'When would you be able to start?' asked Jake.

'Monday morning.'

'Thanks for coming,' said Jake.

Sarah let her out.

When she returned, she said, 'Jake, we've got nothing to lose by giving her the position, and we'll probably gain a lot. One of those references is from a well-respected firm of accountants.'

Jake raised his eyebrows. 'I wonder why she's interested in this job then?'

'We'll probably find out later.'

'I'll give her a ring after six,' Jake decided. 'I'd better go and pick Nick up now. I left him on the job to do the sweeping up.'

When he collected Nicholas, he told him about the woman straight away.

Nicholas very interested. 'What's her name?'

'Mrs Waters. Mrs Abigail Waters. I'll phone her after six to offer her the job.'

Nicholas felt dazed. 'Abigail?' he repeated.

'Yes,' Jake replied. 'But she's very proper, so you'd better call her Mrs Waters.'

'Jake,' said Nicholas, 'don't drop me off at home. I'll come with you to Uncle John's.

'Okay,' Jake replied cheerfully. Now that they had someone to look after the office, a load had been lifted from his mind, and he began to whistle a tune.

Nicholas was silent all the way to John's. He could not wait to have time with his uncle to talk about what he had just learned.

When they arrived at the house, he was relieved that Jake went to have a shower.

Nicholas went straight into the living room and sat on the arm of his uncle's chair. 'Someone's come about the job in the office,' he began.

'That's good news,' John replied. 'They've...'

Nicholas broke in. 'Her name's Abigail.'

'Abigail!'

'Mrs Abigail Waters.'

John shook his head. 'It's got to be a coincidence,' he said without conviction.

'The only person I know called Abigail is the shepherd's daughter,' stated Nicholas.

'It's not a common name,' John acknowledged. 'I've heard of it a few times, but never someone I've known.' He put his head in his hands. 'Oh dear, my head's swimming.'

'Mine is as well, Uncle John,' said Nicholas. 'Do you think Todd's sent her?' he asked suddenly.

'I don't know anything,' his uncle replied. 'We'll have to wait and see what happens.'

Jake appeared in the doorway looking clean. 'Has Nick told you the news?' he asked.

'Yes,' said John. 'Sounds good.'

'I'll just phone Mrs Waters to offer her the job, and then I'll join you.'

Jake disappeared into the hall, and Nicholas could hear the sound of his voice. The phone call was very brief, and he reappeared after only a few minutes.

'That's it,' he said. 'She's starting on Monday.'

'I think I'll have a shower now,' Nicholas decided, and he left Jake and John talking about whether or not Jake would buy a particular piece of expensive equipment, or continue to hire it meantime.

As he stood under the stream of warm water, Nicholas realised that after the initial shock of hearing her name, he was looking forward to meeting Mrs Waters...

Nicholas said nothing to Jake of his interest in Mrs Waters. In fact he said nothing about her at all. He and Jake were on a job for most of the weekend, and so the time he had to wait was filled productively, and passed quickly.

Jake picked him up as usual at about seven twenty that Monday morning, and they arrived at the unit at half past, to gather together the things they needed for the day. Nicholas was loading things into the van when he became aware that someone was approaching. He looked up, and then he saw her. This must be Abigail.

'Hello,' he said tentatively. 'Are you Mrs Waters?'

'Yes, that's right. I'm starting work here this morning.'

'I'm Jake's brother, Nicholas.'

'I'm glad to meet you,' replied Abigail.

She went into the office, hung her coat up behind the door, and began to look through the pile of letters that Jake had put on the desk.

'She's here,' Nicholas whispered to Jake when he appeared with a box full of spares.

Jake put the box in the van and glanced at his watch. 'She's early,' he remarked. Then he went and put his head round the office door. 'Good morning,' he said.

'Good morning,' replied Abigail, hardly lifting her head from her task.

'Put anything you can't deal with on one side, and we'll have a look at it later,' Jake instructed. 'Phone me about any calls you think are urgent.' He pointed to a card on the desk where his mobile number was written. 'Leave me a message if it's switched off. Thanks.'

He went to the van, and they set off.

When they returned to the office around five o'clock, Jake found that everything was arranged neatly. Completed work had been filed away, and there was a list of messages for him, together with a list of questions.

'This makes it very easy for me,' he told Nicholas. 'I hope she stays.'

At this stage, Nicholas was not sure. Her work might be perfect, but he was concerned about any deeper significance of her presence.

Yet as the weeks passed, her quiet consistency lulled him into a sense of ease. She always wore the same kind of clothes, she always arrived early, and she was always thorough in everything she did. And most importantly, Jake found her invaluable.

One Sunday afternoon, a few weeks later, Colin and Sarah had joined Nicholas, Jake and John for a lazy afternoon, sitting in John's garden. The vegetable patch had yielded well, and there were still things left to eat.

'Your friends have worked very hard, Nicholas,' said John.

'I know,' Nicholas replied. 'Once they knew I would be busy working with Jake, they said they were going to do it anyway.'

'I made sure they took plenty home with them,' said John, smiling. 'I heard their parents were pretty impressed, and I believe there's a lot of new activity going on in their gardens.'

'Abigail seems to have settled in well at the office,' Sarah commented. 'Already it's almost as if she's always been there.'

Nicholas shot a quick glance in the direction of his uncle, who said nothing, but inclined his head slightly.

'She's a widow,' said Jake.

'How do you know that?' asked Nicholas, startled.

'Someone told me her husband had been killed in an accident.'

'What kind of accident?' Nicholas pressed. Then he saw the expression on his uncle's face, and said no more. He wanted to ask if she had any children, but he knew he must not. In any case, it was hard to imagine that she had. It would not be possible for her to arrive so early at work.

The rest of the summer was slipping by. Nicholas was beginning to face the fact that soon he would be back at school, and would only be working with Jake at weekends.

He had noticed a change in Jake recently, and he did not know quite what to make of it. Each morning, instead of setting off as soon as the van was loaded, Jake would give him some small task to do in the workshop, while he spent some time in the office with Abigail.

Then came the weekend when Jake told him that he was going to have lunch with Abigail in the museum café.

Nicholas did not know what he felt about this, and spent the time at his uncle's, talking things over.

'He hasn't done anything like this before,' he complained.

'It's about time,' his uncle replied. 'He doesn't need to be like me.'

'What's wrong with being like you?' asked Nicholas.

'I mean he hasn't been told he's not to get married.'

'Jake's getting married!' exclaimed Nicholas, horrified.

'I didn't say he was,' said his uncle. 'All I meant was that he can if he wants.'

'I don't think I want him to,' said Nicholas flatly.

'Why on earth not?'

Nicholas hung his head. 'Er... Well... I won't see him as much.'

'Nonsense,' said John. 'You'll see him, and you'll see his partner – whoever it might be.'

'It's too soon,' groaned Nicholas.

'It might feel too soon for you,' said his uncle, 'but there's more of a risk with Jake that he'll leave things too late. In any case, what do you think will happen when *you* have a girlfriend?'

'Oh! I hadn't thought about that.'

'I thought so. You've been busy enough learning how to be a man. And one day there'll be someone special in your life.'

Nicholas fell silent.

John said nothing further. He took a newspaper from the heap beside his chair, and began to read.

Nicholas barely noticed. He was lost in thought. His ideas of the future had thus far only involved him and Jake running the business, with their parents taking an interest. Abigail had only featured as the person who kept the paperwork in order. Nicholas was worried by the idea of Jake spending more and more time with her. Surely that would mean that he and Jake could not have the same bond? Uncle John's suggestion of his having a girlfriend of his own one day had barely registered. It was only his relationship with Jake that counted. And it seemed that his uncle did not understand his situation.

Nicholas tried again. 'Uncle John, I haven't had Jake for long enough yet,' he began.

John put down his paper. 'Look, Nicholas,' he said firmly, 'Jake won't be rushing into anything... and neither will Abigail I should think. You'll soon find out that anything between them won't get in the way of what you have with Jake.'

Nicholas did not feel convinced, but as his uncle seemed so certain, he was willing to go along with this, for a while at least.

'And there's something else,' John added.

'What's that?'

'I think you'll find that if Jake and Abigail get closer, Jake's relationship with your mum and dad will get even better.'

'You think so?'

'I have no doubts at all,' John replied.

A warm feeling began to replace the anxiety that Nicholas had felt inside himself, and he began to look forward to seeing how things developed between his brother and Abigail. After all, maybe Todd *had* directed her to come ...

Also available from Augur Press

The Poetry Catchers by Pupils from Craigton Primary School	£7.99	978-0-9549551-9-9
Beyond the Veil by Mirabelle Maslin	£8.99	0-9549551-4-5
Fay by Mirabelle Maslin	£8.99	0-9549551-3-7
Emily by Mirabelle Maslin	£8.99	978-0-9549551-8-2
Hemiplegic Utopia: Manc Style by Lee Seymour	£6.99	978-0-9549551-7-5
Carl and other writings by Mirabelle Maslin	£5.99	0-9549551-2-9
Letters to my Paper Lover by Fleur Soignon	£7.99	0-9549551-1-0
On a Dog Lead by Mirabelle Maslin	£6.99	978-0-9549551-5-1
Poems of Wartime Years by W N Taylor	£4.99	978-0-9549551-6-8
For ages 8-14 (and adult readers too): Tracy by Mirabelle Maslin	£6.95	0-9549551-0-2

Postage and packing – £1.00 per title

Ordering:

By phone	+44 (0) 131 440 1690
By post	Delf House, 52, Penicuik Road, Roslin, Midlothian EH25 9LH UK
By fax	+44 (0) 131 448 0990
By e-mail	info@augurpress.com
Online	www.augurpress.com (credit cards accepted)

Cheques payable to Augur Press
Prices and availability subject to change without notice
When placing your order, please mention if you do not wish to receive
any additional information

www.augurpress.com

Mirabelle Maslin
ON A DOG LEAD

Mirabelle Maslin
CARL AND OTHER WRITINGS

LEE
SEYMOUR
HEMIPLEGIC
UTOPIA

Letters to my Paper Lover
FLEUR SOIGNON

Poems of Wartime Years
W N Taylor

Mirabelle
Maslin

tracy

from the author of Beyond the Veil

Beyond the Veil by Mirabelle Maslin
ISBN 0-9549551-4-5   £8.99

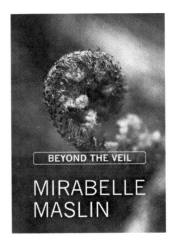

Spiral patterns, a strange tape of music from Russia, a 'blank' book and an oddly-carved walking stick…

Ellen encounters Adam, a young widower, and a chain of mysterious and unpredictable events begins to weave their lives together.   Chance, contingency and coincidence all play a part – involving them with friends in profound experiences, and lifting the pall of loss that has been affecting both their lives.

Against a backdrop of music, plant lore, mysterious writing and archaeology, the author touches on deeper issues of bereavement, friendship, illness and the impact of objects from the past on our lives. Altered states, heightened sensitivities and unseen communications are explored, as is the importance of caring and mutual understanding.

The story culminates in an experience of spiritual ecstasy, leading separate paths to an unusual and satisfying convergence.

Order from your local bookshop, amazon, or from the Augur Press website www.augurpress.com

Fay by Mirabelle Maslin
ISBN 0-9549551-3-7   £8.99

Fay is suffering from a mysterious illness.   Her family and friends are
concerned about her.   In her vulnerable state, she begins to be affected by
something more than intuition, and at first no one can make sense of it.

Alongside the preparation for her daughter's wedding, she is drawn into
new situations together with resonances of lives that are long past, and at
last the central meaning of her struggles begins to emerge.

**Order from your local bookshop, amazon, or from the Augur Press
website www.augurpress.com**

EMILY by Mirabelle Maslin

ISBN 978–0–9549551–8–2   £8.99

Orphaned by the age of ten, Emily lives with her Aunt Jane. While preparing to move house, they come across an old diary of Jane's, and she shows Emily some intriguing spiral patterns that appeared in it just before she, Emily, was born. Clearly no passing curiosity, these patterns begin to affect Emily in ways that no one can understand, and as time passes, something momentous begins to form in their lives.

While studying at university, Emily meets Barnaby. Sensing that they have been drawn together for a common purpose, they discover that each carries a crucial part of an unfinished puzzle from years past. It is only then that Emily's true purpose is revealed.

Order from your local bookshop, amazon.co.uk or the augurpress website at www.augurpress.com

Poetry Catchers by The Pupils of Craigton Primary
ISBN 978-0-9549551-9-9   £7.99

Craigton Primary is an inner-city school in Glasgow, Scotland. It has over 200 poetry-mad pupils, and it is the first school in Glasgow to have its own poetry library!

All of us have written a poem for this wonderful book.

We have picked our favourite poems, and we hope that you enjoy reading them as much as we have enjoyed writing them.

We have been inspired by Michael Rosen and our poetry-loving teacher, Mrs McCay.

Some of the poems will bring a tear to your eye, and others will make you cry with laughter.

Why don't you open the book and see what's inside?

**Order from your local bookshop, amazon, or from the Augur Press
website www.augurpress.com**

Printed in the United Kingdom by
Lightning Source UK Ltd., Milton Keynes
139829UK00001BA/88/P